CONFESSIONS OF A HATER

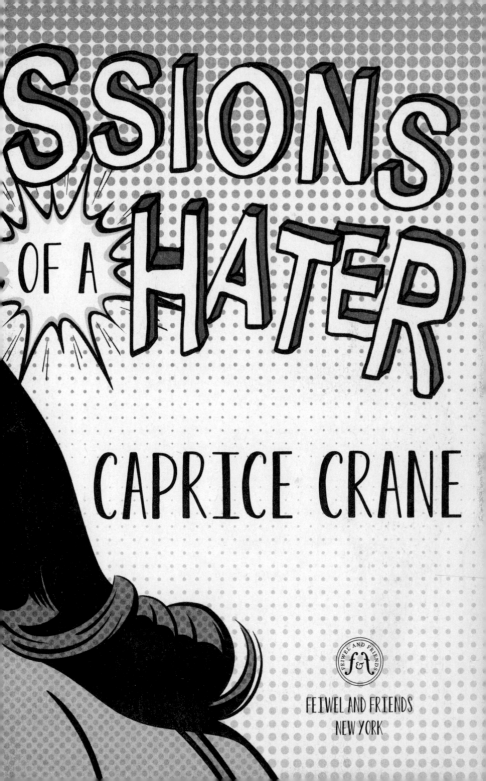

SSIONS
OF A HATER

CAPRICE CRANE

FEIWEL AND FRIENDS
NEW YORK

A FEIWEL AND FRIENDS BOOK
An Imprint of Macmillan

Feiwel and Friends books may be purchased for business or promotional use.
For information on bulk purchases, please contact the Macmillan
Corporate and Premium Sales Department at (800) 221-7945 x5442 or
by e-mail at specialmarkets@macmillan.com.

Library of Congress Cataloging-in-Publication Data Available

ISBN: 978-1-250-00846-6 (hardcover)/978-1-250-00847-3 (ebook)

Book design by April Ward

Feiwel and Friends logo designed by Filomena Tuosto

First Edition: 2013

2 4 6 8 10 9 7 5 3 1

macteenbooks.com

For Invisibles everywhere

Welcome to your life…

—TEARS FOR FEARS

"Everybody Wants to Rule the World"

CHAPTER 1

High school was pretty much like this huge party I wasn't actually *invited* to, but I still had to show up to every day. Awkward much? Have you ever had one of those days when from the second you woke up you just *knew* everything was going to go wrong? Yeah, that was *every single day* of my life during freshman year at Hamilton High. I wish I could tell you I was exaggerating. I wish this was a case of me being the "ugly girl" in a teen movie who wears glasses and overalls and has her hair in a ponytail, but as soon as she changes her clothes, takes off her glasses and lets her hair down—OMG, she's gorgeous, *how did we not see it before?*

Yeah, that's not me.

I've always been one of the Invisibles. I'm not a misfit. (Although admittedly I did go through a goth phase—and still have the tiny hole in my nose to prove it. Unfortunately.) I can put an outfit together without getting laughed at when I roam the halls among the fashionistas (the girls who wouldn't be caught dead in last season's clothes) and the trashionistas (the girls who majorly slut it up). My clothes are cute enough to keep me from hating myself when I catch my reflection, but nothing so great that anyone ever says, "Where did you get that?"

When it came to me and my friends, we were invisible enough not to matter in the grand scheme of the high school hierarchy, but not enough to escape the ridicule of the cool kids when they *did* happen upon us. More important, this was the inspiration for a comic strip character I'd been working on for at least a year—Abby Invisible, the New Kid at School. I'd been scoffed at by haters and called every name in the book at one time or another. (Well . . . maybe every name except "popular.") I had *plenty* of material.

I guess that's the trade-off for having grown up relatively well-adjusted with two parents who loved me. Because if you put your ear up really close to the girls who are extra mean, you can actually *hear* their daddy issues. Oh, what a difference a hug would have made. (Except for the girls who got *too* much hugging from their daddies, but that's a whole other issue.)

My mom said I'd ultimately find my "groove" at my new school. Oh, yeah, I guess I left that part out: That's how it *really* started. My parents announced that we were moving across the country. The move and packing for it was what led to me finding the diary . . . which is what led to everything else.

I was freaking out about the move. My mom was trying to spin it, to get me excited about having a fresh start—but show me one kid in the history of high school who's overjoyed to hear she has to move and switch schools, and I'll show you a leprechaun eating calorie-free chocolate cake while riding a unicorn. Mom said things would be different at my new school. I'd "make *new* friends" and "find my Jake Ryan." I don't know if he's some guy she dated before she married my dad or what, but a) I liked the friends I had, and b) whoever this Jake Ryan is, he has two first names and I never trust a guy with two first names. (I'm looking at you, Kevin

James.) She's a total optimist, my mom. If life hands her lemons, she's not just making lemonade—she's gonna turn her lemonade business into an empire.

My dad's more of a realist. He'd tell me things like "Always follow your head and not your heart. Hearts tend to be *idiots.*" I've always loved that about my dad. There's way too much encouragement from parents in today's world, and most people could use some honest criticism. If parents praise every single idiotic thing their children do, how will kids learn what they're good at? What will make them want to try harder? Think about it. Every time you lie to your kid and tell her that some dumb thing she did is "great," you're potentially creating the next Ke$ha. Half the songs on the radio these days sound like I did when I was eleven years old, singing into a fan.

I respect my dad for his honesty and pragmatism. That said, telling a teenager not to follow her heart is like telling a dog to meow instead of bark. It's, like, physiologically impossible. How else are we supposed to relate to sappy songs on the radio and make the mistakes that shape us? (Although if mistakes are supposed to shape you, which is what I hear, by this point I should be in *much* better shape—like forget six-pack abs, I should have a *solid* eight-pack.)

You know that saying "The enemy of my enemy is my friend"? Well, in high school, your own worst enemy is often yourself . . . which makes sense, because when all is said and done and you've screwed up enough times and you have no friends left, the only friend you have left is *you.* And you have to count on yourself to get it together and make better decisions and become a better person. Or at least a better person than you were yesterday. That is, of course, until you screw it up again in some spectacular new way tomorrow.

It was my last week in Westchester and I was already feeling nostalgic. The cerulean blue lockers lining the corridors, the clusters of cliques with girls shooting sideways glances to make sure the target du jour of the current "breaking" gossip wasn't nearby, the paired-off boyfriends and girlfriends who'd completely forgotten what it was like to roam the halls alone, BC (Before Coupling).

My friend Amy cruised up to me with a huge smile, like we were in on some secret, but I had no idea what the secret was or why she was grinning like a crazy person.

"Like my necklace?"

I looked at her neck and saw a cool metal chain with one of those friendship hearts made of brass. Of course, only half of the heart dangled from the chain. The other half was to be worn by her "best friend." As I looked closer I saw her heart had engraved on it:

Be

Fu

Fri

"Very cool," I said, with equal parts hope and sadness, hope stemming from the idea that the other half was for me, sadness from the worry that she got the necklace with someone else. And why not? I was leaving, after all. I'm not the smartest investment to make at this point.

So I was flooded with relief when Amy held out her fist and opened her hand, palm up, to reveal the other half:

st

cking

ends

Oh, that's my girl. Seriously, that warmed the cockles of my heart. And I'm not even sure what cockles are. (Though they sound kinda dirty, huh? *Amy made my cockles warm.*)

"Really?" I exclaimed. "For me?"

"*Doy*," she said, making the idiot face that went with all variations of "duh," "doy" and a great many other utterances of that ilk.

"I love it," I said. "It's so cool."

"Well, we're cool like that," she said. "So don't forget about me when you're busy hanging out with, like, Demi Lovato or whoever in fancy LA."

"Yeah, right," I said with an eye roll so big you could probably hear it.

Just then, my art teacher stopped me in the hall. Amy tossed me a "catch ya later" and went on her way. She'd never been one for fraternizing with teachers, but here's where Amy should have made an exception: Lana was very different from most teachers. Lana insisted we call her by her first name. She usually wore combat boots and long skirts paired with long-sleeve thermal shirts. She definitely had her own sense of style, and everyone thought she was a cool teacher. But she was more than that to me. She was the first person who really encouraged my artistic talents—so much so that I would eat lunch in her classroom at least a couple of times a week. I'd work on my art projects and she'd tell me about her husband, who was an art director for music videos, and I'd secretly hoped one day he'd show up when I was there so I could ask him if he'd ever met Gwen or Rihanna or Nicki Minaj. Part of me believed I was spending lunches with Lana because it gave me more time to work on my art . . . but the rest of me knew it was because the school cafeteria was a battleground—who sits with whom, who's judging whose eating habits, who fits into what clique and who is a total outcast—and this was a prime opportunity to avoid it.

"I have to tell you," Lana said with the proud smile usually reserved for a parent, "your caricature the other day was truly spectacular."

"Thanks," I said, staring at my shoes, because I was never very good at accepting compliments. There was a spot on my left sneaker. I squinted at it as if I had the power to will it away with a dirty look.

"I mean it, Hailey. I know high school is the time to get caught up in clothes and boys and parties, but you are so talented. I don't want you to lose focus when you move."

"I won't. Believe me, you've got nothing to worry about. I don't get invited to parties."

"There's the spirit," she teased, then changed her tone. "Things will turn around for you at your new school. These are confusing times for sure . . . but interspersed there are wonderful experiences to be had."

"So they say . . . whoever 'they' are. The people who believe that youth is wasted on the young, I guess."

"I don't know if youth is wasted on the young, but fitting into kid-size jeans certainly is."

And that's why she was my favorite teacher—smart and funny.

"You're just so gifted, Hailey," Lana went on. "I can really see this art thing working out for you—and you know I'm loath to ever tell someone they actually *should* be an artist."

"I hope you're right," I said.

"Do me a favor?"

"Sure . . ."

"I feel like sometimes you hold yourself back."

"I do?" I asked. "I don't mean to."

But did I? I wondered. I kinda thought I was pretty up-front with my thoughts and feelings. If I had a nickel for every time someone sarcastically said, "Tell me how you *really* feel," after some very honest (and perhaps not very nice) thing I'd said, I'd probably have a lot of nickels . . . which, if we're being honest—who wants a bunch of nickels? My dad always said it, too: "If I had a nickel for every time blah blah blah . . ." and I'd think, *How about a dollar for every time? I mean, times have changed, people. Inflation!*

"You might not even be aware of it," she said with a reassuring smile. "Just don't be afraid to explore your emotions through your art—especially when you're frustrated or confused or if your move is difficult for you. There's no safer place to express yourself than in your art."

"Okay," I said. "I'll try."

"Good. And I'll try to forget that I saw you in the hall when you're supposed to be in second period."

With a smirk and a wink, she spun on her scuffed boots and walked away.

There is no way the art teacher at my new school is gonna be this cool, I thought.

And with that, my mind was off and running, rewriting history, making mental excuses about the good things at Hamilton—the way you do with a boyfriend who treats you like crap, but since he's the captain of the football team, you don't want to break up with him. (Not that I'd know what that's like; besides kissing Nick Foster during a game of truth or dare, or making out with Danny O'Connell in a closet during a similar party game, I haven't even ever kissed anyone without an audience or the option to instead answer a humiliating question. I've never had a boyfriend.)

But just as I started to feel sad about the move and leaving everything I knew behind, reality showed up and slapped me in the face. It wasn't the bell ringing to signal the end of second period and the rush of students trying to get to their next class. It was *Jemma Gray*: queen bitch of my grade.

As I tried to slide past her, the cobra adorned in J Brand jeans struck.

"Why do you wear boys' underwear?"

Just keep walking, said the voice in my head. I really need to start listening to that sucker.

I stopped, utterly perplexed. "What?"

"Boys' underwear," Jemma repeated pointedly, projecting to the cheap seats like she was playing Madison Square Garden. "Why do you wear them? Are you, like, confused about whether you're a boy or a girl? Do you find them more comfortable? Did you lose a bet?"

You're deluded. Bite me.

That's what the brain said. The mouth part chickened out.

"I have no idea what you're talking about."

"Oh my God, why are you such a liar?!" she said, a crowd gathering now. I was Frankenstein's monster, surrounded by villagers with torches, who all wanted to know why the Creature wore guys' tighty-whities.

Focus. Just deny it. Forcefully. Stand up for yourself and move on.

"Jemma, that's the most ridiculous thing I've ever heard. I *don't* wear boys' underwear."

"Prove it."

A million things went through my mind in the next few moments, and I'd replay all of them over and over for the next week. *Why is this girl such a bitch? What the hell is she talking about? Is that mole on her face leaking nonsense into her brain?*

Hell with it, I thought, *just prove her wrong. That'll teach her.*

Before I could think better of it, I popped the button on my jeans, unzipped and flashed just a little bit of my undies for Jemma. Turquoise Hanky Panky lace underwear: definitely not for boys. Quite fashionable, in fact.

There you go, bitch. The More You Know.

And then there was a brief flash of light. Actually, two flashes:

One appeared in the corner of my eye, the flash from an iPhone camera. The other seemed to come from above my head, a light-bulb appearing as if I were a cartoon character who just figured something out, just like the mouse who took its first and last bite into a hunk of cheese before the lever on the mousetrap swung down and snapped its neck.

Oh, shit.

It only took seconds. As soon as my Hanky Panky panties saw the light of day, Sasha Hendricks—Jemma's "number two"—snapped a picture with her iPhone. As I'd learn just a few minutes later, she immediately uploaded it to Facebook and Instagram and tagged me with the caption:

"OMFG! *Weirdo Hailey Harper flashes everyone in the hallway between second and third period.*"

Sixty seconds earlier, I was just considered a loser and outcast within the halls of this school, which was bad enough. Now I was instantly the Freshman Flasher Freak of Facebook.

I zipped and ran from the sounds of laughter, and it didn't seem to diminish even after I was long gone. My face flushed at the realization I might never escape this sort of humiliation.

I was no stranger to taunting. I'd always felt like school itself was a test and I'd somehow wound up in the wrong classroom. I immediately flashed back to an incident in seventh grade when I was washing my hands in the girls' bathroom:

Sandy Carson was putting on bubble-gum lip gloss while Jessica Landen and Mia Quong were pinching their thighs.

"I just pray they never touch each other," Jessica said.

"Mine won't," Mia answered. "Asians are always skinny."

"Unless they're fat ones."

"It's rare," Mia declared. "Especially in Asian countries."

"What about sumo wrestlers?"

"That's rare! Plus, they're Japanese!" Mia exclaimed. "I'm Chinese! I've told you a million times!"

"Oh, whatever," Jessica said. "Nobody said you're Japanese! But you're right. Most are pretty skinny. God, I wish I was Asian."

Sandy rolled her crystal-blue eyes at the dippy duo, and then turned her gaze to me. I thought maybe we were having a moment. Not like a romantic moment, but like we both realized the conversation was pretty silly. Sandy had never really spoken to me, and it was already the third week of school.

"Hailey, right?" Sandy said.

"Yup," I answered, perhaps a little too excitedly. "That's me."

Definitely didn't need to add that part . . .

She continued, "So we've been wondering . . . Do you, like, *not* wear any makeup because your parents won't let you? Or is it because you think you're *so pretty* that you don't need it?"

The pit I felt in my stomach was confusion, coupled with hurt, tied up in a nice big red ribbon of shame. I hadn't even considered makeup prior to this conversation. Nobody wore it in grade school, and, yes, this was technically middle school now, and we all jumped up a category in the age groupings, but there was no handbook. Were you supposed to wear makeup in seventh grade?

My mouth opened, but nothing came out. I didn't know what the right answer was. I mean, obviously I didn't think I was especially pretty, but my parents hadn't forbidden me to wear makeup either—we'd just never talked about it.

Mia and Jessica erupted in laughter and I willed my eyes away from the mirror so I wouldn't see the crimson shade of red I was turning.

"Well, let me just put it this way," Sandy said. "You're *not* so pretty that you don't need makeup. So if your parents *don't* have a problem with it . . . you should consider running—not walking—to the nearest makeup aisle at Walmart."

Double zing.

The first tear to sneak out of my left eye was considerate enough to wait until they were out of sight. I stayed in the bathroom and cried for twenty minutes. That was a luxury I would only be able to afford for the next twenty-four hours, because the magical world of mascara was about to be introduced into my life—and crying with mascara on is *definitely* not worth the extra pain and suffering it causes (as I'd soon learn).

I took a minute to examine myself in the mirror. Was I really so unfortunate looking that I deserved this kind of attack? I mean, I was *normal*. I wasn't a stick-skinny girl with fake boobs (which I think looks ridiculous by the way), my boobs were proportionate to my body and my nose was fine. In fact, I rather liked my nose. It was smallish and maybe curved up a tiny bit at the tip but not so you could look up my nose or anything. I had dark, dark brown eyes and dark brown hair, very fair skin and freckles that crossed the bridge of my nose. I was average height for my age, I thought. I don't know when you stop growing but I was five foot six. Maybe I could even be considered tall?

But not in that moment. As I stood there in the bathroom after being humiliated by Sandy Carson, I felt like the smallest person in the world. Ugly, uninformed, and completely lost in a world where superficial bitches reigned supreme. Apparently.

The next day I showed up to school looking like a confident, empowered, mature, dynamic, completely self-actualized . . .

Prostitute.

Overcompensate much?

That's right, I'd taken all of my allowance and bought foundation (the wrong shade), lipstick (Hooker Red, naturally), blush (more like Moulin Rouge Regret), mascara (who knew you could look like you had spiders living in and around your eye sockets), eyeliner (hi, raccoon—I think we share a grandparent), and powder (to seal it all in like an embalmer).

On an attractiveness scale of one to ten, I ranked somewhere between zero and your average made-up corpse. Six weeks after the wake.

I didn't even make it to first period before getting my marching orders: straight to the principal's office to explain why I thought it was appropriate to look like a clown on steroids. From there, I was questioned about my homelife and whether there had been any recent "emotionally traumatic" events; once this *Law & Order SVU*-type questioning had determined that nothing drastic had triggered this "acting out," I was ordered to the bathroom to wash my face.

Of course I couldn't have just made it to the bathroom in solitude. I passed right by Sandy and the girls on my way there. And of course they laughed at me, even though I kept my head down and avoided eye contact. And of course Sandy shouted after me, "OMG, your head and neck are two completely different colors!"

What I thought:

This is all your fault, you evil bitch.

What I said:

Nothing.

I raced to the bathroom before my tears could make the Twister game that was my face degrade completely into the look of a notorious crime scene. I desperately just wanted to get this shameful crap off my stupid big fat head—*who the hell did I think I was anyway*—but without any makeup remover, using the awful detergent-like soap in the bathroom, it took forever to clean it away. It felt like I'd laid it on an inch thick, and I rubbed so hard and so fast, desperate to remove it all before someone entered the bathroom to ridicule me further. By the time it was all clean, my face was red and raw, puffy and swollen. Which led me to start crying harder than ever. And when I was all cried out, I swore to myself I'd never make a mistake like that again.

Everything in moderation, I told myself. (To which I'd later add *including moderation*.) Also, I realized, whatever your knee-jerk reaction is when something hits you down where it counts, you're probably better off doing the exact opposite.

So, yeah. The respect and admiration of the popular crowd was as alien to me as self-respect and perspective is to the Real Housewives of Anywhere Ever. And this Facebook fiasco was only the latest in a string of unfortunate experiences collectively known as "my existence."

Of course I could untag myself later, at least on Facebook, but the damage was done. Two things were certain: I would not miss Jemma, and I would not miss Hamilton High.

It never gets better or worse.

—ELVIS COSTELLO

"This Is Hell"

CHAPTER 2

"Please turn your music down!" Mom called from downstairs.

Enjoying the sanctity of my room, I contemplated for a moment pretending I didn't hear her, but then she'd just come upstairs and fling my bedroom door open, one eyebrow cocked, a smirk veering left that says: *We both know damn well you heard me.*

I know this routine. We've done this dance.

I turn the music down.

Packing sucks. Moving sucks. Turning my music down sucks. Everything sucks. You'd think I'd at least be able to rock out while I painfully and methodically box up my belongings against my will.

You'd be wrong.

My parents have tried to spin this move every which way, to the point that every time I find myself in the kitchen with one of them, I preemptively cringe at whatever uplifting nonsense they're about to spew at me.

"This could be the best thing that ever happened to you."

Really? Thanks, Captain Cliché.

"It's a fresh start."

Yay. A chance to be the same outcast at a whole new school!

"You'll make new friends."

Because that's so easy to do when everyone already made their new friends freshman year. And what about my old friends? What about the fact that I was leaving everyone I knew in the entire world?

Parents never get it.

I understand that we have to move. I'm not being a brat about it. My dad got a promotion—that's good. My sister, Noel, is off at college, so even if we stayed here, the house is too big. It's always been too big, because I think my parents wanted a third child, but that sibling never materialized. So now that it's just me, it's that much more obvious.

Not to be mean, but the one good thing about being at a new school is that nobody knows I'm related to Noel—therefore, no one knows how uncool I am by comparison. Don't get me wrong; I love my sister. It's just that *everybody* loves my sister. For my entire life, I've been overshadowed by her.

Noel is pretty much perfect. She has thick, gorgeous, wavy brown hair with natural highlights that regular people pay a fortune to get. Frizz? She's heard of it . . . but never had it. And don't even get me started on her eyes. They're like cats' eyes with Bambi lashes. Now that I think about it, that's a perfect analogy, because she's almost cartoon perfect.

She's taller than me and skinnier than me, yet she's still muscular in awe-inspiring, completely unfair ways. Her sense of style has always been unique, yet fashionable; she'd never be caught dead in anything that says "Juicy."

(BTW, have you noticed you never see sweatpants with "Classy" written across the ass?)

(Second BTW, have you noticed people who wear sweatpants

are never actually *sweating*? Take note, people: If you're not planning on sweating, don't wear the sweatpants.)

(Final BTW, I swear: If you *are* planning on sweating, and it's
not because you're going to the gym, maybe you just shouldn't
leave the house.)

If Noel were just pretty, that would be one thing. Wonderfully
(for her) and unfortunately (for me), she just happens to also be
good at freaking *everything*. Grades? Check. Singing? Better than
your average *American Idol* finalist. Dancing? She was head cheerleader, and since cheerleading has basically evolved into insanely
amazingly choreographed dance routines, yes, you could say she's
also amazing at that.

I could also run down all the sports she can play or list the
awards she won at school or mention the three college scholar-
ships she was offered and it would all be true, but what always
mystified me more than anything else was for two people who
were sisters . . . how completely and utterly *different* we were from
each other. Total freakin' opposites.

Noel and I are nothing alike, and sadly, we were never close.
In fact, I'm pretty sure if we weren't related she wouldn't even talk
to me.

How do I know? Because she once told me exactly that. Point
blank.

I remember it clear as day and that was a rough one. And
given all the rough days I've had, it takes a lot for one to stand out.

So there was no love lost between us when Noel went to college. My mom has always said we aren't close because of the age
difference and that in a few years it'll all change. My dad says it's
because my sister is "stuck up" and he'd "take the brainy girl over
the beauty queen any day."

Great, Dad. Thanks for saying what I was already thinking. I look forward to your self-esteem workshop!

Honestly, my dad is awesome. I know he means well. He's actually really cool. (Don't tell him I said that.) He treats me like an adult and tells it like it is. Always has. The family drama in our house has always been pretty underwhelming and limited to "someone" not doing her homework before she watched *Pretty Little Liars* or "someone" getting her nose pierced (that hole really should be closed up by now) or "someone" missing her curfew (curfews are totally unconstitutional, by the way—check out the Fourteenth Amendment).

Anyway, my dad's a lawyer. He works *a lot* and I guess the bosses noticed because that's why they're moving us out to Los Angeles. He's going to head up their entertainment law department. I guess that would be the silver lining of my life as I know it being completely upended—great weather year-round. Well, that and the fact that hopefully he'll represent some cool famous people who occasionally find themselves in hot water, like Lindsay or Britney or Selena, and then I'll meet them and of course they'll need stable, non-Hollywood friends so we'll become instant besties and then through them I'll meet (and marry) Robert Pattinson.

(What, like you've never had a crush on someone? Someone who was famous? Someone who you'll never meet?)

I'll try to stay in touch with my friends from home—we'll Skype or FaceTime when we can, the rest of the time we'll talk, we'll tweet, we'll text. But how many sad faces can one send before it just becomes redundant? Not to mention that every time I even *use* an emoticon, I hate myself just a little bit more. And add to that, they're all so basic: happy, sad, crying, confused. Where's the emoticon for "utterly defeated"? Add that bad boy in and maybe I'll come to the party.

Emoticons aside, I'm just fooling myself if I think everything isn't going to change and most likely the move will also cost me my friends. Amy's heart necklace says "BFF" and we'll promise to stay in touch, but the truth is this: One thing is king when it comes to high school friendships, and that thing is *geography*. What's that they say about real estate? Location, location, location? Same deal. Without proximity and day-in, day-out contact, the friendship is toast. Burnt.

I'll be starting sophomore year at West Hollywood High. It's supposed to be a good school from what I hear, but school is school: one big popularity contest. There's always a nonsensical hierarchy among students, much like that of Louis XIV's court (which we *do* study at some point, but the irony is lost on the students). You know what else is a popularity contest? Popularity. It's stupid and random and based not on talent or skill but on *rank*—a rank decided upon by no one deserving to make that determination.

But that's how it is. And that's why I'm not looking forward to the move. And probably why I'm packing slower than I should be. (Though it might go a little faster if I could turn up My Chemical Romance to a volume that could be heard by humans and not just dogs.) I know my subconscious also is slowing me down to delay the inevitable. Instead of swiftly sifting through my stuff and deciding what's coming with, what's being donated to Goodwill and what's going in the garbage . . . I'm looking at pictures, moving things from one area to the next, and just generally prolonging my misadventure.

All of which is why I find myself going through an already donation-designated box my parents threw together on behalf of my sister. Some clothes, old CDs she already ripped into her iTunes library, her diary, some junk from—

Wait.

Her *diary*?

Holy crap, Noel kept a *diary*?

I guess I really don't know her that well. Gorgeous, talented and smart—yes, she was all those things, to my undying irritation. But she never struck me as particularly *introspective*.

I wanted to give that some more thought, but I was too eager to open the diary. Of course, this was a deep moral dilemma that I wrestled with for a solid, well-considered eleven seconds before opening to the first page, which read:

HOW TO BE A HATER

In retrospect, it's hard to recall my exact thoughts on reading those first few pages. They seem to blur together somewhat now. Here's what Mom likes to call the *Reader's Digest* version, which is some term she uses for a book that's been cut down to its basic story:

Noel's diary—or at least the few dozen pages I read—was like a self-empowerment guide of sorts. Stuff that had been passed down to her from some girl named Alexa Derringer who was apparently older, wiser, prettier, thinner, sluttier, and better-all-around than Noel—who knew that was even possible? This diary was apparently some kind of legacy passed down to the next protégé each year. It explained how she stopped being so sensitive, how she learned to stop putting up with bullshit. It was a virtual guide on how she became strong and popular and self-assured. Flipping through the pages, I couldn't help but think some of this stuff could really come in handy:

Don't make that stupid duck face in your photos. Just don't.

Her reason was tied to someone named Samantha Jacobsen and her much-mocked modeling debut in the Delia's catalogue. I knew the exact face that she meant. That stupid, lips-pursed face-pose that every girl seems to have in at least three of her Facebook photos.

Noted. I wouldn't make that face in photos with my friends. Once I *had* friends.

> Don't say "deets." If you ask me to "tell you the deets" I will withhold them from you on principle.

That was *so* like Noel. Ruler of cool. Arbiter of what makes or breaks you. Her example stemmed from an unfortunate (for the boy) incident where some guy tried to pick her up in an Exxon parking lot after being rejected in front of her for a pack of Parliaments. When he tried to get her number, he asked for her "digits," so he could text her "the deets" about some party that night. She'd rather drink a bleach cocktail while watching her parents have sex than attend that party.

(Thanks for the visual, sis.)

Her next rule came from an incident with Lana—my art teacher, remember—who she apparently couldn't stand. *Ugh, that figures.*

Turns out she thought Lana was always trying to be "down" with the kids, and she said "OMG" during class one day, inspiring ridicule galore.

> Text "OMG?" Fine. Say "OMG" out loud? No. It's the same amount of syllables as the words you're abbreviating. You sound like an idiot.

Poor Lana. She meant well. And I had to admit, Noel had a point there. I'd never do that. Actually saying OMG out loud should only happen if you're being ironic or asking your phone for directions to the Oklahoma Meerkat Gardens.

So I guess we do share some DNA after all. You just can't tell. Like Alec Baldwin and all the other Baldwins.

> When anyone asks you if you hooked up with a guy, just roll your eyes and laugh. This way you simultaneously avoid looking like a prude or a slut.

She's kind of a genius. I mean, this is exactly the kind of stuff that I'd hope she would tell me if we *were* close and I *was* starting a new school . . . which I was. It was almost like having a virtual big sister—one who *liked* me.

Who knows? Maybe she left the diary behind for me to find it. Maybe it was her way of wanting to help me.

> Don't wear pigtails. If you're not on a Disney show or a porn star (or both), there is no good excuse to wear pigtails past the age of twelve.
>
> Don't wear tiny shorts and Ugg boots unless you're trying out for a Wet Seal catalogue.
>
> Don't go out with a guy who wears his pants below his ass. The only way you should see a guy's underwear before you've kissed him is if he's a Calvin Klein model.

She would know. She *did* go out with a Calvin Klein model. But she's right. I don't know what the deal is with guys wearing their pants like that. It looks ridiculous. I know it's like a "gangsta" thing, but I've heard the real story is it actually started in jails. Guys would wear their pants like that to signal they were "available" and, more important, *willing*. (Even more reason not to date a guy who wears his pants like that.) Though I doubt the guys who wear their pants that way at school have any idea where it all started. I just watch too many documentaries. Sadly, my brain retains useless trivia way easier than Algebra II.

I put the diary down and looked at the box of Noel's clothes. Behind it were three other boxes—all clothes, all much cooler than mine. Before I even knew what I was doing, I'd stopped packing my stuff and started *unpacking* hers, trying things on, seeing what fit.

I thought,

What's the big difference if I keep them, right? They were going to charity anyway—she obviously didn't want them. Maybe some of my wardrobe can go to charity instead? Maybe I need a makeover? And maybe I already have everything I need right in these boxes? Who's to say I can't be just as cool as Noel at my new school? Who would know I hadn't been cool all my life?

Granted, I had no interest in being a "hater" per se, but I didn't want to be a total loser when I made my fresh start. I thought, *This diary could be my roadmap to cool.*

Don't get a "tramp stamp" or a "skank flank." Stay classy.
To that end, don't get a chinese symbol tattoo. No matter what your chinese symbol tattoo says, I'm going to assume the translation is either: "Please think I'm cool" or "The tattoo artist told me this symbol means 'warrior' but it actually means 'gullible shithead.'"

This one was funny because Noel *did* get a tattoo during her senior year. My mom saw it and freaked out. I don't think my dad ever found out. She'd written down part of a lyric from her favorite song by Paramore and had it tattooed on the inside of her wrist in her own handwriting: Shine brighter. I guess some stuff I didn't know about had gone down, because she didn't really get into trouble once my mom got past the initial shock.

Fake it 'til you make it. confidence is king. Act "as if."

I knew this one would definitely come in handy. The power of persuasion is a hell of a thing. Take Kim Kardashian—not that she's a role model (at all)—but before she was a huge megastar, she was just a girl who got peed on in a sex tape with Brandy's rapper brother. (Gross much?) But she went about her business, acting like she was somebody, and next thing you knew, she *was*. To this day I don't know why she's still famous, but there she is with her other talent-less sisters on the cover of the tabloids every other week. And those girls didn't even get peed on! (Well, at least not on video.)

I looked at the clothes just sitting there in that box . . . waiting to be given away to complete strangers, and thought, funny how she'd *never* let me borrow anything of hers to wear but once she grew sick of them . . . it *still* wasn't okay for me to wear them. Well . . . what she didn't know wouldn't hurt her. . . .

I pulled out a pair of Seven jeans from the box. They were a little tight, but I figured I could skip the mac 'n' cheese for a few weeks. Her black Repetto flats? I always knew Noel and I were the same size. I slid into the ballet flats like they were Cinderella's slippers. Perfect.

I turned my attention back to the journal. Some of her scrawl was about the exterior:

If you can see VPL before you leave the house, then don't leave the house.

Perfect a "pretty cry face" just in case of an emergency—nobody likes an ugly crier.

Don't ever wear pants with a word written across your ass. It's not attractive on anyone.

There were tips about behavior and mannerisms:

Don't giggle when a guy makes a dumb joke. You're making it too easy and lowering the bar. Let them earn your laughs. And that goes triple for "everything else."

Don't make YouTube videos of you and your friends dancing and lip-syncing to some song. At best, your only viewers will be creepy old men. At worst, you'll go viral and become a meme. No.

Don't fake an accent. They're like fake boobs. They draw unwanted attention and are hard to maintain. Leave that to the pros. (I'm looking at you, Madonna.)

I agreed with her on all three counts. And by the way, on the subject of fake boobs? I'd known girls in high school who'd *already* gotten them! Really? Plastic surgery in high school? Aren't you scared you'll keep growing and then your surgery won't match the rest of you? You'll look like a Picasso. And for the record, I'm pretty sure he hated women. A nose over here, an eyeball over there. *Thank God* he had a paintbrush, or who knows, he could have been a serial killer, murdering women and cutting them up to rearrange their faces! Yeesh!

Don't tag your boyfriend in every single Facebook status. We remember that you know each other.

No sexting and definitely no naked pictures to your boyfriend's cell phone. Eventually, the whole school will see them and you'll be "that girl." Also? It's child pornography.

Some of her rules were downright ridiculous:

Don't eat garlic or onions around cute guys. Or any guys. Or girls. Ever.

But could *all* of it be my ticket to the new me? (And I'm sorry, but onions aren't all bad. And garlic? Who doesn't love garlic? Besides vampires.)

I found myself opening iTunes and downloading music that Noel liked, songs I'd told her sucked, bands I hated on principle. I was going to open my mind and see if she wasn't so wrong after all.

Dinner that night was my first foray into "fitting a four." That was not one of Noel's little rules, per se, but the only way I'd really be able to wear my new wardrobe would be to get down to Noel's size. Easier said than done. I knew I was a six—a healthy six at that—and honestly, I was pretty okay with my body, but if I was going to wear Noel's clothes, I was going to have to make some adjustments.

"Why aren't you eating your potatoes?" my mom asked.

"I'm just not feeling like potatoes."

"Are you feeling like po-TAH-toes?" my dad jumped in.

"Oh my God, could you be more corny?" I asked.

"I could, in fact," he said. "Wanna see?"

"No, Dad. Please, spare us."

"You love those potatoes," my mom pushed. "I made them with sour cream, chives and garlic."

Garlic. The diary flashed in my head: no onions, no garlic. Ever.

"Noel never ate garlic," I said.

"Noel never ate white food," my dad said. He twirled his index finger in a circular motion next to his ear, and out of the side of his mouth he added, "Noel was a little cuckoo."

"Nick!" my mom said, eyebrow cocked; that was never a good sign. In eyebrow language that meant she was either on to your ruse or you were misbehaving.

"What?" He winked at me. "I'm just saying."

"That's a cute top on you," Mom said, changing the subject.

"Thanks," I said, not wanting to mention that I'd just stolen it from the Goodwill box.

"Is it new?"

"Kinda," I said.

"Well, I like it," she said.

I wondered if she'd notice that all of my clothes seemed new or if (and at what point) she'd notice I'd scavenged Noel's castoffs. Then I worried for a minute about the fact that she liked it. After all, one of Noel's rules was:

When clothes shopping with Mom, always be sure to buy the one outfit she hates the most. There's a reason there's a thing called "mom jeans," and it's not to be forgotten.

"Can I be excused?" I asked. Before they could say anything about me finishing my dinner, I added, "I really need to pack."

In truth, I was just dying to try on more of Noel's clothes. They totally bought it and I was back upstairs in record time, spinning in front of the mirror in Noel's hippie Joie blouse. I was in love. (With the shirt.) The skinny jeans I paired with it? A little too skinny for my taste (ahem, my legs), but no matter—there were two other pairs and I knew one was destined to fit better.

I spent the rest of the night rummaging through Noel's stuff, trying things on and separating everything into piles. By the time I was done I had a whole new wardrobe—I even replaced some of the stuff I took from Noel's boxes with stuff of mine so I wouldn't be shortchanging the donation box. I mean, quality-wise, yes—I'm *totally* shortchanging the donation box—but in quantity, it about evens out. (And I don't mean to be rude, but are the people shopping at Goodwill really going to turn down a lightly used blouse for $4.99 just because it isn't quite *couture*?)

And, hey, she's my sister. I figured that if I don't get someone who has my back and gives me advice and keeps my secrets and does all that "sister" stuff, the least I can get is some hand-me-down clothes and some sisterly advice in the form of one misplaced (and perhaps forgotten) diary.

Yes, I knew that reading her diary was totally uncool, but it's not like I was using this stuff *against* her . . . I was using it for good. I was using it to help myself.

Packing was somehow less of a chore once I had my new wardrobe in place. Same with the stress about moving. And when I got a pre-move haircut and tried on a "new" outfit the next night, when I looked at myself in the mirror I was considerably less bummed and more excited about the possibilities—especially since my mom also took me to get contacts so I wouldn't be going to my new school as Nerdy McFourEyes. Not that glasses are so terrible. I mean, hipsters wear them these days without even having any *lenses* in them. (Another phenom I do not get. In fact I'm pretty sure hipsters are the way they are because their "skinny jeans" are cutting off all the circulation to their brains.) But I looked way better in contacts and for once I just wanted to be normal. Relatively. At least appearance-wise. The truth is, I did like my glasses. They were like an outward badge for brains. I'll never forget (mostly because it was immortalized) the one day in Spanish class when Lisa Myers tossed that old adage at me, "Guys don't make passes at girls who wear glasses," and without missing a beat I responded, "That may be so, but we pass all our classes." That quote ended up in the yearbook—attributed to me. Nerd Burn at its best. But still, I knew it would be nice to not be automatically classified as a bookworm or worse based on a pair of dumb prescription glasses. Which gave me an idea . . .

I took my old Paul Frank skull-and-crossbones lunchbox off the top shelf above my dresser and placed my glasses in it for safe-keeping. Then I added the Hanky Panky underwear I was wearing when that idiot Jemma made a spectacle of me (and them) at school. I was making a time capsule. Not necessarily to remind myself "what it was like," but more as a symbolic effort to bury my old self in order to start fresh.

Into the donation bin went my old iPod Shuffle. (What were you thinking, not even allowing us to select tracks, Steve Jobs? But you were a genius. RIP.) With it went the music that was technically the soundtrack to my miserable life. I'm not saying I didn't still like some of the songs on there, but I had the ones I liked on my updated iPod, and it seemed fitting for this relic to be part of the package.

I also wrote a letter to my future self, detailing why I was making these changes at the time of this move. Finally, I tossed in this year's class photo. I looked like I was about to say something in the picture—which I was, I was asking if I could move the hair out of my eye—but *flash* went the camera, and there I was in the year-book with my left eye partially covered with a growing-out chunk of my unfortunate bangs experiment, my mouth open in the "can" part of "can I move my hair" and looking like a total idiot.

Par for my course. My *old* course.

By the time we moved, I was barely recognizable. New clothes, new haircut (subtle layers—no bangs), new me. Transformation complete.

But the stars look very different today . . .

—DAVID BOWIE

"Space Oddity"

CHAPTER 3

The thing that made everything simultaneously seem both real and unreal was the presence of palm trees. I'd seen them on TV and in movies my whole life, but for whatever reason, they were ingrained in my head as part of some fantasy world. Their sudden introduction to *my* reality made everything seem that much more surreal. The palm trees lined the streets, towering and stately, like the backdrop of a movie—a movie that was now my reality. All that was missing was the beach, the Hollywood sign, and perhaps a stray movie star walking with her Starbucks cup and her boyfriend du jour.

Moving into a new house is exciting and chaotic and frustrating and scary. Sure there's fresh paint and wide-open space and new opportunities to decorate according to your new life, your new plan and, in my case, a new *you*. But it's also completely unfamiliar. You can't sleepwalk to the fridge in the dark without tripping over a box or walking into a wall that didn't exist in your old house. You can't look at a closet and know that on the back of that door is a penciled-in measuring stick with a series of marks that indicate your height over the years. (With all the pounds I'd dropped on my new diet, I should have been pencil-marking my *circumference*.) You can't know exactly where to go for whatever you need because there isn't a place for that yet. It feels almost like you're house-sitting for someone else, but for some reason all of your stuff came with you. It's bizarre.

The day our belongings arrived was eventful, to say the least. Mom and I rushed out to meet the movers when the truck pulled into the driveway, and our next-door neighbors were just returning from the grocery store at the same time. We hadn't had a chance to meet yet.

A woman who looked about my mom's age waved and called out, "Hey there! Hang on, we'll be over in a minute!"

My mom waved back, but I was more distracted by the boy tagging along behind the woman, who looked, luckily enough, to be about *my* age. He was pretty cute even from a distance, and I was eager to show off my improving figure—slimming just the right way in some places, expanding quite impressively in others—and improving the way Noel's clothes were hanging off it. Well, both eager and scared to death.

The neighbors came over after putting away their groceries, and we immediately learned that a) they were the Kellars and b) the boy was definitely cute—maybe a little short, but beggars can't be choosers.

And I'd been begging for a long, long time.

Next to the moving truck, the moms introduced each other, the cute boy lurking behind his mom, me lurking behind mine, stealing glances as discreetly as I could.

Mrs. Kellar turned to me. "What grade are you in?"

"Tenth," I said. "Well . . . going to be."

She perked up. "Andy too! How fantastic. Andy, come say hello."

Embarrassment, party of two, your table's ready.

The old insecurities popped up as usual. I was afraid he'd have a miserable look on his face—*Gawd, Mom, why are you forcing me to talk to this loser*—but he smiled kinda sweetly. Suddenly, he was easily twice as cute.

"Hey," Andy said. His mom shot him a glare, and he continued, "Um, nice to meet you."

"You too," I said with a smile, albeit a carefully practiced smile, one I'd been working on in the mirror probably too much, like Robert De Niro in that *Taxi Driver* movie I sneaked out of Dad's DVD collection one time. *Are you talking to me? Are you talking to me?*

And I *was* talking to this cute boy, my smile avoiding the ever-deadly TMG. That stood for Too Much Gums, another gem from Noel's diary:

> Don't smile like a lunatic. Have some self-control. Girls who smile all gummy look too eager, too excited.
> See also: That shit cray!

I'd always been envious of Noel's better smile, and I was already aware of my gum situation, thus the hours in the mirror that would get me institutionalized if my parents decided to install a secret camera in my room. (Now, *that's* a creepy thought.) I try to be aware of my smile, but the problems come on the rare but wonderful-because-they're-rare occasions when I'm actually *happy*. How backward and unfair is that? And PS, how can you be *real* if you can't even flash an authentic smile? I guess you're only allowed to finally be genuine once you've snagged the boy. You trick them by luring them into your gumless trap and then once they've fallen head over heels in love with you, you unleash the gums. And then you can smile wide and not even worry if there's spinach in your teeth or whether your nose is 100 percent guaranteed booger-free . . . well actually, you *always* hope you're booger-free, but spinach is forgivable and it's nice to have someone who will point that stuff out to you and . . . what was I doing again?

"So you're going to West Hollywood?"

Oh, right . . . *Andy.*

He was talking about my new school, West Hollywood High.

"Yeah. You go there?"

"Yeah."

"Any suggestions? Tips? Warnings? Knowledge is power."

"Is that like a PSA?" he asked, as he inspected the right heel of his sneaker. The gum on his shoe was even more interesting than me. *Remember the diary.*

"Sounds like one, but no, I think it's a Baconism."

"Baconism? As in Kevin?"

"As in Francis. Philosopher."

Oh, hell. I'm nerding him out. I need to save this, fast.

Him: Empty stare.

Me: "Anyway, bacon is bacon."

That's your save? Bacon is bacon? What does that even mean?

Him: Arched eyebrow.

Me: "Um, I'm sure Francis Bacon and Kevin Bacon are somehow separated by six degrees anyway. Most everyone else is and they even have the same last name."

This is not Noel-approved conversation. Stop moving, mouth!

Him: Slight grin, but is he laughing with me or at me?

Me: "Riveting topic, eh? Catch that 'eh'? There's another bacon: Canadian."

Andy chuckled, a good sign. "Okay, well . . . If you take algebra with Mrs. Coletti, don't get caught staring at her mustache. She's sensitive about it."

"Understood."

"I'm serious. You try not to look, but your eyes will get drawn in. It's like a tractor beam."

"What's a tractor beam?" I asked.

The incredulous look he tossed my way was priceless. "You know, a tractor beam. *Star Wars?*"

Now it was my turn to stare blankly.

"The Millennium Falcon gets drawn into the Death Star with a tractor beam? No?"

I gave him a slight shrug and a weak, entirely gumless smile.

He smiled softly, *humanely.* "Never mind."

"Phew. For a second there I was feeling bad about the Francis Bacon stuff, but you totally out-nerded me."

That got a smile. He *did* have a nice smile.

"Out-nerded you? I was talking about the Millennium Falcon. It's *Star Wars.* It's one of the biggest movies of all time. Not to mention a ship that helped bring down the Empire and made the Kessel Run in less than twelve parsecs . . . Okay, yeah, maybe *that* was a little nerdy."

"I'll make a point of watching it," I said.

"Andy," Mrs. Kellar interrupted. "Why don't you help Hailey and her family with the boxes? I need to start putting dinner together."

"That's okay," I offered, wanting to give him an out. I know I wouldn't want to help some stranger move in, new neighbor or not. "You don't have to. We have movers."

But Andy was already lifting a box off the truck, saying, "No problem." Which suddenly made me feel like *I* should take one too, so I grabbed a box that was large but fairly light, spun around and headed for the house . . . and immediately tripped over the edge of the walkway.

I went down hard.

The box went down harder.

It popped open—*what are we paying those movers for anyway, did they even tape these things*—and suddenly I saw why the box had been so light. The contents were my clothes. Specifically, the clothes from my top drawer.

More specifically, my frigging *bras and underwear.*

And now they were all over the lawn.

"Are you okay?" Andy asked, setting down his box.

"No!" I cried, meaning: *No, just keep going into the house, Andy!*

"You're not?" he said, alarmed.

"Yes! I mean no. I mean I'm fine," I said, getting up, but not before . . .

"You take it easy," he said. "I'll get these." Trying to be polite, Andy started picking up my underthings, cementing my mortification. He cradled underwear in one arm and scooped up a bra in another. I leapt to my feet and grabbed for the bra, and next thing I knew we were in a two-second tug of war that he instantly won, the bra popping out of my hands, snapping back at him and striking him, *bam*, right in the face.

Oh God. Let's just move back to Westchester *now*. It's not too late. We can pretend none of this happened.

"Are you okay?" I asked, wincing.

Andy had a hand over his eye, his face scrunched up.

"You're not okay," I said. "I'm so sorry."

"It's okay," he said, removing his hand to reveal a small welt just *underneath* his eye. (*Whew!*)

Thankfully, his attention was grabbed by something in the corner of his eye. We both turned to look.

She was about three houses down, on the opposite side of the street: a girl about our age, with short, dirty-blond hair, fair skin and eyes so big and brown I could see them clearly from the distance. (Thankfully, so could Andy, because I had somehow managed not to blind him.) She wore skinny jeans, Converse sneakers and a flannel shirt with a T-shirt *over* it instead of under. She was very pretty and definitely had her own sense of style, but she looked really cool. My first thought was one of slight panic—*don't be Andy's girlfriend, I just met a cute guy, and I didn't quite make him a cyclops*—but when I looked at Andy's face, he wasn't smiling.

I saw the girl glance at Andy and then me, and I thought I caught a bit of a smile just at the end, before she turned into her driveway and disappeared into her house.

Andy clearly was not pleased. I teased him: "Good friend of yours?"

He didn't answer at first, just finished up scooping up my undies. I almost thought he didn't hear me when he quietly said, "That's Anya."

"Okay . . . I'm guessing you guys don't hang out."

"No," he answered, almost too quickly. "I don't. You don't want to either. You're new, there's lots of cool people at the school. Not her. You should avoid her."

"Why?"

He shook his head. "Don't worry about it."

I shouldn't have pushed my luck with this cute guy, and the old Hailey wouldn't have, but Noel's diary was in my mind. *Be strong.*

"Come on, Andy," I said. "You can talk to me. Sure, we've only known each other fifteen minutes, but, I mean you've already seen my underwear. You West Hollywood boys sure do move fast."

Wow? Did I just say that? Noel's words, her confidence, coming out of my mouth.

He smiled with genuine warmth. "Hailey, stay away from Anya, okay? Trust me. She's a psycho."

"Really? She looked relatively normal."

"So did Ted Bundy."

"Ted who?"

"Google it sometime. Anyway, I know you're new and want to meet people, but don't waste your time with her. Seriously, I know some cool people. I'll introduce you. You'll be fine."

I was confused, but Andy was being sweet and I'd pushed my luck far enough. He was being nice, maybe even a little flirty, and he cared enough to give me the lowdown on this girl who was obviously bad news.

"Okay, *Andrew*," I said, having no idea where *that* came from. "It's a deal. As long as you'll please hand me back my underwear before I die of embarrassment."

As we continued to help the movers unpack the truck, I thought about how odd this all was. Little did Andy know, he'd probably be warning me against *myself* if he'd met me just a few weeks earlier, but somehow he didn't sniff out the Old Hailey working beneath my New Hailey façade—and it still felt like a façade sometimes, but sometimes it didn't. Right then it felt pretty good.

I wondered about Anya, but not all that much; Andy just helped me dodge a Loserville bullet. Noel's diary had become my center of gravity, and her inadvertent "advice" was to be ruthlessly political when deciding whom to befriend:

> Eat fattening foods, you're going to gain weight. Hang out with losers, you're going to become one. Be ruthless when choosing your friends. You are who you hang out with.

I saw Andy only twice more before the first day of school. I was hoping I'd run into him closer to that Monday, just so I could hint that I'd like him to show me around or introduce me to a few people or just remind him that I knew utterly frigging *nobody*, including the (quite possibly psycho) girl who lives just *three doors away*. But no matter how much time I spent lingering in our driveway, the chance run-in didn't happen.

I saw Anya walk by a few times, but I never crossed the street, and neither did she. She'd look over on occasion and smile, and I felt the urge to wave but resisted. I managed a soft nod, because anything less would be a dick move.

She might be a psycho, and I might be New and Improved Ruthless Hailey, but I'm not an asshole.

The last Sunday before my first day at the new school was spent trying on outfits and hairstyles and practicing smiling in the mirror.

"Hi, nice to meet you. Hi, I'm Hailey."

Hand extended. Hand not extended.

"Hey, there. Great to meet you."

Leaning in a little, scrunching my eyes, *why the hell am I scrunching my eyes,* leaning back, eyes wider now, *too* wide, now I really look like a lunatic, "Hey. Hi. Hey, how's it goin'?"

Ugh.

"You talkin' to me? Are *you* talkin' to *me*? You must be talkin' to me, because no one else is standing here. I'm standing here; you make the move. You make the move. It's your move."

I never should have watched Taxi Driver.

"Sweetie, how's it going?" Mom called from outside my door.

"Good," I responded, trying to cover. *No, I wasn't just having introductory conversations with myself. In front of my mirror. Perfecting a casual-yet-friendly greeting while simultaneously making sure not to frighten anyone with my gums and occasionally slipping into classic De Niro mode. That certainly never happened. That would be weird.*

Of the three outfits competing for the new-school debut, I vacillated between the J Brand jeans, Repetto flats and simple white Splendid cap-sleeve T-shirt, and the vintage-inspired Marc Jacobs tiny flower dress with to-the-knee flat boots. Again I thanked the powers that be for giving me the same size feet as Noel's. Ultimately, the jeans and tee won out. It was cleaner. Simpler. Not trying too hard. While, of course, *totally* trying hard not to look like I was trying hard. The delicate balance that I'm guessing never stops.

The night-before-first-day jitters made it impossible to fall asleep. I spent the entire night unintentionally practicing math. *If I can fall asleep* right now, *I'll still get six hours of sleep.* Which devolved into *five hours and nine minutes* and then *four hours and seventeen minutes* and then *three hours and six minutes.* The time I spent counting how many hours of sleep I'd get if I fell asleep right then was probably more math than I did the entire last semester in school.

The digital alarm clock just mocked me.

If I hold my breath until I pass out, will I just wake back up, or will I keep sleeping? Is that dangerous? That's probably dangerous. Yeah, don't do that.

Go to hell, alarm clock.

I eventually wound up negotiating with myself that a "cat nap" is supposedly quite energizing and *if I could just get twenty minutes of sleep, I'd be good to go.*

No such luck.

I wound up convincing myself that relaxing with your eyes closed is good enough—not that I was relaxed. But my eyes were closed.

So there was that.

No one's gonna fool around with us.

—ELLIOTT SMITH

"Angeles"

West Hollywood High School boasted a proud history in Los Angeles for being both excellent in academic achievements and architecturally outstanding. It was everything you'd expect it to be. Perfectly manicured lawns, impressive architecture, the Swim Gym—an indoor swimming pool hidden beneath a basketball court (!) and, inside, an intricate, maze-like infrastructure that guaranteed I would spend at *least* the first few weeks being two things I couldn't stand: lost and late. That's expected freshman year, but I was a sophomore now, so all my peers already went through this. They knew their way around, knew the ins and outs, knew the secret shortcuts, and I knew . . .

Jack crap.

I tried to blend in as I walked up the front steps. I caught my share of glances—who's-the-new-girl looks, I assumed—but nothing disdainful. If anything, just curious. Which was a first. Heck, that's a big-time win in the History of Hailey.

And then something surprising happened.

"I wore my Repettos too," said a girl just to my left. She was dressed in skinny jeans and a multicolored wrap sweater. She was about an inch shorter than I was and had her long blond hair in a simple ponytail, her eyes hidden behind large-framed glasses. "Cute and comfy. Perfect back-to-school choice."

"I know," I said. "It was a no-brainer."

"I'll bet Skyler wears hers too."

"She obviously has good taste," I replied, wondering who the hell Skyler was, or what the hell a Skyler is, and realizing there's no time like the present to ask. "I'm new. Who's Skyler?"

The girl's head tilted and her brow furrowed slightly. "But you're not a freshman, right?" I could sense the tips of her thorns appearing ever so slightly, just beneath the surface of her perfectly tanned skin, ready to surface in case I answered wrong.

Thankfully, I had the right answer.

"Sophomore. I just moved from New York. I'm Hailey."

She seemed relieved. "I'm Jericha."

I smiled but still wondered what she would have done if I *had* been a freshman. We walked together, making our way to the entrance. Going through those massive front doors with Jericha made it about a thousand times easier. Kids swarmed the hallways, navigating their way to their first-period classes.

"Do you know where you're going?" she asked.

"No clue," I admitted.

"Let me see your schedule."

I handed it over, grateful for the moment, our chance meeting, Repetto flats.

"You go to room three hundred," she said. "Go down this hallway and up the stairs. You'll see, the doors are all numbered."

"Okay, thanks," I said, wondering if this meant we were now friends, even just sort of say-hi friends, or if that was my send-off.

She was pretty and fashionable, just the kind of friend I was looking for, but I didn't want to appear needy. I mustered some confidence, like Noel would have had from the get-go, and smiled as I turned to the stairs. "See you around."

I found my first class with a few minutes to spare. I chose my seat cautiously, not wanting to be right up front, but also not wanting to be in the last row. To my right was a girl wearing vintage glasses, dressed like she'd stepped off the pages of a sixties-themed *Vogue* magazine spread. In contrast, to my left was a boy with bad acne who wore a skate-rat hoodie. I smiled and nodded to both of them and got a polite smile back from the girl but only a grimace from the Tony Hawk-a-be. Fine. Be that way.

Our teacher had glasses, curly brown hair and ears that stuck out like a monkey's. He turned his back to us and picked up the chalk, writing a big A on the chalkboard.

"I'm Mr. Preston," he said. "And as of right now, you all have an A in my class."

A few whoops and cheers escaped from the students' mouths, but Mr. Preston held up a hand that clearly communicated: *Not so fast.*

"Your job is to *keep* it." Therein lies the rub.

We did the usual boring introductory stuff you do on a first day at school. Nothing out of the ordinary happened in that class and nothing catastrophically embarrassing happened on my way to or during my next one. Then again, nothing good happened either. I didn't see Jericha again, not that I expected to be instant BFFs, but the only person I knew was Andy and I barely knew him either. I was totally alone.

Sure, I might not have looked like a total outcast to everyone (from what I could tell so far), but last-minute makeover aside, the reality was settling in that I was starting *completely* from scratch. I wasn't popular at my old school, but at least I had people I could be unpopular *with*.

I found myself searching the eyes of students in the halls, looking for a friendly face, waiting for some fairy godmother to magically appear in the form of a benevolent (and preferably popular) student to take me under her wing and show me the ropes.

At third period, she materialized . . . in the form of Andy.

"Hey hey hey," he said.

"Hi!"

"Guess we have history together."

"Good," I said. "I've kinda been feeling a bit loserish, what with not knowing a single person here and all."

"What? That's ridiculous. It's only your first day. And anyway, you know me."

Exactly what I was hoping he'd say.

"Well, yeah," I said as I twisted my mouth into a half smile.

"Hey, meet me at the quad at lunch," he said. "You know where the quad is?"

"I don't even know *what* a quad is."

"It's where everyone will be. I'll introduce you around."

Surely it can't be that easy? I thought.

But come lunchtime, I found my way to the quad, a patio-like area just outside of the cafeteria. There were about twelve individual seating areas with concrete tables and mounted umbrellas overhead. Kids divided themselves into culture clusters as happens at every school—some based on ethnicity, some on a shared love of music, math or meth—your usual self-imposed segregation . . . stoners, rockers, geeks, jocks, the in-crowd, the outcasts and everything in between.

In one corner of the quad I spotted Anya, my supposedly

psycho neighbor. She was sitting alone, wearing headphones and laughing. I felt a strange relief, because I knew that the Old Hailey was so desperate that halfway through the first day of school, she would have given in and tried to talk to the loser girl. (If she is a loser girl. Or a psycho. Or whatever she is.) Sitting there by herself, laughing, most people would consider that rather losery. Perhaps even crazy. The popular kids certainly would.

But New Hailey had higher standards. New Hailey knew how to be a hater. New Hailey was following Noel's diary to the letter, which helped her make friends with Andy, who is going to take her away from all this. Whatever this was. So where the hell was . . .

Andy! I spotted him standing beside a table of four girls, and I had their number instantly. This was a popular group, and quite possibly *the* popular group. You could tell just from the way they sat, the way they talked, and certainly the way they dressed. Sure, every girl picks out something "just so" for the first day of school, but *their* "just so" was just so . . . *amazing.*

They'd all have been BFFs with Jemma back at Hamilton, popular girls, girls who . . . would want nothing to do with me.

That was the old me, I reminded myself, shaking off the butterflies that started buzzing in my stomach. Actually, they felt more like piranhas, but whatever.

Andy caught my eye and waved at me, and the girls looked up. One smiled, two looked me up and down, and the other, I was pleased to realize, was Jericha.

I made my way over and said hi to Andy. He nodded and turned to the group.

"This is the girl I was telling you about," he said. "Hailey, this is Skyler, Daniella, Cassidy and—"

"Jericha," I interrupted. "We met this morning."

"We bonded over shoes," Jericha confirmed, tilting her flats to the heavens.

I wasn't oblivious to the closer once-over Skyler bestowed upon me—of course I was used to popular girls granting them to me with great generosity—but what I wasn't prepared for was the slow half smile that appeared on her face.

"Hailey," she said warmly. "We've heard all about you."

What did she hear? I wondered. About the bra-snap incident? About my lame attempts at flirting?

Chill! What would Noel do?

Go hard or go home.

"*All* about me? Everything? And I've only been here one morning," I said, surprising even myself with the next words to come out of my mouth: "Hell, by Thursday you'll be writing my biography. Just make sure to get the spelling right. There's an *i* in there."

Skyler looked almost shocked, but not a *bad* shocked, more like a *Damn, girl!* shocked, a broad grin appearing on her face.

"Well," she said, regaining her composure. "Maybe we haven't heard *all* about you. Aren't you intriguing, Miss Repetto flats?"

If I wasn't sure Skyler was the alpha dog before, I was now. The other girls sat quietly as she checked me out. This meant I had to tread carefully. Threaten her position and I'm doomed. But if I show fear . . . I'm just as doomed. Given the alternatives, might as well die a warrior. Noel said to fake it 'til you make it, and it was time to go for it.

"That's me, international girl of intrigue," I said, liking that, but unsure how to follow it. I decided to get a foot back on solid ground.

"Andy said you were the who's who of who to know," I said, mentally correcting that to *whom to know* in my head, but knowing how stupid that would have sounded.

"Yeah, that's why we keep him around," she said, giving Andy a smile that looked twice as practiced as mine. She brushed his arm and gave him a knowing look, and I felt a tiny pang of jealousy mixing with my other emotions.

She turned back to me: "Sit." So I did.

Presumably that was Andy's cue to make his exit. "I'll catch you later," he said to the group. Turning to me, he added, "Play nice with the girls. They're fragile."

That got a laugh out of the group, dying out only after Andy left. I was alone with the pack of wolves. The true test had begun.

And it was going *brilliantly*. We had more in common than I could have possibly dreamed, albeit mostly stuff that reminded me of entries from the first third of Noel's diary, which is all I'd read so far. It was almost like these girls had read it—or even *written* it.

They were bitchy, sure, but what Old Hailey considered bitchiness, New Hailey considered *self-empowerment*. They were discriminating, sure, but now that seemed more like *focus*. They knew there's nothing wrong with going after what you want.

This is whom I've been—make that who *I've been—all along,* I thought, reminding myself that perfect grammar was for nerds. *And that's not me.*

It was unreal, I thought. And truth be told, it *was* unreal. What true friendship in the history of friendships was formulated in forty-three minutes? Still, I was happy to live the lie, even if it didn't last.

When lunch was over, I walked with Skyler and the group back to the main building.

"We eat together every day," Skyler said. "If you want to join us, you have an open invitation."

"Wow, formal," I replied.

"You're damn right it is," she said, turning and stopping to face me. The other girls circled around us. "We don't just half-ass our way through life, Hailey. That invitation is highly prized around here, at least by anyone worth caring about. There are juniors who crave that very invitation, even seniors. You understand?"

"Yeah," I said, thinking, *this is a big first day.*

"Look," she said. "This is going to sound harsh, and it *is* harsh, but life is full of harsh realities, and it's kill or be killed. I don't make friends by happenstance. I like you, and so far I think you'll fit in well. But there are rules, Hailey. We keep things just the way we like it, and that means sticking to some policies."

"There's a rule book?" I said, trying to sound light. "It's the first day of school, I'm not sure how many study materials I can handle."

"It's not a book, but we treat it like our bible," Skyler said. "And no one deviates from it, not once, not ever. Don't stress about it, though. We'll talk more later. It's a big first day for you, Hailey with an *i.*"

"Wait," I said, my curiosity piqued. "Can I get a few examples? We still have ten minutes until class."

"Okay," Skyler said. "Don't invite anyone to lunch. If you meet someone in one of your classes who you think might fit in, think again. Everyone who's invited is already on the list."

This brought chuckles from the other girls, but I was taken aback.

So I'm not allowed to have other friends? Haters sure are gonna hate!

This wasn't the time to cause trouble, though. It was only my first day. *Play along.*

"Okay," I said. "What else?"

"Well, I know this is going to sound a little controlling, but it's for your own good," Skyler said. "If you're at a store, like, on Robertson or at Barneys or whatever and you happen to see something you think you like? I need you to take a picture and text it to me before you try it on, let alone buy it, to make sure a) I don't already have it, or b) I don't want it."

"Huh."

"Did I lose you there? You have to keep up. We don't hang back for stragglers."

"Well," I said, slowing my thoughts down, trying to choose my words carefully. "First, I don't know what Robertson is—is that a store?"

Cassidy chimed in: "It's a street."

Then Daniella: "Fairly decent but not, like, couture." I'd come to learn she was the daughter of the famous fashion designer Eliza Hunt, who'd made her meteoric rise in the fashion world on the heels of a scandalous affair with a famous rock star. Nobody knew if Daniella was actually his daughter and nobody talked about it.

"Not a problem," I said, trying to act blasé. "I don't know it and I don't go shopping all that much anyway."

"Then it won't be a problem," Skyler said, then added, "but really, photos first. It's a good rule to live by . . . because even if I don't want it, you'll want my opinion."

"Or mine," Daniella added.

It was weird. I didn't know what it was like to have these kinds of friends and I didn't want to rock the boat because in the hierarchy of popular girls, Skyler was obviously the Queen Bee and we were lucky to be part of her posse. This wasn't how I was used to friendships going down. But at this point I was grateful to have any friendships, let alone the most coveted ones in my grade. I wasn't about to screw this up.

"Give me your phone," Jericha said, palm extended.

"My phone?" I asked. "Why?"

She looked at me like I was a child. "Duh. So I can put our numbers on your speed dial."

"Umm . . . okay," I said, reaching into my bag and handing her my clunky iPhone 4, several years old but still kicking. Normally I wouldn't have been self-conscious—so what if I didn't have the latest gadget—but I worried that they'd notice and think less of me.

"Whoa," Jericha said. "Antique much?"

And there it was. "Yeah," I said with a wistful sigh, and suddenly the lies came pouring out. "It was my boyfriend's phone. He died in a car accident and his parents gave it to me and I transferred my service to it. I know it's totally outdated but . . . I don't know, I just can't let go of it."

"Oh my God," Skyler said. "That's so sad."

It *was* sad. I felt like a total asshole for lying, but when I weighed the pros and cons in the millisecond before my lie came flying out of my mouth, dead-boyfriend sob story trumped out-of-touch loser with an outdated iPhone.

"What happened?" Skyler asked, her brows furrowed, her hand now clutching my arm either to show support or check my blood pressure—her grip was so tight I wasn't sure.

"Um, it was a fire," I started to say, already screwing up the story I *just* invented. *What the hell! My poor, dead, mythical boyfriend deserved so much better.*

I tried to recover: "I mean, his car caught fire after the accident, so he technically died in the fire. Smoke inhalation mostly. He was unconscious. He didn't suffer. I really don't want to talk about it. It's still too painful."

"What was his name?" Cassidy asked.

I froze for a minute as I tried to pick the perfect dead-boyfriend name—*Edward, Jacob, Conan, Shia, OMG, what's wrong with me*—but thankfully Jericha took pity.

"She just said she doesn't want to talk about it. It's obviously still painful for her. *She's carrying his phone.*"

"It's still a little fresh," I said, and then looked away, hoping a new topic of conversation would be hovering just over one of their shoulders.

"We totally get it," Cassidy said. "And we're here for you."

I felt so stupid lying like that, but just as the clothes I was wearing weren't mine, neither was this new persona.

I was still ironing out the wrinkles.

Be my friend.

—SIA

"Breathe Me"

CHAPTER 5

If the most boring person in the world married the most socially awkward person in the world and they had a baby and that baby grew up to have adult acne, wear tie-dye and become my new art teacher, you'd pretty much have the picture. Miss Hoyt: art teacher exBOREDinaire.

Holy snoozefest, was this class tedious. This was like watching paint dry on a wall in a retirement center being covered live by C-SPAN. (You know C-SPAN, right? That channel you flip by as quickly as possible to get to the comparatively action-packed C-SPAN 2.) Considering my love of art and that my future plans for world domination were somehow focused around art of some kind, this did not bode well. I weighed the pros and cons of sleeping through the class for the whole year, wasting precious time— but catching up on the rest I wasn't getting at night—*or* seeing if I could transfer out and maybe get a free period instead.

But then there was Chris Roberts. Piercing blue eyes, fair skin, perfect red lips and a couple of freckles on his adorable nose. He looked like Ian Somerhalder but less vampirey—not that I'd mind being bitten on the neck by him either. He was by far the best part of being in that class, which was terrible considering it was my favorite subject. I could only gawk at the cute boy for so long before it would become obvious and stalkerish. Plus, he caught me looking at him once already. Second day of class. He glanced over at me and I felt like I was busted staring at him so I rolled my eyes at him, as if to say, "Could this class possibly be more boring?" but never having spoken to him prior to that moment, for all I know he could have just thought I was just some eye-rolling weirdo. I made a habit of not looking at him during class after that. Ditto for PE, which we also had together. Talk about an uneven playing field— pun intended if you're into that, but whatever—putting me in shorts and a T-shirt next to Chris in all his golden-goddedness. It was patently unfair. He looked like a *Men's Fitness* cover model from every angle. Whereas I remained of the opinion the only way I looked even semi-okay was if I rotated my torso exactly twenty degrees to the left while flexing my right calf just less than halfway while turning my head fifteen degrees to the right while also lifting my chin just high enough to reduce any appearance of a double chin but not high enough to show everyone the inside of my nostrils. And it's *really* hard to get through school maintaining that pose the entire day. Let alone even trying to walk.

I stuck it out for the first week, working on my cartoon for almost the entire class, eyes down (to avoid Chris Roberts), taking full advantage of the fact that Miss Hoyt at first seemed physically incapable of actually wandering more than five feet away from her desk. I secretly wondered if she had an ankle sensor that would alert the LAPD if she took one more step in our direction. *What did you do to get desk arrest, Miss Hoyt? Did you kill the real art teacher, the one who knew the difference between Manet, Monet and Mo'Nique?*

Yep, that was pretty much the whole period, until we had five minutes left. Then I'd flip my sketchbook to a fresh page and bang out whatever lame assignment she'd asked us to do, and I'd do it better than anyone else in the class. (Gauging from her examples, that included *her*.)

Unfortunately, each day Miss Hoyt started venturing farther from her desk—*guess her lawyer got her acquitted, but I hear that's LA for you*—and tried to sneak peeks of what I was *really* working on. By Thursday, she just flat out asked me if she could see it.

I wasn't thrilled at the idea, but that felt like Old Hailey behavior, being self-conscious and wary of disapproval. New Hailey wouldn't give a crap what this tie-dyed lady thought, so I handed her the sketch pad.

My comic was a variation of my character Abby Invisible— but my move had given me new insights and, I suppose, a more biting sense of humor. I was working on a five-panel strip in which the popular girl gets hit in the face with a volleyball during PE. Her nose is swollen and crooked. All of her "minions" appear to be horrified. . . . But there's a twist. Suddenly, swollen, crooked noses are all the rage, as minions line up outside of Dr. Fredrick B. Utcher's plastic surgery office for their "fix."

"See me after class," Miss Hoyt said. That was it. No strong reaction to my cartoon either way. She walked back up to the front of the room, yammered on for a few more minutes that felt like nine days and then the bell rang.

I bet I won't be calling this art teacher by her first name, I thought. *Whatever her first name is. What was it again? Mothra? Widow-maker? Prometheus?*

I gathered my things and walked to the front of the class.

"You seem to have your own ideas of how you'd like to spend this hour," she said.

"Sorry," I said, then added, "I do your assignments."

"I know. But you're obviously bored."

"Yeah, kinda," I said, looking everywhere but at her.

"I'm recommending you for the school paper," she said matter-of-factly. "The newspaper staff meets at the same time as this class."

"Oh," I said, a little bit taken aback and a lot pleased. "That's cool."

"I thought you might think so. Perhaps you can do your comic for the paper."

"That would be awesome."

"No," Miss Hoyt said. "You know what's awesome?"

"Uhh . . ." I wasn't sure where she was going with this. "I guess not?"

"Childbirth is 'awesome.' The fact that we can travel to space is 'awesome.' Transferring out of a class is a lucky break—it's not 'awesome.' If you can't learn anything from me in art class, let me at least teach you *this*: Your use of the word 'awesome' is not awesome. The way everyone overuses that word has desensitized it so much that you have no words left when you experience something that truly *is* awesome. And as the *writer* of your comics . . . words matter."

I stood there for a moment taking it all in: the lackluster teacher with the shrewd and valid point. And she was confident enough to recognize her limits and want me to be able to excel at my art through the school paper. There was no ego. She was a better person than I'd given her credit for. And I felt awful for my behavior, my judgment, for making my boredom so obvious.

Though she wouldn't be the one to inspire my art, she'd be the person who taught me a lesson I needed, beyond the whole "awesome" thing: Don't judge a book by its tie-dyed clothes and adult acne.

On my way home from school, I noticed Anya standing by her mailbox. She smiled at me, so I smiled back. A smile was okay, I figured. I'm not going to be a total jerk. But then she turned ever so slightly and I saw something that changed everything: a black T-shirt showing a guy holding a microphone with the quote, "I don't mean to sound bitter, cold, or cruel, but I am, so that's how it comes out."

Maybe this was going off script, but I had to investigate. I walked up and pointed at the quote on her shirt.

"Holy crap, that's Bill Hicks, right?"

"Yeah!" she said, seemingly surprised to have someone actually recognize the quote. "You know who he is?"

"I love him! Well, I never saw him when he was alive—mostly because I wasn't born yet—but my dad used to play his CDs all the time."

"I know. So unfair. You know people who are like, 'I was born at the wrong time,' but they're talking about a whole era like the sixties or something? I'm, like—how about just ten years earlier, so I could see my comic heroes? He was brilliant. He's why I want to be a stand-up comic someday."

"That's so cool," I said. "I would never have the guts to get up on a stage. But I do draw comics—like comic strips."

"Now *that's* cool," she said. "I can't even draw stick figures. Do you know Mitch Hedberg?"

"No," I said. The name sounded familiar but I wasn't certain.

"Okay, you need to come over right now," she said. "We are going to—"

She stopped abruptly.

"What?" I asked.

Her face wrinkled a little. "Well . . . I mean, if you want to. If not that's cool, I get it . . . honestly."

I figured it out. She'd seen me with Andy, with Skyler and the crew, and wondered what my deal was, this girl from just down the street.

I didn't know how Noel would handle this, but she would do something empowered, right? She'd do whatever she thought was right.

"I'm Hailey," I said, extending my hand. "I'm sorry I didn't say hi earlier."

"Anya," she said. "But I'll bet you know that."

"Yeah," I said a bit sheepishly. "Anyway, I'd love to come in."

"Really?" she said, brightening. "Good call, neighbor. I'm about to change your world."

And like that, what felt like my first *real* friendship in LA was born. We went inside, Anya introduced me to her parents, and we spent the next three hours listening to bootleg CDs of Mitch Hedberg and Bill Hicks, two of the world's most brilliant comics (who both, sadly, died way too young). We laughed our asses off.

Spending just a little time with her, I could tell Anya would be great at comedy. She made these biting, hilarious comments that made me wonder: *Is this why Andy thinks she's a psycho? Just because she has a brilliantly dark sense of humor?*

We spent three hours quoting jokes and listening and laughing and bonding. Part of me felt conflicted about "fraternizing with the enemy"—I mean, not only was she deemed uncool, I had specifically been warned away from her. But I couldn't help it. She was cool. She was real. She was exactly the kind of person I'd be friends with if I weren't in the midst of this transformation. And it also felt pretty good to let down the hater façade and just be me. I figured it was time to address the elephant in the room.

"Hey, what's the deal with you and Andy?"

"The deal? Why? What did he say? Wait: Let me guess. He said I was a nutjob and to keep your distance."

"Pretty close."

"How close?"

"I think the word 'psycho' might have popped up."

Anya actually laughed a little, but it was the saddest, most bitter laugh I'd ever heard. Suddenly I wished we were listening to Bill and Mitch again.

"It's okay," I said. "We don't have to talk about it."

"That's alright," she said. "Do you like Andy?"

"You mean, like, *like* like?" I said. "I don't know . . . he's cute, sure, but really I'm just glad to meet a guy who's friendly and who's introduced me to people. It's tough being new, you know. I've made a bunch of new friends through him."

"Like Skyler and Jericha and that bunch. I've seen you hanging out with them."

"Yeah, them."

"They're all assholes. Andy too. Trust me, if anyone knows, I do. I'm sorry. I know you're new, but—you'll see."

"Okay . . . ," I said, unsure exactly how to process this. I really liked Anya, and I already felt like I could trust her, which left an unsettling feeling in the pit of my stomach. I'd worked hard to get in with a popular crew and wasn't keen on choosing sides.

Anya was silent, looking out the window.

I dove in: "So what do you mean that if anyone knows, *you* do?"

She took a deep breath and twisted her mouth a little as she thought about her answer. She looked at me for a few seconds, and I felt like she was trying to gauge whether she could confide in me.

Then she just went for it.

"I was a cheerleader all through middle school, and freshman year too. Skyler was my best friend. Jericha, Cassidy—all her 'minions'—we were all tight. That was the clique. Which means, as you've figured out, that was *the* clique."

I looked at her blankly. Was this a joke?

"Hailey, you should probably be thanking me. That seat you're enjoying on the quad at lunch, that used to be *mine*."

Nothing about Anya, other than her natural beauty, suggested that she used to be a cheerleader. Everything in her room and her wardrobe screamed counterculture, right down to the Converse sneakers with the not-so-carefully-drawn anarchy symbol emblazoned in ballpoint. This girl did not scream "cheerleader" at first glance. Or fourteenth.

"You seem surprised," Anya said. "What, the group doesn't spend lunch period reminiscing about all the great times we had together?"

I cleared my throat. "They've never even mentioned you."

"Could be worse," she said. "They could be running around telling all the new kids I'm a psycho."

I cringed a little at her jab at Andy but let it pass. And before I could say anything else, Anya dropped the bombshell.

"I got pregnant," she said. "I was stupid and careless and it was awful."

Stunned, all I could respond with was, "Wow. I'm sorry."

It also occurred to me that there was nothing about Anya's room, or her house, to indicate that she was a mother. No crib, or a bronze shoe, a cute onesie with a clever saying—something like "iPooped" or "This is what happens when you forget the condom" or "I lived in a belly for nine months and all I got was this stupid onesie."

I'd never been in a conversation like this and didn't know what to say, what was appropriate. What fell out of my mouth was a generic, "What happened?"

"I didn't want to have an abortion. I also knew I couldn't see myself being a mom at fifteen—just one episode of that *Teen Mom* show was enough to convince me of that. I talked with my parents, they were upset but understanding. We decided I'd keep her and put her up for adoption."

"Wow," I said again, noting the word "her." "When . . ."

"Last year," she said. "I found out early freshman year. I had to drop out of cheerleading. I didn't want anyone to know—other than the father, I only told one person. I said I had a chronic hamstring problem, which also helped me get out of PE, and thus having to undress in the locker room. I covered up the baby bulge with a carefully coordinated ensemble, as all good undercover teen moms should, until I really started to show. Then I left. I told everyone my dad was sick and I was doing homeschooling for a few months to take care of him."

Information overload. So many questions and thoughts popped up in my mind: *What's the baby's name? Was her dad actually sick? Speaking of dads, who's the father of the baby? Is it that really handsome Mediterranean-looking guy in my biology class, because he looks* way *too old to be a sophomore, like he's a seventeen-year-old exchange student or something. I bet he can grow a full beard. Wow, this was heavy stuff. Poor Anya. The worst thing* I've *ever experienced was my DVR not recording the season finale of* Pretty Little Liars.

"So, the baby . . . ," I said, prodding just a little.

"Yeah," she said, her eyes misting the tiniest bit. "She was fine. The delivery went great. She's . . . she's with a very nice family."

She stopped there. I waited.

"So . . . everything went according to plan, as much as you can plan something that was completely freaking unplanned. I wanted to get back to school for the last few weeks of freshman year. I've always been in good shape, so I had just a little extra baby weight, nothing too obvious. So I went back in May."

"Sounds . . . okay," I said.

"You'd think. After going through all that in your personal life, you might think school doesn't matter so much anymore. But it's not true. My life, the baby, my parents, the adoption, all of that—my whole world was turned upside down. I was looking forward to school, to—you know, pretentious as it sounds, the whole social structure there. It was familiar. It was comfortable. It was . . . safe."

It was dawning on me. "But the one person you told . . . or the father . . ."

"Not the father," Anya said. "He kept his trap shut. I'll give him that."

"But the one person you told . . . Skyler."

"Ding ding ding!" Anya said. "The news was *everywhere*. And it wasn't just the pregnancy—I'm not the first teenager to get knocked up, I won't be the last—but she'd made up all this horrible stuff, that I'd been sleeping around, I didn't know who the father was, all this bullshit. I wasn't just a teen mom, I was the biggest slut in the history of the school."

"Wow," I said. "I mean, are you sure that all came from her? Why would she do something like that?"

"I don't know," Anya said. "That's the thing. She wouldn't tell me. After I found out I was pregnant, she just acted like everything was fine, 'Let me know if there's anything I can do,' all that stuff. As soon as I went on leave she didn't come around, wouldn't take my phone calls or messages, so I thought something was weird. It hurt. I thought everything would be better when I got back to school. Then I found out she'd betrayed me, called me all sorts of horrible things, you name it. It was devastating."

"I can't even imagine."

"Yeah. The whispers, the stares—I couldn't take it. After everything I'd been through, I just needed—here I go with the shrink talk, I know, but I needed a support system. And a few people I know came up to me and tried to be supportive, but I was already dealing with the emotions from the adoption and—I just left. I finished out the last few weeks in homeschool."

I figured I should try to come up with something more constructive than "Wow." I didn't want to pry too much about the baby and the father, so . . .

"Look, obviously I don't know Skyler very well," I said. "And I get that she can be kinda vain and self-serving and all, but that's your average popular sophomore right there. I didn't get the vibe that she'd do whatever she could to destroy her best friend's life for no apparent reason."

"She's complicated," Anya said. "I wouldn't have expected that either, but on the other hand . . . well, she's complicated. Hang around her long enough and you'll see."

"You expect me to keep hanging out with her after what you told me?"

Anya shook her head softly. "I'm not stupid, Hailey. You have a lot going on. You're pretty, you dress well, you're smart and funny, and you have the good fortune of catching on very quickly with the school's most popular clique. You're a very lucky girl. You'd be an idiot to just throw all that away."

That was a lot to digest, even as Anya's compliments warmed my heart. No one would have ever said that about Old Hailey. Had I really transformed so much, so quickly? Noel's diary really did have amazing powers.

"I don't know," I said. "If Skyler treated you—her *best friend*—like that . . . I can't imagine . . ."

"What she'd do to someone she hardly knows?" Anya said. "Exactly. So be careful, Hailey."

"I will. I'm so sorry to hear about what happened. Do you want to tell me more about—"

"No, not right now," she said, offering a tiny smile. "No point in bumming us both out any further. Maybe sometime later, cool?"

"Cool," I said, a crazy mix of conflicting emotions bouncing around inside me. "Thanks for turning me on to Mitch Hedberg. He's awesome." *And that time, Miss Hoyt, I meant it.*

"'Dogs are forever in the push-up position,'" Anya said, doing her damnedest to break the mood.

I played along: "'I am wearing a vest. If I had no arms, it would be a jacket.'"

We laughed, and it was a good, cleansing laugh, reciting a few more Mitch Hedberg lines. I wished it could go on forever, because I had *no* idea how I was going to handle school tomorrow.

The next day was going surprisingly okay. I mean, if you can separate out the anxiety of having to get into a bathing suit in front of the whole PE class—the class, once again, that happened to include a certain super-sexy slab of studly hotness named Chris Roberts, a guy so intimidatingly handsome he could make Miss Teen USA feel like Miss Teen Wolf. Oh, and also take out that moment when I thought he was waving "hello" to me on my way to the Swim Gym and I waved back and it turned out he was waving to Tyler Colgan—not embarrassing at all. (Kill me.)

But once we got to the pool and I looked around, I noticed something—or maybe I noticed a lack of something: my requisite humiliation and self-loathing (which was usually accompanied by tears and much cupcake eating later in the day). I actually felt almost comfortable in my own skin, and that was a first. My newfound confidence allowed me to focus more on swimming and less on finding the best angle to hide my problem areas . . . which is not to say I didn't still take issue with certain zones. (Pizza, why can't I quit you?)

I was on fire—or whatever the equivalent of "on fire" is when you're "in water." (*En fuego* sounds *awesome*. *En agua*, not so much. No offense, Michael Phelps. Or Aquaman. Or Nemo.) I was practically flying back and forth in laps, and people were noticing—even Coach Dalton. He was even trying to get my attention, so I raced to the shallow end of the pool and stood up . . . noticing a breeze as I did. The terminal velocity or whatever physics equation applies when you're *in hell* had caused the fabric of my bathing suit to somehow rebel against me. Somehow, without my noticing, either the material crept down or my left boob crawled out—or the two conspired against me in a moment of bathing suit/boob mutiny.

Long story short: My boob was out! Can you say *most embarrassing moment of your life*?

So much for feeling confident. *That* was why Coach Dalton had been trying to get my attention—not because my speed was so mighty (though it was impressive). He only had to clear his throat before I felt the draft, looked down and realized what had happened. I was pretty sure I was going to die from mortification. If I'd still been in the deep end I would have just sunk to the bottom and stayed there.

Seriously, God? Was it not bad enough that I did the mistake-wave? Not humiliating enough? Had to whip out a boob just to make sure I didn't get too confident? Well, mission accomplished.

Luckily, not too many people saw. Less luckily?

I was pretty sure Chris Roberts *did*.

"Hey!" I heard, as I turned slightly to see who was shouting. Yep, of course. It was Chris.

Chris Roberts.

Chris *oh-my-God-it's-Chris-Roberts* Roberts.

Nope. Not gonna fall for that one again. I'd turn around and say, "Hey!" and then I'd see and hear whoever he was *actually* talking to say "hey" at the same time and then I'd want to crawl under a rock and do a tiny high five with a snail over how much of a loser I was.

Not this time. Not again.

I sped up, repeating one of Noel's rules over and over in my head:

When in doubt, do nothing and say nothing.

"Hey," he called again, even as I attempted to flee at breakneck walking speed. "Hailey, wait up!"

He knows my name?!

I stopped, kinda thrilled, kinda terrified, running my hand quickly over my chest to make sure the girls were tucked all safe and snug in their beds. Then I took a deep breath and turned.

"Oh, hey," I said. I tried to remain cool, calm and collected, a virtually impossible task, but one I tried to make easier by completely avoiding eye contact. No way could I look him in the eyes. His piercing blue eyes. His beautiful blue eyes that had just witnessed the dastardly escape of my renegade boob. *Damn you, boob!*

"Relax," he said. "Nobody saw. Don't be embarrassed."

"Kinda impossible to not be."

He shook his head gently and flashed a soft smile. "Don't sweat it. These things happen. Jeez, play enough sports and you'll see stuff flopping out all over the place. It was just a couple of seconds, and honestly, we've all had worse things happen."

Wow, he's actually kind of sweet!

"Um, thanks," I said.

"Besides," Chris said, now flashing a much wider smile. "You have *nothing* to be embarrassed about."

Whoa! Was he flirting with me? Did he like my boob? Did he want to see the other one?

I was stunned. He saw that I was stunned. And he took it the wrong way.

"Oh God, I'm sorry!" he said. "That's not what I meant. I didn't mean you had *nothing*—you have *something*. You have a really nice something! You . . . you have a couple of nice some—"

"No, no," I found myself saying, laughing as I did. "I got it, Chris. I got what you meant the first time."

"Oh, good," he said, wiping pretend sweat off his brow.

Suddenly the embarrassment was melting away, replaced by all sorts of warm fuzzies.

"So," I said, "stuff flopping out all over the place?"

He laughed. "Well, sorta. Sports, the gym, PE—like Mark Montero, his shorts split when he was climbing the rope last year. Turns out he wasn't wearing underwear. Full-on b-hole exposed to everyone below."

"Gross," I said, laughing.

"I'll say," he agreed. "Or like your buddy, Cassidy."

"Cassidy?" I asked. "What about her?"

"Well, she had a . . . I guess what you girls call a 'chicken cutlet'? One day at basketball, hers fell right out of her bra. *Splat*. Flat on the court. And . . . just as flat on her chest."

(Chris was talking about the clear silicone implants you can stuff your bra with. Luckily, I didn't need them, but most of my friends had them.)

"Oh God," I said. "Poor Cassidy."

"Exactly. And then there's all the people who have gotten pantsed—"

"Okay, okay," I interrupted. "I get it."

"So, don't be embarrassed."

"Fine," I said begrudgingly.

"Fine," he said back with an air of cockiness/adorableness.

"Anything else?" I asked.

"Not presently," he said.

"Okay, then," I said.

"Okay, then," he said, flashing that gorgeous smile one more time. Then he was off to his next class.

I was in an oh-my-God-Chris-Roberts-just-spoke-to-me haze when I passed by Skyler and Cassidy on my way to Room 251 to do my new free period. I gave them a quick wave and was almost inside when . . .

"Where are you going?" Skyler asked.

"I transferred out of art. I'm working at the school paper. I think it's this way."

"Really?" Skyler asked, her face scrunched up in the most unattractive way. "Hailey, are you a nerd?" she asked. "I hate to break this to you, but *nerds* work at the school paper."

"A nerd? Last time I checked, no," I said, standing my ground. "Wait, hang on—let me make sure."

I gave myself a once-over, even did a little spin, making a show of my fashionable clothes and my sharp look. *I sure as hell don't look like a nerd,* I thought. *At least not anymore.*

I smiled. "Nope. Definitely not a nerd."

That at least got a chuckle out of Skyler. Cassidy laughed too, following Skyler's lead once she knew it was okay.

"Then why on *earth* are you working for the paper?" Skyler asked. "Are you taking pity on the freaks? Were chess club and the role-playing-games society already full?"

I flashed her a confident smile, gears turning in my head. How do I spin this one?

"Really, Skyler? I'm surprised this move never occurred to you." *That's it, put her on the defensive.*

Skyler looked confused. "Um, what never occurred to me?"

Yeah, Hailey, what?

Shut up, inner voice! I'm working on it!

"Newspaper staff takes all the pictures and chooses what goes in the paper," I said, a mountain climber scrambling for a toe-hold. "How else do we make sure that they use good pictures of us? Plus, they put together the *yearbook*. You do *not* want to leave that to the losers."

Skyler paused for a second, then a smile spread across her face. She approved.

"Taking one for the team," she said. "I like your style. Can't say *I'd* ever do that . . . but hey—it'll be good to have someone on the inside of Dork Central. Just try not to catch anything."

What I thought: *Like intelligent thoughts?*

What I said: "I'll wear a hazmat suit."

I cringed as the words came out of my mouth. It's fun to be with the in crowd, I thought, but did they hate themselves as much as I was hating myself right then? This popular stuff was complicated.

On the other hand, isn't this what real life was like? My dad had told me before that you need to have a wide range of friends, and you have to act according to the situation. *Be whatever you need to be for the person in front of you,* he said. *That's how you'll become president.* We always laughed about that, but now I really started thinking about it. I can do that. If Dad could, and Noel sure could, I could too.

And then it all went to shit.

Because lunchtime rolled around, of course, and after I picked up my how-the-hell-can-you-call-this-pizza lunch tray, there was Anya in her usual spot, sitting alone. And out of the corner of my eye I saw Skyler waving me over to *our* usual spot. *Is that what it was now?*

And I just stood there while the cartoon Angel Hailey and Devil Hailey popped up on each of my shoulders.

Devil Hailey: *Do you really want to do this now? Maybe tomorrow. Go sit with Skyler.*

Angel Hailey: *Screw Skyler. She's a bitch! Sit with Anya!*

Devil Hailey: *You don't know that Skyler's a bitch! Maybe Anya's lying about everything! Maybe she really is a psycho! Maybe she never was a cheerleader, never had a baby! You're taking her word for it! You don't know!*

Angel Hailey: *You know. In your heart, you know.*

I don't even remember making the decision. I just suddenly found myself sitting next to Anya.

She looked up.

"What the *hell* are you thinking?"

"What?" I asked. "I need a place to sit and eat this overcooked blackboard eraser they call pizza. Here's as good a place as any."

Anya leaned in. "This is the 'social suicide' stuff you read about in books or see in movies. Jason is in his mask and he's right behind you, about to kill your blossoming popularity and crush your prom-queen dreams."

"Whatever," I said.

"Bullshit," she said. "It's not 'whatever.' I'm serious. They're staring at you right now, doing all their devious mental calculations and trying to decide whether treason is punishable by death even in tenth grade, and believe me, they think it is. Get your ass up right now and go over there and tell them you only sat down here so you could tell me I smell like roadkill and ask why I can't get around to bathing more than once every leap year."

"But—"

"*Seriously*, Hailey," she said, her eyes pleading. "I'm fine. I'm good. You don't have to do this. Don't—"

And then we were surrounded: Skyler, Daniella, Cassidy, Jericha. I noticed Skyler giving Anya the evil eye. Anya, staring back, scratched an itch on her nose . . . with her middle finger.

Skyler turned to me. Once we caught eyes, I knew things would never be the same. She said: "Did you *not* see me waving at you?"

I decided to play along for now. Maybe there still was some way to salvage this. Maybe I had the unique ability to walk this line. Hell, you never know 'til you try.

"Hey, Skyler," I said pleasantly. "Did you need to talk about something? Or . . . something?" I was hoping for a good reason to leave Anya other than a popularity contest.

"Actually, yes," she replied. "It's important."

"Okay," I replied, and as I grabbed my tray and got up, I mouthed the word *sorry* to Anya, who replied with a soft, understanding nod that made me feel ten times worse.

We returned to the table, where the something Skyler wanted to talk about turned out to be . . . nothing. I expected some sort of grilling for my impudence, that I dared to sit next to the outcast Anya, but it wasn't even discussed. It was as if Anya wasn't even worth talking about, as if the girls felt they would be poisoned by even letting her name cross their lips.

Because they had far more important things to discuss, like clothes, and shoes and bangs, and *Holy crap why am I sitting here?* I thought. Fact is, girls live in an endless loop of:

1) contemplating bangs
2) getting bangs
3) hating a recent bangs decision
4) growing out bangs

. . . but that doesn't mean they need to be discussed every single day.

"Bangs are a commitment," Daniella said. "You have to really know what you're in for. And always carry bobby pins, because at some point they will drive you crazy and you'll need to do damage control."

"I'm just so not a bangs person," Cassidy said. "They make my forehead sweat and I totally break out from them. Blech. I mean, they look great on you—super cute—but not on me."

As I listened to the riveting bangs discussion, I knew Anya was telling the truth about everything. That's when I also figured out that the minions were just as bad as Skyler, if not worse. And I realized it doesn't *get* any worse than Skyler.

I started to determine my course of action, but Skyler, once again, took care of that for me.

She leaned over and whispered in my ear: "Hailey, I'm letting it go this time because you're new. Just this time. You only get one warning." Then she leaned back and rejoined the increasingly vapid conversation.

I sat there steaming, then spoke:

"Warning?" I asked, not whispering, loud enough for everyone to hear.

"Excuse me?" Skyler said, turning.

"I don't think I quite understand what you're trying to say."

Skyler looked aghast, then irritated, then . . . *dark*. "I was saying, 'You're welcome for me saving you from that loser's table.'

What I was saying was that if you hadn't come with us right then . . . you would have been done."

"Just like that?" I asked.

"Even quicker."

"Wow."

It was like everything Noel's journal had taught me was lead-ing up to this moment. Noel would certainly be Team Bitch Squad, I knew that much. But as I thought about it for a moment, there really wasn't a decision to be made—I couldn't *stand* these people.

"You know what?" I picked up my tray again and stood, a weapons-grade smile spreading across my face. "I guess I'm 'done' then."

Skyler confirmed it: "*So* done, Hailey. Big mistake. You think you look good? You look *okay*, Hailey, and guess what? No one notices *okay*."

I balanced my tray in my left hand and turned away. As I walked off, I lifted my right hand and extended it back toward them in a familiar gesture.

"Do they notice me giving you the finger?"

The Hater Tots chimed in, hurling insults at my back. I could hear the barrage of insults being hissed in my direction, but I didn't stop or turn around. I felt like an action hero in a movie, walking in slow motion as buildings behind me exploded in my wake. Those buildings being my fleeting brush with popularity, but I didn't care. I walked back and sat down next to my one true friend. The first real friend I'd made at my new school: Anya.

She looked up, and I smiled. "This seat taken?"

Funny how we make new friends.

—WILCO

"Can't Stand It"

CHAPTER
6

"The Breezeway is this covered walkway between two of our school buildings," Anya explained. It was a warm afternoon, and we occupied the children's swings in the park, twisting the chains we hung from into impossibly tight spirals and then kicking up our feet to spin like Tasmanian devils. "That's where kids and teachers who think they're cool smoke."

"Which is not to be confused with Stonerville," Xandra chimed in. "That's where the partiers skip class and smoke pot."

"Got it," I said. Getting the lay of the land was proving to be almost more complicated than some of my classes. Luckily, my friends list was growing, and my new friends were happy to catch me up on the *real* deal. My brief foray into popularity didn't exactly prove helpful in learning about my surroundings or how to get around. With the Bitch Squad, the most important thing impressed upon me was that I wasn't allowed to go shopping without an ankle bracelet that would alert the freakin' police if I tried on an article of clothing that Skyler might want.

In the week following Lunch Rebellion, Anya introduced me to

Xandra, Emily and Kura. Xandra's a theater geek, known for developing impossible crushes on gay boys. She planned to be the next Natalie Portman. Academy Award? Yes, please. (Starvation diet to achieve Ballerina Body . . . no thanks.) Xandra would buy up all the tabloids every single week, not realizing (or caring) that half the stories were manufactured nonsense. The stories that were true were worth it—any tips she could glean were welcome. Between building sets and actual rehearsals, Xandra was busy three days a week after school. The rest of her time was ours—at least when her nose wasn't buried deep in an *Us Weekly*.

Emily is a bit of a contradiction. She's a staunch vegan who made it clear to everyone that "Fur Is Murder," and, yes—she won't eat anything related to meat or dairy, so in that sense she's socially conscious . . . but get her near a mall, and she suddenly turns into Winona Ryder on a theft-bender.

Kura (short for Sakura) is basically a genius. Never mind that she takes all advanced placement classes, but she also takes satellite classes at UCLA, which is kind of a big deal considering that's college and she's only a sophomore in high school. She actually tested *out* of high school because she's so smart, but she's staying because of studies that show problems with many genius kids who test out and enter college way too soon: They not only miss out on crucial life experiences in high school, but many grow up to be socially awkward. While Kura is unquestionably a "brain," she also happens to be drop-dead gorgeous. Her dad is Irish and her mom is Japanese, and she looks like she could be a model. Well, she could if she dressed better (she doesn't), styled her hair on occasion (she's busy studying books that confuse me just in the table of contents) or ditched the biggest and ugliest pair of eyeglasses you've ever seen. Consequently, her beauty remains a bit of a secret to the rest of the school.

All the girls had horror stories about the different ways they'd suffered humiliation at the hands of Skyler and her minions. We bonded over lunches and after-school frozen yogurt runs, and I'd wince at their tales of trauma, thankful that I escaped before any of that evil rubbed off on me. Sure, I thought about how far I'd strayed from what would have been "approved" friends according to Noel. But those brief what-if moments were far outweighed by how nice it felt to have friends I could just be myself with, though I would get a little self-conscious about the lie I still perpetuated when they'd mention how strange it was for a "popular" girl to suddenly hang out with the nobodies. Everyone knew the story of how Skyler betrayed Anya, of course, but why would I give up a seat in the Queen's Court, as it were, to hang with the misfit crew? I usually just shrugged it off, said "Nobody tells me who my friends can be," and left it at that.

Even though I'd been exiled by the Bitch Squad, I wasn't ready to let my guard down completely with my new clique—though I was loath to call it that, we were turning into a clique of sorts—one of lonely girls, unpopular girls, randoms, pretty much anyone who didn't already have a clique.

Emily put it into terms that resonated especially with me: "Before we all started hanging out, I always felt invisible."

I related all too well. "That's so funny, because I have a comic I'm working on, and the main character is called Abby Invisible."

"She's like a totally sick artist," Anya said, which made me feel good.

"We should call ourselves that," Emily said. "The Invisibles."

Anya knitted her brow. "Isn't that a bit too self-deprecating?"

"Well, I'm pretty sure the Beatles is already taken, and it's kind of like taking ownership of the term," I said.

"Like we're invisible because we damn well want to be," Anya said.

"Exactly!" Emily said.

"Well, when you put it that way," Anya said, "I love it!"

And so our little group of misfits became a part of something bigger than just the individuals. It was nice to be surrounded by acceptance and encouragement.

One afternoon that week, Anya and I were at Yogurtland (OMG, red velvet cake frozen yogurt—I live for you!), and I felt a tap on my shoulder. I figured it was Anya telling me to back away from the self-serve pump—bad idea, Yogurtland, you don't know what depths I'm capable of—but when I turned, it was Andy.

"Hey," he said, as a drip of deliciousness trickled onto my finger. I leaned down to lick it off. "Hey back."

"You girls and your frozen yogurt."

"Everyone has a weakness. Achilles has a heel. Tiger Woods has a . . . well, it's not his heel that's the problem there. For us, the promise of less calories than ice cream and the multitude of ridiculously tasty flavors sucks us in."

"They should hire you to promote it."

"I'd eat them out of business."

"I don't doubt it," he said, motioning to the mountainous cup of yogurt I had in my hand.

"Hey now," I said in a mock-upset tone. "Are you calling me fat?"

"No," Andy said, smiling, "I just meant—"

I wasn't sure why he stopped talking until I turned and saw Anya. She'd headed over but stopped about ten feet away, keeping her distance.

"Huh," Andy said.

"Um, huh what?" I asked.

He twisted his mouth as he weighed his answer. "It's just . . . so you're still hanging with Anya. It wasn't just that one time at lunch."

"Absolutely," I said, giving zero ground. "Anya's great. I really like her. We actually have things in common."

"Okay," Andy said. "It's just . . . I mean, it's not my business, but I just thought when I hooked you up with Skyler and those girls that you kinda found your groove. And obviously that didn't work out, and I took a little crap from Skyler and the rest for that, but—"

"Really? They gave you a hard time?"

"Well, I kinda vouched for you," he said. "Skyler wasn't exactly celebrating after you basically told her to go to hell."

"But I've seen you still hanging out with them," I said. I glanced over at Anya, motioning for her to just give me another minute.

"Yeah, they can't do much to me," he said. "They'll take it out on someone else."

"I know," I said. "Why didn't you warn me that they could be so cruel?"

"I don't know," he said. "Look, they're still my friends. They just have their ways, and I know they can play rough. But there's a lot to be gained from being part of that. Which is why I'm surprised you'd rather be hanging out with, you know, randoms."

If my raised left eyebrow could talk, it would have said, "Randoms?"

I think the message got across, because Andy started to back-pedal.

"I mean, look—I don't know most of the people you're hanging out with, but I do know Anya." When he said her name, it was quieter than the rest of his words—more carefully measured, like when you're trying not to say a bad word or something. "I *told* you about her."

"Yeah, you did. But I like to make my own decisions. From what I can tell, she's damn sure not a psycho. So you lied to me."

He let out a huffy sigh, and for a second I thought he was

going to storm off. But he settled himself and said, "Okay, 'psycho' may have been a little harsh."

"Well, Andy, I don't know. Maybe you're right. I mean, if 'psycho' means 'funny' or 'smart' or 'not a sheep like that idiot clique you introduced me to,' then yeah, she's a total psycho. And for that matter—"

"Stop it!"

We spun around, but we already knew the voice: It was Anya, who decided enough was enough and joined us.

"You two realize this isn't a sitcom, right?" she asked. "I'm standing ten feet away. I can hear every word you're saying. Andy, I am *anything* but *random*, and you damn well know it. Hell, I'd rather you stuck with *psycho*."

As Andy stammered, I started to say, "That's right," but Anya cut me off.

"And, Hailey, I appreciate you standing up for me, but I can fight my own battles, thank you very much. I'm not a cheerleader anymore. I've had just about enough standing on the sideline, okay?"

My yogurt was now fully dripping down my hand, and out of the corner of my eye, I could see the Yogurtland manager giving us the evil eye.

Andy looked down and then at Anya, then back to me, shook his head and started to walk off.

"No!" I yelled, loud enough to startle Andy and Anya and the increasingly upset Yogurtland manager. I grabbed Andy's arm and pulled him back to us, and said in a firm, measured voice: "No one is leaving Yogurtland until you two call a truce. Got it? *No one leaves Yogurtland.*"

I realized that I'd come to genuinely like Andy. I liked the idea of all my friends being friends. And it was obvious that Andy transcended the clique thing. He was friends with all sorts of people—I'd seen it in the brief time I'd gotten to know him. He didn't care about who fit into what group, and that was one of the things I liked best about him. Of course, it also occurred to me that if Skyler and her crew of rabid wolverines remained his buddies, it might not hurt for him to be just a *little* more exclusive.

"Look, you two," I started in. "Can't we all just get along?" (Yeah, I know. But we'd just studied Rodney King in history, and I was evoking my inner Rodney—well, my inner Rodney post-beating, but pre–*Celebrity Rehab*.)

"You guys," I continued. "Anya, you're not a psycho. Andy, you're not an asshole. So whatever the deal is with you, let's put it to rest." (I figured that knowing nothing of what happened made me an excellent decider on the matter. Ignorance is bliss, and I'm one blissful kind of girl.)

I could see the muscles flexing in Anya's jaw. It looked like she was clenching her teeth together, which made me wonder if she grinds her teeth at night like I do, and if she had a mouth guard, and which one, and if she liked it . . . but we probably had bigger fish to fry at the moment.

"Fine," Anya finally uttered. "Why not? It's a new year, right? It's nothing so earth-shattering or life-changing that we can't bury the proverbial hatchet, right? I mean, assuming I'm not the 'psycho' you apparently tell everyone I am, and I'm not actually wielding a hatchet under my coat."

She leaned in toward Andy. "Don't worry; I'm not. I leave my hatchet home on Tuesdays."

I wasn't sure how much of that was intended to be friendly, but it seemed like most of it was.

"Fine by me," Andy said. "Since Hailey is apparently in charge of who is friends with who, I guess it's her world now, we just live in it."

"Great!" I said, pleased with myself. "It's about time. Wanna shake on it? Wait—even better, maybe you could hug it out."

Dead silence in Yogurtland.

"Um, let's work up to that," Anya said. Andy just stared at his shoes—*Shoegazer! Shoegazer!* I oddly thought, but kept to myself—and he chuckled uncomfortably.

"Fine," I said. "Baby steps."

Oh, crap, I thought, even as I was finishing the second word, realizing that's the last thing I should have said around Anya.

I glanced at her to catch any reaction, but thankfully that's right when Xandra sauntered in, distracting everyone from me trying to pry my foot from my big fat mouth with a crowbar.

Xandra was wearing a cashmere hoodie, black leggings and metallic Ugg boots. *I bet an Ugg boot would fit in my mouth right now.*

"Hey hey," she singsonged. I glanced at the shimmering eyesores adorning her feet, thrilled at the opportunity for my wit to wipe away my gigantic brain fart. "Xan, when aliens finally wipe us out, it's gonna be because they couldn't get past our wearing Uggs."

Andy laughed and Anya nodded with approval. But Xandra was impervious.

"I like them," she said. "And they're comfy."

"Don't let Emily see you in those," I said. "She'll call PETA."

"Let her," Xandra said. "I'll call mall security next time she goes 'shopping.'" Xandra made air quotes when she said *shopping*, and we all (except Andy) knew exactly what that meant: Emily's penchant for five-fingered discounts. Speaking of Andy, Xandra spun in his direction and said hi.

"Hey," he replied.

Xandra waited for it to dawn on Andy that he should proffer a little more. "I'm Andy."

"Oh, I know," she said coolly. "I'm Xandra. We have chemistry together."

"Oh. Right. Sorry. It's—you know, a big class."

"I sit right next to you."

"Right," he said, flailing. "I just get so focused on my studies—"

"You're barely passing the class. You've cheated off my paper five times. On the semester midterm, when Mr. Spaid was distracted by the fire alarm your buddy Frankie tripped just for kicks, you actually leaned over and asked me what a covalent bond was."

"Um, right, and I meant to thank you for that, but I'm just, you know, not great with names."

Xandra chuckled. "So you know a lot of Xandras?"

Andy turned red. I worried for a second that he would get pissy with her, especially coming right after my forced Andy–Anya intervention, but he was impressively diplomatic: "No. Look, I'm sorry. I'm just—"

"You're busy with your friends. Like Skyler and . . . *the others*."

She said "the others" portentously and followed with a smile, breaking the tension. Andy laughed with relief. I wondered whether he watched *Lost* and if that was what Xandra meant by the foreboding "others" reference, or whether it was unintentional.

The four of us walked outside. We were a few blocks into our walk when Andy suddenly turned to Anya.

"Anya," he said tentatively. He started to speak again and stopped. We could all hear the gears grinding as he tried to select his words.

"Look. I owe you a huge apology. Skyler told me to spread the 'psycho' term around school. It's no excuse, but . . . I just didn't have the balls to tell her off."

Anya looked genuinely touched.

Andy continued, "It was really wrong. I just . . . I don't know, there's just been so much stuff and—"

He stopped, glancing at Xandra and me, and I suddenly felt like my presence was unwanted, like I'd just walked into the boys' bathroom. I glanced down, staring at my bracelet as if I'd just discovered the secret to eternal life etched in it.

Anya took mercy on him, classy and cool as ever: "Hey. It's okay. Really. It takes even bigger balls to apologize and admit you were wrong."

Andy looked up appreciatively. "Thanks."

Then again, Anya being Anya, she took only another second to bust those very same balls: "So if you just remind me every day for the next two weeks that you've been a *complete* dick, I'm willing to start over. If you are."

Andy burst out in laughter. "I am."

Anya: "And . . ."

Andy sighed. "And I am a *complete* dick."

Xandra chimed in: "Okay, dude, you're totally winning points. So I have to know: Why do you even hang out with those *assholes*?"

Andy pondered. "You mean Skyler and her clique?"

"All of 'em. Skyler and the 'others,' sure, but also the jocks, those jerks who make life hard for anyone whose only goal in life isn't to letter in three sports and win a district championship."

Andy laughed. "I can't deny the assholeness of that crew." He gathered his thoughts again. "But they're my friends. They are. I know how they can come off, and I know the way they act gets old, but it's just, you know—"

I pitched in: "Insecurity?"

"I guess. I mean, underneath the meathead exterior of those guys . . . is *another* level of meathead idiocy . . . but underneath *that*, you have some good guys. They just have to put up a front, you know? Everybody does that sometimes, right?"

They sure do, I thought, feeling a little gross about myself.

"And the bitches?" Xandra asked. No beating around the bush for her.

"*Definitely* insecurity," he said.

"True dat," I agreed.

Turns out Andy was a lot smarter than I'd given him credit for. (His ineptness with protons and electrons notwithstanding.) Seeing him bring his guard down, I liked him more now than ever. In fact, his loyalty to the idiot crowd was endearing. And a shrewder purpose came to mind: His ability to navigate easily between a variety of sociological groups could come in handy down the line.

It was a gorgeous Saturday in September. I was in the kitchen trying to decide what I wanted to snack on when my dad walked in with a picnic basket.

"Hey there, Little Red Riding Hood," I said.

My dad smiled his easy grin and placed the basket on the counter. "Is there anything in there worth munching?" he asked.

"I was just trying to decide."

"Well, if not, we're going to Bay Cities and getting sandwiches to go."

"I vote for that," I said. "What's Bay Cities?"

"What's Bay Cities?" Dad was making his incredulous face, which always made me laugh. "You mean to tell me none of your new friends have taken you there yet?"

"Uh . . . nope?"

"These are not friends," he said. "Bay Cities has by far the best sandwiches in the city. Messy and delicious."

"Oh, really?" my mom said as she entered the kitchen. "How

do you know who has the best sandwiches, and why haven't *you* taken us there?"

He thought about it for a moment. "Well, for one, it's in Santa Monica—which isn't far, but it's not exactly on the way to any of our local haunts."

"We have haunts?" I asked.

"Oh, we have haunts," he said. "Yours is the refrigerator. Anything new in there since you last looked ten minutes ago?"

"No," I said. "I always think that something will magically change, and yet it never does."

"Get used to it, babe," Dad said. "Life lesson *numero uno*: Nothing changes. People. Refrigerator contents. Nothing."

"Well, unless someone goes shopping," Mom said.

"For refrigerator contents or people?" I asked.

"Well, that settles it," my dad said as he stood. "We're getting sammiches at Bay Cities, and then I'm taking you to Hollywood Forever Cemetery."

"I'm sorry, *what*?" I gave him my alarmed face, and it was totally sincere. "*Cemetery?* You think that a) I want to go to a cemetery, and b) I want to *eat* there? Uh . . . no."

"Oh ye of little faith," my dad said, flashing his usual Cheshire Cat grin.

My objection was filed for the record and otherwise ignored, as usual. We got the sandwiches and headed for the cemetery, and though I protested most of the way, I was mildly curious as to what the hell my dad had planned.

But when we got there, it turned out he wasn't necessarily the one who had done the planning. They actually have this ridiculously cool thing at the cemetery where they show classic (or cult) movies on the side of a huge mausoleum, and people bring blankets and picnic baskets and make a night of it. A DJ spins records to set the mood or just entertain people while they wait until it gets dark. Then they start the movie around nine p.m.

That night, the movie was *Pee-wee's Big Adventure*. I'd never seen it, but my dad had always said it was one of his favorites, and we tended to share the same taste in movies. It was *so cool*.

Part of me wished my mom hadn't had plans with Andy's mom, so she could have experienced it with us, but the other part of me was glad Mom was making friends and glad that my dad and I kind of had a new thing. Not that I planned to spend every weekend night out with my dad, but it was pretty fun, plus this was something my friends and I could do as well.

Oh, and the sandwiches were damn good too.

I told Anya about it the next day, and she wanted to go, but two nights in a row were a bit much for me, so we made plans to get a bigger group and go next weekend. Plus, Sunday was a school night, so Saturday made more sense. Ever think about how much that sucks? Sunday is the weekend, but it's also a school night. Kind of ruins the whole day. Like if you get quiet enough on a Sunday night, you can almost hear Monday taunting you with the theme from *Jaws*.

In fifth-period English, we were being quizzed on Ray Bradbury's *Fahrenheit 451*. The question posed by Miss Mercer: "How much power should a government have?" Considering all the unrest and protests we'd lived through the past few years, it would seem like a legitimate answer might be "less than it currently has." I expected even *Skyler* to say as much when she proudly raised her hand.

Not so much.

"Um . . . ," Skyler said. "I feel like we need to be protected. Like, is freedom more important than safety? All the hippies who get crazy over their 'rights' and have so much free time to stand outside and protest don't seem to have jobs. So how much does their opinion really matter?"

Of course. Spoken like a true girl of privilege.

She continued, "I think government should have more control, actually. Like wouldn't it be nice if someone could step in and make sure Hailey wasn't wearing a Marc Jacobs shirt from two seasons ago? Like, embarrassing much?"

God, *really*?

Several kids turned to look at me and my Marc Jacobs shirt. Even though intellectually I knew she was making an ass of herself, no one let my subconscious in on that. Old insecurities rose up, and I could feel my face getting hot. I heard a few laughs, and I felt even more embarrassed as some guy I didn't know put up his hand to high-five Skyler. (The only saving grace? She didn't raise her hand to meet his—apparently she's above high fives. I can't say I'm a fan of them either, but I digress.)

The Old Hailey would have sunk down in her chair and prayed for the moment to pass, but I decided to take this one head-on. I could hear Miss Mercer starting to admonish Skyler for her attitude, but the last thing I needed was a teacher defending me. That's the sort of thing *no one* lives down.

"Guilty as charged," I said. (I mean, it was true. The shirt I was wearing *was* one of Noel's castoffs—new to me, but not to the fashionistas of the world. Apparently.) "This shirt was *not* purchased at full retail from an overpriced boutique within the past few weeks. I didn't know clothes had an expiration date, but thank you for teaching me they do."

"My pleasure," Skyler replied, unrepentant. "I do what I can to educate the less fortunate. It's a calling."

Suddenly, a boy's voice chimed in: "I've had this shirt for a couple years." I turned to see it was Chris.

Holy crap, Chris was looking right at Skyler, eyes boring holes through her. "I'd like to personally apologize to everyone for wearing this ancient shirt to school today," he said. "I guess I'm *'like totally'* out of fashion."

Skyler pursed her lips, steaming. She said nothing.

"Beyond," I said to Chris. "I don't know how you can even walk these halls."

"I probably shouldn't," he said with a smile. "Miss Mercer, can I be excused? I have to go home for the day. I'm wearing clothes Skyler doesn't approve of."

Marry me now.

Skyler exhaled an exaggerated sigh. "Chris, I didn't say anything about *your* clothes."

Miss Mercer was now conspicuous in her silence, letting this whole thing play out. She even seemed to be enjoying it. Power to the people, I guess. Less governing, more Bradbury.

"I should probably be excused too," I told Miss Mercer. "It was my shirt that started this. I don't want to offend anyone else's delicate fashion sensibilities. It could lead to, I don't know, anarchy. Human sacrifice. Cats and dogs living together. Mass hysteria!"

Chris laughed. I didn't know whether he got the ancient *Ghostbusters* reference (one of my dad's favorites) or just thought it was funny. I didn't care, just as long as he was laughing.

"Well," Miss Mercer said, "in the spirit of our lesson plan, perhaps I should abdicate power and leave it to the people. Show of hands: Who thinks Hailey and Chris should go home because their clothes aren't as up to date as Skyler would like?"

Hailey and Chris. I didn't mind the sound of that at all.

We looked around the room. No hands were raised. (Which was good, but wouldn't it be awesome if we could leave for the day? We could go to the mall, grab some frozen yogurt, compare favorite bands . . .)

Skyler sunk down a bit, but she wasn't totally chastened. She raised her hand. *Only Skyler.*

"Well," Miss Mercer said. "That settles that. It seems Skyler is the only one bothered by this. Nobody gets excused. But, Skyler, see me after class."

Skyler rolled her eyes and then just looked down. I mouthed, "Thank you" to Chris, and he winked at me. My face felt hot again, but this time it most definitely wasn't from embarrassment.

It was a perfect California day: seventy-five degrees and sunny. I'd come to learn that meant the smog layer wasn't so brutal for a change—today, you could actually see things more than fifty feet away.

Emily, Xandra and Anya had come over after school. I was preparing myself for a confession. Maybe it was how honest everyone had been, or maybe it was because I've never been a really good liar—so much for my career in politics or big business—but I felt I needed to come clean.

"You guys?" My voice was meek, maybe more so than I'd intended.

Anya looked up. She'd been attending to the sole of her Converse sneaker, coloring in part of it. Emily and Xandra sat perched at attention.

"I kind of need to tell you something."

Anya's eyebrow cocked.

Emily sat patiently.

Xandra piped up: "You're a man."

"No!" I blurted, and everyone cracked up.

"It's okay," Emily said, joining in. "We're all friends here. We don't care that you have boy parts."

"They have *lots* of great support groups for that," Anya said. "Especially in California. You sit in a circle and everyone tells their stories."

I smiled.

"Guys, seriously," I said, trying to steer this back on course. "It's not like a huge deal or anything, but it's kind of an interesting thing, I guess, and I just feel I owe it to you to be totally honest. Because we're really friends now."

"Oh my Christ," Anya said. "This is something serious? What's the deal? You're not actually a man, are you?"

"Lesbian!" Xandra announced. "Lesbian? It's lesbian, right?"

"No, I'm not a lesbian."

Emily: "But if you were, you'd totally be into me, right?"

I sighed.

"Oh, spit it out," Anya said. "You can tell us anything. Unless it's that you like Nickelback."

"Oh God, no," Xandra said. "Not that."

"I'd rather hang myself than listen to that band," Anya added.

"Stop it, you guys," I said, laughing. I took a deep breath and exhaled. "It's none of those things. It's *definitely* not Nickelback. Here's the thing: I, well, I wasn't always popular. Like at my last school, I wasn't popular at all." I thought about Amy and got a pit in my stomach as soon as I said that, making a mental note to Skype with her later. I'd been pretty bad the last few weeks about staying in touch.

Nobody said anything. Maybe I made too big a deal out of that popularity part. Technically, I had only been popular at West Hollywood for a few days, but still.

I continued, "I wasn't just unpopular; I was a total outcast. People made fun of me and it sucked and I hated school and, so . . . yeah."

"That's it?" Emily asked.

"Well, yeah, that's it in a nutshell, but—"

"Gawd!" Xandra said. "What a disappointment!"

"Xan, I know. Look, I am so sorry, I should have told you ear—"

"Not *that*, dumbass. I thought for a second you had some devastating secret that had haunted you for years, something good, but all you got is 'I was a huge dork. Now I'm, you know, slightly less of a huge dork.'"

"We don't care," Anya said. "We're outcasts too. You know that."

"Well, it's just a little more complicated," I said. "I kind of transformed myself before I moved. I have a sister who's like *perfect*."

I rolled my eyes as I said it. Still didn't take away the sting of its truth.

"In the spring, I found her diary."

"*Oooh*," Xandra cooed, eyes gleaming devilishly. "Diary!"

"Now we're getting somewhere," Emily agreed. "So *she's* a man?"

"Come on, guys." I sighed. "It's just a diary, but it's an amazing diary. The info in it is pretty much a how-to-be-cool manual. In her words, it's *How to Be a Hater*, but the fact remains . . . it's a roadmap to a better place."

"Says who?" Anya asked.

"Says the girl who got instantly accepted into the cool crowd after following a few easy steps."

Now Anya was the one rolling her eyes. "Hailey, seriously now, why on earth would we care about that? *I've* been there. *You've* been there. It *sucked*. It wasn't a whole lot of fun when Skyler kicked me to the curb, but I adapted. I would rather spend the day with you guys in an Iraqi minefield than spend it with Skyler and her minions at a day spa."

"I know, Anya," I replied. "But I'm not saying we use it to become one with the haters. I'm just thinking maybe we can use it to beat them at their own game."

"Or at the very least, step up *our* game," Emily said.

"Maybe it's just me," I said, "but having Skyler humiliate me in English because my shirt isn't from this season? It felt pretty crappy."

"From what I heard, that little play blew up in her face," Anya said.

"Sort of, but it still sucked," I said. "I don't want to constantly be a target, constantly be on guard. I'm thinking we can make her ridicule less valuable somehow, and what better way than by building our own self-esteem? What's the harm in that?"

"Amen to that!" said Emily.

"It's not just you," Xandra said. "They've been taunting us all since grade school. Well, except Anya, given that she was a card-carrying member of the Dark Side."

Anya seemed taken aback. "I was never mean to you, was I?"

"No, not really," Xandra said. "But I was still scared of you."

"I'm sorry, Xan." Anya looked down at her hands. "I think I've blocked a lot of that stuff out. It seems like a whole different lifetime. So much has happened since then."

Emily put a hand on Anya's shoulder. "Hey, it's okay. You were still figuring yourself out. People get older. They get smarter. Except for Xandra."

"Hey!" Xandra cried, giving Emily a soft love tap in the side.

"Cut it out," Anya said. "I mean it; I'm sorry that I was ever a bitch to you guys. Standing by silently while Skyler ripped you apart wasn't right. I should have spoken up."

"And now we can't get you to shut up," Xandra said with a smile. "Really, Anya, it's cool. Anyway, it sounds like our new best bestie has a plan to give 'em a taste of their own meds."

"Yeah, so what's the plan, Hailey?" Emily asked.

"Everyone goes around scared of these girls, and it makes *no* sense," I said. "Nobody should be scared of them. We all just grant them that kind of power, because they're used to acting like it's their birthright. It's not real, and they don't deserve it. Why can't we just be a better version of them? Just as cool, you know, but not tyrannical bitches."

"I'm down for that," Emily said.

"Second," Xandra said.

"We can help other girls too," I said, turning my attention mostly to Anya, who was obviously the hard sell. "Personally I think it's *way* cooler to be smart or funny or creative than vapid, popular and 'perfect.'"

Anya sighed. "Look, I see your point. I just—I don't know. I'm already pretty happy now. Weird as it sounds, I'm fine with just you goobers. I don't need more friends. I sure as hell don't need to be 'popular.'"

"I know," I said. "We're going to do this our way. It will be a good thing. Trust me."

"Okay, Hailey," Anya said. "I trust you. I'm in."

You got your head in the clouds…

—ADELE

"Rumour Has It"

CHAPTER 7

I'm certain beyond a shadow of a doubt that the eight minutes allotted by my alarm clock's snooze button and eight minutes of "real" time are two completely different things. There's just no way eight minutes goes by that fast. If I'm in class and the bell is supposed to ring in eight minutes, it takes, like, a century. Snoozing in my bed, trying to get a tiny bit more rest? Boom. Over.

Waking up at six a.m. makes you wish three things:

1) You weren't awake at six a.m.
2) There was a tiny Starbucks in your bedroom and a barista waiting to make your latte just how you want it (extra hot, no foam, one pump of vanilla).
3) See #1.

We had planned an after-school meeting to go over our new plans for world domination—or at least partial-world domination, the part that began and ended at West Hollywood High (which for all intents and purposes *is* the whole world when you're in high school).

I tucked Noel's diary into my bag and took one last look in the mirror before heading off to school. That was one of Noel's decrees:

> Before you leave the house, turn your back to the mirror and then quickly turn around. Whatever catches your eye first is probably "too much." If it's not legitimately covering you up, take it off. You're trying too hard.

Buh-bye, sparkly barrette. The Queen has spoken. (She did have a point.)

And in the grand tradition of the space-time discrepancy between snooze time and real time, the day just dragged on and on while I waited for our first official meeting of the Invisibles. Like anything, when you're excited for it, it seems to take forever to come. Case in point: summer vacation. Waiting for it to come—waiting an eternity. Then as soon as you're having fun during vacation . . . tick-tock, school is suddenly right around the corner.

Our calculus teacher was a transplant from England: Mr. Davies. His face looked like it never fully formed. He's got this tiny weird pug-like nose that forces you to look in his nostrils when he's in front of you. And when he's to your side. And when he's seated at his desk. Seriously, there's like no angle where you can't see the man's nostrils, which wouldn't be as awful if he paid sufficient attention to grooming his nose hair—but he most certainly does not.

Mr. Davies is like the stoner guy from *The Breakfast Club*, Judd Nostril—I mean, Nelson. Actually, Judd Nelson had a pretty big schnoz, but Mr. Davies? His actual nose looks skeletal, like Michael Jackson after something like his seventy-third plastic surgery. Mr. Davies has barely a nose, but nostrils to spare. Totally gross.

Even sadder, he thinks he's hot stuff. He's super-satisfied with himself ever since he got his teeth fixed, and he likes to show them off constantly with the goofiest smile you can imagine. Creepy. He reminds me of the senior girls who have boob jobs already. (There are five that I know of.) They're always bragging about how "real" they feel. News flash: They don't feel or look real. Because big boobs on skinny girls don't exist in the real world. Even if a girl used to be bigger and had proportionate boobage, the minute she loses weight and gets skinny, the first things to go are the boobs. It's a sad, cruel fact of life.

In today's class we're studying sequences. The current sequence we're looking at is

$$\{x_n\}_{n \geq 1}$$

Mr. Davies had written on the board that it's

increasing, if and only if, $x_n < x_{n+1}$ for any $n \geq 1$,

or **decreasing**, if and only if, $x_n > x_{n+1}$ for any $n \geq 1$.

"If one of these properties holds," Mr. Davies said, "we say that the sequence is monotonic."

You ain't kidding, Mr. Davies. *Your entire lecture is monotonic.* If watching paint dry is supposed to be the most boring thing in the world, then listening to Mr. Davies teach—while simultaneously creeping everyone out with his huge fake-looking teeth—is like watching paint dry on a giant set of disturbing veneers. Brutal.

Class finally ended and I made my way toward the Invisibles' meeting spot du jour, the IHOP. I ate a bag of Peanut M&M's on the way because a) I had them in my bag and b) *delicious.*

People who love dark chocolate are always so snobby about it.

Relax. It's just chocolate, you elitist ninnies. Yes, I know dark chocolate supposedly has antioxidants, so it's better for you, but I'm not gonna be mad if a regular old candy bar winds up in my chocolate-loving hands. (Honestly, I prefer milk chocolate to dark, but it seems so uncool to actually admit that—why, I have no idea. It's probably those lactose-intolerant freaks. We all know there's nothing cool about intolerance.)

The first official meeting of the Invisibles was scheduled for us to set goals and go over some basic ground rules, but most important, it was for me to show everyone the diary—our Holy Grail.

I only expected the five of us: me, Anya, Emily, Kura and Xandra. But when I walked in, there were in addition a couple of girls I thought I recognized from school but hadn't met. They were all talking about some fight, and I was trying to figure out who they were talking about and what I'd missed without bluntly interrupting them and asking outright.

"It was epic," Emily said. "Like, I swear, I thought I saw her head spin."

"I could hear her yelling all the way from the theater," Xandra said. "We actually stopped rehearsal so we could eavesdrop but then Mr. Coogan clapped his hands and made us get back to rehearsal."

"Well, they did used to date, so I can see why she was mad," Anya added. "I'd be pissed if I were her too. Him defending our girl over here, pretty much humiliating Skyler in front of the whole class was a bold move."

"Wait, whose girl over here?" I interrupted, because it seemed almost like Anya was motioning to me when she said it.

"You!" she said. "Duh!"

"Wait, back up," I said. "And hi," I said to the two girls I didn't know. "But back to the issue at hand, who defended me?"

"Chris Roberts!" they all said at the same time.

"Wait—what? Chris? He dated Skyler?"

Holy news flash!

"Yes," Anya said. "They were the 'it couple' freshman year, but they broke up this past summer and nobody knows why."

Figures no one felt the need to mention this to me before. It's like how Yoda was chilling out and training Luke to take on Darth Vader without mentioning a little thing like, "Hey, just as an FYI, that guy I'm teaching you to slice up with a light saber? Funny little coinkydink: He's your *dad*!"

(Yes, I got around to watching *Star Wars*.)

Of course Skyler dated the one guy who made me feel like there was a parade of butterflies practicing for Cirque du Soleil in my stomach. It had to be him.

Total nightmare.

Anya said, "The story got around school like wildfire, and the more Skyler heard about it circulating, the more pissed she got. She yelled at Chris right in the middle of the quad. It was one thing for everyone in your English class to know, but once it started to become headline news, Skyler lost it."

"I can't believe they dated," I said, somewhat under my breath, still stuck on that one detail. *She's horrible! He's smart! I would have thought he had better taste.*

Then reality set in even harder. "So now she must *really* hate me."

"Ohhhhhh yeah," Emily said.

"All signs point to yes," Kura said, quoting a Magic 8 Ball.

"Perfect," I said. "As if I weren't already on her shit list."

I didn't want to mention the fact that, in addition to Chris being my knight in shining banter that day, he was also the cutest guy I'd seen at school. Knowing that he dated Skyler (and dumped her) made the idea of him that much more intriguing, but also flat-out terrifying. If she were his type, I definitely wouldn't be. But then, he did dump her, so that had to mean something. If *he* actually dumped *her,* that is. Then again, if *she* dumped *him*, then she shouldn't care if we end up going out and then getting married and having ten babies—of course we'd be super-famous by then and the tabloids would refer to us as "Chrailey" or "Hailis." And they'd lie about us being on the verge of breaking up, but we'd know it was just to sell magazines.

More to the point, why the hell was Anya snapping her fingers in my face?

"Hello!" Anya said. "Earth to Hailey!"

"Huh? Did you say something?"

"Told you we should have slapped her," Kura said. "That took too long."

"You don't go slapping your friends," Emily said.

"They do it on TV all the time," Kura said. "People zone out, slap 'em. People get hysterical, slap 'em."

"That's why I don't watch TV," Emily said.

"Really? I thought it's just because you couldn't fit one in your purse."

"Hey!"

"Ladies," I said, having sufficiently cleared my head. "Let's get down to business."

I looked at the two new girls and then at Anya.

"They're cool," she said with an easygoing shrug, and that's all she needed to say. If you check out with Anya, you check out with me.

I extended my hand to the girls. "Hi, I'm Hailey."

The blond girl shook my hand, saying, "I'm Dahlia." She had a pierced nose, an adornment that suited her well. Dahlia wore ripped jeans with red tights underneath, Vans sneakers with black-and-white checkers and a Tegan and Sara T-shirt underneath a hoodie, which she wore with the hood up.

"I'm Grace," said the other girl. She had brown hair and brown eyes, and she was what a polite person would call "big-boned." She wore an oversize T-shirt, jeans and sneakers.

"Hey, Dahlia. Hey, Grace," I said warmly. "Welcome to the Invisibles."

"Thanks," Dahlia replied. Grace nodded and smiled.

"Woo hoo!" cried Emily and Kura, clinking their glasses. Kura immediately sucked down her entire glass of Diet Coke through a straw, then tried to catch a server's eye for a refill.

"Uh . . . thirsty much?" Xandra asked. Kura looked a little embarrassed.

"I'm not allowed to drink soda at home," she said. "I get a little crazy when I'm finally in a place where my parents can't monitor my soda intake."

"Drink up," Anya encouraged.

"Same goes for sugared cereals," Kura went on. "I see their point, I guess, sugar isn't good for you—but if you deprive me, I'm so going to want it!"

"Next stop, hard drugs," Anya said.

"A life lesson to parents everywhere," Emily said. "Too bad none of them are here to take it in . . . on second thought, I take that back."

"Plus," Kura went on, "I mean, I'll bet Cristina Yang drinks a ton of Diet Coke. And someday when I'm in an OR standing on my feet for nineteen hours straight, trying to save a life? I think I might need a little caffeine. *I'm saving lives, people!*"

Anyone who knew Kura knew this: She was obsessed with the character of Cristina Yang from the TV show *Grey's Anatomy*. It was because of *her* that Kura planned to be a cardiothoracic surgeon. (Well done, Shonda Rhimes! I'd say that's about as positive an influence as any.) Studies show that less than one half of one percent of American medical students currently show interest in pursuing training in cardiothoracic surgery. (See, I know stuff. And you thought kids today don't read.) In fact, each year there are fewer graduates applying for residency positions in cardiothoracic surgery than the number of open positions. This is supposedly because the training is longer than regular surgical residency (which is already long), and it's pretty brutal. It also leaves students with higher educational debt from covering the med school costs.

Regardless, Kura remains undeterred. She lives, sleeps, eats, breathes Cristina Yang. Thank goodness Yang isn't an actual person, because I'm pretty sure if she were real, Kura would literally stalk her to see if she could glean any little bits of wisdom.

"Well, let's go, Hailey," Xandra said with her typical theatricality. "Let's solve the Da Vinci Code or whatever you have in that book of yours."

I removed Noel's diary from my bag. The way all the girls' eyes widened, you'd think I was pulling out something magical, and in a sense I was. I also had the forethought to bring a yearbook of Noel's and some pictures of her so they could see who they were taking advice from.

"This is Noel," I said, distributing the photographs, which the girls all passed around. It felt weird to be making such a legend of my annoying sister, but as long as she didn't know about it, her ego wouldn't get any bigger.

"Wow," Anya said. "She's gorgeous."

"No kidding," I said. "Imagine growing up in the shadow of *that*."

I'd tabbed the pages of the yearbook that highlighted all of her excellence. The photo of her up in the air, spiking a volleyball, wearing a bikini top and tiny shorts—a pose that any normal person would look awful in—looked almost choreographed. Her muscles showed, her hair was perfect, the expression on her face was determined but happy. It was annoyingly awesome. A photo of her onstage in the lead of our high school's musical *Legally Blonde*. She of course played Elle Woods and nailed it.

I opened the diary and read a couple passages to them:

> If your boobs dominate 85% of your Facebook photo, all those comments about how "gorgeous" you are have nothing to do with your face. Don't be pathetic.
>   If you're going to sleep around, everyone is going to know. That's just how it is. If you genuinely like being a bit of a slut . . . own it. Don't pretend to be innocent and don't get offended when people call you a slut. Just do *you*. (Apparently everyone *else* is.)

That got a laugh from the girls.

"So, I think maybe we should have some kind of 'buddy system,'" I said.

"Like kindergarten?" Emily asked.

"Exactly like kindergarten," I said. "And don't think of that as a bad thing. We are kindergartners in a sense, aren't we? We're relearning the basics so we can better function in society."

"Kind of like a halfway house for newly released felons," Anya said, eliciting chuckles.

"It makes sense, I guess," Emily said.

"It makes total sense," I said. "This diary is going to be invaluable for being less loserish day to day, but we can—and should—also use each other for support. I mean, I'm certainly sick of being humiliated whenever the Bitch Squad is in the mood. I'm sure a few of you wouldn't mind being spared that indignity."

Grace chimed in softly: "I've been made fun of since I was in second grade. The idea of walking through the halls and not being called names is like . . . I don't even have the words, because I can't imagine it."

It was heartbreaking and invigorating at the same time. This being the first time I'd even met Grace, I could only guess she was teased relentlessly about her weight. Kids are going to be mean. "Haters gonna hate," as they say all over the Internet. But that doesn't make it any easier to deal with.

We weren't using Noel's words for evil. This was about self-preservation, about building confidence; the modifications we were going to make could go beyond school and, potentially, be genuinely life-changing.

I looked at Grace, her cheeks flush, her big brown eyes hopeful, and then took a look around the whole table—everyone was there because they had been made to feel "less than." As angry as I had been about being uprooted and having to change schools, for the first time, I felt really glad I did.

"You know it's going to get bad soon," Anya said.

"Why?" I asked.

"Ugh," said Emily. "That's right. Spirit Week."

"What happens at Spirit Week?" I asked.

"It's a ritual," Anya said. "On the fifth day of every Spirit Week, anyone Skyler's crew defines as 'losers' gets humiliated in some grand fashion."

I rolled my eyes at the thought. I could only imagine.

"You know Skyler," Anya continued. "It's like there's an engine inside her that runs on other people's tears, anger and embarrass-ment. She's found some scary-ass ways to fuel that engine."

"Well, that's not going to happen this year—at least not to us," I said. "I don't know how much we can accomplish in that window, but we can make sure we're a long way from being the biggest nerds by the time Spirit Week rolls around. At least that's a start."

"I'll drink to that," Kura said, flagging down the waitress. "Could I please get another refill on Diet Coke?"

"Honey," the waitress said, "that would be your seventh one."

"Zero calories," Kura replied.

"Yeah, but you've had six of 'em."

Kura furrowed her brow. "You know what six times zero is?"

The waitress shrugged. "I never was very good at math."

It's times like these, you learn to live again...

—FOO FIGHTERS

"Times Like These"

CHAPTER
8

The fact that summer break is even a thing totally screws us up as far as preparation for adulthood goes. Not that I'm complaining—I'm not, not at all. But it sets up an unrealistic expectation for life. One would be led to believe that as an adult you work for, like, nine or ten months and then you get three months to screw off with your friends. Not so much. My dad never got time off—not even Christmas break. He was always in the office or at a meeting or doing something lawyerly like checking to make sure I completed my homework. Why? Is someone going to sue me if I skip my social studies reading? Honestly, it's depressing. I mean, I always did all my work, but our first-quarter lesson plan involved comparing the *Exxon Valdez* spill with the BP spill in the Gulf of Mexico. You can only take so much truth before closing your study materials and pondering if the ecosystem is even going to exist when we grow up. (And those poor oil-covered birds!)

Anyway, adulthood seems pretty tricky. I guess in my limited experience I'd define it a few ways:

1) Adulthood is when your friends start getting pregnant . . . on purpose.
2) Adulthood is the freedom to eat breakfast for dinner whenever you damn well please.
3) I reserve the right to add to this list.

My parents had been acting kind of weird. I caught my mom—who never cries—crying at a commercial. *Don't worry . . . Tide is gonna get the stain out. Have faith!*

It wasn't actually a Tide commercial—that would be ridiculous—but it was a commercial, and my mom's not usually that emotional. (Not even during her time of the month.) Me, on the other hand? Forget it. If I don't have an arsenal of chocolate and Midol, I will go legit insane. We all have our favorite acronyms for PMS. I'd have to say some of the funniest (and truest) I've heard are "Pass My Sweatpants," "Pardon My Sobbing," and "Potential Murder Suspect."

Dad wasn't coming home for dinner as much, and that was kind of always our thing. In fact, he was the one who insisted it was super-important to maintain that ritual. He'd say, "Family dinner keeps a family together." (A little redundant, but it gets the point across.) So what does it say if the person who hammered a saying into your head stops caring about the very thing that inspired it?

I guess it's not fair to say he stopped caring, and when I thought about it, it made more sense to me. He must have been busy with work—we did move across the country for this new, very important position, so I had to give him some leeway. But I was in school, making friends, and my dad was at work—not necessarily making friends, but certainly interacting with people—and I did feel a little bad for my mom since she didn't have an organic place to go and, consequently, people to meet.

Still, I worried about my mom and asked her if everything was all right.

"Peachy keen, jelly bean!" she said.

"You sure? You can talk to me, you know."

"Honey, the last thing I want is for you to worry about me." She brushed my hair out of my face and smiled.

She seemed okay, thank goodness. "If you could have anything, what would it be?" I asked.

"Hmm . . . are we talking genie? Like three amazing wishes? Or something realistic? Like to find my favorite sweater—which I know I packed, but it doesn't seem to be anywhere."

"Genie wishes," I said.

She thought for a minute. "I want my daughters to always be healthy and happy."

"Don't be such a *mom*," I said.

"Fine," she said, paired with a sideways glance. "The first thing I want is a big chocolate cake that I can eat by myself and not gain a single ounce. Better?"

"No," I said. "Selfish. You're not going to share your cake with me? You have magic chocolate cake you can eat and not get fat, and you're not going to even share it with your daughter?"

"Get your own genie!" she said. I stuck out my tongue at her and knew she was telling the truth—everything was okay.

Then, a familiar sound—the chirp of an instant message on my computer. I went to my room to see who was summoning me.

Lo and behold, it was . . . Anya. Anya's great, but I was a tad disappointed. More on that later.

ANYA: u there?

ME: si senorita

ANYA: what r u doing tonight?

ME: gonna work on new comic strip. want it in next week's paper

ANYA: well i don't want to interrupt your brilliance

ME: you're not. haven't started. arguing with mom over imaginary calorie free chocolate cake she won't share. rude.

ANYA: totally rude. in other news . . . Skyler spreading around school that evan birnstein has three balls.

ME: !!! WHAT?

ANYA: she got stuck with him in '7 mins in heaven'

ME: and she put her hand down his pants?

ANYA: he IS on the football team

ME: but he looks like a mutant!

ANYA: ANYWAY . . . she said she couldn't find his dick and thought he had three balls and then she realized that one of the balls was his dick . . . just super-tiny

ME: OMG this is so tragic

ANYA: so she basically told entire world and now guys on the football team r calling him '3ball'

ME: poor guy! who told u?

ANYA: i still have moles on the inside. hear stuff now and then. that one's making the rounds tho. pretty much everyone's heard by now

ME: she's so evil!!!!

ANYA: all in a day's work 4 her. the sun rises . . . skyler plots to destroy

ME: ugh. ok, i'm going to draw

ANYA: later sk8er

I closed the chat window and pondered the Three-Ball situation for a moment. I couldn't imagine going so far out of my way just to hurt someone, but it seemed Skyler wasn't just out to hurt other girls . . . she'd hurt anyone she didn't deem "worthy."

I decided to make the new comic strip about a game of Seven Minutes in Heaven, since it was fresh in my mind. The game hasn't changed over the years. In middle school it's your standard fare: seven minutes in a closet, blindfolded, with whoever you're randomly paired up with. In high school, the only modification is that sometimes seven minutes becomes thirty, and instead of kissing and touching, sometimes people go . . . well, a whole lot further. What you do in the closet is up to you and your partner. I've only played twice in my life.

The first time I played Seven Minutes in Heaven was actually the first time I french-kissed a boy: Danny O'Connell. He'd just eaten a patty melt, and I was trying to pay attention to the kiss and which way I tilted my head and where our tongues went and not to embarrass myself too badly, but all I could focus on was the fact that he tasted like melted cheese and grilled onions and rye bread and was that a rye seed stuck between his teeth and should I try to help dislodge it or just leave it be? This was a lot to ponder during a first kiss. In fact, I remember none of the kiss and all of his sandwich. I should have just had a sandwich.

Sadly, the second time I played was only the *second* time I french-kissed a boy. Sensing a theme? No, I haven't ever kissed a boy when I wasn't dared to. But it's *not my fault*! Maybe I'm a late bloomer. (Fine. *Obviously* I'm a late bloomer. No maybes about it.)

I was hoping my fortunes would improve with the tweaks I'd

made thanks to Noel's (unintentional) help, and indeed things did seem to be looking up. Which is to say, in the school hallways the past week, I'd found myself regularly looking up to see Chris making eye contact with me, often paired with a smile. (Which made me happy. Although the times he wasn't exactly smiling made me even happier, because it was just kinda hot.)

It started with a few random chats here and there, e.g., "Isn't that teacher boring?" directed at our science teacher who was like "human Ambien." Or, "Can you believe they call that stuff pizza?" regarding the atrocity they served in the cafeteria. (Come on! This is Los Angeles . . . land of the famous, home of the privileged—why so skimpy with the cheese?!) But as the days passed, our chats became more than an observation-and-agreement exchange, and after we chatted one day for about fifteen minutes on the front lawn after school on a Thursday, it finally happened.

I was wearing my new "boyfriend jeans" (they're actually called that—but was it a sign?), a plain white T-shirt and my pseudo army boots (with buckles strategically arranged in three places—none of them actually functional as there's a zipper on the inside to get in and out). We were talking about Matt McCarthy and how he'd used the word "whorehouse" in class just before the bell rang and how Miss Mercer interrupted his story and suggested that he use the word "brothel." Classic. How *that* segued into Chris and I trading information, I'm not even sure, but it *happened*. We traded emails, instant messaging IDs, Twitter handles, you name it. Then he asked for my phone number. Which was a little scary, coming from a super-cute and super-popular guy who also happened to be Skyler's ex.

Not wanting to seem nervous, of course, I made a joke out of it.

"It's, um . . . 555 . . . 1212."

"Okay," he replied. "Is that 310 area code?"

Oh God, he didn't get it?

"Um, sure," I said. "What's yours?"

"Mine's 1-800-ASK-GARY," he said.

I giggled. "Is that so?"

He smiled. "Yep. You're sure your number's 555-1212?"

"You know, I might have gotten that wrong," I said, and then gave him the right number. And he gave me his. And he told me that a huge concert venue outside Tampa had sold its naming rights in 2010, changing from the Ford Amphitheatre to the 1-800-ASK-GARY Amphitheatre, and that was the lamest thing he'd ever heard of in his life, and I agreed, and I couldn't wait to tell Anya, partly so she could share our disgust for corporate greed but mostly so I could tell her *Chris and I traded numbers!*

Noel's rules of texting started blinking on a neon sign in my brain:

Never text the boy you like right back until you're for sure in couple-mode, and even then . . . make him wait every third time. Keep him on his toes. If he gets an attitude about it, make him wait every other time he texts. He'll never bitch about it again.

Chris and I had texted a few times, but that was it so far. I'd followed Noel's rule as best as I could but come on—it was Chris Roberts! Had it run through my mind that I would like him to be the third guy I french-kissed? You bet. Was I confident that kiss would be patty melt free? Largely.

But it would have to wait, because I had work to do tonight: the comic strip. How could I incorporate Seven Minutes in Heaven . . .

let's see . . . it involves a closet . . . bingo! There was the answer. I drew the strip.

In the strip, a popular, stuck-up girl arrives at a party where they're playing the game. Abby stands against a wall off to the side, watching the proceedings. The popular girl immediately eyes a really cute boy she doesn't know. He's wearing a football jersey with the number 12—a quarterback number! She spins the bottle, and—jackpot! It lands on the boy! The popular girl is ecstatic, but then she looks in the closet. The music from the shower scene in *Psycho* plays as she sees all the clothes in the closet are from *last season,* some even *older!* She can't be seen in a closet with those clothes—no way! She openly insults the outdated wardrobe in front of everyone, then asks the boy if he'd like to go outside. He tells her to go to hell, grabs another girl's hand and those two go into the closet, slamming the door behind them. Offended, the popular girl wonders aloud to the group, "What's *his* problem?"

From the corner, Abby Invisible replies, "Well, dummy, that's *his* twin sister's closet!"

It took a while for my comic strip to find its voice, but the path became clear when I realized my daily experiences at this new school were providing me all the material I needed. Satirists have always existed to comment on the absurdity of society, and few things were as absurd as what I'd been witnessing at my school. Anya's biting views also proved inspirational. The first quarterly paper was coming out soon, and I finished the artwork in time to get my work published, but I wasn't prepared for the reaction it would get.

Who run the world? Girls!

—BEYONCÉ

"Run the World"

CHAPTER
9

$\mathbb{S}$kyler and her sheep were obviously pissed off. I'd shined a light on them—and kids like them—and cut them down to size (at least gauging by the response I'd received from the other Invisibles). How dare I poke fun at Skyler's royal court?

Cassidy and Jericha stopped me in the hallway before third period.

"So, your cartoon wasn't funny at all," Cassidy said.

"Like, what's the deal?" Jericha asked. "Are you *trying* to make us hate you even more?"

"I don't really care how you feel about me one way or the other."

"Yeah, right," Cassidy said with a roll of her eyes and a smirk.

"Cassidy," I said, looking her right in the eye, "I don't want to be you. I *was* you—for as long as I could stand it, which obviously wasn't long. Keep in mind, I wasn't pushed out; I *jumped.*"

Jericha leaned in, speaking in the most serious tone possible for a girl who spends most of her time tweeting Ke$ha lyrics: "Just don't do it again."

"For real," Cassidy said. "Don't, like . . . use us as material."

"I'll think about it," I said, pausing for a half second. "Okay, thought about it. Sorry. Can't guarantee anything."

Jericha flushed. "Hailey, you *will* be sorry if you do it again."

"Well, I can tell you now, *Abby Invisible* isn't going anywhere."

"What gives you the right?" Cassidy started back in. "We aren't bothering you—"

"What?" I couldn't believe my ears. "You're bothering *everybody*—at least everybody who isn't a member of the homecoming court or a regular presence in the paper's prep sports stories. You all try to lord over the school like we should be flattered to be in your presence. You tear a new one into anyone who isn't interested in looking like you, dressing like you, or freaking *being* you. If you guys don't want to be material for my comic, *stop giving me a reason.*"

"Or else?" Jericha asked.

I glared at her.

Jericha shook her head at me slowly. "You have no idea what you're getting yourself into. Keep drawing your little pictures. That's gonna go well for you."

They turned and left. I could only imagine how that was going to go down when they reported to Skyler. I'd like to say I couldn't care less, but that wasn't true.

I felt a little chill run up my back, suddenly feeling a bit vulnerable. I had laid down the gauntlet once again. It was like getting up from the Bitch Squad's lunch table and making the choice all over again. But isn't that life? A series of gauntlets being laid down by you or before you? Choices you make then defining your character? How *could* I back down now?

"Hey, you're Hailey, right?"

It came from my left, from some girl I didn't recognize. She wore track pants and a T-shirt, and she looked extremely fit. My mind started racing. *Another unhappy customer? Maybe an enforcer for Skyler? Does Skyler have enforcers? Am I about to get my ass kicked by some chick in track pants? Does she know krav maga? If she does, I'm screwed.*

Oh, well. Let's get this over with. "That would be me."

"*Loved* your comic," the girl said. "So brilliant."

Oh, thank goodness. I don't have to learn krav maga. Yet.

"Thanks," I said genuinely.

"Hey, I'm Lauren," she said. "I'm on the track team, and . . . well, I'm on the track team. I'm otherwise pretty invisible. I totally related to Abby."

"That's so nice," I said. "And you're not invisible. You run. *By choice.* That makes you some kind of warrior woman."

Lauren laughed. "I love it. If I'm mad or frustrated . . . running totally makes me feel better."

"Running makes *me* feel mad and frustrated!" I said. Which was true. Oh my God, did I hate running. "And tired. And miserable. So thanks for doing it so the rest of us don't have to."

I told Lauren I'd catch her later and headed to class. As I walked, some girl called out, "Abby Invisible rocks!"

"Yeah, she does," boomed a deep voice behind me.

Chris! I spun around, spinning straight into—

—Andy.

I tried not to let the disappointment show on my face.

"What's up, squirt?" Andy asked. "You making more trouble?"

"Nope!" I said. "I'm keeping my nose totally clean." I tapped it with my finger. "See? It's shiny!"

"Yep, it looks very shiny," he said, then making me self-conscious about my nose.

"Really shiny?" I asked. "Like I need to powder it?"

"I'm a guy," he said, with his mouth pursed sideways and his head tilted, reminding me of a confused puppy. "How do I know if a girl needs to powder her nose? You're the one who said it was shiny!"

"I meant clean," I said. "Squeaky clean. Out of trouble."

"Right," he said. "You and your nose are staying out of trouble. It's Abby Invisible who's causing all the ruckus."

I wrinkled my still-shiny nose, really wishing I had a mirror. "'Ruckus'? Really?"

"Play innocent all you like, Hailey. I know a couple of the girls already gave you a little shit about it."

"So I shouldn't have done it?"

"I'm not saying that. I thought it was hilarious. Just keep in mind who you're messing with."

"Is that you talking, Andy? Or is it a message from Skyler?"

He looked hurt for a second. "No! No. I'm your friend, Hailey. I'm just looking out. Don't want anything bad to happen to you. Or . . . Anya. Or your other friends. Skyler . . . well, let's just say she doesn't handle rebellion too well."

"Thanks, Andy," I said. "I appreciate it."

"Wait, one more thing," he said. "If there's any way I can help, you know, let me know."

"Okay," I said. "I will."

It was almost impossible to walk the halls those first few days after the comic came out without having someone say something flattering. Outside of Skyler and her minions—who shot me dirty looks, flipped me the bird, and generally tried to make daily life unpleasant for me whenever they could—everyone who mentioned the comic to me was appreciative. The Invisibles loved it. It was like Abby was their spirit animal. And the fact that it had such a positive response from almost all of the school somehow made them feel better about themselves. I was psyched.

And then I got called to our guidance counselor's office.

Okay, that's nowhere near as worrisome as getting called to the principal's office, which comparatively is nowhere near as worrisome as getting called to see the school resource officer, which is a pleasant term for the police officer—who can actually arrest you, with handcuffs and everything!

Still, my mind was flooded with concerns and questions as I headed to see Mr. Muñez. I never mentioned the true targets of my scorn in my comic, but it was pretty easy to put two and two together, even for the faculty. Sure, we have free speech, but ten minutes on Google will tell you that some schools try to give you a lot less leeway on how much free speech you express in their publications.

Maybe this was all too good to be true. After all the attention and praise, I'd pretty much convinced myself I was about to get in trouble for mocking the fortunate: an ironic twist.

My fears seemed to be confirmed from the second I sat down.

"Thanks for coming over, Hailey," Mr. Muñez said. "I'll get right to it: People are talking about your comic strip."

"Oh, really?" I replied nervously.

"Yes," he said. "It certainly caught the students' attention, but some teachers pointed it out to me as well."

"The newspaper staff approved it," I stammered, quickly adding, "A lot of students actually liked it."

He looked at me oddly.

"Well, yeah," he said. "They should . . . it's *quite* good."

Now I looked at him oddly. "Does this mean I'm not in trouble?"

"That depends on how you define 'trouble,'" he said.

"Pretty much the standard way, Mr. Muñez. You know, detention, in-school suspension, out-of-school suspension, jail, prison, Mrs. Long's advanced calculus class."

"No, none of that," he said. "I—"

"Mr. Muñez," I said quietly. "Seriously, please just don't take the comic strip away. I'm sorry if some people got upset, but I think it actually does some good. It's my way of speaking out for kids who don't feel they have a voice at the school. It's—"

"Hailey . . ."

"No, really. Please. I'll do whatever you want. I'll clean the toilets with a toothbrush. I'll—I mean, I'll even *run track*."

He looked puzzled. "*Run track?*"

I sighed. "Yes. If I have to."

"So you'd rather clean toilets with a toothbrush than run track?"

"I *really* hate track."

"Eh, artists." He sighed. "Hailey, let's take this from the top. I wasn't clear before: You're not in trouble. I'm just the guidance counselor. The only way a student in my office is in trouble is if she wants to get a scholarship to be an opera singer, and she sounds like Mr. Spaid."

We both laughed out loud at that, and I instantly relaxed. Mr. Spaid's voice was a running joke around the school. The science teacher sounded like Batman from *The Dark Knight* but with walking pneumonia.

Mr. Muñez continued, "But just because it's 'art' doesn't mean it should be hurtful. The girls were upset by it and there is a line, albeit a fine one. Make sure it's satire and not too specific. But otherwise, have fun with it."

"Thanks, Mr. Muñez," I said, turning back just before leaving.

"But there is just one thing."

"Yes?"

"I'd better not see a 'Mr. Muñez' in there," he said with a big smile. "But if he is, he'd better be *awesome*."

I smiled. "He will be. And don't let Miss Hoyt hear you use that word."

"What word? Why?"

"You'll have to ask her," I said.

I remained on a high all day. Nothing could bring me down, not even the more-than-occasional vicious glances from Skyler and the rest of the Hateful Harem. All the way home, I balanced my lot in life with theirs, and mine was looking up. They'd never be more than shallow shrews. Someday their looks will dry up, and they'll be nothing but bad attitudes with good hair. Extremely wealthy bad attitudes with good hair, but whatever. Maybe their parents would get convicted for tax evasion.

It was really nice to have my art be appreciated. I hadn't even been aware of how much I really needed a pat on the back or a few flattering and encouraging words. The last month or so had been an emotionally taxing stretch. Dad was busy with work all the time, Mom seemed more stressed than usual, and even though Noel and I hadn't been close in a long, long time, I missed her. She'd replied to a few of my emails with curt replies, while others weren't answered at all. Mom said Noel was just super-busy with school, and I believed that, but having read her diary, I couldn't help but wonder whether Noel was blowing me off because I wasn't worthy of her time. She didn't know how much better I looked now, how I'd used her journal to become more confident. As far as she knew, I was still a loser—and she, true to form, was being a hater.

So all this was racing through my head when I approached my house and saw two cars in the driveway. That *never* happened this early in the day. There might be no cars, or there might be one car (Mom's, and actually it's a minivan-SUV hybrid, not technically a car, but whatever). But there was my dad's car, right there next to what I liked to call Mom's "SUVan."

What the hell was he doing home?

I approached the front door nervously and slowly opened it, peeking through as I did, and—

"Holy shit! You're home!"

(In my defense, the s-word was out of my mouth before I could even form a thought. That's what you get when you've barely seen your dad the past few weeks and suddenly he's standing in the foyer when you walk in, arms crossed, staring at you.)

Dad was stone-faced. "Apparently I'm going to need to keep a closer eye on you, if that's the sort of language you're throwing around lately. What a way to greet your only father."

Oh, thank God, I thought. I knew when Dad was messing with me. And Dad was messing with me.

I set down my book bag and pointed a finger at him. "Well, if I saw you more than once every sixty days, if I had, you know, a strong paternal role model in my life, maybe I wouldn't have to resort to such gutter language as—"

"Whoa, whoa, whoa!" Dad said. "I get the picture."

"Dad, so what *are* you doing home so early? And where's Mom? Her car's in the driveway . . ."

"Oh, she's next door at the neighbors', you know, with the lady, her son's your friend . . ."

"Yeah, Andy," I said.

"Right. They're doing . . . uh, I don't know." He smiled. "Chick stuff."

I laughed. *Man, I'd really missed him.*

"So, Dad, what's up? Why are you home so early?" Had the school called him?

"Hailey," he said, "I know this move has been rough on you, and I've felt bad that I haven't been around much, so I moved a few things around today. I thought maybe you and I could go do something. I mean, if you don't already have big plans with . . . um, Channing Tatum or Taylor Lautner or some other Hollywood hunk or something."

Oh God. Dad memorized those names just to make that joke. He must have googled "Hollywood hunks" and gone with whatever he found.

I rolled my eyes, but really I found it sweet. Just the fact that he took time to set up a dorky little joke for me meant he still cared. And honestly I'd been beginning to wonder.

"Actually, I have a little soiree with Zac Efron set up, but for you, I'll call and let him down easy," I said.

Dad looked confused. "Zac? Um . . . is he . . . a boy from class?"

I shook my head and laughed. "You're a sad old man, old man! Where are we going? Make it good . . ."

Dad smiled. "Well, I happen to have two tickets to the Egyptian in Hollywood, which is showing a classic film tonight."

"Yeah? What's it about?"

"It's about a man who's stuck in a rut, he can't escape his daily existence, he's doomed to go through the same boring, unfulfilling life forever . . ."

I liked where this was going. "And who's in this fine film?"

"Well, there's a young man named Chris Elliott, and a lovely actress named Andie MacDowell, and the star is a young up-and-comer by the name of—"

"Bill Murray!" I squealed.

Dad chuckled. "Yeah, I *think* that's his name. You in?"

"I'm in."

"Is Mom coming?"

Dad shook his head. "Oh, you know her. She knows how much we love *Groundhog Day*. She's going to let us go have fun together. We'll get pizza and ice cream too. Just like old times."

I paused for a second. "Nope, not *just* like old times."

"What?" he asked. "We've watched this movie fifty times. You *love* this movie. And pizza . . . and ice cream."

"I know," I said. "But let's do Chinese chicken salad instead of pizza. And frozen yogurt instead of ice cream. I don't know if you've noticed, but—"

"Wow," Dad said, apparently just noticing. "You've been dieting. Yeah, of course I've noticed." He stood up, leaned over and kissed me on top of my head. "You look amazing, sweetheart."

And even though I knew he was covering for not noticing before, he still somehow made it all better. I wished I saw him more, but we were going to have fun that night. And we did. It was the first time I'd ever seen *Groundhog Day* in a theater with an audience, and it was a blast.

I worried that these opportunities to just be a kid with my dad were becoming a thing of my past, but for that night, I just sat back and had a great time.

The following Monday—my eyes not entirely open after having two glorious days to sleep in—I was in the main hallway, heading toward my locker.

That's when I smelled it.

Fish.

The entire main hall stunk of disgusting, rotting fish. Every face I passed had the same expression, the one I could only assume was involuntarily plastered on mine: *blegh.*

"Oh my God," one girl said, and held her nose.

"Ugh," another student groaned.

My eyes were almost watering from the stench. I neared my locker with the plan to get in and get out as quickly as possible, because something was rotten in Denmark—that much was certain.

In retrospect, it should have tipped me off that the stench only got more pungent as I neared my locker. By the time I was turning the lock, it was downright suffocating. And when I opened my locker, yep, that's right:

Shakespeare only had it *half* right. Something sure was rotten, but it wasn't in the state of Denmark . . . it was *in my locker*!

I felt myself simultaneously turning green from the stench and red from anger and embarrassment—I have no idea what color that makes, but it's probably good that I couldn't see my face.

My locker and all its contents—books, notepads, backpack, you name it—were all coated in fish guts, parts of fish, whole fish, the whole enchilada. (My mind flashed on an *enchilada* and that turned into a *dead fish enchilada* and I felt a little vomit rise up in my throat, then choked it down.) It was like someone was trying to catch a great white shark with all the chum in my locker.

But wait: Just like in every terrible late-night infomercial, *there's more!*

Dangling from a hook above the marine massacre that had become my locker were two Barbie dolls tied together in the sixty-nine position.

If that were not charming enough, the scissor sisters had a note attached to them:

Hey Lezbo! Since you obviously love Anya's tuna so much, here's a snack we KNOW you'll enjoy!

I stepped back, woozy and nauseated. I didn't need CSI to determine who was responsible for this disgusting prank. Skyler and her crew had to know that breaking into a locker is considered serious stuff, out-of-school-suspension level at most schools. That's not even factoring in the juvenile and obviously homophobic implication of the message.

Had these dumbasses even heard of hate crimes or gay bullying? *And if I'm not even gay,* I pondered, *is it still gay bullying? I'm pretty sure it is. What assholes.*

And PS, If we were gay? We'd make a damn *hot couple.*

They went above and beyond the call to hit me below the belt. It looked like things were only going to get uglier.

The rest of the school day was (thankfully!) uneventful, and I was exhausted when I got home. I hit my bed and figured I'd be out like a light until dinner, but even though I couldn't move a muscle, my mind was racing. There was so much going on. Every single day was a new adventure, good, bad and everything in between.

Something occurred to me: Before we moved, things usually sucked, sure, but they sucked in a fairly *predictable* way. I mean, there were no expectations. Every week was kinda the same: No boy would be interested in me, most of the girls would be bitches, the teachers would be an uneven mix, maybe one good one, definitely one shitty one, and the rest treading water in a sea of mediocrity.

I remembered a saying my social studies teacher told my class once: *May you live in interesting times.* The meaning seemed a little deeper when he said it actually was a Chinese curse. I didn't understand why then, but I kinda did now. Even when your life sucks, some stability and predictability is . . . hell, I don't know . . . comforting, I guess. My times were definitely interesting, but they sure as shit weren't *comforting*.

My stomach hurt. I'd been lying on the bed for hours, totally spent but also wide awake. And Mom was calling me downstairs for dinner.

"Just us again?" I asked, sliding my roast beef around the plate like it was a ship at sea. My mashed potatoes sorta looked like an iceberg, and I found myself re-creating the *Titanic* disaster. *It's okay, Leo. You can grab on to the peas until the rescue boats arrive.*

"I think we're just going to have to get used to it, honey," Mom said. "I've gone from cooking for four to cooking for two. We're going to have to get a dog before we both gain fifty pounds. But then, you're doing fine in that department."

"Yeah," I said, barely listening, killing rich seafarers with every slide of my fork.

"Especially if you don't eat any of your dinner," Mom said.

"Yeah."

I didn't really catch the next few things she said, having totally tuned out, the million things going on at school zipping through my stressed-out bean. I just heard the *dink-dink-dink* sound like someone was making a toast, and my mom yelling at me: "Hailey!"

"Huh?" I said, looking up, noticing the *dink-dink-dink* again, and looking down. I was making the sound. My hand was shaking so hard that it kept clanging the fork against the plate. Peas and potatoes were everywhere. *Too late for the lifeboats.*

"Whoa," I said, putting down my fork. "Sorry, Mom. Can I be excused?"

"Hailey, you should eat something. You're too skinny these days as it is."

"Yeah," I said, ignoring her point and heading upstairs. *Do people get ulcers in high school? Will I be the first?*

That night, I decided to email Noel. Our communications had

been sporadic at best since she left—a brief email here, a text there. When she and Mom would talk on the phone, I'd invariably be called over to "say hi to your sister"—whether either of us wanted to or not. We'd exchange small talk for a minute or two, tops, before finding an excuse to jump off.

Which was all sort of weird, I realized, given that I was using Noel's journal to totally reinvent my life. But that was different. Noel's journal didn't even sound like Noel, exactly. It's like seeing a movie star on the street. He's one guy when he's kicking the ass of an invading alien force with all the CGI and the soaring orchestra and all that, but then you see him coming out of Whole Foods wearing a ball cap and an ill-fitting sweatshirt, and he's just some dude.

I started writing Noel an email. It was weird, because we've never been given to heart to hearts. I almost scrapped it, like, five times, but that's Old Hailey behavior, right? So I toughed it out and put it all out there. I didn't mention *How to Be a Hater*, of course—that might piss off Noel enough to come home and beat me to death with the journal—but I told her how tough school was, all the haters and all the crap. How the few friends I'd made (following an incredibly brief and self-destructive flirtation with the popular crowd) were as invisible as I was. Everything up until today. I laid it all out and hit send.

Now I was more exhausted than ever. My stomach still hurt. I was all stressed out. But I felt strangely better for getting that off my chest. When would Noel answer? Tonight? Tomorrow? Maybe Noel would have some really good ideas! Those are all through her journal, after all. Maybe this would kick off the start of a closer relationship with my sister. She could start telling me all about her college adventures, I could go to her for advice on boys, we could be a team for once, dealing with the haters and the bitches and the—

Plink!

There was a sound I know by heart. It was my computer notifying me there was a new email in my inbox. It was a reply to my email to Noel.

Huh? That was fast. I had just sent it, like, five minutes ago. Even assuming Noel pulled it up and replied immediately, what could she write that fast?

Before I opened it, visions of various possible replies ran through my head:

Dear Hailey:
Fuck off.

———————————————

Dear Hailey: You're adopted.
So we're not actually sisters.
Also, fuck off.

———————————————

Dear Shithead:
You don't even deserve a response, but I wanted to respond just so you'd know that you don't deserve a response.
P.S. You're adopted.
P.P.S. I meant to mention this earlier, but fuck off.

Have you ever been afraid of opening an email? I mean, how pathetic is that?

I took a deep breath and opened her actual reply.

It wasn't anywhere near as bad as those examples...but it also wasn't what you'd call good. It didn't even start with a Dear Hailey or Hey Sis or anything.

It just said:

Sorry youre having tough time. High school sucks, but could be worse. You have no idea. Talk to mom & dad. Theyll help. Gotta run. Well catch up.—N

I spent the next hour trying to parse out the meaning of twenty-eight words. I stared at my monitor so long my eyes ached. And after all that careful analysis, my well-considered conclusion was this:

WHAT THE FUCK?

I write three full pages telling Noel everything (well, almost everything) going on in my life, and this is the bullshit I get back? Something she banged out on her phone in thirty seconds? Noel's a good writer—even in her journal, something she wrote just for *herself*, there's barely a spelling or punctuation mistake in there. Now she can't even spend an extra second to send me something with *apostrophes*?

As bad as the possible responses were I had in my head, they at least indicated she gave a shit about me one way or the other. But this? I've written unsubscribe-me-from-your-list emails with more emotion.

I plopped down on my bed, and the next thing I knew, I was crying. Not crying like blubbering and choking and snot all running from my nose, but crying like you just feel tears running down your cheeks from out of nowhere, like something says, *You need to let this out whether you want to or not.*

It wasn't just the letter. It was everything. It was the stress, the haters, the pressure to do something great with *Abby Invisible*, to stay in shape, to look good enough every second I was at school so the haters wouldn't have an opening. So, so much pressure. And Journal Noel has helped me navigate it a little, but Real-Life Noel couldn't care less about me.

I lay down and eventually faded into sleep, with this thought running through my head:

I definitely live in interesting times.

This is what you get when you mess with us.

—RADIOHEAD

"Karma Police"

CHAPTER
10

Much like frozen yogurt—and just as sweet—revenge is a dish best served cold. So the Invisibles decided to meet and plot world domination—or, at the very least, some divine humbling for those bitches—at Pinkberry.

It had been three days since I got the blow-off email from Noel, which still annoyed me, but I'd calmed down about it. I'm sure she's just busy. Maybe she didn't understand how much the move and this new school were kicking my ass. Maybe I'm not so good with words; I should have drawn her a comic strip!

Anyway, I decided not to get so down about it, especially since I had bigger fish to fry—pun intended. It had also been three days since the fish incident, which Anya almost immediately began referring to as the "Fishcident," and the rest of the Invisibles fol- lowed suit.

The lone holdout (at first), me. I was a little hurt Anya was making light of an incident that actually was a bit traumatic, but Anya set me straight:

"Look, Hailes, we're all about taking ownership of our situation, right? That's why we call ourselves the Invisibles—because we're 'invisible' to the so-called popular crowd. We're going to own that shit. So Skyler and her scum squad turned your locker into a scene from a *Saw* movie? So they're so screwed up they think gay jokes are funny? They think we're going to get embarrassed just because they like to pose Barbie dolls together, you know, something most people grow out of when they turn seven? Screw that. We're not going to run scared."

She was totally right. "And we're gonna turn it back on them," I said.

"Damn straight," she added.

"Or not," I said. "We can hold hands in the hallways."

"Oh, you know it," she replied, sporting the most wonderfully evil grin.

I wasn't going to even mention the Fishcident to a teacher or any other adult, but word got around quickly, largely because the stink tracked into several nearby classrooms. I ended up in front of the dean of students, who was pretty riled up over both a locker getting burglarized and the fact that two janitors and five gallons of bleach still didn't completely kill the smell.

She pressed me to tell her of anyone I suspected of the offense, but I played dumb. It's not like you can dust fish guts for fingerprints, and the school was replacing the replaceable contents of my locker (and my lock) already.

Plus, we already had our own plans to exact some justice.

As far as our revenge plans were concerned, we'd decided on Pinkberry between third and fourth period, and sixth period, all of the players knew where to go. Why? Because Invisibles don't do anything halfway. We had cool meetings at fun locations, and there was a unique order and fun hierarchy to our meetings. Ever seen the movie *Dead Poets Society*? We were like a modern-day version of that group, but instead of using poetry to seize the day, we were using our own unique talents.

Everyone had a voice, and no matter what, we had one another's backs. We were an all-inclusive bunch, and there was a specific way for each of us to contribute. Though *we* may have seen ourselves as outsiders, the truth was that our group was composed of the most interesting, funny, creative, artistic kids in school. To name just two, among our members was Taylor Witt, who did T-shirt screenprinting, and Dahlia Charles, a computer whiz so brilliant she could walk into Apple or Google immediately and be running the place in no time flat. Dahlia set up a secret message board for us to communicate privately online. I designed our own logo: a pair of lips, sealed with a zipper; Taylor screened us all T-shirts with the logo.

When we passed each other in the hall, if we needed to meet or discuss something, we'd mimic the zipper: two fingers, crossed, horizontally held across our lips. (Our inside joke: The first rule of the Invisibles is you do not talk about the Invisibles.) The zipper gesture signaled to its recipient to check the online board if she hadn't yet. That was how everyone knew to meet at the Pinkberry that afternoon.

It was almost like Noel was there with us, reminding us of her credos: Always have a plan. Always have a comeback. Never be intimidated. Or in Noel's words:

Picture the person who intimidates you most. Now picture them crouched like a dog, pooping on the sidewalk, looking up at you, all vulnerable. We all poop. Maybe not on the *sidewalk, but nobody is better than you and don't let them think they are for a minute.*

We discussed our plans for more than three hours, going over the details until everyone knew what they had to do and where they had to be.

"I feel like I'm not being utilized to my full capacity," Xandra said. "I mean, I *am* in theater."

"Fine," I said. "Xan, you switch with Emily."

"That's not fair," Emily protested. Being vegan, she was always good for a protest.

"Then work it out between yourselves," I said. "Moving on . . ."

"What if we don't get it on the first try?" Anya asked.

"We try again," I said. "We try another way in. Another question. Another lead-in. We do whatever it takes."

"You're sure your information is good?" Anya asked me.

"Yeah," I said. "Aren't you?"

Anya sighed. "I think so. I think we can trust Andy. If he says they'll be where they'll be, that's the spot . . . yeah, I think he's for real."

"Me too," I said. "Me too."

"This is gonna be so good," Grace said.

Kura didn't say much. She was too busy enjoying her yogurt.

Once we had our plan solidified and collected our gear, we slowly began to execute. It was an intricate plan—much more complicated than buying some fish at the grocery store and depositing it in some poor unsuspecting person's locker. (That was pretty pedestrian. Disgusting, sure. But definitely lacking creativity.) Our plan required multiple people all executing their assignments, working together to achieve one thing:

Payback.

. . .

A person's greatest strength can sometimes be their greatest liability, and so it was for Skyler. She had become Miss Popular in large part due to massive self-confidence born from being the most narcissistic person ever in the history of ever. Skyler's list of most important people started with Skyler, ended with Skyler, and found room for exactly one person in between: Skyler.

Which is why it turned out to be *so* easy to spy on her.

Seriously, when your whole mind-set is focused on yourself— and just maybe the tiny group of friends you deign suitable to breathe your rarified air—you don't even *notice* all the "commoners" around you. (Unless you're looking for a target to humiliate, obviously.) I learned quickly that pretty much anytime I needed to, I could listen in on Skyler from just a few feet away, and she wouldn't even notice. (It doesn't hurt that I happen to have kick-ass hearing. You can blow a dog whistle and I'll come running.)

It was Wednesday afternoon between second and third period. Skyler, Daniella and Jericha were chatting by Skyler's locker, which was the perfect place and time—for a few reasons. And we knew them thanks to our own personal, adorable double agent:

Andy.

As Andy explained to us, Skyler and Jericha have Miss Kramer for third period, and Miss Kramer's like this old-school hippie free spirit who doesn't care if anyone's late, or early, or whatever. So they're always late. (And we'd be late for our classes, but oh well. We'd take a little slap on the wrist if needed for sweet, sweet revenge.) We found a great hiding spot just around the corner from Skyler's locker, one where it's really easy to watch what's going down undetected, so the three of us—me, Anya and Xandra— were able to listen in for the perfect time to make our move.

As always, Skyler looked good: hair perfectly done, makeup

applied to achieve beauty without looking too made-up, Rag & Bone skinny jeans paired with a Vince thermal, ankle boots to match. You couldn't deny she had style. (Too bad she lacked class.) There was something almost Noel-ish about her, if I was being totally honest. It was hard not to envy her a little bit, with her perfect clothes and perfect life . . . though the minute she opened her mouth you'd get a reality check.

Meanwhile, an asset of being one of the Invisibles is being, well, invisible! Skyler had never met Xandra—that would require at least some slight interest in the arts—and I felt pretty sure Skyler and her minions had no idea Xandra was my friend. We'd done a few test runs in recent days where Xandra had crossed Skyler's path, and she got no reaction from Skyler. That was promising.

Xandra was dressed in cobalt blue jeggings, a Union Jack long-sleeve T-shirt and Adidas sneakers. Oh, and a baseball cap. A *very important* baseball cap.

"I'm so obsessed with your shirt," Daniella said to Skyler. "Obsessed. It's so simple but perfect. Totes amaze."

"I know, right?" said Skyler as she looked down and admired herself.

"I wish I'd got one," Daniella said.

Xandra and I looked at each other. Even from our hiding place, we could feel the arctic chill blow through. *Wrong answer, Daniella.*

"Why?" Skyler asked Daniella, bitchiness factor increasing by the second. "So we could wear it the same day and be *humiliated*? No thanks."

"My mom did those last season anyway," Daniella said, a weak attempt at a face-saving dig. She closed her locker and headed off.

"She's kind of being a bitch," Skyler said. "I'm tempted to not do any locker decoration for her birthday—if anything. Teach her a lesson."

"*So* mean," Jericha said.

Skyler just gave her a look, and you didn't need to be psychic to get it:

How. Dare. You.

Oh, yes, locker drama. Here, we need to take a moment to examine the issue of lockers. (More specifically, lockers that don't still stink of bleach with just a slight remaining hint of fish guts.)

There was *always* locker decoration drama to be had if it was someone's birthday. Since who knows when, locker decorating had become the thing to do for a birthday. There would be notes, and collages, and flowers, and balloons, all of them attached to the "birthday locker." But that's where the politics kicked in. (Yes, birthday locker politics. Sad, huh?)

If you gave three balloons to Kristin, but Sophia only got two— well, Sophia would feel slighted, and it would become a big deal. (Sophia now feels she's only two-thirds as important as Kristin, but that's presuming Sophia can do math, which is total speculation when you're dealing with hypothetical girls, but whatever.) There was an unwritten rule among friends: All decorations had to be equal . . . or *else.*

Locker placement was also key. This was the case at my last school, and even *more so* at West Hollywood. You had to have your locker in the coolest hall (in this case it was the main hall, which was creatively named Main Hall), and you needed to be near your friends.

Now, don't shoot the messenger, but this is how it was according to Noel:

Locker placement is basically the first time you figure out your place in the social pecking order. It's all about having your locker in the primo hallway. If you get a locker far away or in a desolate area where there's not a lot of foot traffic, you're pretty much screwed. You won't ever hear the good gossip or know what's going on, and nobody will want to come hang out at your locker. (Or, even worse, only the other social pariahs will hang out at your locker.)

You have to make sure all your friends have lockers near you. If you get a random weirdo, nerd or simply someone from another social circle stuck between you and your friends, like some weird loner ending up in your cabin on an amusement park log flume ride, you need to gently (but firmly) get them out.

The key to getting the best hall is that someone from your group has to go to school over the summer and scope out where you want your lockers to be, writing down all the locker numbers in the good group. Chances are, a lot of groups will want to claim the best lockers, so someone from your group must come to school early with all your locks and stake your claim first. You want to have your locker next to those of all your friends. Even if it's in the right hall but you're on the "wrong side" of the hallway, that can suck. You might miss out on stuff, and you could end up feeling left out.

It's also important to have other cool groups near your own.

(I know this all sounds nuts, but it's high school—of course it's nuts.)

For instance, once you get into the right hallway, you might want to migrate over a few lockers, or across the hall, depending on which guys have lockers near you. You also might want to avoid conflicting groups, necessitating a little more sliding over. Basically, you have about forty-eight hours to lock down and finalize your locker placement. Then you're pretty much stuck. One or two people may be able to move, but as a group, you will be there for at least a semester.

This brings us back to the new revolution when it came to the decorating of lockers. This had become such a "thing" that people were spending, like, ridiculous amounts of money to decorate their lockers. Okay, can I just say one thing?

It's a freaking *locker*!

It's a place to keep your books and your jacket and maybe to keep a mirror just to do the after-lunch spot-check to make sure you don't have a poppy seed in your teeth from that poppy-seed-lemon loaf you snarfed down before class. (I *had* a mirror in my locker, but when it's covered in fish guts, it loses a lot of its usefulness.)

Sure, I suppose decorating a locker is a way to express your individuality and make that space your own, but I've heard it described as "nesting." (What? Are they planning on moving into their lockers?) I've seen with my own eyes, like crazy excessive decorations. Not just wallpaper and standard crap, but like... *chandeliers*. I mean, *really?*

Getting back to the mission at hand: From the look on Jericha's face, she realized she shouldn't have questioned Queen Skyler—once you're out, you're out, as Anya and I know perfectly well—and she must have wanted to change the subject. She pointed to a magazine Skyler was holding. Skyler was reading various horoscopes aloud.

I wonder what Skyler's astrological sign is, I thought. *Probably Cancer. It should be Cancer. Hey, Skyler, what's it say for Cancer? "Today, you will be a total bitch?"*

"Read *mine*," Jericha said, mouth full of a banana-nut muffin, crumbs dotting her all-too-carefully considered ensemble.

"You know, you may as well be eating cake," Skyler said with her usual disdain.

"It's banana-nut," Jericha said.

"I don't need to see it half-digested. Chew and swallow. Then speak."

Jericha swallowed. "It's healthier than a chocolate muffin."

"Look, eat what you want. But when you start crying because you can't fit into your skinny jeans, um, because you're no longer skinny? Don't expect me to feel sorry for you."

Jericha said nothing for a moment. "Are you going to read mine?"

"*Fine*," Skyler sighed. "What sign are you?"

"Gemini!" Jericha gasped, never so great at learning her lesson. "Still Gemini! These things don't change! I tell you *every week*."

"Like I'm supposed to *memorize* it?" Skyler said, rolling her eyes like she was training a puppy. I swear, if eye rolling burned calories, girls would never have to work out.

Anya giggled softly, so I pressed a finger up to my lips, and she swallowed her amusement. If we were detected, it would blow everything.

Skyler looked for the horoscope. "Gemini. Here it is: 'If you've been wondering why someone seems to act a little strangely whenever they're near, you may be about to find out. Don't be surprised by the sudden revelation that they have romantic feelings toward you.'"

"Oooh, I wonder who it is," Jericha said. She seemed genuinely excited. *I'll bet she believes in unicorns too. Hey, Skyler, tell Jericha her new beau's a unicorn.*

"Maybe it's Mr. Davies," Skyler said, sharpening her claws right on cue. "Maybe you can stare into his nostrils from up close!"

"I'd rather make out with my grandfather."

"Ew," Skyler said, but you couldn't tell if it was directed toward Jericha or the fact that Xandra had emerged from our hiding place and was heading toward them.

As Xan marched forward, I felt my phone vibrate in my hand. We'd all checked our phones several times to make sure the sound was off—can't have a poorly timed ring tone exposing us at the worst time—but now I was thinking I should have just turned it off. I glanced down to see a text from Chris: **hey you, whats up?**

Boy, will I have a story for you, I thought. *Someday.*

Skyler watched Xan approach with the look of a child being spoon-fed spinach. *You can make all the airplane noises you want to, Mom, but it's not gonna make that green crap any more appetizing.*

"Hey, Skyler," Xandra said, as if they'd been best buds since kindergarten.

Skyler looked confused. God, I love that look on her. "Hey . . . person I don't know."

"What do you have fifth period?" Xan asked, undeterred.

"I have . . ." Skyler thought for a second. "Spanish. Why?"

"Oh," Xandra said. "Well, our 'Elizabeth' dropped out of Drama. And we can't very well do *Pride and Prejudice* without an Elizabeth Bennett."

Skyler looked at her blankly. "This conversation is actually *worse* than Spanish class. Speak *English*! What are you trying to say to me? I don't know who Elizabeth Whoever is, and why are you telling me this?"

"She's a character. I thought you'd be perfect for the part," Xandra said. "They're having auditions during fifth period, so I thought maybe you'd want to try out."

"You thought wrong," Skyler said. "Like, I'm going to spend my free time in the auditorium with a bunch of theater geeks? Um . . . no."

"Okay," Xandra said, fearless and right in character. *She really is good.* "I had to try. It's just so sad. Kristy got into so much trouble, and well . . . her mom pulled her out of school so suddenly. She was going to be a great Elizabeth. So crazy. Such a tragedy."

"Tragedy?" Skyler replied, and I turned to Anya. We could barely hold it in, but we quietly high-fived. *She's on the hook!* There's no way Skyler's passing up some good gossip.

"You didn't hear?" Xan asked, deadpan.

"Of course I didn't hear! I don't know who she is! What's the tragedy?"

"She got herpes," Xandra said.

"What?" Skyler's eyes widened and her jaw dropped.

"Yeah," Xan said. "Her parents didn't even know she was having sex yet, much less with—"

"With who?" exclaimed Jericha, seemingly desperate to get in the conversation. A deadly glare from Skyler ended her curiosity just as quickly.

"Oh . . . nobody," Xan said, just to annoy the shit out of them. "It's nobody you know anyway."

"Screw it, who cares?" Skyler said, laughing. "They found out she was having sex *and* she has herpes? OMG, that is *amazing*. I wish I knew who you were talking about, but whatever. Herpes, huh? Gross."

Xandra smiled.

"Why are you looking at me like that?" Skyler asked. "You look like a psycho."

"I just think you're *really* great," Xandra said, unable to keep the grin off her face. I couldn't help but worry for a second: *You did great, Xan, don't blow it!*

"Well, I think you're really *weird*," Skyler said. "Also? Bright-colored denim isn't 'in' anymore. Thought you should know."

"And thanks for that," Xandra said. "So that's a no on tryouts, right?"

"A definite no," Skyler said. "Feel free to stay away from me in the future."

"My pleasure!" Xandra said, and then walked away, practically bursting from excitement.

Xandra rounded the corner, and she, Anya and I quickly slipped down a separate hallway. We ducked into an empty class-room and regrouped in the back.

"I got it!" Xandra said.

"We know! You fucking rule!" Anya said.

"You're sure you got it all?" I asked.

"All and then some," Xandra said. "She ad-libbed some true gems!"

"Okay," I said. "Let's move."

We glanced into the hallway to make sure the coast was clear—if Skyler saw Anya or me with Xan, the jig was up—and then the three of us walked to the media lab. Dahlia was waiting alone amid a sea of computers, Avid digital-editing machines and other equipment.

"Hey, ladies," Dahlia said. "Did you bring me some candy?"

Xandra took off her hat and handed it to Anya, who turned the hat upside down, fidgeted with it, and plugged in a USB cable connected to a computer.

Voilà: We had Skyler on video!

The initial question about fifth period was to get her saying "I have" on video. The rest . . . well, that was soon to become the talk of West Hollywood High.

The groundwork we laid would pay off the next morning. Anya, budding comedian that she was, had landed the morning announcements gig at school. She treated it like a combination open mic/morning radio show, and she handled it beautifully: entertaining enough that no students took issue with it, but school-friendly enough that the administration left her alone.

Even though she only had five minutes, she always tried to make the most of it. We had TV monitors in five places around our campus in case anyone wanted to watch (typically, nobody really did), but the audio was broadcast throughout the halls.

This time, we were going to make sure people actually watched. I arrived twenty minutes before school started with lattes for Anya and me, so we'd be properly caffeinated and happy as we took Skyler down. Anya was in the media room, practicing, going through the rigmarole:

"Remember that it's Taco Tuesday in the cafeteria."

"Friday is a half day, not that you'd forget that."

"Whatever heathen thinks they're above flushing in the third bathroom stall on the second floor in Chem Hall needs to seriously check herself."

This morning would be just a little bit different.

"Uno venti mocha latte, por vous," I said.

"I think you just managed to incorporate three languages into that sentence," Anya said, accepting her latte.

"I did, didn't I?" I felt rather pleased with myself. "You ready?"

"Oh, you have no idea," she said. "I never really had the chance to get her back for making my life hell."

"Payback's a bitch," I said. "And so is she."

We toasted with our Starbucks cups, and Anya put on her headphones. I moved out of view.

"Morning, everybody," Anya said. "We have a little change in our scheduled programming, just one quick special announcement. Don't worry, it's not a natural disaster or an unnatural disaster. And unlike the glee club's performance last night in regionals, it's not a *total* disaster. Well, actually, I don't know *what* it is, but I just got the tape, and I'm told it's extremely important, so everyone needs to watch it carefully, *right now*. Enjoy!"

With that, time was immediately of the essence. Anya pressed a button, and the video of Skyler began to play. Well, you could call it a mash-up of sorts. A "best of" remix from her conversation with Xandra.

Skyler, looking directly at the camera: "I have . . . herpes. Thought you should know. Feel free to stay away from me in the future."

Aaaaaand . . . *scene*.

That's right, Dahlia's seamless editing skills turning Skyler's words to our advantage in our (hopefully) seamless plan.

153

Anya took the mic again. "Huh. Well, that's not exactly what I was expecting. Skyler Brandt has herpes? Wow, just saying the words sounds so strange: *Skyler Brandt has herpes.* I guess it's some sort of public service announcement. That's—well, I'd say that's a pretty brave decision to put it right out there for the good of the school. And considerate. Thank you, Skyler! Thank you for caring enough about your fellow students to make this news public so people won't unknowingly contract this painful and recurring STD. Everyone be sure to thank Skyler today when you see her!"

Anya turned off the mic and whipped around to find me. I stood there, grin plastered on my face, shaking my head. "She is going to *freak.*"

"Oh, I know," Anya said. "We should probably start counting now because—"

Before Anya could even finish her sentence, we heard it: the guttural scream sailing down the hall, courtesy of one pair of lungs, belonging to one *Skyler Brandt.*

"You do know her well," I said.

"I *did,*" Anya answered, and I could detect a hint of sadness. She was glad we'd gotten her back, but in her heart of hearts, she probably wished none of it ever happened—the pregnancy, the rumors, the dissolution of their friendship. Wouldn't it be nice to go back to a simpler time? I know sometimes I'd think to myself, *I'd like to go back to a time when my biggest problem was Cap'n Crunch destroying the roof of my mouth.*

We were collecting our things and heading for the door. If the principal or dean of students got here while we were still together, it would make our "escape plan" a bit more complicated, but we'd planned for that contingency—they were in a meeting on the other side of campus. It was more likely we'd be intercepted by—

Skyler. She had just stepped inside the doorway, and the look on her face was priceless. She was beet red, with her fists balled and her face twisted into a mask of hatred.

"Get on that thing *right now*," Skyler seethed, "and tell everyone you lied."

"But I didn't lie," Anya said. "*You're* the one who said it."

"I *didn't* say that," she said through gritted teeth. "You edited that to make it look like I did."

"I most certainly did not," Anya said.

"Well, *someone* did, so fix it!"

"Morning announcements are over, Skyler," Anya said. "My work is done here. And I have to get to class now."

"How could you?" Skyler said, going for the heartstrings—because threats certainly weren't working.

"I could ask the same of you," Anya said, referring to past transgressions. When Skyler provided no response—and encouraged by my energetic gesturing to *hurry up, we need to roll*—Anya walked toward the door.

"*You,*" Skyler said to me just before we could get out. "This is your fault. Anya never would have done something like this before you got to her."

"Sorry," I said hurriedly. "I don't control my friends. Anya is her own person."

"Yeah," Skyler said. "Right."

We needed to get out of there, but I couldn't help myself. "Anyway"—I turned one last time and threw Skyler my best fauxsympathetic look—"sorry to hear about the herpes. That must be a *real* drag."

"*I. Don't. Have. Herpes!*" Skyler shouted after us.

Sure I felt a pang of guilt—I'm not a *monster.* And it wasn't lost on me that I'd gone "Skyler" on Skyler and two wrongs don't make a right blah blah blah but you know what? It's called survival. Maybe now she'd realize she'd messed with the wrong girls. Maybe now she'd quit being so awful. And maybe there would be a calorie-free red velvet cupcake that would not just keep you slim, it would clear up all your zits with its miraculous ingredients! Hey, a girl can dream.

'Cause you know sometimes
words have two meanings.

—LED ZEPPELIN
"Stairway to Heaven"

CHAPTER
11

If you ever decide to rob a bank, commit a murder or hold some hostages, I can tell you beyond a shadow of a doubt that the person you want as your partner in crime is Anya Delaney.

(For the record, please do not rob a bank, commit a murder or hold hostages. Even if you can do them all at the same time. Not all multitasking is good multitasking, you know.)

We didn't figure that Anya's awesome announcement would go over big with the administration, and give us points for this:

Holy shit, were we right.

As Anya later explained it, only seconds after we separated and she entered her first-period class, she was told to report to Principal Dash's office *immediately*.

That wasn't surprising. Well, maybe just a little surprising; we kinda figured The Man would have closed in on her before she made it to first period.

If you haven't noticed anything else about US public school administrations in the twenty-first century, you've probably noticed this:

They are gigantic chickenshits.

At the slightest hint of controversy, like a half inch of your underwear exposed by your low-rise jeans (and by the way—the whale tail is just not a good look—nobody ever looked at a plumber's ass-crack and said, "Hey, that's fantastic!"), or a school newspaper running an editorial that questions the dress-code policy, or a big Stephenie Meyer fan feeling "invalidated" because someone wore a T-shirt that reads TWILIGHT SUCKS!, a school district will hold thirty-seven "emergency" meetings and pass forty-six new no-tolerance policies to ensure that no one ever does anything interesting ever in the history of ever.

That's one reason I had been pleasantly surprised that my shots at the self-involved popular crew didn't get *Abby Invisible* eighty-sixed. This school had proven itself a bit more tolerant of self-expression than I expected.

But satire is a completely different story from broadcasting over the morning announcements that one of the most popular girls in school has (mythical, but whatever) herpes.

Even if everyone knew she *totally* deserved that shit.

Anyway, Anya put herself squarely in the crosshairs for us, so we did everything we could to coach her up for her eventual interrogation. Anya's always had an appreciation for performance art anyway—what else is great stand-up comedy than performance art—so she came correct with the aptitude. Xandra helped out with some of her acting tricks, and we all pitched in by trying to hit her with every torturous interrogation tactic we could think of— short of waterboarding, bamboo shoots under the fingernails or watching an entire season of *Toddlers and Tiaras*. I swear those kids and their makeup are scarier than evil clowns! I just hope someone will document at least one girl's evolution from *Toddlers and Tiaras* to *Teen Mom* to *Intervention* to *Hoarders*.

Anyway, of course, Anya kicked the living shit out of it. I so wished I could have been there to watch but from what it sounded like, her performance was *inspired.* I'll relate what happened as best as I can recall what Anya explained to me:

Anya sat outside Principal Dash's office for forty-five minutes, which Anya said felt like approximately three weeks. Eventually, the door opened, and Skyler walked out. She walked up to Anya, smiled slightly (hinting at Anya's impending demise), then walked right out the door. About a minute later, Principal Dash called Anya into his office.

Inside were Principal Dash and Mr. Muñez, and the looks on their faces told Anya this would not be a pleasant conversation. I won't bore you with the play-by-play, but they took turns trying to wear her down about Operation Herpes, which Anya says she found odd—hadn't Skyler already provided them with the whole enchilada?

Here Anya was, like, totally ready with her whole defense, and these guys are still asking *where the tape came from*?

"I don't know!" Anya replied, for the fifteenth time. (She might have been exaggerating there—I'll bet they only asked her twelve times—but that's what she told me, so whatever.)

"Anya, you really expect me to believe you have no idea where the tape came from?" Principal Dash asked.

Xan had trained her well. Anya explained that someone had stuck the DVD through the slats in her locker on the morning of the announcement, with the note:

ANYA, THIS IS TIME-SENSITIVE MATERIAL THAT MUST BE
PLAYED ON THIS MORNING'S ANNOUNCEMENTS. IT'S VERY
IMPORTANT, SO MAKE SURE EVERYONE LISTENS. THANK YOU.
-PRINCIPAL DASH

(We'd created the actual note, of course, for the little bit of extra *oomph* that hopefully gave our story. Plus we totally knew he'd ask for it.)

"And you really thought that was a note from *me*?" Principal Dash asked.

"Well . . . yeah!" Anya said. "You're busy with, you know, principal stuff. You even had a meeting this morning, right? I figured you just dropped it off in my locker."

"And when you watched it, you didn't wonder why I would ask you to play a DVD on the morning announcements in which an underclassman supposedly declares—to the entire school—that she has an incurable venereal disease?"

"I didn't watch it before I played it on the announcements," Anya said.

"What?"

"I didn't *watch* it, Mr. Dash. I'm sorry. I was running late this morning, and I was afraid I'd be late for the morning announcements entirely, and I don't want to lose the gig."

Mr. Muñez shook his head. "So, Anya, you just played something, without any idea what it was, over the morning announcements?"

"I thought it was from Mr. Dash!" Anya said. "The note didn't say *watch* it. It said *play* it."

"You know that any major changes to the morning announcements have to be cleared by the administration," Principal Dash said.

"I thought you'd already cleared it, because I thought you wrote the note," Anya replied.

"Anya, that's a little hard to believe," Mr. Muñez said. "Look, we know you and Skyler used to run in the same circles. And we know that all changed once you came back to school after your . . . um . . . extended absence."

"My pregnancy," Anya said, taking the opportunity to put them on the defensive.

"Um . . . well . . . right," Mr. Muñez said.

Anya relied on the principle we had drilled into her over and over, the principle that, if anything, best defined the Invisibles:

The best defense is a good offense.

"Look," Anya said defiantly. (Well, she *said* it was defiantly, and knowing Anya, it was *definitely* defiantly.) "I got a DVD in my locker. It said it was from the principal, and that I *had* to play it on the morning announcements. So I did. And then it turned out to be some prank from someone trying to make Skyler look bad. I'm really sorry that happened, but I don't know who made this video."

That's when she pulled out the move Xan had taught her, step by step: Anya closed her eyes and bowed her head, then made the sign of the cross over her chest, and said: "I swear to God. I swear to my Lord and Savior, Jesus Christ."

(Sure, *we* know Anya's a total atheist, but these faculty goobers were totally taken in by that stuff.)

(Well, mostly.)

"Anya, given what we know, that's still a pretty hard story to swallow," the principal said.

Emily had warned Anya about this move, the we-can-prove-you're-not-telling-us-the-truth maneuver. Credit Emily's experience with having to talk her way out of more than a few questioning sessions with Paul Blart types at the local malls.

Don't fall into that trap, Emily had told Anya. *They're trying to mine information from you. Play dumb and try to get information from them.*

"Mr. Dash," Anya replied, "what are you talking about?"

"We talked to Skyler," Mr. Muñez interrupted. "She told us everything that happened."

"Great," Anya said. "So what happened?"

"We want you to tell us," Mr. Dash said.

"Um . . . I just told you I *don't know*. Skyler does, right? What did she say?"

As Anya tells it, the men just looked at each other in silence. And that's when Anya knew it for sure: Skyler hadn't told them *anything*. Why, she had no idea. But for some reason, Skyler played dumb.

This was way better than we could have ever hoped for. We'd already set up Xan with a whole defense, but she never even got called in to the principal's office. She walked away scot-free and so did I and Dahlia too.

Anya wasn't as lucky. We figured she might face some punishment, and indeed she did. Obviously the principal didn't completely buy her story, but she was helped immensely by one thing:

He couldn't actually *prove* she was full of shit.

That made it pretty tricky for Mr. Dash to throw the book at her, despite how public and huge the Herpes Humiliation had been.

He called Anya back into his office later that day and laid out his ruling: one week of in-school suspension (ISS), plus one day of detention *every week* for the rest of the semester. His rationale was that Anya should have known better than to broadcast something on the morning announcements sight unseen, that she shouldn't have taken for granted that something came from him without speaking to him in person, and that running late that morning was no excuse for being party to something that so embarrassed one of the students.

He had a point there—I mean, half the school was referring to

Skyler as "Vicky Valtrex" by fourth period, and that doesn't even include the ones calling her "Suzie STD" or "Becky Blisters." (If you included our crew, she was being called all three.)

Mr. Dash wrote out an apology and "correction" that Anya was mandated to read the next day on the morning announcements, advising that the "student-related announcement from yesterday was entirely false, the result of a cruel unfortunate prank, the likes of which will not be tolerated at West Hollywood." She concluded by saying she would be taking an indefinite (and, of course, also principal-mandated) leave from the morning announcements.

It was pretty tough, but it was in line with what we expected, and what Anya had been braced for—she knew it was a calculated risk, and she expected she'd be doing some sacrificing for the cause.

We'd all made that commitment to the Invisibles. No risk, no reward, right? There was no point in banding together if we didn't put ourselves in positions where we had to put up or shut up.

And we sure as shit weren't going to shut up.

Not anymore.

Still, it would have been a whole lot worse if not for Skyler's inexplicable refusal to sell us all down the river. We had elaborate plans to minimize that damage, sure, but we never had to bother with them.

Word got around that Skyler's family was *furious*, they wanted Anya expelled from school and worse, but the other shoe never dropped. Still, we all felt for Anya. The after-school detention part sucked, but getting out of classes for a full week didn't seem too awful—even if you were stuck in the library.

The worst part of it was she was going to miss driver's ed, and with no chance to make up the class before the test, she was going to have to take it again and wait until next semester to get her driver's license. We all promised to be her chauffeurs during her waiting period—it was the least we could do. She *had* taken one for the team.

Anyway, in light of the herpes announcement, whether or not it was indeed a prank, the school implemented a new zero-tolerance rule. (Like I said, schools love zero-tolerance rules. Don't force us to think or use any discretion, just lump everything into one pile! Zero tolerance!)

This one regarded pranks. There would be a zero-tolerance policy for anyone who did anything remotely resembling a prank. Nothing surprising there.

When Chris and I caught up after school, I braced myself for the worst.

"Wow . . . go big or go home, huh, Hailey?"

I gave him a slightly sheepish look. "You mess with the bull . . . you get the horns?"

"Yeah, but you didn't say she had horns," Chris said. "You said she had herpes."

"Technically, it wasn't me," I said, not even trying to sound sincere. "It was some video stuck in Anya's locker with a note—"

"Nice try," he said, "but you know no one buys that. Got away with it though, huh?"

"I hope so," I said.

He looked a bit pained, which bothered me, then he stepped closer, which thrilled me. Though I was really worried about what was coming next.

"Look, Hailes," he said, giving me some weird variant nickname I immediately loved, "I'm not mad for *me*. I mean, no one thinks I have herpes. No one thinks *Skyler* has herpes. It was obviously a prank, and it was pretty smooth, I gotta say."

"Um, thanks," I said. "So if you're not mad for you, you're mad for . . . *Skyler*?"

"I'm not mad at all," he said. "Mad isn't the right word. It's just . . . look, I know Skyler can be awful. I mean, awful. I mean tripping blind orphans who are sightseeing at Grand Canyon awful."

"Probably not the best group for sightseeing," I said.

"Valid point," he said.

"So what's the *but*?"

He sighed. "*But* . . . I don't know. I'm not saying she isn't ripe for pranking—she deserves to get as much as she gives—but . . . I don't know. Guess I can't help but feel sorry for her a little."

"Really?" I replied. "That makes sense. Like watching the *Harry Potter* movies and feeling bad for Voldemort."

"Yeah, I've never seen one of those," he said, and it didn't look like he was kidding. "Anyway, it's cool. It's just—you're really smart, Hailes. You're really funny."

"Thanks," I replied. *Hailes.*

"And you're a killer artist . . . you have all this potential."

"Thanks again . . ."

Chris looked me dead in the eye. "So don't fuck it up." And he walked off.

So I was knocking that around for the following few days. In fact, it was still fresh on my brain when I returned from school one day to find a real surprise outside my house:

Skyler Brandt.

It had already been ten minutes and nothing drastic had happened. Curiosity was getting the best of me so I finally just asked Skyler what was going on:

"So when do your friends jump out of the bushes to beat the

crap out of me?" I asked, suggesting we were in some kind of chola gang war. "Force-shampoo my hair with something to make it all fall out? Kidnap me and force-feed me cupcakes for a week so when I get back to school I'm fifteen pounds fatter? Actually that sounds kinda good. I'm amenable to that."

Skyler chuckled at my remark. It was a surprisingly understated response from her, possibly the first genuine-sounding thing I'd ever heard pass her oft-venomous lips. You'd almost think she was human—if you didn't know better.

"No one's in the bushes, Hailey. It's just you and me."

"I knew I should have patted you down."

"Don't worry, I'm unarmed. You're mostly safe. Really, all you can get from me is herpes—right?"

Ouch. Nice touch. Skyler was a bitch, no question whatsoever, but she wasn't exactly stupid. Too bad she always used that quick wit for evil.

We walked to the small park down the street. I really didn't know what to expect, though getting duct-taped upside down to a tree—a picture that would be immediately uploaded to Facebook by one of Skyler's minions—certainly crossed my mind.

Her humor reminded me of a section of Noel's diary:

Don't take yourself too seriously. Being able to laugh at yourself is super-important. If you're someone who can't laugh at yourself, other people are probably doing it for you. (And they're not laughing _with_ you, they're laughing _at_ you.)

It was almost like Skyler had been privy to the diary as well— but I knew she wasn't. I guess charm and the how-to's of being cool came naturally to the Skylers of the world. I knew she *had* to be infuriated over the Herpes Hoax, and I was right at the top of her hit list.

Then again, Noel wouldn't have backed off or run into her house, terrified of the evil meanie. She would look her in the eye, cool as ice. So I played along, followed Skyler to the park, braced myself for the worst, and then . . . nothing.

At least so far.

"Can we get on with it, Skyler?" I asked. "I don't have all day. I'm sure you want revenge. Do your worst. I can clean fish guts off my shit six days a week and twice on Sunday."

She smirked. "We don't have school on Sunday."

"I wouldn't put anything past you."

Skyler chuckled again. It sounded genuine. *Again*.

"Hailey, like, you expect the worst," Skyler said. "Of course you do. You should. I've, like, destroyed girls' *lives* before, left them broken and pitiful, and they hadn't pulled anything as *fucked up* as what you pulled on me."

I had no idea what to say. So I didn't say anything. *What would Noel do? Stare her down.* So I stared her down, looking as tough as I could, but mostly thinking, *Please don't duct-tape me to a tree. Go the cupcakes route if you need to do something drastic. Red velvet is my favorite but I'm open.*

It seemed like she was still waiting for a response, so finally I gave her one. "I didn't start it," I said. "You could have left me alone. Just because I didn't want to be part of your clique—"

"That's *exactly* what started it," Skyler said. "You're a pretty girl. You dress decently. I know that. I know everything that's going on. If we hadn't met, you think I would have spent a single extra second concerning myself with you? With all the freaks and fashion tragedies, all those Walmart ensembles, cluttering the halls at West Hollywood? Gawd, they could keep me occupied for *years*."

"So what's the issue?" I asked, now genuinely curious.

"You turned your back on me," she said. "It was, like, betrayal. I barely knew you, but I took a chance on you, and you—well, you 'dumped' me. I don't *get* dumped. I damn well don't get dumped in front of the whole school."

"Yeah, but—"

"Let me finish. I know what you're going to say: 'Yeah, but you're shallow and whatever, and I'm all deep and I'm an artist and I'm all funny and shit.' Fine. Great. Whatever. You think I don't get you? *I get you*, Hailey. You think I would have let you in if you didn't have something going on? I'm not an asshole, Hailey. I get you. The problem is, you don't get *me*."

Now it was my turn to chuckle, especially because any concealed minions would have attacked me long ago. *I think.*

"Really?" I asked. "You're a shallow, bitter, style-obsessed bitch. What's not to get?"

Skyler flashed a shark's smile, reminding me who I was talking to again. "Well . . . why do you think you're not suspended from school? Like, why do you think your buddy Xandra wasn't suspended? Or how about Dahlia?"

Shit. She knew Xandra's name now. Mental note: Warn Xandra.

"Yeah, Hailey, I know who Dahlia is, and I know she edited the video. And my old pal Anya, my old *bestie*? Why isn't she looking forward to taking the GED at *this very second*?"

The shot at Anya infuriated me. "You did way worse to her."

Her face was placid, unfazed. "You weren't here then, sweetie. But . . . yeah, maybe I could have handled that better. Like, sometimes I just start talking and I'm surprised what comes out. You know how that is. Like you and your buddies telling the whole school that someone has a fictional case of herpes. It just comes out—*whoops*! Or . . . like me telling the administrators that if they check the cameras in the media center—they have security cameras in there, you know—they might find out how your little broadcast came to be in the first place."

I felt my stomach drop. Skyler didn't keep what she knew to herself to protect us. She was just looking to prolong the agony. And she had us dead to rights.

All of which must have been illustrated on my face.

"Wait, Hailey, don't worry!" Skyler exclaimed. "I'm sorry, I really am. My tongue gets away from me sometimes."

No shit.

"Skyler, seriously, what the hell?" I asked. "Why are we here? You want to say whatever you want to say to whoever, I can't stop you. You claim there are security tapes to nail us, congratulations, we'll see. Far as I know, it's still our word against—"

I stopped.

"Are you recording me, Skyler? Taste of my own medicine?"

"No! Hailey, I—"

"You know, it's illegal to record someone without their knowledge," I found myself saying. I saw that on an episode of *Law & Order*.

"Oh, is it?" Skyler said. "Really, that's illegal? Because . . ."

Oops.

And then we caught each other's eyes and both broke out laughing. Yes, laughing. Me and Skyler, laughing together. Oil and water, Cain and Abel, Jennifer Aniston and Angelina Jolie.

How the hell did this happen?

"We're not all that different, Hailey," Skyler was saying, and for some reason, in that moment, it almost made sense. "We, like, both want to, I don't know, *define* ourselves. You were looking to do it from the second you stepped into our school. I saw it. I get it. I know the new-girl-in-town thing. Seen it, like, a million times."

"Okay—"

"So let's just end this now."

What?

"End it?"

"Yeah," she said. "Right here, right now."

Oh my God, we're going to fight to the death. We're going to fight to the death right now. I really should have learned krav maga . . .

"So is that cool?" Skyler asked.

What did she say?

"Huh?" I asked.

"Is that cool? Peace. Like, a seize fire. No more crap."

Cease fire, I thought, but didn't say it.

I also didn't quite buy it.

"Skyler, no offense, but . . . I don't get it. I don't know why you'd play nice with me, and after the morning announcements thing—not to say you didn't deserve it, because you sure as hell did—the last thing I expected was for you to be declaring a—"

Say it. For everyone's good, just frigging say it.

"—'seize fire.'"

Skyler reclined against a tree, which was as unlike her as anything I'd seen in my life. She had a gorgeous cashmere cardigan wrapped around her, and why on earth she would let cashmere touch tree bark was beyond my comprehension.

Maybe I'd had her wrong all along? Sure, she'd done some awful things, but maybe she wasn't awful to the core?

Or maybe her family just had so much money it could shit cashmere?

"Like I said, Hailey, you're smart. I'm smart too. I might not know a lot about stuff you'd see on *Jeopardy!*, but I know people. I know there's nothing to be gained by making an enemy of you. We might not all be besties, but there's no reason we can't . . . um . . . what's the word? Co . . . habitate?"

"I don't think that's the word you mean."

"Co . . . shit, it's on the tip of my tongue."

"You mean *coexist.*"

"Yeah! Coexist!"

Good Lord. "Coexist. Well, yeah, Skyler. We all just want to co-exist. We want to coexist without someone making us feel second-class all the time. And it doesn't matter what you think of me. You make any of my friends feel like shit, that's a shot at me. I have friends with weird interests. I have friends who don't look like run-way models. I know kids who get their clothes from Walmart, because their parents can't afford anything else. Our school is full of artists and actors and gay and straight and weird and unique and funny and a million other things that don't fit into your tiny box of what's acceptable."

I paused for effect. (Hey, we've all learned something from Xan.)

"You want to 'seize fire'?" I asked. "You leave them alone."

Skyler put her palms out toward me, a classic sign of surrender.

"Hailey, I'll do you one better," she said. "I'd like to invite you all to a party."

Turn yourself around, you weren't invited.

—YEAH YEAH YEAHS

"Honeybear"

CHAPTER 12

"Oh, bullshit."

Yeah, that was Anya. Which was pretty much the response I expected from Anya, but still . . . I wasn't sure. People are all, like, multifaceted, right? So maybe Skyler had more facets than I'd given her credit for. It wasn't impossible.

The party was at Skyler's amazing house in the hills. Other than Anya, none of us had ever been to Skyler's house. Actually, other than Anya, none of us had ever been to any amazing house in the hills.

I'd pretty much predicted Anya's response to the invite, and she came through with flying colors:

"No way. It's a trap."

Couldn't blame her. Anya knew Skyler much better than I did, after all. They were close for a while, whereas I was hardly more than a weekend guest of the Clique of Evil.

Still . . . Skyler had really seemed *genuine*. Some of what she said made a lot of sense. It wasn't really in her best interests to make enemies of the Invisibles. She'd learned that firsthand. And I have to admit, the idea of being invited to a party at Skyler's seemed a tiny bit cool to me, and it was beyond the realm of anything many of the Invisibles had ever thought possible.

The girls had adopted a certain sense of pride for fighting back. When we got the invite, they felt they'd finally won the respect of the popular kids. Once Skyler realized we wouldn't be pushed around, the girls reasoned, she figured there's no reason we couldn't all be friends.

It actually made sense. Maybe this was actual *acceptance*, our "coming out" party as equals? The truth was, we'd grown in numbers, and the lines between who was popular and who wasn't were starting to blur.

The popular kids want to stand apart and be known. But from the outside, you'd never really know who was or who wasn't in the Invisibles. And when push came to shove, the popular kids weren't entirely sure who or what they were up against. Even worse: You can't be a popular kid without the "normal" people in school thinking you *are* popular.

Were things really balancing out? I wasn't so sure.

So there we were, Anya on the defensive, after school at Chipotle, where we'd agreed to meet for some burritos and bitching. What started as a discussion turned into quite the heated debate among the Invisibles over whether or not to go to the party.

"How is this even a discussion?" Anya scoffed.

"Maybe because we can see the good in people?" Kura suggested.

"Cristina Yang would never, *never* believe this crap," Anya said to Kura. "She would know it was bullshit. She'd be the first one to *call* bullshit. So if you want to be a Yang, you need to grow a healthy dose of reality check."

"Anya," I said, "I understand why you're skeptical—"

"Yeah?" she said. "Then why the hell are you going along with this, Hailey?"

"I'm not. I mean, I am. I mean, I don't know what I mean." I paused. "Look, I'm just telling you what she told me. She seemed sincere. She seemed to realize there was no point in letting this go any further."

"Yeah, funny how that works after your cooch crawlies get blasted all over the school," Anya said.

For the oddest second, I found myself wanting to defend Skyler. And before I could stop myself . . .

"She could have gotten you expelled, Anya," I said.

"Oh, bullshit," she repeated. "We had that covered, Hailey. Just because you bought her line about the security cameras and shit—"

"Okay, maybe that's a load. It's probably a load. But she knew about Dahlia. She could have told them all about Xan and Dahlia and me, and she didn't."

"Because she's not stupid, Hailey. She's horrible. Not stupid."

Xandra chimed in: "We can't always be cynical. Why can't we accept that maybe they want to become friends with us?"

"Because people are evil," Anya said. "People are just the worst. That's a fact. We are an ugly, terrible species."

"Like a ray of sunshine, you are," I said.

"Thanks, Yoda," she replied. "Look, I would love nothing more than for Skyler to just fuck off and leave all of us alone. That's my greatest wish. And that would be so much better than this. Just let me live my life. I don't need Skyler to invite us to some 'fabulous' party."

"But maybe some of us do want that, Anya," Emily said. "God, I've never been to a nice party, and I don't know if I ever will. What if Hailey's right? What if Skyler's for real, and she's really okay with us coming?"

"Well, I didn't exactly say I was sure—" I started.

"Well, Chris sure knows her well," Anya said. "What did he say?"

I'd been keeping my burgeoning thing with Chris pretty quiet, so maybe this was Anya's way of putting me on the spot. Kinda uncool, but anyway . . .

"He doesn't trust her," I said. "But she isn't really talking to him. I think it's because she's seen me and him hanging out. He isn't even invited to the party."

"But if she's cool with us," Anya said, "wouldn't she be cool with Chris too?"

I sighed. She *did* have a good point. "How the hell should I know? She's a nutjob."

"Exactly," Anya said. "And you know what Andy said . . ."

"What did Andy say?" Emily asked.

"He said he didn't know of anything specific, but that Jericha, Daniella and the rest have been really quiet lately," Anya said.

"So maybe they're just chastened," I said. "We got 'em good, and now they're laying low."

Anya rolled her eyes. "I know Skyler," she said. "I know her way better than you do. And I trusted her. I trusted her with the secret that was most dear to me in the world. And she turned around and used it to disembowel me."

There was a long pause and then Emily said, "And that's awful. But that's also why you'd be the last to notice if she's changed."

"Fine," Anya said. "If you guys want to give these bitches the benefit of the doubt . . . let's just see what happens. I'll go. I'm Team Invisible, for better or worse. But I have a pretty strong feeling that it's gonna be 'for worse.'"

Grace had been quiet for most of the discussion, but she finally piped up: "*I'm going.* I want us all to go. But dammit, I'm *going.*"

We were all too stunned to speak.

"If she really hated us, would she invite us to her house?" she asked. "I wouldn't want people I hated at my party."

"Well, if it were a trap," I said. "Maybe."

"I've known Skyler since second grade," Grace went on. "I've never *once* been invited to her house. I've heard about her parties for ten years. When we were in fourth grade and I didn't know better, I actually asked her why I wasn't invited to her pool party, because I thought it must have been a mistake."

"Oh boy," Anya said, seeing this one coming.

"And?" I asked.

Grace put her hands on her hips. "Skyler said I was 'so fat I would *drain her pool* if I jumped in.'"

"God!" I exclaimed. "She was even a monster back *then*?"

"Well, that was when my thick phase began," Grace said. "And I guess at this point we can't really call it a 'phase.' But who would seriously care about something like that in *grade school*?"

"Skyler!" several voices rang out, a chorus of Invisibles.

"Seriously, Grace," Anya said, "she's been such a dick to you for ten years, calling you fat in *fourth grade*, so why *would* you be pumped to go?"

"I mean . . . it's *still* a Skyler Brandt party, right? You must have gone to her parties when you two hung out, right?"

Anya shrugged. "Yeah."

"And they were amazing, right?"

Anya considered it for a second. "I guess. I mean, yeah. Definitely. At the time, they seemed like the sweetest shit ever. All the coolest kids, that gorgeous house, and damn, I don't know where she gets the budget for those things, but every event, every occasion, it's pretty wild. Actually, I guess I *do* know where she gets the budget."

"Her parties have names!" Emily said. "Like her C-and-C party, which she threw at the end of last year."

"C-and-C?" I asked. "Like the clothing brand?"

"No." Anya laughed. "It stood for Cocaine and Champagne."

"Jesus," I said. "Welcome to Los Angeles!"

"This is my point!" Grace said. "So to actually go to one would be epic. I've *dreamed* about going to her parties. Now we're actually invited. We at least need to give it a shot, give her the benefit of the doubt."

Emily chimed in: "Yeah, her parties are legendary! Like every room is a hookup room, right, Anya?"

"Well," Anya said, "that might be a bit of an exaggeration, but . . . it's not too far off."

"So," I interrupted, "basically she calls it a 'party,' but really it's a free sex motel? Doesn't she have *parents*?"

"That never came up between you two?" Anya asked me.

"We didn't hang out that long," I said. "And basically every conversation was about what to wear, what not to wear and what to never ever wear under penalty of torture, execution or having to shop at Walmart. Which is why we didn't hang out that long."

"Her dad's out of the picture," Anya said, "and her mom isn't around a whole lot, but she makes sure Skyler is well funded at all times. Your basic super-enabler. Plus she's got some *serious* issues."

"Like what?" I asked. "You can't say that and just leave us hanging!"

"Her mom is . . . kind of a mess," Anya said. "She slept with the PE teacher and everybody knows it. Then there was that one night when she chaperoned the freshman dance and got smashed on bourbon in Mr. Mitchell's car and came back in screaming 'I'm still hotter than all of you bitches.' She hasn't been asked to chaperone since."

This was new information. And in a way it made me feel sorry for Skyler. I mean—that is embarrassing. And here she was extending the olive branch.

"Look, guys," Kura said. "Sure, Skyler's been überbitch to all of us. But she came to Hailey and she sounded sincere, right? So we can do the cynical thing and keep this war up forever and think the worst of everyone and miss out on a kick-ass party. Or we can show up and see what happens. That's what Noel would do, right, Hailey? Even if she thought it might be a trap, she'd show up and adapt, right?"

She had me there. Which is probably why I said, "You have me there."

"Fine, then, it's settled," Kura said. "Let's hope it's not a trap."

You'd think that meant it was actually settled, but not so much. We kept debating it for a couple of hours. It wasn't until the staff at Chipotle was passive-aggressively sweeping around us and removing the hot sauce bottles from our tables that we realized they were closing soon and we'd overstayed our welcome. Then again, they also could have been annoyed by Kura's frequent trips to the bathroom. (Something was up there, and I made a mental note to look into it.)

Ultimately, hope triumphed over cynicism and we decided to go. Best-case scenario? We'd have new friends, we'd no longer live in fear at school and everything would turn out wonderful . . . just like the last five minutes of your favorite hour-long TV show. Worst-case scenario? The bitch squad would've come up with new and improved ways to humiliate us and we'd go home covered in pigs' blood.

Personally, I found myself torn, but I was leaning toward the former. Maybe it was just my improved confidence since following the lessons in Noel's *How to Be a Hater* journal, but I really did consider myself a force to be reckoned with. Skyler really did have to believe she shouldn't mess with me, right? She didn't build her little cult of personality without being savvy about threats to her position. She knew diplomacy was the smartest play, so she went with that. And we could take pride in the fact that we forced her hand. We had the *cojones* to go toe-to-toe with her, and she blinked. That's why we deserved to break bread with the glitz-and-glamour crew.

The next few days were fairly uneventful. Skyler and her minions had done nothing at school to make us think she wasn't being genuine and didn't really want the "seize fire." The only thing that made my heart skip a beat was when I got called into Mr. Muñez's office. I thought I was going to get in trouble for something I hadn't done, which I had to admit would be sorta karmic, given my luck at avoiding trouble for stuff I had done. Not that I was in any hurry to get my yin and yang balanced out. I had no idea what it could be . . . but I wouldn't be shocked in the slightest to find the Hater Tots secretly orchestrated something. And I was sure it would be vicious. And cruel. And embarrassing.

Give 'em credit: For a crew of teenage twits, they sure had shown off a green thumb for evil.

So I braced myself for the worst. Turned out it was nothing of the sort. Not even *close*.

Mr. Muñez's smile betrayed my good fortune before he said a word.

"I called you in to tell you about a possible opportunity I'd like to recommend for you . . . if you're interested."

"Sure," I replied. "What is it?"

"It's a summer internship. Previously, it's only been offered to college students, but they're opening up a special workshop this year to mentor exemplary high school artists."

"Wait—what?"

"Here's the thing, Hailey." He gestured broadly with his hands as he spoke. I got the feeling he must accidentally whack passersby in the face now and then, and the thought forced me to stifle a giggle. "I've enjoyed your last few comics, and your talent is certainly undeniable."

"Thank you," I said, still thrown a bit. If I were being honest, and not humble at all, *Abby Invisible* really had improved since its first incarnation. And it was still getting a great response from other students.

"I'm sure you're familiar with CalArts?" he said.

Of course I was familiar. CalArts was the very first arts college, i.e., the first collegiate institution in the United States, to grant degrees in both visual and performing arts. Okay, so maybe that doesn't lift your skirt. Try this: It was founded by *Walt Freakin' Disney.*

"Yes," I said, trying to stay cool. "I'm absolutely . . . familiar."

"Great," he said. "How would you feel about a CalArts internship this summer? I can't guarantee your placement, but I can certainly recommend you. I believe in fostering talent when I see it, and provided you do a good job in school the rest of this year, I think this would be a wonderful opportunity."

"It would be incredible," I said, thinking, *This is so far* beyond *incredible.*

"I thought you might think so," he said. "It's rare to see such distinct talent so early in a student's academic career, and when I do spot it . . . I try to nurture it."

I was floored. "I don't know what to say."

"You don't have to say anything. Just study hard, do all your homework, be a good person and we'll take it from there."

I practically floated out of his office. What an amazing feeling. I'd directed my artistic skills and social commentary into a project that actually meant something to me, people liked it, and bonus: I was getting offered opportunities I couldn't have even dreamed up!

By the day of that party, I'd managed to convince myself almost completely that Skyler's invite was genuine—apparently "seize fire" really was in full effect. If they were going to make a move, they'd have made it by now, right? It seemed like everything really was looking up.

Meanwhile, I had to field about fifteen calls from the girls, all trying to decide what they were going to wear that night. Dahlia had gotten highlights and needed to be reminded of what Noel had said about hair:

Don't change your hairstyle/color more than once every three months, so that you don't look schizo or like early-Madonna.
Exception: If you get a really bad color job, change it ASAP, _never_ stick with something that looks bad.

Emily was the most concerned, yet considering her extracurricular thieftivities, she had the least to worry about. She had the best clothes out of any of us—or at least the most current.

"I can't decide between jeans and a cute top or a dress," Emily said over the phone line. "I've literally tried on both outfits like twenty times."

"I'm sure you look great in both," I said.

"Well . . . what do you think Andy would like better?"

I couldn't help but smile. I thought I'd noticed some flirting going on between those two but this made it official. *She liked him.* "I think Andy will like you in whatever you wear," I said, "but wear a dress—why not show some leg?"

Emily giggled as my caller ID flashed: *Anya.*

"Can you hold on a second, Em?"

"Totes!"

I clicked over to Anya. "Hey."

"Do you remember what Carrie wore to the prom?" she asked.

"Carrie Bradshaw?"

"No, not fucking Carrie Bradshaw. Carrie—"

"Yeah, Carrie. *Carrie* Carrie. I get the reference. And also— *really?*"

"I have a dress that looks similar, but my concern is the shoes. Can I wear combat boots?"

"I think you should," I said. "Why not put your own spin on it?"

"I'm thinking about wearing a tiara," she said. "Do you have a tiara?"

"Of course I don't have a tiara," I said. "Shit, I forgot I have Emily on the other line."

"Good! Ask her if she can steal me a tiara!" Anya said.

"Yeah, I'll get right on that," I said.

When I clicked back over, Emily had decided on a Jill Stuart dress, and thankfully my work was done.

After one last look in the mirror (seriously, I'd been so involved with everyone else's wardrobe choices I'd barely had time to focus on my *own* clothes), I finalized my outfit: a short-sleeved Marc Jacobs cream-based top patterned with multicolored finches (cute!), rust-colored Rag & Bone jeans, a vintage denim cutoff vest and booties (all courtesy of Noel). I fussed with my hair for just another minute and then made my way downstairs to say good night to Mom. She was at the dinner table and my dad was seated next to her. I hadn't even heard him come in.

"Hey, little lady," he said, standing and giving me a hug.

"Hey, mister," I said. "Anyone ever tell you that you look just like my dad? I think so, at least. Haven't seen him in a while. I think we have some black-and-white photographs somewhere. . . ."

Dad grunted. "This new job's a lot of work, honey. Have to make a good impression in your first year."

Mom laughed. "As many hours as you're putting in, you should be the CEO by now."

I piled on: "Yeah, Dad, where's the corporate mansion?"

"You might never see it," he said. "It's reserved for appreciative daughters who respect their elders."

"Then she'll *definitely* never see it," Mom said with a smile.

"Yeah, yeah," I said.

"I thought maybe we could hang out tonight," he said, "but you're obviously dressed for—" He turned to Mom. "A date?"

"A *party*," Mom said. "I didn't have a chance to tell you."

"Uh-oh," Dad said. "Do we know these people?"

"It's just some friends from school, Dad. It's fine."

"Uh-huh," he said. "So you'll be in by ten?"

I looked at Mom. She turned to my dad and said: "We agreed on eleven. No later."

"What, eleven?" he said, sounding genuinely shocked. "At your age? That's—"

"—earlier than you get in some nights," I said before I could stop myself. *Well, it was true.*

He sighed. "Alright. But not a second later. Promise?"

I gave him a hug and headed for the door. "Promise!"

. . .

Skyler's house was hidden high in the hills, off windy roads and multiple turns, tucked away behind a gate. Which is to say, it's not exactly a place you could stumble across. Hell, delivering a pizza would probably take an hour, guarantee be damned.

Once you gained entry, let's just say you'd never look at your own home the same way again. "Humble abode" took on a whole new meaning.

Her house? Gorgeous. Crazy insane gorgeous, like you had unlimited funds in one of those virtual reality games and just decided to design your own Sims Mansion that was intended purely for Sims Parties and Sims Bridal Receptions and Sims Royal Weddings and basically the most ostentatious shit you can Sims-imagine. It was your typical "house in the hills," like everything you've seen on TV. Everything you'd expect from the over-privileged.

Gate to keep out the riffraff? Check. Circular driveway with ridiculously overpriced cars scattered about? Check. Perfectly manicured hedges with flawless blooming flowers? Check.

You might say we were a hair intimidated as we neared the house.

Grace already had her license, so Anya, Grace and I took one car. (Yes, Anya wore the *Carrie* dress and her combat boots.) The second we made that last turn and pulled up to Skyler's house, we immediately saw Cassidy and Jericha out front, leaning against an Audi. Dahlia and Emily pulled up right behind us; Kura was nowhere to be found.

Xandra too, but she had texted:

No way in hell I wanna b face-to-face with Skyler, in her home. Esp. so soon after the videotape incident. Have fun n get me TONS of gossip!

"Hi, girls," Jericha said.

"Hey," we all said back.

"So, we're all so glad you could come tonight," Jericha said. "Cassidy, do you have their party favors?"

"Yep," Cassidy said, seemingly buzzed and distracted by trying to screw off the top of her pop-top beer (a Corona). "Party favors. They get special party favors."

She reached into the trunk of the Audi and pulled out a box, then opened the flaps, saying, "Here you go, girls."

We stepped forward, and even as we did, I had this terrible feeling. I tried to bite it down—I told myself it was just my old insecurities rising to the surface. It's not fish guts, I told myself. It doesn't *look* like fish guts. It doesn't *smell* like fish guts. It's just . . .

Clothes?

The box contained red vests and little red bow ties.

"Now, don't worry," Jericha said. "We made sure these were all professionally dry-cleaned first. We need you to look professional when you valet park all our friends' cars."

It's one thing to feel horrible for a single mistake. Like, let's say you borrowed your buddy's bicycle, and you promised you were only going to ride it up the street to the supermarket, but instead you took it mountain biking. And then you smashed it into a tree and it's totally wrecked forever. You feel bad about what happened, but you feel worse because you promised one thing, and because you lied, you've ruined something important to your friend.

I felt horrible for a variety of mistakes. Like trusting Skyler. Like convincing my friends it was worth showing up to this party. Like letting them get their hopes up—for some of them, the first time they'd trusted in anything for a long time—just to have the horrible bitches rip their hearts out—right now, on their turf—even as my friends are wearing their carefully selected outfits, the ones they looked forward to showing off in front of the other party guests.

And now these bitches wanted us to tear off our awesome outfits and wear valet costumes.

And park their fucking cars.

"It's not that complicated," Jericha said. "There's a nice, fully landscaped plot right down the street that Skyler's family owns. You saw it when you came up, where the blue flashing barricades are? It's only a half mile down, maybe a hair more. Just park the cars there, then jog back up to park the next car. And then hang out to retrieve the cars tonight. You might even get *tips!*"

My heart sank and my stomach dropped. Everything inside me ached for my friends. And that was all multiplied when we heard the laughter. It came from the few kids who'd arrived early and witnessed the blessed moment. They all thought it was hilarious. Emily stormed over to her car and the laughter only got louder. It seemed that Skyler had struck a mighty blow.

I saw tears start to well up in Grace's eyes. Under her breath she said, "I want to drain her pool. I want to jump in and cannonball and drain her fucking pool."

I couldn't let this happen.

I wouldn't let this happen.

They want us to wear this stupid shit?

Fine. We'll wear your stupid shit.

I was the first to grab a vest and bow tie. I slipped into the vest as if this were totally normal and turned to Anya as I tried to affix my bow tie: "Is this crooked? I don't want it to be crooked."

Anya smiled and adjusted my tie, then she grabbed a vest and put it on. One by one, all of the Invisibles put on the vests and bow ties—even Emily walked back from her car to join in, not knowing what the hell we were thinking, but still acting a team player.

Jericha finally walked up to me, amazed that we were actually going to *do* it. "God, what is wrong with you? Don't you know we were just—"

"Wanting us to park cars?" I replied. "Got it. On it. No prob."

"No, but, see, it was—"

"Right, like an initiation," I replied. "Or a hazing. We get it. We have to do this so we can gain favor. That's cool."

"No," replied Cassidy, who still had no clue how to open her beer, despite seeming far from sober. "See, it's—you aren't—it's, like, wait, see, it's, like—it's, it's."

"We're good," Anya said. "We're going to park cars." By now, almost everyone was dressed in their valet outfits.

"Actually, I don't think—hang on, let me call Skyler," Jericha said.

"No need!" I said. "You have tickets, right?" I asked. "Because otherwise, how will we keep track of keys and cars?"

Cassidy looked at Jericha: *Do we have tickets?* Cassidy looked in her box and sure enough, she did.

Just then someone pulled up: Brian Caldwell, captain of the football team. He slowed to a stop when he saw us.

"I'll take it from here," I said, opening Brian's door for him. I helped him out of the car and handed him a ticket.

I drove Brian's car slightly down the hill, going until I was just out of sight, parking it in front of a perfectly lovely fire hydrant.

Once I returned and put his keys in a safe place, Jericha and Cassidy had vanished. I presumed Jericha was satisfied that their prank had turned into a legitimate valet-parking service for the party, and was looking forward to reporting this to Skyler. Would Skyler shut it all down? Would she just let us go ahead and valet? Either way, I presumed that Cassidy would be vomiting all over herself within minutes, given that she looked pretty wrecked.

Skyler never emerged, so that's how we spent the party.

Parking cars.

Wherever the fuck we felt like parking them.

It wasn't until the party was in its waning hours that Skyler would realize her "valet parking crew" was nowhere to be found. We'd left all the keys for them, but the cars?

That was a different story. We all took turns parking the cars ALL. OVER. TOWN.

Anywhere and everywhere.

Cars in front of hydrants? Hell yeah.

Cars parked right in front of the ordering sign in the KFC drive-through window? You'd better believe it.

Cars parked in sandboxes in children's playgrounds? That might well have occurred.

One on the fifth floor of a mall parking garage? Yep. One at Dodgers Stadium? You know it.

Yes, this wasn't the smartest thing, considering most of us didn't even have our licenses. Still, yes, there was at least one car parked in a mud pit by a lake, where it would require a tow truck to pull the car free. (But in our defense, that dick was using a disability tag, probably belonging to a relative, and he's a perfectly healthy letterman in three sports. So eat it, Eddie Bauer.)

Andy was inside at the party. He never saw us (or Emily in her dress) because he'd arrived early before it all went down, but he'd heard rumblings about the valet gag they'd pulled on us, and he texted me to see if it was actually true. I called him back to confirm and to let him know what happened. He was steaming mad, but I talked him into playing it cool.

"Stay there, have fun, be our ears," I told him over the phone during one car drop-off. "See what you can do to keep Skyler inside or Jericha or whoever. The longer it takes them to figure out what we're doing, the better."

"Okay," Andy said. "Be careful."

"I will, thank—"

Suddenly, I heard another voice over the phone, somewhere in the background:

"Are you *kidding* me? Oh my GOD, it BURNS!"

It was a girl's voice. Familiar, but I couldn't quite place it.

"What's going on?" I asked.

"No clue," Andy said.

The voice again: "*Ow! God!* What the hell!"

"Andy," I said, "is someone on fire over there?"

"No, I don't know—some of the girls are in a bathroom, the door's closed, but they're still—"

"Really fucking loud?"

He chuckled. "Yeah."

"Okay," I said. "I'm—"

The voice again: "I told you we should have used vanilla! Not *citrus!*"

This night just keeps getting more interesting. I signed off with Andy and got back to "work."

At all times, at least two of us were using our own cars to pick up the girls depositing the cars. Now, we're not total assholes—and we didn't want anyone calling the LAPD and accusing us of stealing cars per se—so we made a point of noting everywhere we'd parked cars on handwritten lists, with brief descriptions of the cars and where they were left. We left behind our lists and all the keys. If the partygoers had to call cabs or catch rides to get to their cars, so be it.

After a couple of hours, we headed out for good, and we kept the damn vests and ties. We figured we'd worked hard for them.

Later, we found out that not everything had worked out like we expected—it actually turned out *better.*

Apparently, shortly after we left, Skyler popped out to check on how we were doing. She found the keys and the notes and maps. To try to save face and keep the partygoers clueless about the situation, Skyler, Daniella and Jericha (Cassidy was having her own drama) each had to frantically drive all over town picking up cars. Because they had to drive the cars back, they had to take *taxis* to each car, costing them a minor fortune. They also missed the rest of their own party.

Cassidy, we learned, had an even *worse* night. She'd decided to try out the latest *supposed* craze of using vodka-soaked tampons to get drunk. Yeah, that's quite possibly the most idiotic thing I have ever heard of. They say it gets into your bloodstream quicker than drinking vodka and saves you the stomach upset (and calories), but from what I overheard, Cassidy did not have a pleasant experience. And it didn't help that Skyler, Daniella and Jericha had to abandon Cassidy and her corrosive cooch in her moment of panic to solve the car situation.

Even though they found many of the cars in time, some hadn't been retrieved when people needed their cars (because of curfews or whatever). The whole thing was a mess, and everybody blamed Skyler because the "valet joke" was her mean-spirited idea to begin with.

The party was a bust. Skyler's crew was a laughingstock. That went double for Cassidy, who got out of car-retrieval duty but spent the rest of the night with a carton of Ben & Jerry's between her legs.

And now, more than ever, Skyler was *pissed.*

Next time you point a finger...
I'll point you to the mirror.

—PARAMORE

"Playing God"

CHAPTER 13

Life doesn't do much to prepare you for finding out someone isn't who you think they are—more specifically, seeing what someone you like and respect has dwelling in the inner sanctum of his iPod.

Like, how do you deal with knowing the guy you have a massive crush on likes really shitty music?

One option: Pretend it never happened. Pretend you never even touched that iPod and you definitely weren't scrolling through it when you happened to find the offending Miley Cyrus song (which is to say, *any* Miley Cyrus song).

Another option? Torment your boy-crush until you feel you have shamed him enough to satisfy your inner Simon Cowell. (However, that way might make him hate you, so if you have hopes of any kind of boyfriend/girlfriend action happening, you might want to skip this option.)

Last but not least, you could very calmly let this person know that you have this tidbit of information in your back pocket and that you can and might use it against him should he ever piss you off. This one runs close to Option B in that it's mildly threatening, so you have to weigh your tone and keep it playful. It's still a little bit risky.

I chose Option A when I found a Miley tune on Chris's iPod. I decided that he had to have a very good reason for this terrible offense, that he was innocent until proven guilty of ever listening to or (about a million times worse) actually enjoying it. I would just pretend I never saw it. (Kind of like how girls always have to pretend we never see guys adjusting their balls, which they seem to do every 8.5 minutes. What's going on in there, anyway? It's not like one's threatening to bounce out of their pants or anything. Is it?)

We were having a study session. It was just Chris and me in the quad, chilling at one of the cement tables, umbrella overhead. There was a test coming up on Friday and it was going to count for a third of our grade that semester. I was trying to focus on the books, but Chris was so cute, it was making things difficult. He was wearing the jeans I loved on him, my absolute favorites, the ones that had a tiny hole just starting on his right knee, and I wondered whether I could track the progress of this developing flirtation by how big the hole grew.

Would I be around long enough for his whole knee to be exposed? Maybe eventually his calf? (I hoped so: He had *really* nice calves. Although that suddenly made me think of little baby cows. They're so cute. But then I thought of hamburgers and steak and chili, and that made me a little sad. *Comfort me, Chris Roberts. Save me from the sadness of sloppy joes.*)

He had the nicest eyes too, brilliantly blue, brought out by an orange T-shirt with a logo on it that I couldn't quite make out, with a red, yellow and orange flannel shirt over it. Noel would definitely approve.

"What are the odds we'll ever need to use this information as adults?" he asked me, noticing I was zoning out, thinking of our future life together.

"I'd say slim to it-will-never-come-up-again," I replied. "Slightly better than the odds of glee club making regionals next year. Or ever."

"Exactly," he said, and shook his head. Oh, that smile. *He has perfect teeth. I love those teeth. Our kids would never need braces.*

"I think school is a conspiracy to just keep us out of our parents' hair so they can work and do stuff until we're old enough to go work and do stuff," I said. "We're all just worker bees being groomed to replace the current worker bees."

"Well, that's depressing," he said.

"Yeah," I agreed. "But you can always choose a fun profession. Like Jay-Z grew up to replace Run-D.M.C., right?"

"I can see my mansion now . . . ," he said.

"How many cars will you have?" I asked.

"Probably thirteen," he said. "It's my lucky number."

"And how many girlfriends?" I boldly asked. *Please say just one. Please say me. I would make a good baby mama. Together we could bask in your rap star glory.*

"Just one," he said, as if he could read my thoughts. *Yes!*

I was imagining an MTV *Cribs*–style home for us and getting lost in his eyes, the same blue as our swimming pool, which would be shaped like a dollar sign, of course, when I heard her.

"Is that a hole in your nose?"

I looked up to see Skyler standing before me, looking none too pleased to see me sitting with Chris. But then, I'm sure these days I could save Skyler's entire family from a horde of zombies and she'd still want my head on a stake. A bamboo stake from Gucci, of course. Do they sell stakes?

"Guilty as charged," I said, loud and proud, though it was totally embarrassing. I hated the hole in my nose. I wished I'd never had it pierced. Among other things, when you no longer have a stud in there, it's basically indistinguishable from a wee acne scar.

"So, *what*, did you like, used to be a goth or something?" she prodded.

"It was a phase," I said.

"I never noticed," Chris said, now inspecting my nose, and I'm thinking, *Stop looking at my nose, Hannah Montana lover!*

"Aww, it's cute. Looks like a freckle."

Whew.

That's much better than a wee acne scar. Isn't he sweet? (Answer: Yes, he is.)

"Cute?" Skyler said. "About as cute as the mustache she's sporting. Ever hear of laser hair removal? Or at the very least waxing? Should we take up a collection for you?" Skyler reached into her pocket and pulled out a five-dollar bill. "Here's five bucks," she said, placing it on my notebook. "Get a Bic razor in the meantime."

God, what an asshole! I *didn't* have a mustache, but I didn't expect little things like reality to divert Skyler from her mission to destroy me at all costs. On top of everything else, I was sitting with her ex-boyfriend. He thought my nose-hole was "cute," so she decided to go for my throat—well, actually, my upper lip.

But Skyler had a way of making "Old Hailey" emerge from deep inside me. I knew she was just being a bitch because—well, just because she's a gigantic freaking bitch.

It reminded me of that old fable about the scorpion stinging the frog that had agreed to carry it across a river. Just before they both drown, the frog asks why the scorpion did it. The scorpion replies: *It's my nature.*

Skyler the Scorpion, I thought. Now, that might make a good target for *Abby Invisible.*

Still, my insecurities were welling up. I wanted to disappear. But first, I wanted to get my hands on a mirror. *Did I suddenly start growing a mustache between this morning and now? Did I have a huge mustache? Did I look like Dr. Phil?*

Of course, all of that occurred in my head in all of two seconds. It was washed away the moment Chris said,

"Shut up, Skyler."

Thank God, I thought, both to have Chris defending my hopefully-still-mythical mustache and saving me from even having to think of a comeback. (I'd probably have one by eighth period, but that might be a little late to the game.)

"Wow," Skyler said, her eyes boring into Chris. "How the mighty have fallen."

Then something happened. It seemed like it was happening in slow motion, but I'll just assume it happened in real time because I'm not in a movie or on a TV show—even though I *do* often feel like there is a soundtrack to my life, and in that soundtrack, the audio at this particular moment was my exaggerated heartbeat.

Chris reached up to my face—*oh my God oh my God oh my God*—and picked at something on my upper lip. He held it out for display.

"Oh, *this*," he said. "You win, Sky. I can't believe I didn't notice it sooner."

It was a tiny wisp of brush hair, nothing more.

"Happens to my sisters all the time. It's from a makeup brush—though I can't say if it's for eye shadow or blush."

My hero. Again.

"Hailey," Chris said to me.

I lifted my head and my eyes met his. I was swallowed up in that sea of blue.

He continued: "I don't know why you thought it was okay to

actually go out in public at only ninety-nine-point-nine percent gorgeous."

At this point I'm probably beet red. And that's okay.

"It's all good, though," he said. "Now you're back to your usual hundred percent."

Now Skyler was turning red. And as much as I *loved* everything Chris just said, I was letting this damsel-in-distress act become a bad habit.

I turned to face my tormentor.

"You know, Skyler," I said. "If you spent a third of the time studying that you do being a total bitch, maybe you could end up being more than the dumb stereotype that you are."

"I'm *not* dumb," Skyler said. And I knew that was true—though she could definitely brush up on her studies—but that wasn't the point. I needed to hit her where it hurt. I couldn't call her ugly; that would obviously be a lie.

"No?" I asked. "You just handed me five dollars—and thanks, by the way, I'll keep it—in an effort to humiliate me when you didn't even have your facts straight. So now you not only look stupid . . . you're out five dollars."

"Like I *care* about five dollars?" she said desperately.

"You don't? I just thought it might come in handy, considering all those cab rides you had to shell out for, retrieving your party guests' cars the other night."

The look on Chris's face—hands over his mouth, trying hard not to laugh out loud—made me (the now-100-percent-gorgeous me, according to Chris, that is) feel all the more empowered. So I continued, "I guess when you don't value people's feelings, money doesn't matter either."

"Whatever, Hailey," Skyler said in a moving-on-now tone.

"Oh, good. So we're done here?"

"We were done a long time ago," Skyler said, looking at me, and then Chris. Her meaning was clear.

I watched her walk away and wondered how long this was going to go on. We were only sophomores. Were we going to just attack each other for the next two and a half years? Would it ever get old? I was certainly over it, but would she ever stop?

"That was awkward," I said.

"She's gotten worse," he said.

We watched as she disappeared into Chem Hall. I so badly wished I knew exactly what he was thinking. Was he missing her at all? What did they actually share? What were they like as a couple?

Not having gone to West Hollywood for my freshman year, I missed out on so much. *This was information I needed!*

Of course, I was still floating a bit from the 100-percent-gorgeous bit—not even Skyler could completely wreck that. But my curiosity was killing me, and Chris had opened the door with the "she's gotten worse" comment, so I figured I'd see if he cared to expand on that thought.

"What do you mean?" I asked.

"Just . . . she didn't used to be such a total bitch," he said. "I mean, yeah, she wasn't the *nicest* girl to people who weren't her friends, but it got worse and worse and that was part of why we broke up. She started to become . . . like . . . a monster."

"But she's kind of . . ." I stopped to gather my thoughts, but the truth was, I couldn't even conceive of her being any other way.

So I said as much.

"I mean . . . she's *Skyler*. I can't imagine she was ever that much different from who she is now."

He shrugged and looked down at his book, but he sure didn't

208

look like he was reading anything. I decided to press my luck a little.

"What *did* happen with you guys?" I asked.

"Like, why'd we break up?"

"Well, yeah, I guess." I said. "If it's too personal, you don't have to tell me."

"No, it's fine," he said, and kind of scrunched up his face as he gathered his thoughts. "She was pretty, you know? Obviously. So, at first I was attracted to that . . ."

"She *is* pretty," I agreed, while thinking *only on the outside*. I actually felt myself biting my tongue.

"And we had the same friends, so hanging out was always convenient. And I guess there was a part of me that felt cool because I was dating her."

I let out a chuckle and immediately wished I hadn't. Chris looked up and tilted his head. "What?"

"No, I get it," I said. "She's the most popular girl, so it would be cool to date her."

"But it wasn't," he said. "I mean, at first it was because she wasn't always so bad. Sure she was a little snobby, but it wasn't until things got weird at home for her that she started to get really nasty. I'm still not even sure what the deal was—she never told me. But that's when things got bad."

About 75,000 questions filled my brain, but I resisted the urge to interrupt him.

"And it wasn't that she was mean to me," he continued. "She was fine with me. It was when I saw how she treated other people that I got uncomfortable."

"Because you're a good person," I interjected.

"I guess." He shrugged.

I was dying to know more, but I tried to play it cool. We were still getting to know each other. Better not put him on the spot, not after he rescued me from mustache-hole-in-the-face hell. I jumped straight to:

"So what was the final straw?"

"She was all excited about Spirit Week," he said, and of course I immediately sat up extra straight. "She was planning a prank, and it was so brutal . . . I just was like—whoa . . . *not* cool."

What was the prank? What was the prank? What was the prank?

"Did you tell her that?" I asked.

"Yeah," he said. "I told her it was totally out of bounds. But she didn't care. She thought it was funny."

"What was it?"

Chris sighed. "She was planning to hold her very own Westminster Dog Show."

"Huh?"

He looked me in the eye. "She was going to Photoshop pictures of the unpopular girls' heads on different breeds of dogs, poking fun at them based on weight—and other potentially humiliating characteristics—and then post them all over school."

Wow.

"That's pretty awful," I said. "Like . . . for Spirit Week *this* year?"

"Yeah," Chris said. "That was the other thing. It was so long ago, and she was already planning how to hurt people that far in *advance*. Like, forget doing well in school or looking at colleges and starting to think about your future—she was all about embarrassing people."

"That's . . . I mean, that's seriously messed up."

"Totally. That's when I finally saw Skyler for who she had become: someone with this deep-seated need to make other people feel bad. Who cares how pretty she is on the outside if that's who she is on the inside?"

"No argument here," I said.

Then he looked at me with a look I wasn't used to. He almost looked a little embarrassed. "Especially when there are people like you, who are pretty on the outside *and* the inside," he said.

Oh my God.

I didn't think things could get better after 100 percent gorgeous, but I was thrilled to be proved wrong. I didn't know how to respond to that. Was I supposed to respond? What's the protocol when the Cutest Boy Ever has just paid you yet another major compliment?

He saved me the trouble of figuring it out.

Chris took my hands.

"Hailey . . . this has been fun, the texting, the calls and all—"

Oh my God, no! That sounds like he's breaking up with me. Is he breaking up with me? He's breaking up with me! We're not even going out and he's breaking up with me!!!

"Chris," I sputtered. "Chris—wait, I, um—"

Oh no oh no oh no . . . why did he change his mind? Now we'll never go out and I'll never get to see that hole in his pants get bigger and I'll only get to take secret peeks at his calves at PE and baby cows and—

"What?" I asked.

He looked puzzled. "Didn't you just hear me?"

Not if you're going to just dump me again.

"Um . . . sorry," I said. "What was the last part?"

Chris smiled. "I said, it's been fun texting and calling and all, so let's go do something, like, this weekend? Is that cool?"

Oh, thank God. Thank you, God, thank you, baby cows, thank you, mythical mustache.

"Yes," I said a little too quickly.

"Cool," he said. "I know Andy was thinking about asking Emily to hang out, so maybe we can all hang out together?"

Really? I thought. *Emily and Andy? That's cool!* But there were far more pressing matters at hand.

"Sounds good to me," I said. And the butterflies in my stomach were going so crazy, I was scared one was going to literally fly out of my mouth. Which would be weird. And then Chris would probably take back his invite, because—butterflies or not—who wants to hang out with a weird girl who has insects flying out of her mouth?

Luckily, nothing warranting a terrible Syfy Channel movie came fluttering out of my mouth, and even more luckily, I was eventually able to get the picture out of my mind of caterpillars slowly metamorphosing in my stomach, and much, much *more* luckily . . .

I had a *real* date with Chris Roberts coming up!

I was so stoked about my date with Chris that it didn't even seem super-weird that Mom had left me a note on the table when I got home:

Book club tonight. Your dad's working late, so heat up the leftovers in the fridge. I'll be back by 9. Love you!
Mom ☺

Had Mom told me she joined a book club? That must have slid right past me. This whole lack of family dinner was a big change—I don't think Dad had been home for dinner in a week, but Mom almost never missed dinner with me. Maybe that's just how it is when you get older. It might have bummed me out a little if my thoughts lately weren't pretty much all *Chris Chris Chris Chris Instagram Chris Facebook Chris Twitter Chris Chris Me & Chris. Chris.*

Mom got in around nine thirty. I'd eaten every last bit of the yummy leftovers—funny how sometimes they're better than a fresh-cooked meal—and was studying when she got back.

She dropped her purse on the coffee table. "Your dad's not home?"

Duh, I thought. *His car's not in the driveway.*

"Nope," I said. "He didn't call you?"

She glanced at her cell phone as she walked into the kitchen. "No. He didn't call here?"

"Nope. That job must be really kicking his—" I stopped myself. "Um, butt."

I expected a laugh, but Mom just said, "Thanks for doing the dishes, honey. You should get ready for bed."

"Uh," I said, "but it's only—"

Mom had already vanished into their bedroom and shut the door. I shrugged it off and tried to study, but my thoughts wandered back to Chris, and then back to the Invisibles.

After a lot of soul-searching, I decided to call a meeting of the Invisibles the next day.

I realized we'd been going about this whole thing wrong. We'd been trying to *not* get noticed. We were trying to make sure we flew under the radar, didn't get made fun of, didn't get publicly humiliated . . . but what good was a life where you strive to *not* be noticed? We deserved to be noticed. And be *liked*. And it was already starting to happen anyway.

And really, wasn't that more in the *How to Be a Hater* spirit in the first place? Noel was never interested in being a wallflower. Her journal was about taking action. Sure, there's something revolutionary about working *against* the system, but isn't it just as radical to find a new way to work *inside* the system?

Each of us had pretty cool qualities that, in my humble opinion, made us way cooler than the "cool kids." So why couldn't we turn the tables?

Forget just not being the biggest losers at Spirit Week . . . we could beat them at their own game.

"So in the movie of our lives, this is the makeover moment?" Anya asked.

"Pretty much," I said.

"Do I get to give thumbs-up or thumbs-down as you all try on new clothes?" she continued. "Because I'll do that, as long as it's set to some really cheesy pop song. But if you think I'm gonna go out and buy a pair of J Brand skinny jeans and whoever makes the Top of the Moment, it's not gonna happen. I like how I dress."

"I'm not saying you have to change how you dress," I reassured her. "I like how you dress too."

"I wouldn't mind a few pointers," Dahlia said.

"I'm in theater," Xandra said. "I'm supposed to dress all artsy. Plus, none of my gays would let me walk around looking like a total loser."

"None of your *gays*?" Anya said. "Okay, *Kathy Griffin*."

"I don't think it really matters how I dress," Grace said in a defeated tone.

"That's not the attitude we want," I said. "Remember one of Noel's cardinal rules: 'Fake it 'til you make it.' We're gonna run with that one."

"Did you ever ask Noel why the diary stopped so abruptly?" Kura asked.

"Yeah," I said with a heavy dose of sarcasm. "I called her and said, 'Hey, Noel, me and a bunch of my friends have been combing through your diary, reading your innermost thoughts—you don't mind, do you? Anyway, we've been using your wisdom as a kind of how-to and, well, it stops abruptly, so we were wondering what happened or if you had any further tips you might want to share with us—'"

"Okay, okay," Kura interrupted. "I see your point."

But she did bring up a valid issue. Noel's diary stopped short. I did wonder what happened. We were sort of left to our own devices a few pages after:

Ugly or bitchy. you can only be one.

Short and sweet, that one. Then there were her movie guidelines:

Do not EVER watch horror films when home alone. However, watch Disney movies in PRIVATE ONLY. Related: Do not watch Michael Bay movies _anywhere_.

The gym etiquette:

Never be the girl wearing a ton of makeup to the gym. you look desperate and ridiculous. Related: Never flirt with guys who wear jewelry at the gym or anywhere. They are desperate and ridiculous.

Timing:

Be confident and funny. But also know when not to be. Timing is everything. cracking jokes at a funeral is not a good look. Neither is dancing like nobody's watching.

And then:

Don't try too hard, no matter the situation. Everything in moderation—including moderation.

That was the last sort-of rule she'd put down, and I did wonder what happened, why she stopped keeping her diary and if there was more to the story. I already felt like I barely knew my sister at all, but after reading her diary it was even *more* clear how close we *weren't*.

The makeover plan wasn't about compromising who we were; it was about embracing it. As usual, we were at odds. Whereas during our discussion pre-Skyler's Partypocalypse, it was me and Anya who were the most anti, and everyone else pro, this time it was Grace and Anya who were against it.

(Sometimes I wondered if Anya just liked to go against the grain no matter what, which could be a little frustrating at times, but, hey, that's also what made Anya Anya.)

In a moment when we'd gotten off topic, I asked Kura what happened the other night, why she wasn't at the party.

"It was really stupid," she said. "I'm sorry I wasn't there."

"Yeah, you missed an interesting night. But . . . what happened?"

"Yeah," Emily said. "We were concerned."

Kura stared straight at the ground, and I knew that look. Like that look your dog gives you when *someone* went to the bathroom on the living room rug, and it's only the two of you there, so you both know *you* didn't do it.

She sighed and looked up, but she still didn't look me in the eye. "I just wasn't feeling too hot."

There used to be a Hailey who would have taken that bullshit for an answer, but that girl was long gone.

"Kura, what's the deal?" I asked. "You can tell us. We're here to help each other."

She sighed again. "You know Adderall?"

"Sure," I said. "You have ADHD?"

She shrugged. "Don't we all?"

"Pretty sure we don't."

"Well . . . ," she said, "I . . . snorted some."

She paused, presumably gauging our reactions. Emily didn't seem to react at all, and I wasn't sure what to think. So Kura continued.

"I know. Look, I had this crazy big test I was studying for Thursday night. I really needed something to get me through. But maybe I did too much . . . I don't know. But I didn't feel great the next day."

Emily stepped forward and put an arm around Kura, to my relief, because I didn't have a clue how to handle this one. "Babe, that's really dangerous," Emily said. "Please don't do that again."

"I won't," Kura said. "I swear. It was a one-time deal. Can we get back to the task at hand?"

I was far from convinced, but this really wasn't the time or place to get into it, so I turned my focus back on our strategy. Most of the Invisibles were all for the new plan. They loved the idea of knocking down the popular kids a peg or two (or twenty). We might not be able to become *the* popular clique, but we could certainly jump a few rungs on the ladder while making *their* clique look ridiculous. It might be wishful thinking, but maybe we could eventually make Skyler & Co. obsolete altogether.

It had been steadily happening anyway. Lines were starting to blur as we were becoming more confident. People had been starting to notice us, and boys were paying attention. Hell, Emily and I were about to have a double date with two of the most popular boys in our grade!

I am human and I need to be loved...

—THE SMITHS

"How Soon Is Now?"

CHAPTER 14

Little did Mr. Hecht know that when we studied the physical properties of leaves and the physiology of the leaf cells, his students would be so inspired they'd take it upon themselves to grow their own science project in the planters along the walkway, just outside the cafeteria.

I mean, a plant is a plant is a plant, right? It takes just as much effort to analyze the structures of a fern as a daisy, a rhododendron as a daylily, a sunflower as . . . well, that interesting little plant in the corner—three plants, actually—each an annual, dioecious, flowering herb with a distinctive formation that clearly identified it as—

"Pot? *Pot!* Your kids are growing *pot?* On *campus?*"

I wasn't actually there for the principal's response when Mr. Hecht laid that revelation on him, but that's a pretty accurate report of his reaction, according to the word on the street.

For us, the "word on the street" came from having an Invisible as a student assistant in the principal's office for three periods a day. Grace actually sat just outside the principal's office, and he closed the door for conversations such as this, but the door was so thin Grace couldn't help but overhear what was going on, even if she wasn't trying to listen in. Which, of course, she was. All the time.

Yes, some remarkably green-thumbed prankster had decided it would be rather awesome to deposit three fine examples of the female *Cannabis sativa* plant in the school planters. Given that a good portion of the marijuana had been harvested by the time the plants were discovered, they clearly had not gone entirely unnoticed by some of our classmates, and almost certainly some of the faculty: Everyone knew Mr. Mitchell—the pervy driver's ed teacher—could sniff out bud from a half mile away. (And the less he had to buy from his students, all the better for him. Heck, the guy had a super-secret invitation-only Super Bowl party every year, and the "bowl" part had nothing to do with football.)

But the gig was up, and the administration called everyone into the auditorium so Principal Dash could reprimand the crap out of us, even though 97 percent of the school had no idea where the pot came from (or where some of it went).

You can figure out where it went from there. Lots of threats about juvie and stuff being on your permanent record. Sure, you didn't want to consider any of that for your potential fate, but the fact remained that someone had the balls to plant three pot plants right there on campus. It was kind of hilarious. Not to mention that every time Principal Dash said "weed" or "bud" or any other slang variation, the entire place would erupt in stifled laughter—and even though we were all trying to stifle it, the combined result came out like a cacophony of snorts.

Note to anyone who plans to eventually be an authority figure supervising teenagers: Don't try to use hip terms or references to "relate" to the kids. You'll just make a fool of yourself. In a case like this, don't say "marijuana," which sounds stupid (like saying "intercourse" instead of "sex"), just say "pot." Simple. Classic. Everyone knows what you mean. And most definitely don't say . . .

"It appears that some not-so-clever students fancy themselves budding Snoop Doggs."

Oh, no, Mr. Dash. You did not actually say that.

Snickers rose up through the auditorium. From somewhere around the middle of the auditorium, a kid mimicked a stoner's voice, shouting: "He said *'budding.'*"

The entire place erupted with laughter.

"This isn't the time or place for *jokes!*" Mr. Dash said a bit too loudly. He paused to compose himself, then said, "When we find out who did this—and we will—those students involved will face very serious punishment, up to and including expulsion and criminal charges. Right now, I'm calling on anyone involved to speak up. The first person to come forward can still avoid the most severe penalties by confessing and telling us who else was involved."

"Don't roll over!" came a voice from a ways behind me.

"But if you do, roll it *tight!*" yelled another student.

Another eruption of laughter. Even at this distance, I could see Mr. Dash steaming. His head looked like a cherry tomato.

I could relate, at least to some degree. Chris was seated one row over, and every time we made eye contact, I could feel the blood rush into my cheeks. We were going on our double date with Emily and Andy that night, and if the day could have gone any slower, it would have been some kind of space-time continuum feat worthy of a scientific journal somewhere. (In this month's issue of *Boring Shit by Boring People*, "Electrons: Hot or Not?") Granted, this impromptu assembly was eating up third period quite impressively, but still, it seemed like this day was taking *forever.*

The only distraction was, well, actually sorta gross. Kura sat two rows down from me, and though I invited her to squeeze in next to me, she mumbled something about not feeling great. I guess not, because she kept wiping her nose with tissues and then quickly stuffing them in her purse. She must have gone through a dozen of them. It was weird because she wasn't sneezing and she didn't sound stuffy or anything. At first I started to wonder whether she had some sort of weird OCD addiction to Kleenex, like those people who wash their hands every fifteen minutes. (I mean if she wasn't a little bit weird, she wouldn't be an Invisible.) But then I remembered her having mentioned the Adderall thing and I made a mental note to start keeping a closer eye on her. That was *not* cool.

The assembly finally ended, albeit somewhat abruptly, after Mr. Dash made the mistake of working in a few announcements about other school-related events, specifically the Environmental Club, aka the "Green Team." You can imagine what happened from there. I guess Mr. Dash felt his precious time was wasted. (Like, *totally wasted.*) And after what seemed like nine years, the school day finally ended. It was time for our sorta-kinda (but hopefully a) date.

I'd carefully planned my wardrobe and changed my mind sixteen times before the day began. I wanted to wear something to school that could also transition to cute-enough date clothes. I had settled on these dark turquoise, almost teal skinny Hollister jeans and a burgundy button-down thermal by Joie. I wore flat brown riding boots (courtesy of Noel) and had my hair in a messy ponytail (purposely styled to look like I just threw it up casually, with wispy tendrils that hung loose to flatter my face on either side). The messy low ponytail was one of Noel's commands. Like it said in her journal,

Tease your boys, not your hair.

I made sure my pony was mid to low on my head because—
while the Southern credo went, "The higher the hair, the closer to
God"—Noel had her own version:

The higher the ponytail, the more varsity
boys she's slept with.

I didn't want to send the wrong message.

I met Emily by her locker and the two of us walked down the
stairs, through the main hall and out to the front lawn, where Chris
and Andy were waiting for us. The second I saw Chris, I got this
warm, fuzzy feeling, and I could tell I was smiling way too big—
totally breaking the cardinal no-gums rule—but I couldn't help it!

He was so perfect. And there he was waiting for me.

How did this happen?

When we finally caught up with them (sixty-three steps, not
that I was counting), something happened that I did not expect:
Chris grabbed my hand. In public. Right there on the front lawn.

I felt a jolt of electricity course through my body as we secured
our now-entangled fingers. We were holding hands like a "real"
couple. *Were* we a couple now? Did this make it official?

I mean, in high school there's no real "dating" like older people
do. There's a lot of hanging out and going out in groups, and if you
hang out with one person all the time, it pretty much makes you a
couple—but I still felt this overwhelming sense of shock that it was
me on the other end of Chris Roberts's hand. It was stunning. I'd
gone from the never-been-kissed-unless-it-was-a-dare girl to the
girl who was holding hands on the front lawn with the most popular boy at West Hollywood. I mean, we still hadn't kissed!

Was I being crazy? Getting ahead of myself? The kiss had to
come today, right? A million questions were running through my

head, but I just had to tell myself, *calm down, head!* And then I started to worry about my hand getting sweaty, and it getting all slimy and gross in Chris's hand. *Calm down, hand!*

"How are you doing, ladies?" Chris said.

"Great!" Emily said. "How are you boys?"

"Rockin'," Andy said. "We're just chilling out here on the *grass*."

"But it's kinda hot out here," Chris said. "We're trying not to get *baked*."

Both boys chuckled. You could tell they'd spent the last several minutes plumbing the depths of every pot joke they could think of. It was juvenile, but adorable. Then again, anything Chris did while holding my hand would be adorable. He could sentence a litter of kittens to death by chainsaw* and it would be the sweetest thing I'd ever seen, just as long as he was holding my hand.

(*Okay, that's not true at all, unless they were, like, really, really evil kittens who beat up and tormented other kittens or declared war for no reason on some other kitten nation. In which case, justice must be meted out. Gawd, even then it still sounds like a bad example. So, no kitten-killing, but yes to Chris holding my hand.)

"Are we ready to go?" I asked.

"Yep," Chris said. "By the way, Hailey, you look really pretty."

"Thank you," I replied.

"And, Emily," Chris said, "you look awesome too."

If I weren't head over heels already, that sealed the deal. Chris not only took the time to compliment me, but he also complimented *Emily*, and I knew how much that sort of thing would mean to her, especially coming from someone as popular (and as *gorgeous*, IMHO!) as Chris.

"Aw, um—thanks!" Emily stammered.

"You both look hot!" Andy blurted, trying to desperately catch up, and we all laughed.

We wound up at the ArcLight Cinemas, the coolest theater in Los Angeles. I hadn't been yet, but I'd heard all about it. They have pre-reserved seating (which we sure never had in Westchester), and you don't have to wait in lines, and it's really clean, and it's not like any other movie theater. They have two different kinds of popcorn, regular and caramel—both fresh-popped, from what I'd heard. Also, movie stars go there, so there's a chance of a random spotting at any given time. (And I mean *real* movie stars, not just reality TV freaks on shows like *Dancing with the Extreme Couponing Bad Girls Club of Toddlers & Tiaras*.) I'd yet to have my brush with fame since moving to Cali. Maybe tonight was the night?

Then again, who could care about seeing some star when they were with Chris Roberts, who, by the way, was *still holding my hand.* It would pale in comparison. (Unless it was Robert Pattinson or Channing Tatum or something, then I might want to sneak a peek, but only if Chris wouldn't see, because I wouldn't want to get into a fight and have him break up with me before I even knew if we were a couple, and certainly not before I had my first on-purpose kiss!)

Emily and Andy were in line for the popcorn. I was peeking over at them, and they seemed to be getting along great. I was happy for them, though it would take nuclear Armageddon to bring me down right now. Chris and I were standing by the theater entrance, discussing the pros and cons of movie theater candy.

"You've never dumped M&M's into your popcorn?" he asked.

"No, because I dip my popcorn in mustard!"

"That's disgusting," he said. "And messy. How do you manage that?"

He did have a point. It was a careful balancing act I'd honed over time. I'd take two lids for soft drink cups (granted, one risked the mustard seeping through the perforated + on top), and layer them. I'd squeeze all the mustard into the lid. Then I'd either hold the lid with one hand and reach, dip and eat with the other, or I'd rest the mustard lids on the armrest, but this risked spillage, and to try to count how many times I'd ruined my clothes this way would be fruitless (though mustardful).

"We can try it your way this time," I said. "But I'll make a believer out of you one of these days."

"Definitely not today."

"Well, obviously. We're getting the caramel corn. Something tells me that mustard and caramel corn would be major yucko."

"*You're* major yucko," he said, though his smile belied the statement completely.

"Oh, really?" I said.

"No," he said. "Not really . . ." and then he pushed me toward the wall.

Oh God oh God oh God oh God

My breath caught. He held my shoulders and guided me to where I found myself pinned to the wall, looking directly into those insanely gorgeous eyes, and then at his lips, his perfect lips.

I couldn't focus on anything else around us—it was like time stopped and everything was silent and we weren't in the middle of a movie theater, but we were in our own flirt-bubble where he had me pinned to the wall and I was waiting for him to lean in just a little bit closer with those lips. His eyes darted from my eyes to my lips, and I bit my bottom lip for a second and then quickly let it go, because I didn't want half of my top teeth getting in the way of the kiss I was certain was coming.

Then he leaned forward and his lips brushed against mine softly, his right hand leaving my shoulder and tracing my arm to where it found my hand. He looked at me once more before he closed his eyes completely and our lips met in what felt like the most epic kiss of all time. I squeezed his hand and he squeezed back and we kissed for I don't know how long because suddenly I heard—

"Any time you guys are done would be cool to go get our seats."

Andy's voice. Chris and I turned to see him standing there, smile plastered on his face. Emily was right beside him with her mouth slightly agape. The sounds of the theater came rushing back to life, and I remembered where we were.

My first real kiss. I'd remember this moment forever—nestled in there, surrounded by the lyrics of about a zillion songs. How is it that I can remember all the words to practically every song ever written, but I'll forget the rule on a simple algebra equation? I'd never understand *that* logic.

As the four of us headed to our seats, Emily and I kept sneaking looks at each other, bulging our eyes and putting on our best "OMG!" faces when we could. And when the lights came down and the previews started to show, Chris winked at me as he dumped the entire pack of Peanut M&M's into our caramel popcorn and shook it around. Then he took a handful and fed it to me—incredible! But even if it tasted like garbage, I probably wouldn't have noticed. I was too giddy from the recent turn of events. I'd never felt happier.

It was a great night throughout. We had fun at the movie, and while Chris and I were (of course!) most focused on each other—and Emily and Andy did the same—the four of us also had fun in general. I was happy for Emily and, well, completely *freaking thrilled* for myself.

After the movie, Andy drove Emily home, and she seemed like she was on cloud nine. He was holding her hand as they left, and I'd hoped those two had worked in a kiss of their own at some point—I'd honestly been too lost in Chris to really notice. At the very least, I felt confident their drive would be eventful. I was happy for Andy too—whatever Emily's occasional issues, she was a sweetheart, and I thought she'd bring out the best in Andy.

Outside my house, Chris and I were saying good night. He had walked me to my front door, and I was ready for another kiss. I was getting used to them. We'd kissed three times during the previews and then once during the movie, that one for a pretty long time, which was incredible and magical and made me contemplate never doing anything else for the rest of my life except for kissing Chris Roberts. But I'd probably eventually need to do things like eat and sleep and I couldn't go to classes with my face attached to his and then I'd never graduate and everyone would think we were conjoined twins who couldn't have been separated because we shared a single mouth or something so I rethought that plan in the same minute I hatched it . . . but it was still nice to think about for that brief moment.

There's a section of my hair that always fell in my face, and my hand was constantly finding its way to push that section behind my ear, but when it fell that night, that wonderful amazing unbelievable night in front of my house . . . it was *Chris* who reached over, tenderly but confidently, and pushed it back in place.

God, I loved that.

"I'm really glad we started hanging out," he said.

"Me too," I said back. *Understatement of the century.*

"I gotta admit something, Hailey."

Oh no, I thought. *He has a girlfriend. Two girlfriends. Five girlfriends. He's too cute and wonderful and perfect not to have a girlfriend or five.*

He continued, "I was a little worried when I got to really know you that you were gonna be kind of weird."

"Okay . . . weird, how?"

"Well, when I told Andy I wanted to ask you out, he told me about your thing."

I was totally confused. "My thing."

"Your thing."

What? What's my thing? Does he think I have a penis or something? A tail? "Um, what's my thing?"

"Well . . . you know. He told me . . . that you're autistic."

"What?!"

"I mean," he stammered. "I don't think anything of it—honestly, I'm not even sure I understand what it means, because I thought autistic people were supposed to be hypersensitive to certain things and—"

"Chris, wait—"

"Like maybe I'm not supposed to touch your ears or—"

"No, Chris—"

"—but that it's also kind of awesome because you can count all the jellybeans in a jar and it's almost like a superpower so maybe we could win a prize at the fair or, hell, we could go to Vegas and clean up—"

"Hold up!" I yelled.

He held up.

"Chris, I'm. Not. *Autistic.*"

"You're not? But . . ."

I sighed. "What did Andy say? Exactly."

Chris thought for a moment. "Well, it's when I said I thought you were pretty and you seemed really cool, he said you were. He said you were 'really cool and autistic.'"

"Oh God," I said, and couldn't help but laugh.

"What?" Chris asked.

"I think you misheard him. Or he misspoke. Or somebody mis-somethinged. Is there any chance he told you I was cool and *artistic*?"

"Oh man," he said, turning three shades of red. (That was turning into a theme for the day.) "Yeah, that must have been it. Because then he started talking about your comics and that your work is really creative, and I thought he was just trying to change the subject because he'd said too much and maybe it wasn't my business."

I was relieved, and also more than a little pleased that Andy had talked me up so well. I owed that boy a kiss. A super-platonic kiss on the cheek, of course, because there was only one mouth in this town for me, which was too bad for Andy because I *was* feeling pretty good about my newfound smooching success.

"You might want to get your hearing checked," I teased.

"Hey," he said, grabbing my jacket collar playfully. "Be nice to me. I was willing to date you even when you were autistic."

"How considerate," I said with a major smirk. On that, he leaned in and kissed the smirk right off my face. There it was. The good-night kiss I was waiting for.

Perfection.

Even after the Pot Planting Proceedings, here's how well Principal Dash's zero-tolerance prank policy was working out:

Chris and some guys on the track team had come across a discarded couch on one of their morning practice runs, so like all good environmentally conscious youth, they deposited it at the bottom of the steps in front of the school, right smack on the lawn.

Yes, a couch. Like a big living room couch. And adding fuel to the (very true) rumors that Chris and I were now a couple, he asked me to meet him on the front steps a half hour before first bell. That's where I found him, relaxing on the oddly placed couch, just like he was kicking back to watch some TV or play Xbox or whatever else you do on a couch on a lawn. He had two coffees from Starbucks—smart boy, currying my favor with caffeine—and breakfast sandwiches for us both.

"What is this?" I asked, regarding the couch.

"Breakfast?" Chris said.

Arriving students were all pointing and staring, laughing at the couch and the way Chris was relaxing on it like it wasn't weird at all.

"Um, whose *couch* is this?" I asked.

"Ours?" he said, shrugging with feigned innocence.

"I'm so confused!" I said, hesitantly taking a seat on the couch next to him. "Seriously, whose couch is this? And what's it doing here?"

Chris looked around and then leaned in close—*damn, that never gets old*—and in a hushed tone, he said: "Me, Matty and Jacob found it, and we brought it to school."

I know another thief, I thought, but didn't say it out loud, for fear I'd be compelled to name names. *Oh, Emily. Why?!* I thought back to the assembly: *Don't roll over!*

Chris leaned in again. "Don't tell anyone it was us, though."

"I won't," I said. "But us sitting on it, much less *eating breakfast,* doesn't exactly make you look *innocent.*"

"It was here!" he said, smiling. "We thought it was first-come, first-served."

"You're nuts," I said. Ten thousand thoughts started racing through my head. *Really—whose couch was it? Why did they discard it on the street? Did someone die on this couch? Am I sitting on a couch with death germs all over it?*

"Yup," he said, handing me a coffee. "Made it how you like. Soy milk—*blegh*—and two sugars."

"Thank you," I said. "Very kind of you."

Did you bring a coffee for Deadsy McDead? Former couch-owner?

Current potential haunter? Did you check under the cushions for spare change? Rats? Used syringes?

"Very kind, indeed," a voice boomed from behind us.

Shit. I knew that voice.

We turned to see Principal Dash, hands on hips. Does anyone stand like that when they're *not* pissed?

He spoke slowly, his tone filled with unspoken menace: "Whose couch is this and *what* is it doing on our lawn?"

"We don't know," I said, immediately needing to protect Chris. "It was just here."

"You don't know," Principal Dash repeated, not looking at me, his glare aimed point-blank at Chris.

"I swear," Chris said with angelic innocence. If I didn't know better, I would have believed it myself, and I found myself filing it away in my head:

Remember this moment. The boy can lie. Keep that in your back pocket and don't forget it.

Mr. Dash spoke into his radio, calling for a maintenance man to meet him out front urgently. He turned back to us: "Please enjoy your breakfast *elsewhere*."

We quickly gathered our things and left without looking back.

"That was terrifying," I said.

"Nah," Chris said. "Me and the guys already took a bunch of pictures with the couch. It'll go down in school history."

"Yeah, those photos won't prove your guilt at all," I said.

"In time," he said. "The photos are for us. They won't be going up on anyone's Facebook wall."

"You're still nuts," I said.

"About *you*," he said, and he snuck a quick kiss.

By the time lunch rolled around, the news had spread like wildfire: Hailey Harper and Chris Roberts were a couple. Andy Kellar and Emily Marsh were also a newly minted twosome—*Go, Emily*, I thought—and that meant two popular boys had been converted to the other side, at least the way I looked at it.

But I soon learned that it also meant something else.

I was walking back to my locker and saw Anya. As soon as we made eye contact, she immediately turned back to whatever she was doing in *her* locker. That was so unlike her, I knew in all of a half second that something was seriously wrong.

Anya kept yanking her books in and out, slamming things around. I walked up right next to her, and she didn't even look up at me once.

"How was your weekend?" she asked, still not looking up.

"Um . . . it was good," I said. "Great, even. I want to tell you all about it."

"Really? You didn't reply to my text."

Shit, I thought. I *had* seen a text that I meant to reply to and I'd just forgotten about it. "I'm sorry, I was just really busy and I totally spaced."

"I'm sure you were," she said. "How's Chris?"

So that's it. "Chris is . . . amazing. I think . . . I think we're actually a couple now."

"Oh, you're a couple, alright," she said, finally turning to look at me. "Did you have fun on your double date?"

"Yeah . . . it was fun," I said, now measuring my words. I didn't know what I'd done wrong yet, and I didn't want to trigger an even-more hostile reaction. "Hey . . . what's going on?"

"Why didn't you tell me Andy and Emily were going out with you?"

Huh? "Um . . . I didn't know you'd care." I was confused and feeling bad. "I'd have invited you if I knew you wanted to go. I'm sorry."

"I wouldn't have wanted to be a fifth wheel," she practically hissed. "Please."

"Well. What's wrong, then?"

"Forget it," she said, slamming her locker shut and turning away from me.

"Anya, wait!" I said. I practically chased her down the hall. "Slow down."

"I said, *forget it.*"

"Yeah, like that's gonna happen." I dragged her into the bathroom with me.

She checked every stall twice before she turned to me. She opened her mouth like she was about to tell me something, but then closed it, pressing her lips together tightly.

"It's Andy and Emily," she finally said.

"You like *Andy*?" I said, wondering about all the weird looks and bad blood from before—if it was all because of a secret crush, which made it hurt even more when Andy shunned her for the Bitch Squad.

"No, I don't like Andy," she said, like the thought of that was totally ridiculous.

Now I was totally lost.

"Um," I said, "you like *Emily*?"

I was trying (and failing) to add a little levity to the situation. (I knew Anya well enough to know she only swung one way. At least I *thought* I did . . .)

Anya cocked her head to the side and arched an eyebrow, her patented "Bitch, *please*" look.

"Then what?" I probed. "I don't know what I did. Or what *they* did. Just *tell* me."

Then Anya did another check around the bathroom—she'd already checked every stall, but I guess she had to be sure.

"Come on, what's going on?" I asked.

"C'mon, you know. You have to know."

"You *do* like Andy?" I repeated. "You *did* like Andy? You—"

They talk about things hitting you like a ton of bricks, but I've never been hit with a ton of bricks. Hell, I've never been hit with *one* brick, which I think would be more than enough.

But if I ever had been hit with a ton of bricks—it probably would feel a lot like this. All the issues with Anya and Andy . . . the weird looks, the uncomfortable silences, the anger . . . but then that *other* thing you sometimes noticed when they looked at each other.

Anya saw it on my face.

"Oh," I said.

"Congratulations, Sherlock," Anya said, bitterness oozing out of every syllable.

Andy is the father of Anya's baby.

"Fuck, Anya."

She laughed, though it sounded more like a grunt. "Yeah, well, that *is* how it all started." Always the comedian.

I looked at her with as much empathy as I've ever felt in my life. "I'm sorry. I had no idea."

"I know," she said. "I mean, I realize you didn't know. But . . . ugh. It just sucks, you know? It all sucks. I mean, I'm over it—as much as you can get over something like that—but seeing him be normal with another girl when I feel like I can never be normal again . . . it hurts."

"You can be normal," I said, hoping that was the right thing to say.

"I don't want to be *normal*," she barked. "Gross. What's more boring than being 'normal'?"

"I don't know what to say. I want to say the right thing and I don't know what it is. But if you tell me what I can say or do to make it better, I will."

"That's just it," she said. "There will never be anything you can say to make it better. It happened. I got through it. And now I go to school and see him every day and since the Invisibles became a 'thing' I even *interact* with him—which is something I never thought I'd do, by the way."

"That must be weird," I said. "I didn't mean to make you feel weird. If I'd have known—"

"No, it's good you didn't know," Anya said. "If you'd known, maybe you wouldn't have pressured us to push past all the bullshit going down, and really, I'm glad that's not going on anymore. I don't want things to be like that with him. You know, I'm actually glad we're talking again—most of the time, anyway. But there's a lot of history there. And seeing him with Emily and hearing about your date . . . man, it's just . . . there's stuff I've had locked up down there a long time."

"I get it," I said. "I'm sorry."

Her eyes welled with tears, and I pulled her in for a hug. "I'm so sorry," I repeated.

"Wait." I stopped, wondering for a moment exactly how things went down. "Was he a dick about it? Did he toss you aside when he found out? Do I need to punch him? Because I will—"

"No," Anya interrupted me, sniffing back would-be tears. "If anyone was the dick, I was. I was scared and of course it wasn't anything we planned for. I totally assumed he'd freak out, so I just kind of pushed him away. I really thought I was doing him a favor. I mean, I didn't want to be the girl who was like, 'So what if we're barely sixteen, let's get married! No pressure!' So, I just ignored his calls and texts . . . and eventually he just stopped trying."

"That's so hard. I know you were trying to spare him."

"I *was*. But I'm sure he felt like I didn't want him to have to do anything with me. Or the . . . you know." She sighed. "The *baby*. And then, I guess a small part of me was mad that he didn't fight harder to get me back. I don't know. It was just all a mess. And when you experience something that huge . . . it's just really frickin' hard to accept that the guy you went through all that shit with is now dating one of your friends."

It was then that her first tear finally escaped. She shrugged, helpless to fight it, allowing her truth to be real, allowing the pain to show.

It felt like any words I could locate would be insignificant. That was okay. I knew she understood I was on her side, and the unspoken promise in that fourth-floor bathroom was that we'd figure it out together.

Can you help me remember
how to smile?

—SOUL ASYLUM

"Runaway Train"

CHAPTER 15

If you had recorded all the times my parents fought during my lifetime, I don't think you'd even have enough to fill a greatest hits album—which is in no way implying there was any hitting going on. (And if there were, it certainly wouldn't be great—my mom didn't care to lift anything heavier than a can opener, and I'm pretty sure I could kick my dad's ass at arm wrestling. Or just in general.)

My parents rarely fought—they barely even had a disagreement—and if they did, it was never over anything serious. When I was a kid, I just always assumed they were the perfect couple, always in love, always just thrilled to be in each other's presence. Even when they disagreed, it seemed playful, just for laughs. As I got a little older, I realized that couldn't be totally true, but they always seemed to get along great, nothing ever really bothering them, like a husband and wife on a sitcom: They occasionally do wacky things, right, but they're always inseparable again by the end of the show. The stupid little shit that happens from day to day is no big deal. If there was ever friction between them, I never, ever saw it. Maybe they were great at keeping their arguments hidden from Noel and me?

Whatever Jedi mind tricks they'd used to achieve that status quo, it had abruptly changed.

Yes, I'd noticed that my dad wasn't around as much, and I thought it was because of the new job . . . but it didn't get past me that when we *did* have dinner together, the conversation was awkward and stilted. The playfulness seemed to have dissipated.

There was something going on. I tried not to worry; hopefully it was something small. I had enough shit going on in my life as it was, although I was pretty happy that my personal life was mostly on a serious upswing. I almost didn't want to know the deal—let them work it out—but everything seemed just a little off with every conversation, every interaction.

So when I swung open the door one afternoon and overheard my parents arguing in the kitchen, not noticing I'd come in, it wasn't entirely unexpected. What *was* entirely unexpected was the weight of whatever was happening.

This wasn't something small.

"We moved our entire life for you," my mom said.

"I know," my dad answered. "You don't think I know?"

"I don't know what to think."

Then they were quiet. I stood there waiting for what would come next, wondering whether I should let them know I was there. I did not want to be there right now. But I also did.

"I don't know what I'm supposed to do here," my mom said.

I couldn't take it any longer.

I walked into the kitchen. My dad stood by the refrigerator, my mom on the other side of the kitchen with that kitchen counter thing—I think they call it an island, but I'm not sure why—between them. Each stood with their arms crossed over their chests. They looked, I don't know—exhausted, I guess.

"What's going on?" I asked.

Now they looked startled.

My mom's body language changed immediately. She crossed the room to smooth my hair. "Nothing, sweetie," she said. "Daddy and I are just having a discussion."

"Sounds like *more* than a discussion," I said, thinking, *I wouldn't have called them on this six months ago, but that seems like a long time now.* "Mom, I'm not a child."

My mom smiled, and her eyes welled up a little. "But you *are*," she said. "I know you're not a baby, but this is between your father and me, and it's nothing you need to worry about."

"Really?" I asked. "Because it kinda seems like it is."

My dad wasn't saying anything. He wasn't even looking at me. I couldn't recall the last time that happened. Actually, I couldn't recall that *ever* happening.

"Honey, why don't you go to your room and let your father and me finish this discussion, and then we can all talk later, okay?"

What I thought: *You're getting a divorce, aren't you?*

What I said: "Okay."

I walked upstairs to my bedroom, staring at my feet. Each step I took, I'd have a memory flash, one for every time my knockoff Marant wedge sneakers touched a stair. Step: palm trees. Step: the front lawn at school. Step: packing up my old clothes and stealing Noel's castoffs. Step: Chris Roberts. Step: my BFF necklace from Amy, who I'd totally lost touch with.

When I got to my room, I saw an open IM on my screen.

Oh, welcome distraction.

ANYA: what r u doing?

ME: freaking out. something's way up with my rents

ANYA: ?

ME: i don't know. they were fighting when i got home. they never fight

ANYA: . . . in front of you

ME: no srsly. they don't. something big is up

ANYA: ☹

ME: what r u doing?

ANYA: nada. brianna is here. wanted to see if you wanted to come over?

ME: what's a brianna?

ANYA: duh. she's in your science class. she's also STANDING RIGHT HERE

ME: oh. way to have someone I don't even know read shit about me that's none of her business

So much for a distraction. Maybe the next one would be a spy satellite falling out of orbit and right through my ceiling.

I closed the chat window without a good-bye—*Anya will understand, or she won't, and who gives a shit anyway*—and threw myself backward onto my bed, where I lay for all of five seconds.

I felt antsy and nervous and annoyed with Anya and worried about my parents and wondered what Chris was up to because I needed to think about something that wouldn't give me a headache.

Wondering wasn't cutting it, so I texted a "hey" to Chris and after a few back-and-forths he was outside my house, waiting in the driveway. (The fact that Chris had a car was a total bonus.)

"Where are you going?" my mom called out as I slid out the door.

"Just for a drive," I called back, not looking back or waiting for approval or even a follow-up question.

Chris leaned against the car, contemplating whatever was on his phone, but he looked up with his bright eyes and a wide smile that comforted me, if just a little. I think those eyes could cure cancer. Or at least a mild flu.

"You got here fast," I said, trying to put all my parents' stuff behind me.

"I was worried about you," he said.

"Yeah, I know. And thanks. Something is totally up."

Chris took my hand and lifted it to his lips, kissing it with amazing tenderness. He led me to the passenger door, opening it, helping me in and closing it behind me.

Guys, keep that in mind: It's the little things, the small reminders that you care and that we're important to you, that make all the difference.

Chris continued to hold my hand as we drove . . . who knows where. Who cares? No matter what was going on with my parents, in that moment I felt happy and safe. We didn't speak that much as we drove into the canyons. I was still trying to get my bearings in the city, but I think we were in Laurel Canyon. Either way, we ended up on Mulholland and the views were just breathtaking.

We listened to music and drove around the twists and turns, and as luck or fate or random timing would have it, we were near an overlook when the sun was setting, and we had pretty much the most perfect view I'd ever seen. Then again, Chris directly in front of me was pretty perfect too.

We parked, and I leaned my head on his shoulder and we watched the sunset, playing with each other's hands, tickling, tracing the edges of our fingers, outlining the lines on our palms.

"Do you want to talk about it?" Chris asked.

"I don't even know what it is," I said truthfully. "My parents were in this fight and they never fight and it was tense and big . . . it was just big. Something big was going on."

"That sucks."

"Yeah. They sent me to my room so they could keep talking, but before I interrupted, my mom played the 'we moved for you' card, so . . . I don't know."

"Do you think they want to move back?" he asked, his brow wrinkled. I liked that the idea of me moving away worried him. I felt my heart swell and ache in the same moment.

"No," I said, but—what did I know? Jack shit. "Actually . . . who knows?"

He sighed. "I'd be really bummed if you left."

"So would I!" I said. For as much as I didn't want to move before, now I was loving life. I had friends, I felt confident, the weather was *uh-mazing* and I had a boyfriend. A real boyfriend. Not just real, but really handsome, and funny, and a popular guy who didn't think being popular meant being shallow and vapid and—there's probably another good word there, but I'd only just added *vapid* to my vocabulary recently (it's a pretty useful term in Skylerland), so that's good enough, right?

Life was good, and with my track record, that's not something you take for granted. I did *not* want to give this up. I shook my head to rid my brain of the thought, as if enough shaking could will it away forever. "I'm not moving. I mean, there's no way."

"Good," Chris said. He slid his hand under my chin and lifted my face to his.

I adjusted myself to a better kissing position and got lost in delicious kisses for I don't even *know* how long. His hands went under my shirt and found my breasts, and with some agile maneuvering—*this isn't his first rodeo*, it occurred to me—he unhooked my bra. But it was *my* first rodeo. My breath caught as he touched me, and my heart was racing as we explored each other's bodies. I felt myself divide, half of me completely lost in the moment, the other half thinking, *Holy crap I am totally fooling around with my boyfriend!*

I wondered how far we'd go, and I worried about moving too fast too soon. I mean, we'd only been together for a month at this point. I definitely wasn't ready to go all the way . . . but I also didn't want to be an "Everything But" girl on our first real hookup.

Everything But girls do everything but intercourse, and sometimes Everything But girls even do it in the butt! (Which I guess makes sense as a pun but makes absolutely no sense otherwise.) Can you tell me how that somehow makes you feel like you're maintaining your virginity? Insane. Anyway, I wasn't going there yet, or *there* probably ever. And Chris wasn't pushing me; another thing to like about him. He was just frisky enough without overstepping. We'd talked about this a little before, dancing around it before finally getting perfectly frank. He must have known I still had my V card, so he wasn't being gross about it, and he certainly wasn't going to try to deflower me in a car on Mulholland Drive. Although with this view, I'm sure that had happened many times with many couples before. This place was basically View Viagra.

By the time we pulled up to my house, I felt much better than when we'd left, for obvious reasons. I kissed Chris one last time and kept my eyes open to remind myself that I was kissing Chris Roberts. Heaven.

It lasted until he pulled away. The unsettling feeling sank in even as my feet hit the doormat, a goofy little thing my dad and I picked out together a few years ago at an outdoor market. It was inscribed PEOPLE WALK ALL OVER ME. It was tacky but adorably so. I hadn't thought about that for a while, but it was one of my favorite memories.

When I walked in, my mom was there in the living room. She

had to be waiting for me, because there's no other reason she'd be sitting there on the couch, no TV on, no radio, nothing. She looked up and her eyes were red, and there was no doubt as to why. The only other time I'd ever seen her cry was when our dog Mildred passed away. (RIP Mildred ☹)

"Hey," I said. "Are you okay?"

"I am," she said with a tiny sniffle. "Come, sit with me."

I crossed the room to join her on the couch, and she smiled and smoothed back my hair. I always loved that. She'd done it ever since I was little, and there's just something so comforting about your mom smoothing your hair. But I felt like I was supposed to be the one comforting her. She was the one with bloodshot eyes . . . unless mine soon would be bloodshot too.

It was just like that for what was probably thirty seconds and seemed like thirty minutes. I guess I just wanted a little longer of this time, this time before whatever came next, because whatever came next obviously wasn't *good*, and I guess she wanted that too.

I steeled myself, exhaled, and turned to her. "Mom, what's going on?"

"I'm going to ask you some questions," she said.

"And *then* tell me what's going on?"

"Honey, I don't know what's going on, entirely. But what I do know is that you seem happy here. Are you happy here?"

I was. I was not only aware of it, but it made me realize how unhappy I was back home. Not that life was terrible, but it certainly wasn't exciting. For all the good *and* bad of my California experience, I was *involved* now—in a lot of ways. I had new friends and despite the fact that I'd known Amy back home since I was nine, Anya and I already knew each other so well we could have entire conversations through facial expressions. And the fact that she was asking me this question made me think there was a chance we were moving back.

"Yes," I said. "I am happy here. Very. Happier than I've ever been."

"Good," she replied, followed by a weak smile. "I'm glad."

"Did something happen with Dad's work?"

"No," she said. "His job is secure."

This was exasperating. "Then what the—"

I caught myself before saying *what the hell*, which she probably could have handled, but I didn't want this to turn into an argument. I stopped, exhaled, started again: "Mom, if there's a problem, I need to know. Please. I can handle it."

She paused for a second, then said, "If there is anything you need to know, I promise you I'll tell you. But knowing that you're happy here makes me happy, and everything else will work itself out."

God, this is frustrating! I felt like I was a detective on one of those cop shows, trying to get the suspect—I'm sorry, I mean *person of interest*—to confess. But this wasn't some crackhead who'd shot a pizza delivery guy to score his—whatever they score—crack, I guess.

I'd rather grill the crackhead.

I figured I'd just get what I could for now, especially the most important thing: "So we're not moving back?"

"Nope," she said. "You won't move anywhere you don't want to."

I let the relief sink in. It didn't sink in too deeply.

My mom gave me a playful jab in the arm. "So you were with Chris?"

Change the subject much?

"Yeah," I said. Despite the situation, I couldn't help but smile.

"I was in the tenth grade when I had my first boyfriend too."

"What was his name?"

"Mick," she said. "His parents were big Rolling Stones fans."

"What happened with him?" I asked.

"I met another boy who didn't go to our school and he stole me away."

"You cheated?"

"No!" she said quickly, like *really* quickly. I looked at her like she was a space alien, and she smiled and continued.

"I just knew I liked him better—Jackson—so I broke up with poor Mick. Your grandfather was so funny. He told me, 'I like him better *too*.' And when I asked him why, he said, 'I like his earring better.'"

Now I gave her a double space-alien look. "Huh?"

Mom smiled. "He was teasing me. Both boys had pierced ears. Well, one ear pierced. The left. That was the thing when I was in high school. Especially with musicians."

Mom seemed to feel better, and that made me feel better, and she *had* answered the million-dollar question: We're not moving. I wouldn't say I was satisfied, but the whole drug-deal-gone-wrong-quadruple-murder confession could wait.

It wasn't until later, when I was lying in bed, alone with my thoughts, that I felt the uneasy feelings return.

This is why you should never be alone with your thoughts, I thought. *Your thoughts are shitty company. They eat all the pizza and don't help clean up and they make you get all freaked out about the future.*

Mom's words echoed in my brain: *You won't move anywhere you don't want to.* Now I *really* felt like a lawyer, trying to cross-examine witness testimony. I asked her if *we* were moving, and she said, "*You* won't move," almost like . . . we weren't a package deal.

Was I reading too much into that? Did she just happen to

answer it that way? Was I making way too much of one word? Should I have pressed her on it?

Did I *really* want to know the answer?

My stomach was in knots. I watched the clock most of the night, trying to fall asleep and failing miserably. It was like the night before the first day of school all over again.

But shittier.

The next day at school . . . you can imagine my disposition. I was totally exhausted and in the worst mood. I needed an outlet, some constructive way to harness the frustration, confusion and anger I was feeling. Since I didn't do krav maga—*I really need to learn krav maga*—I fell back on what's worked so well recently: plotting against the bitches who were undoubtedly plotting the same for us.

I gave the signal to the girls I saw in the halls, and I put a note on our message board for everyone to meet at the Grove after school. I'd been mulling over the Westminster Dog Show prank that Skyler had planned on pulling, and I'd come up with an idea. Actually it was *Skyler's* idea, just taken to the next level.

"BitchBook."

We had assembled by the fountain, and I said it just like that: "BitchBook." A few puzzled looks from the girls, and then Grace said:

"Like Facebook?"

"Exactly. There's already a DogBook app; it's a part of Facebook for *actual* dogs. And that's not as awesome a name as Bitch-Book anyway. So we create a site called BitchBook. It's Skyler's 'brilliant' idea, but better. We don't just plaster pictures on the Homecoming Wall like they were going to. We go high-tech. We create pages for each one of them with pictures and descriptions of what kinds of dogs they are—and why."

"Harsh," Anya said.

"They were gonna do it to *us*," I replied. "They still probably are!"

"Well, sorta," she said.

I gave her the space-alien look.

"Well," Anya continued, "they were going to do it to a bunch of people—whoever they thought they could get away with humiliating—during Spirit Week."

"And you don't think that would include us?" I asked.

"Well, sure, *now*," Anya said. "These days we're A-Number-One with a bullet on their list. I'm just saying—"

"That doesn't matter," Grace said. "It could have been some of us, some other girls, all of the above. It's still messed up and awful."

Anya sighed. "I know. I'm not saying they're not assholes—I've been the biggest victim of Skyler's bullshit; she's a fucking sociopath—I'm just saying a lot's changed. The Invisibles didn't even exist when Skyler concocted her Evil Plan of Evil. Hailey wasn't even here. Things are different."

I turned to Anya. "Are they all *that* different? Did Skyler turn into Mother Teresa overnight? The same girl who looked me right in the eye, told me she wanted to make peace and then had her minions hand us valet uniforms for her party? You think she's not going to do everything in her power to humiliate us? Jesus, after everything that's happened, she's going to be ten times more Vengeance Bitch than she was before. Right?"

Anya nodded. "Yeah. That's probably right."

"So we beat her to the punch," I said. "Best defense is a good offense. We do the same thing to them a week early, and we not only take away their prank . . . we do it better."

"I like it," Dahlia said.

Anya shrugged. "Well, it is right up *your* technical alley."

"Why does that sound dirty to me?" Xandra asked.

"Because *everything* sounds dirty to you," Anya said.

Xandra shrugged now. "True."

"We can allow comments and post check-ins," Dahlia added. "And we can make it so other people can leave comments, add pictures and share."

"Is it too mean?" Grace asked.

Was it too mean? I thought before answering. No. How do we know what they have planned? Part of me still felt responsible for the party incident, and sure we turned it around in the form of the valet parking from hell . . . but I would never forget the look on Grace's face when they shut us down outside. This was finally her moment to be accepted. And she was humiliated. Again. We all were. I didn't care what they had planned for us this time. I wasn't going to let them win.

"I repeat," I said, "it's *exactly* what they were going to do. Just a more technological version. Because we're smarter than them. We—"

The words lodged in my throat as I witnessed the oddest thing: A trickle of blue snot ran from Kura's nose to her upper lip. We all saw it.

Kura wiped it away quickly, but it only smeared blue across her cheek.

"What?" Kura asked, but she looked at her hand and saw blue.

"I thought you were going to stop that," Emily said.

"I did!" Kura said.

"Uh . . . not quite," Emily said.

Kura glared at Emily. "I did, but then I got all depressed, I guess, from being used to it, and I have a big test and I need to focus," Kura defended.

"And you can't just take your Adderall like a normal person?" Emily asked. "You have to snort it?"

"Works faster that way," Kura said.

"It's dangerous," Emily said.

Oh Jesus, I thought, then said, "Says the person who risks getting thrown in jail twice a week."

"Wow," Emily said, turning to glare at me. "What's *your* problem?"

I'd regretted that knock right after it came out of my mouth, but I was in no mood to show weakness. I was in no mood to tolerate anything today.

"Sorry, Emily," I replied, "I'm just saying. It's not exactly the *smartest* thing to pilfer a new ensemble every time something at Urban Outfitters strikes your fancy."

"But it doesn't risk my life like snorting Adderall," Emily snapped. "Why are you attacking me?"

"Why are you attacking Kura?" I said, not even sure where I was in this argument—*maybe I should have stayed in bed today*—because I actually agreed with Emily on that point. Kura definitely shouldn't be snorting her Adderall.

"Time out!" Anya yelled. "Just stop it. What's going on here? Why are we fighting?"

Emily: "*I'm* trying to help a friend—"

"And so am *I*," I interrupted. "Look, I don't think Kura should be snorting *anything*. But I don't think you should steal either."

"Awesome, so it's parenting time," Anya said. "We'll be closing out today's session with Hailey doling out allowances and chores for the week—"

I felt myself about to go off on Anya, but I saw the look in her eyes, and just shut my mouth. My head hurt. My stomach continued to feel like it was being invaded by my rib cage.

It was dead silent for a few seconds, and as the de facto leader of this little crew of outcasts, rebels, drug abusers and thieves, I needed to step up to the plate.

"Look," I said, "we all have our issues. I'm sure Emily meant well, and I meant well, and—"

Kura's looking at me like I just kicked her dog.

"—we all . . . appreciate the pressures everyone's under. So let's just—"

"Let's just *do it*," Dahlia said. "Let's get back to talking about the *real* bitches and how we're gonna digitally destroy them."

"Yeah," Grace said, her head down. "Let's do that." She didn't look up, and if she was particularly enthused about the BitchBook plan, it wasn't apparent in her voice.

Outside of the wonderful oasis that was my visit with Chris, this obviously was destined to be the most frustrating twenty-four hours of my life. First my mom clams up like a Mafioso, and now my brilliant BitchBook plan—and it was brilliant, damn it—was being met with less-than-universal acclaim.

Oh, and I can't keep one girl from shoving shit in her backpack and another one from shoving shit up her nose. *Yay me!*

"If you guys don't want to do this, we don't have to," I said. "It's not up to me. We're in this together. If you want to just say fuck it and let them go ahead with their posters and do nothing about it, then, hey, that's an option too."

"No," Anya said. "You're right, Hailey. We can't let them get away with that shit. We've put too much on the line already. We're . . . in it to win it."

Everyone laughed for a second. That was one of Anya's deadpan ironic lines. She loved tossing clichés into everyday conversation. You should hear her do *It is what it is* or *We need 110 percent out of you.*

Thank goodness Anya provided a clean break for us. Now we needed something to bring us together.

The truth is I had emailed Noel the night before. I wanted to get her opinion on the idea. Of course she hadn't responded, so I just decided on my own: *Yes, it's perfect.* Plus I was pretty sure it wasn't my imagination that Skyler had been holding glances at Chris a little too long lately, and if she thought she was going to get him back she needed to be put in check. Because that? Was *not* happening.

"Why don't we take a vote?" I asked. "Anyone who is *not* in favor of the new plan, raise your hand."

A long pause, and then Grace raised her hand.

She looked around.

No one else joined her.

For a second, I thought maybe I should say something—maybe just straight out ask Grace what she was so concerned about. But I didn't. A part of me didn't want any more debate, any more discussion. I was sick of trying to balance other people's concerns, sick of knocking this around. It was time for action.

And Grace slowly lowered her hand.

"Okay," I said. "I guess that means we're a go."

I made it through the wilderness…

—MADONNA

"Like a Virgin"

CHAPTER 16

Over the next few weeks, Chris and I became one of those couples everyone makes fun of for being joined at the hip—though I should clarify that our hips had not yet actually joined, much to our growing frustration. But our relationship *had* deepened, and I felt closer to him than I probably had ever felt with anybody.

We'd pretty much spend every day together after school and we ate lunch together at school . . . and sometimes snuck off campus. I even created a comic character in his honor, though he didn't have a name or thought bubbles or storylines—okay, maybe I was just drawing him over and over again—my version of writing CHRIS + HAILEY = ♥ all over my notebook.

I felt guilty about ignoring my friends, especially Anya, but she understood and didn't seem to be resentful that I wasn't available much lately. She understood how it was when you were in a relationship and the unspoken resignation to hang out when the boyfriend or girlfriend was otherwise occupied. She'd had relationships before—had she *ever*.

In light of her experiences, it was Anya I turned to when I needed advice of a somewhat sensitive sort.

"Oh God, really?" she said. "We're really gonna do this?"

"Well . . . ," I stammered. "I don't want to be . . . bad at it."

We were on the outdoor basketball court, giving PE our usual level of devotion, which was none at all. I'm not anti-sports, I'm just anti-getting-all-sweaty-at-school. It's one thing if they gave you enough time to shower and dress and do your hair and makeup, but . . . ten minutes before the bell just doesn't cut it. Why do they have to cut all the arts and music classes? Cut frigging PE!

Anya put a hand on my shoulder. "Trust me. He'll just be happy you're doing it. I don't think I've ever heard of an instance where a guy complained about getting a blow job."

"Don't make me beg you. This is embarrassing enough."

"Fine," she said. "Freeze two bananas."

"Seriously?"

"Seriously. Remember when we watched *Fast Times at Ridgemont High* and they practiced on carrots by just moving them in and out? Well, that's just about the most boring technique I've ever seen, and carrots are kinda gross and a banana is a much more realistic size, so just get two fucking bananas and freeze them, okay?"

"Fine," I said. But couldn't help myself: "Why *frozen* exactly?"

I've never seen a human being make a more grandiose act of rolling her eyes.

"Jesus," she said. "Was I this stupid when I was a virgin? Did I have like twenty-five IQ points hidden behind my hymen?"

Ugh, this is aggravating. "Come on, Anya. I just want to be sure I understand exactly what I'm getting into."

"You mean what's getting into you."

"Whatever."

"Well, Hailey, here's why it needs to be frozen: because the male penis, when aroused, is as chilly as an icicle."

I glared at her.

"You have to be careful. You can get your tongue stuck to it, like licking a frozen flagpole in the winter."

Double glare. Considering Chris's last name wasn't "Cullen" and considering vampires don't actually exist, even I knew better than that.

"*Anya . . . ,*" I growled.

She smiled. "Jeez, Hailes. Because a banana at room temperature is soft and it gets mushy and it will get even more mushy in your mouth and do I *really* have to explain this to you?"

"Okay, okay, I get it," I said. "I just wanted to make sure I wasn't missing anything."

"Like the fact that dicks are banana flavored?"

So I punched her. Just playfully. At least we got *some* physical exertion out of PE.

And when I got home, I froze two bananas.

The next day, Anya came over, and we went over technique.

"Okay," she said, holding the banana to her lips. "Now, you don't want to forget to use your hands."

"But I thought the whole point was it's *not* a hand job!"

"Oh, young grasshopper," she said. "You use both. Like this . . ."

Anya showed me on her banana what to do and in between intermittent giggling fits, I got the basic gist.

"And eye contact," she said. "They like it when you look up at them."

"Why?" I asked. "That's embarrassing. I'm embarrassed looking at *you* right now!"

"You *should* be. You're fellating a banana."

"I hate you."

"Just look up at him every now and then when you're doing it," she said. "Yeah, you don't want to stare at him the whole time—that would be creepy—but they love it when you hit 'em with those puppy-dog eyes, big and wide, every once in a while while you're tending to their needs."

"Okay, that just creeped me out a little," I said. "Guys want puppy-dog eyes? Like I'm a dog?"

"No, that's not what I meant. Just think, like, big, wide eyes, like anime or something."

I'd seen some examples from Anya's anime collection, and that didn't make me feel a whole lot better either, but I just played along. This whole year had been about stepping out of my comfort zone. Now I was about to take a giant leap out of the fucker.

Once Anya and I had gone over the basics and I felt I had a good hand (and mouth) on it, we moved on to the subject of spicing it up. This hadn't even crossed my mind. Good thing I had Anya.

"Ice cubes," she said.

"Like . . . during?"

"Well . . ." She looked thoughtful for a moment. "No, probably not. But if you have one in your mouth right before and *then* do it, your mouth will be really cold and they like that. It feels good."

"Okay," I said. Ice cubes. Noted.

"You can also try mints," she said. "Having a couple mints in your mouth is supposed to be mind-blowing."

"Any special *kind* of mints?"

"Breath mints. Like Altoids."

"Before?" I asked, trying to clarify, feeling like an idiot, but there were so many rules: ice before, not during. Mints=during. Practice bananas=frozen.

"No, during," she said.

"Okay," I said, slightly skeptical but willing.

We were at Chris's house on a Tuesday when I finally decided to go for it. We'd been an official couple for over two months now, and since I still wasn't going to go all the way, I decided that particular Tuesday was as good a time as any for me to blow his mind, not to mention his—

Did I really just make that joke? Even just in my head? Who am I? Suddenly, I have a gorgeous boyfriend and he's sweet and cool and he's totally into me and I'm making jokes about something I've never done, but I really want to do this for him because I know guys are supposed to love that and—

Well, you get the picture.

His parents weren't home, but we'd locked his bedroom door anyway. We got down to our usual business, but by now, that was all—I don't want to say *routine*, because it was thrilling and incredible every time—but it was ground we'd covered before. It was safe. We were on his bed, rolling around, kissing, touching, over the clothes, under the clothes, grinding . . . everything that had been part of our typical repertoire. Our comfort zone, if you will . . . in more ways than one.

His body was reacting. And my body was reacting. Though the evidence of his body reacting was harder to hide.

Way, *way* harder.

So, I finally got the courage to pull his jeans all the way off.

"Hailey," he started, and he looked confused and concerned, like, *we haven't talked about this.* But I silenced him by putting my finger over his lips and smiling.

If Chris knew me better—sure, in ways he knew me better than anyone else in my life, but I'm talking life experience here—he'd have known that smile. It's the smile I throw on whenever I'm scared shitless but desperate to convince you otherwise.

I'm really good at it too. I get that confident look in my eye, lift my chin just a hair and turn up the corners of my mouth with a presence that says *I've got this*, while in my head I'm actually thinking, *How the hell am I ever going to pull this off?*

Oh, well. Like Shakespeare said, *Once more unto the breach*, though I'm pretty sure he wasn't talking about this, and I'm honestly not sure what that means anyway, and even as those thoughts were racing through my mind I was suddenly *going down on Chris*.

My heart rate felt like it went from zero to sixty in seconds, though it probably wasn't zero in the first place because then I'd have been dead, and, yes, I was freaking out a little, so these were the things that were going through my mind even as I kissed and licked him on his thighs and near and around the . . . um . . . goal zone.

He was loving it, no question about that—it would have been obvious if he were acting, but just the sensation of my mouth in that area had him shuddering and letting out small gasps. In retrospect, this was a good thing. But at the time, I would have put fifty-fifty odds on whether I was pleasing him or killing him.

I wasn't *used* to these kinds of gasps. In my tenure on this planet to date, gasps were generally limited to "Somebody farted at a fancy dinner" or "Oh damn, yet another kid got slammed in the crotch on *Tosh.0.*" This whole existence of I'm-loving-this gasps was road less traveled for me. So it took a minute for me to register that these were *good* gasps, and that I wasn't doing something wrong. (My uncertainty probably messed with the flow, but seriously, cut me a little slack.)

Being so close to the "target" was awkward, I'm not gonna lie. It was like, THERE IT IS! Right *there*, up close and personal. And I wouldn't be me if I didn't analyze the living shit out of it, so my inner monologue was basically going:

Holy crap, this is really happening!

Please don't let me be too lame at it . . .

Then again, if I were a total pro, that would probably make me a slut, so maybe it's better that I'm inexperienced . . .

But then again, he knows I'm not experienced, and would he really think it was a bad thing if I were great at it . . .

No, he'd be psyched. So let's get back to please don't be lame and . . .

Holy crap, this is really happening!

I felt like I was Christopher Columbus, exploring new lands full of—hell, I don't know—penises.

Actually, it was more like whoever explored Area 51. Not to say that Chris's, um, *business* looked like an alien per se. I recall thinking it was pretty standard fare as far as my entirely limited knowledge went, and then I recall thinking that I needed to—

STOP THINKING! Just do it! (Thanks, Nike. I'm sure that's exactly what you had in mind for your campaign. Just like Shakespeare.)

So I did. I just did it. I kissed it and I touched it and I, well, got acquainted with it. It was a little weird at first, like going to another country where people drive on the left side of the road and eat their French fries with mayonnaise, not that I've ever been to another country but I hear that happens and you just have to . . . *adapt*, you know? So that's what I was doing. Adapting. He has stuff and I have stuff, and granted, this stuff looks like totally different, but as best I could tell, his stuff was not at all objecting to my stuff, and thank God because I had no idea what I was doing, but I seemed to be doing a pretty good job, so . . . I just kept doing what I was doing.

Chris arched his back and closed his eyes, and he was obviously having a wonderful time (believe me, I would have known otherwise, and quickly), and yet I knew that was my opening, so I . . .

. . . snatched five Altoids from the outside pocket of my bag and quickly popped them in my mouth.

You thought that part was good? Get ready for a "Curiously Strong" blow job.

After some more touching and teasing, I delicately took him into my mouth, looking up at Chris's face, noticing how excited he was. It made me even more excited to do a good job. I can't say I felt completely comfortable under the circumstances—no amount of practice with Anya and fruit could equate with the reality of the situation—but I think I adapted remarkably well, all things considered. I even started feeling a little—I'm not sure if this counts as a pun, so bear with me—*cocky*. So when Chris's eyes were closed, I slipped one more mint in my mouth. You know, to make it *extra* special.

Because just plain special wasn't enough.

God, I'm an asshole.

Anyway . . . I was doing what Anya had shown me with the banana, using both my hands and my mouth, but I was having a bit of a hard time navigating all the mints plus him in my mouth. That's a lot of stuff to have in your mouth at one time. So there I was, doing this thing I've never done before, and I'm trying not to gag because I know that will make him feel bad and worry about me, but I've also got all these freaking mints in my mouth, and as I'm moving on Chris they're moving in my mouth and it was a lot going on all at once. Kind of like what I imagine Las Vegas to be like. Not that Vegas is all Altoids and dicks but, you know, just like sensory overload.

Anyway, Chris seemed to still be really happy, and I didn't want to screw that up, so I tried to breathe through my nose and . . . boy, was it getting minty strong. My eyes started watering and I was getting overcome with minty goodness, but it wasn't goodness, it was just *really fucking minty* and I thought, *I might have overdone it with the mints,* and that's pretty much when that concern was—

Completely, brutally and horrifically confirmed.

You know when they say someone turned on a dime? They're going one way and then, *bam*, they're going the other.

Chris turned on a dime.

He suddenly grunted—a bad grunt, a really clearly *bad* grunt, obviously nothing like the good grunts he'd been making earlier. It was a grunt like he'd just stubbed his toe or touched a hot burner on a stovetop. There was no mistaking it for anything but a Make-It-Stop-Right-Now grunt.

Chris suddenly looked . . . *scared*?

I felt my skin get cold and I pulled away from him slowly, looking up at him. Chris was bug-eyed. I'd never seen him bug-eyed. He's a ridiculously good-looking young man, but I can tell you this: *No one* looks good bug-eyed.

"What's wrong?" I asked.

He'd already looked pained. Seconds later, he looked ten times worse.

"It burns!" he yelled, suddenly pulling away, standing, looking around helplessly, panicked, terrified.

And then it dawned on me.

Shit.

I should have gone with the ice.

Dammit, why didn't I use the ice?!

I hope I haven't destroyed Chris's penis. What am I going to tell his mom? "I'm really sorry, I meant all the best for your son's penis. Seriously, I was a big fan."

Chris started to bounce up and down, shaking his arms, confused, reaching down to touch himself, yanking his hands back, totally freaked out.

"I'm sorry," I mumbled, though I didn't mean to mumble, realizing my words were mumbled because . . .

"What's in your *mouth*?" Chris asked.

I slowly opened wide, shamefully revealing the hearty sum of only-somewhat-melted Altoids still resting on my tongue.

"Why?!" he cried as he raced to the bathroom.

The confused and bewildered look on his face as his eyes widened was something that will be burned into my memory forever:

The day I burned my boyfriend's penis off.

Why did I listen to Anya? She *is* the girl who got knocked up freshman year, after all. Getting sex tips from her was like asking Amy Winehouse for advice on how to use drugs safely.

I heard Chris turn on the shower, and I sat there, waiting for him to wash off, feeling like the biggest idiot on the planet. I was half feeling stupid and half genuinely concerned that I'd permanently injured him, but as a whole it was just pretty much the worst.

He'd been in the bathroom for close to ten minutes (but it seemed like at least six weeks), so finally I knocked on the door.

"Are you okay?" I asked.

The longest pause in the history of ever. And then, eventually, a voice:

"I guess."

I stood there awkwardly and waited for him to say something else, but he didn't.

"I'm so sorry," I said. "Can I come in? Or will you come out?"

Finally he opened the door. He was soaking wet, and he looked so cute . . . but not exactly welcoming.

He stepped forward, towel around his waist, and sat on the edge of the bed. I slowly steeled myself and sat down next to him, softly placing a hand on his thigh. He didn't say anything. I didn't say anything. And then—

"What were you thinking?" he asked.

I didn't have any great answers. I went with what I had.

"I wanted it to be special."

"Oh, it was special, alright."

I sighed. "Look . . . I asked a friend for tips. I just wanted it to be good. I wanted you to *like* it. It was supposed to be tingly and awesome. I guess it wasn't. . . ."

Chris pondered this for a moment. "I noticed the tingle before it got bad," he said. "I've never done that before, but I've heard about it. It wasn't bad at first. In fact, it was, you know, kinda good. But I think the idea is you're just supposed to do a little. Not—"

"Like a mouthful."

"Right. Definitely—*definitely*—not a mouthful."

I don't even know where the tears came from, but they were flowing before I even realized it. I guess it was a mixture of the anxiety and fear and the stress of this turn of events, and—I don't cry often. That's just not me. But it wasn't like I was even crying. I was just there with Chris and my face was all wet, and I could taste the salt on my lips, and I started wiping the tears away, and—

"Hey, it's okay," Chris said, wrapping an arm around my shoulders, pulling me into his body, which immediately seemed like pretty much a remedy for any problem anyone's ever had.

He continued, "Don't worry about it. You just don't know these things until they come up. Like last year, I had this pulled muscle in one of my shoulders from baseball, so I was rubbing all this Bengay on it—you know what that is?"

"Yeah. Muscle stuff. Gets . . . hot, then cold, sort of."

"Right. But that's just on regular skin. What you might not realize is that you don't want to immediately touch anywhere around your eyes or any, um, sensitive areas while that stuff's still on your hands. But I used it and then I went to pee, and . . ."

"Not good?"

"Not good," he said. "Burned like hellfire for a while, then went totally numb."

"Worse than tonight?" I asked.

"Um . . . well . . . kind of the same. Once it really kicked in, at least."

More tears were welling up, but I tried to hold them in. "Oh God! Chris, I'm so sorry. Are you mad? Of course you're mad. I'm *such* an idiot. I'm so, so sorry!"

"No," he said. "I'm not mad. I was . . . surprised. And, you know, terrified."

He delivered that with a smile that demolished me. With love, and guilt, and . . . probably some other stuff, but it's a little hard to tell when you're demolished.

I took a deep breath, wiped my eyes to stem the tide and turned to him.

"I'm sorry," I said. "I can't say I'm sorry enough."

"Hailey, it's okay. It wasn't bad, well, for a while, at least. But next time . . . no tricks, no props. You're all I need. Just you."

"Deal," I said. "Promise. I won't even brush my teeth that day."

We both laughed, and virtually at the same time, we both said, "*That* would be gross."

He was really sweet after that. We spent a little more time on his bed just hanging out, cuddling, talking about things. I still felt somewhat mortified, but Chris had a way of making it better. He made me feel safe. He made me feel calm. He made me feel at peace. But despite all that, one thing remained foremost in my mind:

I wanted to kill Anya.

The next day at school, Andy stopped me in the hall.

"Hey, Hailey," he said. "Got a mint?"

Ugh.

"Very funny, Andy," I said. "Now I have *two* people to kill."

"Huh," he said. "*Two?*"

"Don't ask," I said. "I can't believe Chris told you."

"Oh, come on, don't be mad. He only told *me*, nobody else, and he was totally chill about it. Said you two had a good laugh about it after."

"Yeah, I suppose."

"So, seriously: How many did you eat, like, twelve?"

"Five!" I said, and Andy just laughed.

"Just so you know: Nobody likes creative pizza or creative blow jobs. They're good just the way they are."

"Duly noted," I said. "Now if you wouldn't mind minding your own business, I have a person to kill."

"*Two*," he reminded me, walking off.

In our quest for equality (or, you know, popularity . . . whatever) we decided it was time to throw our own party. All this we're-so-lucky-to-be-invited crap was yesterday's news. We had come into our own. We *were* cool. We *had* friends. So when Xandra said that her parents were going out of town for the weekend it was a total no-brainer:

Party at Xandra's.

(Sounds like the title of a skin flick, doesn't it? Not that I've ever even seen a porno, not a real one, anyway—and I'm not sure they actually make whole movies anymore in the Internet age, from what I've heard—but you have to admit: That would make a pretty good title. Anything with "Party" and an "X" word in the title is a good porn title.)

You should have heard us trying to plan the thing. We wanted it to be really special, and while we wouldn't have the funds or the historical legends of Skyler Parties, we did have creativity and a whole bunch of it. We took over a picnic table at a city park near the school and hashed it out over a bagful of take-out burritos (no sour cream or guac for me—stupid diet).

"What about a Les Mis party?" Xandra asked.

"Les *no*," Anya and I said simultaneously.

"*Lay* down and think of something better," Emily said, playing off the pronunciation of *Les*. "We do want *straight* boys to come too."

"Heh-heh," Anya said. "You said 'we want straight boys to *come*.'"

"Settle down, Beavis," I said.

"Point taken," Xandra said. "I'm not good at this stuff."

"Heh-heh," Anya said. "You said 'point taken.'"

"I don't even get that one," Kura said.

"Xandra wants to . . . um . . . take in a point," Anya said.

"Perv!" Xan said.

Cue more friendly shit-talk for another fifteen minutes or so, until we finally got back on point:

"How about a Pimps and Hoes party?" Dahlia said.

"I'll be a pimp," Grace said.

"You'd make a fine pimp," I nodded.

"And you—" Grace started, turning to Anya.

"Done and *done*," Anya groaned, pelting her with a chip.

Grace swung around to me. "And you a fine ho," Grace said. "Emphasis on the *fiiiine*."

Emily chimed in: "What about a White Party?"

"Racist!" Kura yelled. "I want to go too!"

Commence more laughter and pelting.

"No White Party," Anya said. "Too P. Diddy."

"A Black-and-White Party?" Emily offered. "That could be cool."

"We could do our own C-and-C party," I said.

Everyone stopped and stared.

"Dude, I do *not* have that kind of bank," Emily said.

"Our *own* version," I clarified. "Not Skyler's. Cupcakes and Cocktails."

"I'm not mad at that," Grace said.

"They're all too gimmicky," Anya said. "We can have cupcakes, and of course we'll have cocktails, but what about just having a fun party?"

"Okay," I said. "But it would be fun if we did something besides 'Party at Xandra's.' Karaoke?"

"I have a karaoke machine!" Emily screamed. "My sister got it for her engagement party and she and her fiancé didn't want it, so it's at our house!"

"*American Idol* party?" Anya said. "What's better than getting drunk and butchering your favorite songs in front of all your class-mates?"

"Nothing?" Grace said. "Well, pie. Pie is better. Cupcakes. Cake. Pizza. Those little puff pastries, I forget what they're called. Doritos . . ."

"Thanks for that, Grace," I said. "I'm eating a fucking burrito with no guacamole or sour cream and she wants to throw a Let's Get Type-Two Diabetes party."

"Shut up, you're rocking an eight-pack and bitching about extra calories," Dahlia protested, punctuating her point with a three-chip barrage.

"Sure, *AI* party," Anya said. "Can I be Simon Cowell?"

"He's not even on the show anymore," I said, "but, yes, I'd ex-pect nothing less."

"I like this," Emily said. "You guys?"

"I'm game," I said. And it was decided. A simple party with a karaoke machine and some good vibes was the move.

Word spread around school that we were having a party, and by the end of that day, it looked like we were going to have a full house. I'd told my mom we were having a study session/sleepover and, well, technically it was half true. I was sleeping over at Xandra's—all the girls were—we just weren't studying.

We all chipped in and bought alcohol—for the record, there's just no "legal age" when it comes to most stores. (Sorry, parents. I'm sure you're totally shocked, seeing as how you were all getting hooked up by the corner store when you were sixteen too. Sure helps that most of the attendants are only a couple of years older, they're making minimum wage and they're easily swayed by a couple of pretty girls and a ten-dollar tip. Which is not to say I'm promoting underage drinking. I'm just saying it happens. Buying alcohol when you're underage is as easy as taking candy from a baby—which, aside from the fact that it's probably not all that difficult, is a cruel saying. What kind of monster are you that you want to take away a poor baby's candy? Buy your own candy, asshole!)

So, yeah, we put together a pretty good collection of booze, while also agreeing upon some ground rules: Cut off anyone who's overindulging, an unfortunate reality at any teen soiree, and collect car keys as needed, just like John Cusack was the key master in *Say Anything*: "You must chill! You must chill! I have hidden your keys! *Chill!*" (One of my dad's favorite movies, and later one of mine as well.)

Grace and I spent all of Friday and part of Saturday together baking cupcakes, which was actually really fun (though I ate so much frosting I almost hurled), and the end result was about 150 cupcakes that looked good and tasted even better. (We'd know; we started with 156.)

Decorating was less about beautifying and more about hiding the china and the expensive stuff. We've all seen *Risky Business* (another of Dad's faves), and not that there were any insanely expensive crystal eggs—or hookers expected to arrive—but we didn't want to take a chance and get Xandra in trouble. The idea was to minimize all possible risk while creating the best party space possible.

By eight we were all there, waiting for our first guests to arrive. It was me, Anya, Grace, Kura, Dahlia, Xandra and Emily, hanging out in the kitchen, eating Doritos, playing Celebrity.

For the uninitiated, Celebrity is a game in which you have two teams of however many, and each member of the team writes the names of ten different celebrities on ten different slips of paper. Then they're all folded up and placed into a hat or a bowl or some such receptacle. When the game starts, one person will pick a name from the hat and give clues about who the celebrity is while the team-mates have to guess. Each team has one minute to guess as many names as they can and when the hat/bowl/planter/fishbowl/what-have-you is empty, whichever team got the most right is the winner.

We'd played three rounds when we noticed it was eight forty-five and nobody had arrived.

Great, I thought. *Skyler got the whole school to pretend they were coming and then bail on us.*

But I didn't dare say that out loud. *This is being a leader,* I told myself. *Do what Noel would do. Stay strong. Never show fear. And burn down Skyler's fucking house if—*

Which is when the doorbell rang.

Oh thank God.

But when I got to the door it was only Chris and Andy.

Now, don't get me wrong, Chris and Andy were two of our favorite boys—certainly mine and Emily's—but did they really count as party guests? Technically, while they straddled many groups of friends, they were also kind of part of ours.

But in the end . . . who cared? We had everyone we knew well right there. Everyone we liked. Did we need the drama and the judgment and people looking around, inspecting our party and @imatotalfuckingbitch tweeting "Lame Sauce!" whatever the hell that meant? No. Sure the boys were outnumbered, but when do boys *ever* bitch about that? (Maybe the gay ones, understandably, but not these two.) All that meant was that we wouldn't do too many duets.

So just like in *Risky Business* when Tom Cruise's character says, "Sometimes you just gotta say, 'What the fuck?'" we just said, "Fuck it! This is our party, and we're gonna make the most of it, eat a shitload of cupcakes—call this my cheat day for the next month or so—sing our asses off and have a good time." Sure, it was kind of the opposite because in *Risky Business* the party got out of control, and in our life, this party was more controlled than a church picnic, but the sentiment was the same.

And so we ate, and we sang, and we danced, and we had fun. *A lot* of fun.

But then another thing happened. People started arriving at the door. Much to our nerdy and punctual surprise, the party wasn't a flop. It was just the opposite. Pretty much everyone came. Turns out that being late isn't just fashionable—it's how parties work. Want to get your party cranking at eight? Better start that fucker at *five*. Soon the door was opening and closing so often people didn't even bother ringing the doorbell or knocking. There were people we knew, people we didn't (we were all inclusive with the invite, seeing as how that was what we were all about), and by eleven, the place was jam-packed.

Once the party started filling up, everyone was having a fun time, but it wasn't exactly "blowing up," whatever that means. That all changed with one brilliant observation by Anya. Looking over the karaoke catalogue, she noticed that only about two percent of that sucker ever gets used, and there's a *ton* of crazy shit in there—everything from old pop standards to traditional country music to hardcore thrash metal to Motown to Southern rap—you name it, it's in there. But people were just singing the songs they liked (or at least knew the words to). The usual suspects.

So Anya turned everything on its head. She declared that Karaoke Night was over—and "We Pick It" Karaoke Night was about to start. Here's the deal: Everyone had to perform at least one song, but the singer couldn't pick the song. The crowd got to pick. And of course, the crowd picked what (they assumed, at least) would be the weirdest thing for that person to sing.

First up was sweet little Sammi Wu, a straight-A student and all-around perfect daughter, who was required to sing "Get Low" by Lil Jon, a song where the rapper goes on about "till the sweat drips off" his private parts, and—believe it or not—it gets even nastier in places. (Google it if you're curious.) A macho ROTC student named Eric Bryant ended up with "My Neck, My Back" by Khia, a female rapper who goes on about the many places on her body she demands to have licked—and her neck and her back are only the beginning, trust me. Just like Sammi, he gave it his sincere best effort, and it was *hilarious*.

After that, it was on, with everything from a girl who never listened to anything but Black Eyed Peas (I know, and I'm sorry) wrestling with Hank Williams, Sr., and a girl whose record collection started and ended with Taylor Swift doing her best with a tune by a band named Cannibal Corpse. It was all awesome (yes, for real awesome), and everyone at the party was totally losing their minds. They were recording everything and uploading it to YouTube on the spot.

But it got even better when the "performers" surprised everybody, like when Dante Lopez took the stage. (His real name was

Carlos, but everyone called him Dante, because he played bass in a death metal band, was covered in ink from head to toe and had so many piercings he was practically bionic.) We tossed Dante a Clay Aiken tune . . . and he totally fucking *killed* it!

He wasn't the only one. We had the goth chick who turned out to be a secret Toby Keith fan, nailing "I Love This Bar," every line just perfect. Then there was D'von Jordan, the starting tailback on the football team, and more than a few of us assumed he wouldn't have a clue about a Florence + the Machine song, and of course he totally crushed it. Seriously, everyone there lost their minds on the spot.

There were a few more like that, and *a lot* more humiliating but funny failures, but overall, it was totally epic. Everyone got into it, the trash-talking was all in good fun, and it just turned into the weirdest and most hilarious "concert" ever.

Before the party was even over, some of the performances were blowing up on YouTube. Performances were getting shared and liked on Facebook pretty much in real time and anyone who wasn't at the party sure as hell must have wished they were.

It couldn't have been better. I found myself bonding with people I never would have had the courage to even speak to a year ago, and the other Invisibles were doing the same. Everything was different. It was beyond amazing.

And then sometime between one and two a.m. the cops showed up!

Yes, I know this sounds über-dorky, being excited about having the cops come to break up your party . . . but for me and the Invisibles and especially Xandra, who is drawn to drama in all shapes and forms, having a party so successful that the cops had to break it up was a badge of honor. (It helped that her super-cool uncle Christian—yes, that's his name—came by to smooth it over with the cops, which was no surprise because he stuck around to drink and flirt with every teen girl who'd talk to him for even five seconds.)

Nothing too totally insane happened. No one got married to a stripper, no one stole anything from Mike Tyson, and there was no sequel party that just repeated the exact same shit that happened at the first party. But it was still kick-ass, everyone got home safely (if somewhat the worse for wear) and it was a massive success that was *the talk of the school* come Monday.

You could just tell how much things had changed that next week at school: We had finally secured our place. The lines between who was popular—hell, what popularity even *meant*—were officially blurred.

Our little group has always been...

—NIRVANA

"Smells Like Teen Spirit"

CHAPTER
17

Spirit Week was fast approaching. The theme was "candy," but each day was going to have a specific motif and the students in each grade had designed their own color and candy-themed T-shirts for Friday.

The freshmen were Kit-Kats. Their red T-shirts had pictures of Kit-Kats with the caption, GIVE US A BREAK! WE'RE ONLY FRESHMEN! The sophomores chose white, and the standard Hershey's Milk Chocolate Bar was our candy, but our shirts showed it nestled between graham crackers and roasted marshmallows. Our slogan: YOU KNOW YOU WANT S'MORE OF US. The juniors went the obvious route: green shirts, Junior Mints. Their slogan: MINTY FRESH WITH ONE YEAR LEFT! Not their best work, IMHO. (You'd think juniors would be the most spirited of all, but they seem distracted by all the shit that goes on right in that sixteen-seventeen range that they half-ass a lot of this school stuff. Wonder if we'll be like that next year. Probably.)

As for the seniors, they chose black shirts with silver Hershey's Kisses. Slogan: KISS OUR ASS GOOD-BYE! . . . Well, that was the *first* caption, at least, as in it lasted for all of first period. After that, Principal Dash put out an announcement that any seniors wearing the shirt needed to either cover up "ass" completely with masking tape or, preferably, change shirts if possible. More than a little bitching commenced from the seniors, but almost all complied by lunchtime, probably not wanting to do anything that risked their upcoming graduation.

Of course, that struck me as massive dumbassedness, and maybe material for an *Abby Invisible* down the road—hopefully with enough details changed that the administrators wouldn't notice until after it published. I can turn on my TV any time of day and hear fifteen words worse than "ass." I can go on the Internet and find stuff in ten seconds that would make Lady Gaga blush. What exactly was West Hollywood High shielding us from?

Like Anya would say to me later, "They don't give a shit what we wear. They're just terrified that some soccer mom who watches Fox News and *The 700 Club* religiously will lose her shit if the school let her kid wear a shirt that says 'ass.'"

A day later, the seniors were sporting a new Hershey's Kisses shirt around school, one that simply stated "KISS US GOOD-BYE." Well, that was the new *official* shirt. Once off campus, a number of daredevil seniors could be seen at local malls, coffee shops or fast-food joints wearing the Super-Special Senior Spirit Week Variant T-Shirt, which pictured West Hollywood burned to the ground and the caption: PRINCIPAL DASH, KISS MY ASH. As an artist, I had to admit some appreciation for that one.

Speaking of artistry, I was busy working on my latest cartoon, content in the knowledge that the rest of the Invisibles were finishing up work on the website. Everything at school felt like it was happening in Technicolor and I was totally cataloguing the random bullshit that goes down day to day at school for the strip. I'd overheard Skyler in the locker room talking about her hair appointment and inspiration struck.

In the opening frame, the Popular Shallow Girl "Tyler" is sitting next to her friend "Maddie" at lunch. Abby Invisible is eating lunch by herself off to the side. Tyler asks Maddie when she's getting her hair done for the underage club that night. Maddie replies that she's looking forward to it—"It's only ten dollars to get in tonight!"—but she'll just be styling her hair at home.

Tyler says that's the worst thing she's ever heard, and she starts rambling about how she'll be at the salon for three hours after school: "Nico is giving me highlights here, lowlights there—I call them all 'hotlights' though, because they make you feel hotter."

Maddie says that must cost a lot. Tyler says, "Oh, it's only two hundred dollars—just this week's allowance."

Next frame, Maddie walks away with the thought bubble "Jeez . . ."

Next frame. Off to the side, Abby chimes in, "I'm sure your hair will look amazing for the club, Tyler." Tyler replies, "Oh, I can't go to the club. I'm out of money."

Then we have a completely silent frame showing the two characters, followed by the final frame, as Tyler turns to Abby: "Hey, can I borrow ten dollars?"

I showed it to Chris during lunch and held my breath for his verdict.

"It's very funny," he said, but he hit me with a little side-eye as he did.

"What?" I asked.

"What?" he replied, playing dumb.

"I saw that look."

He weighed his reply for a second. "Hope I never piss you off enough to end up in one of these."

"Hey!" I said, feeling slightly hurt. "I'd never."

"I hope not," he said.

It's funny how paranormal romances had been all the rage for the past decade. Forget navigating a relationship with a vampire or werewolf—it was hard enough to have a relationship with a normal human boy!

"You're not fodder for my comic," I said, then raised my eyebrows. "I have much better uses for you."

"Oh, yeah?" he said, smiling, leaning closer. "Like what?"

"Full-time kissing partner," I said.

"I like that one." He leaned in and kissed me sweetly; we both smiled.

"I'm glad."

"Hey, I have something for you," he said, reaching into his pocket.

"What?" I said, trying to angle myself to get a better view of his hand.

"Close your eyes," he said.

I tried to maintain my smile so it didn't get too unwieldy as I closed my eyes. He took my hand and placed something in it, then he closed my fingers around it.

"Okay, you can look now."

I opened my eyes and my hand. In my palm was a silver chain with a guitar pick on it, and on the pick was an engraved I PICK YOU with a little heart underneath.

It was the most adorable thing I'd ever seen.

"Are you kidding me?" I said, now certain that I was in full-gums-mode, but there was nothing I could do. I was too happy. "This is the cutest thing ever! Where did you get this?"

"I'm not telling," he said. "You like it?"

"Love," I said, and if he wanted to read into it he could go ahead and apply that word to how I felt about him too.

He smiled. "I'm glad."

"What's the occasion?" I asked. "Because if it's an anniversary or something—clearly I screwed up."

"No occasion," he said. "I just saw it and thought, 'Too bad neither Hailey or I play guitar because that would be a damn cute gift if one of us did,' and then I thought, 'Fuck it! We don't have to play guitar. I still pick you, dammit!'"

I laughed and leaned in to give him a kiss, and then I spun around, pulling my hair up and out of the way.

"Help me put it on," I said, and he obliged, and I was happy. Really freaking happy.

"I pick you too, in case you're not sure," I said.

"You better!" he said with a smirk, and I wondered to myself if this was the way people in love songs felt. I might not play any instruments, but I could definitely come up with some super-cheesy romantic lyrics right then.

Meanwhile, Dahlia ratcheted up our plan to a new level of virtual viciousness by creating a Web application designed to deliver an emotional gut punch Skyler's crew would never see coming. Proving that even her amazing tech skills were virtually outweighed by her creativity, she'd created a What Kind of Dog Are You? application that allowed people to answer a few multiple-choice questions to find out their answer. Seems innocent enough, right? Kind of like one of those Australian dingoes, those really cute wild dogs who look all cuddly and sweet, but they're not anything like cool domesticated dogs like Benji or Beethoven or Air Bud, so if you catch the wrong one in the outback, it will tear out your throat or eat your baby or tear out your baby's throat while eating you, and long story short, you should really just think twice before petting a dingo.

So Dahlia had designed, appropriately enough, the dingo of all What Kind of Dog Are You? sites. Looks like a nice, fun way to pass a few hours, until you wake up a few hours later to find it gnawing the flesh off your femur.

It was inspired. And it worked like a regular application for the majority of users, providing nice, innocent examples of dogs that met the criteria based on how the users answered the questions. Dahlia's application required users to sign in with their actual Facebook accounts, so we knew exactly who signed in and when.

When anyone from the Bitch Squad signed in, the user experience was completely different. It didn't matter how they answered the questions; they always got the same predetermined result, and when it popped up, the application changed in appearance, color, font and everything else, with the name "BitchBook" suddenly appearing at the top.

Now, that would be fun even if only Skyler and her minions could see it, but it's *way* more fun when everyone can. Which is why when each user signed in, the permissions let the application share the results with everyone else. Thus everyone who participated got a BitchBook sidebar with their results that showed the top BitchBook results. You could click on any of them and get the results for Skyler, Jericha, et al. And of course, most people did, because everyone was a lot more interested in clicking something called BitchBook, featuring everyone's favorite bitches, than the rest of the application.

Skyler was a Yorkshire terrier, tiny but mighty. Yippy and bitchy. Long silky hair and obsessed with what to wear. History taught us the Yorkshire terrier was developed in England during the mid-nineteenth century, and the dog's main purpose was to control the rat population in the coal pits and cotton mills. This was fitting if you considered that Skyler had deemed anyone who was not completely vapid and met her beauty standards to be a rat. Her purpose was to destroy the spirit and self-confidence of those she targeted. Yorkshire terriers are known to have a "big dog" attitude (yup), and a self-assured, important manner (double yup). (Actually, make that *yip*.)

As you might have figured, we had indeed Photoshopped Skyler's head on to one of the ugliest, nastiest-looking Yorkshire terriers we could find. It helped that a fairly unflattering picture of Skyler had made its way into last year's school yearbook—I guess that point I made to her forever ago about controlling your image by controlling the yearbook wasn't complete bullshit after all. So we had a bad picture of her on one extremely nasty Yorkshire terrier, which was—well, what's the most polite way to say this— taking a dump. Yep, that's the most polite way I can think of. Plus Skyler has this sort of constipated look on her face in the picture, so it worked perfectly.

The Skyler entry was the most inspired, but we didn't let her loathsome ladies off the hook at all.

Cassidy was a Pekingese. These lion dogs live a pampered existence and hail from China. They're known to be aloof with strangers but loyal and protective of their home. Substitute "Skyler" for "home" and there you had it. Pekes are known to be stubborn, but if you remain in charge, training will eventually be successful. And Skyler had trained her well.

We had snagged a great cheerleading pic of Cassidy throwing her head back during a cheer, with a look on her face of great, let's say, pleasure. So when we also tracked down a picture of a Pekingese being mounted by another dog, well—we knew we'd struck gold.

Jericha was a basset hound: short legged, with long sweeping ears. (Her ears weren't long, but her hair sure was.) The breed is known for working best in packs—and so was she. Not having an opinion of her own unless it was Skyler-approved, she was a perfect third or fourth to have around to reaffirm whatever nonsense Skyler was shilling on any given day. The perfect follower, a total mindless "yes man"—but a girl. A "yes girl." Which, rumor had it, was an accurate term for Jericha on more than one front.

To fulfill the metaphor, we'd considered putting Jericha's head on a dog at the back of a sled dog team—unfortunately, it turns out there aren't any basset hounds in the Iditarod or any other sled dog races.

Thankfully, we did come across a picture of a basset hound sniffing another dog's butt, which was good enough. Thanks to Dahlia's mastery of all things both technical and artistic—seriously, she should be working for James Cameron—we ended up with an amazingly realistic image of Jericha with her face up a dog's ass. It was perfect. It was seamless. If Jericha's mom had seen it, she would have asked her daughter, "Honey, why on earth did you have your nose up some dog's ass? Oh, and when did the rest of you turn into a basset hound?"

And then there was Daniella. With her parental pedigree hailing directly from the fashion world, it only made sense that she was a "designer dog." Status is everything to owners of these dogs, and the Maltese-Poodle mix was perfect, because it's completely contrived. Small in stature, the Maltipoo—also known as the Maltepoo, the Malt-A-Poo, and other insanely stupid shit—is occasionally mischievous. You know, like buying a dress that Skyler saw and wanted first. Despite its mischievous streak, this contrived hybrid dog is also kind of a dopey, runty little dog, sure to get its ass kicked at any dog park or simply when visiting a playful kitten.

The only downside to this call is that Maltipoos really are cute. Like crazy adorable cute. And it's hard to find a viciously funny photo that involves a Maltipoo. Well, unless you have a team of girls working day and night to find just the right photo and an amazingly talented computer genius/Photoshop queen running the show. In which case . . . it's not all that hard to rig a believable image of a Maltipoo with Daniella's head lapping up some highly questionable pile of something on the side of the road. What is that pile of something? A tossed-away half of a hamburger? Road-kill? Dog poop? All of the above? Hard to tell, but the Daniella-poo is lapping it up like caviar out of a silver spoon, which presumably has been her morning breakfast since birth.

Overall, it was brilliant, a smash success. It not only humiliated the skanks, but it ruined their *own* opportunity to pull the prank on us and/or anyone else Skyler had targeted—basically anyone who objected to bulimia as a necessary evil or dared to have an independent thought on occasion. The application was being tweeted and Facebooked around the school at a furious pace, and once the Bitch-Book sidebar popped up and everyone saw the Bitch Squad results, it went "viral" in no time flat. The whole thing spread around school faster than food poisoning at an all-you-can-eat salad bar. Everyone was eating it up . . . well, everyone but the Bitch Squad, presumably. As of fourth period, I had yet to cross paths with anyone from the Skyler Squadron, but I could imagine how it was going down.

What I hadn't imagined was the reaction I'd get from someone who was (currently, at least) outside Skyler's circle, someone who meant the world to me, someone I never expected this would bother.

"What were you *thinking*?"

Chris glared at me, arms crossed over his chest. We sat at a corner table in the library, a free period for us both. I was trying to read his face, but I'd never seen it like this before, what looked like equal parts anger and disgust.

I sighed. "I was thinking we were going to beat them at their own game."

"Jesus, Hailey," he said. "That dog show prank—I told you about that in confidence."

"I'm sorry," I said. "I didn't think you'd be mad."

"You didn't *think*—that's sure right."

I wasn't sure what to say. Obviously, I hadn't told Chris about the plan ahead of time, and all this time I told myself I didn't want to bother him with the details, that he wouldn't be interested in our silly little girl-drama. That this was between me and Skyler, and it's not like I expect to be consulted every time he gets into a fight with some dude at PE.

Well, that's what I'd been telling myself, anyway. I guess there was another reason I hadn't told Chris what we were planning: I didn't want him to object, to try to talk me out of doing it. And also, if I'm really honest, I didn't want him to see the meanness that I was capable of. But Skyler *deserved* what she got, and so did the rest of them, if only for enabling her.

Still, I didn't expect Chris to be this upset.

"Chris, I'm sorry. You're right. That was private and between us, and I shouldn't have used that information to . . ."

"To do what she was going to do, only ten times *worse*," he finished for me. "That was a total Skyler move."

"You're right," I said. "I'm sorry."

"You remember how that conversation happened, right? It was me telling you why I broke up with her. Because I didn't want to be with someone who would go that far out of her way to hurt people."

"Chris—it's not like that. Jeez, this was *her* idea. She's done awful shit to a lot of people, and this was going to be the cherry on top!"

"Yeah. But she *didn't* do it."

"Only because we did it *first!*"

"No," Chris said, staring at the library carpet like he was counting every hideous blue fiber. "She wasn't going to do it."

"What?"

"She'd changed her mind," he said. "That's the word I got. Decided it wasn't worth it, that all this pranking shit had gotten out of hand. So I thought we'd have a nice, chill Spirit Week, we'd all just have fun and screw around and have fun, and now . . . this."

I just sat there feeling crushed. We'd put all that work into the BitchBook prank, sweating over every last detail, trying to strike a blow for everyone Skyler had mocked, teased and ridiculed, and now Chris was making me feel like an Al Qaeda operative.

And what really hurt was that I was realizing he might be right.

"Chris," I said softly, feeling around for some common ground. "I know you're upset, and I'm sorry. I didn't know she'd changed her mind. For all I knew, she was planning something that would have crushed a lot of girls, most likely including me and a lot of my friends. You know what she's capable of. We felt we had to—"

"Don't tell me about what 'we' felt, Hailey," Chris said. "They do what you tell them to do. *You* wanted to do this. A little payback on Skyler, one more shot at my ex, whatever. You could have talked to me about it, but you didn't. You took something I told you, betrayed my trust and put together this little operation behind my back."

I felt sick. I literally thought I was going to throw up. Everything he was saying was true. I wished I had a time machine to go back and do it all over again—or rather, not do it in the first place. Everything was suddenly different. The way he looked at me, the way he felt about me, and I deserved it. I'd ruined everything.

"You know what's even worse?" he asked.

"There's something worse?" I couldn't imagine what that could be.

"It was shitty, the way Skyler acted and the things she did. But at least I understood why she did it. I could recognize where some of her insecurities came from." He looked down at his sneakers and shook his head. Then he looked me dead in the eyes.

"You *have* no excuse."

He walked away, and I opened my mouth, but nothing would come out. There was nothing to say. He was right. And he obviously knew more about Skyler's family issues than he'd let on. Probably because he knew how to keep private things private, unlike me: Asshole Extraordinaire. Maybe that should be my next comic. Captain Asshole: able to break trust and ruin relationships in a single bound!

It felt like all my internal organs had been removed and replaced with rocks. I staggered from the table, feeling like I'd been hit by a car, and you'd think I would have been able to escape the library without any more incident, but you'd be wrong.

I'd only made it eight steps. Skyler Brandt stood right in front of me.

That's it, I'm totally going to learn krav maga.

Looking at Skyler though, I didn't think any martial arts would be necessary. While it wasn't too hard to figure out Chris's face—furious would be a good catch-all term for that—I'd never seen Skyler look like this before. I had no idea what to make of it. She looked . . . I don't know, I guess older somehow. That's the only way I can phrase it.

"Hailey," she said.

"Skyler," I replied, having no freaking idea what else to say.

She moved in close, until she was less than a foot from me, and looked me right in the eye.

"I knew I saw something in you, way back last fall," she said. "That was a really good prank. A little . . . um, *derivative* is the word, I think—and yeah, I do know words of more than three syllables— but really well done."

Get my defenses down and then stab me in the gut with your switchblade, I thought. *Might as well. Nothing but rocks in there right now anyway.*

I'd gotten all of my apologizing out of the way with Chris. Betraying Chris's trust was wrong, no question, but I had no interest in doing the same for Skyler. For all I knew, she was still planning something horrible before the week was out.

"Thanks," I said. "Learned from the best."

"Oh, Hailey." Skyler grinned. "You didn't learn that from me." She leaned in close, a couple of inches from my ear, and I briefly worried she would bite it off. Instead, she simply whispered:

"Being vicious comes naturally to you."

And then she was gone, leaving behind only a faint trail of Lolita Lempicka perfume.

I left the library, closing in on my locker, just hoping at this point to get through the day. The rocks in my stomach now felt replaced by a huge swirl of emotions, and I could feel myself on the edge of tears. Someone grabbed my arm and spun me around, and for a second I thought my nonviolent interaction with Skyler had just been a prelude to her getting five guys from the wrestling team to beat me up.

Instead, thankfully, it was Anya.

"Nine-one-one," she said.

"No shit!" I replied, barely holding back the tears.

"Wait, what?" she asked.

"Emergency!" I said. "Everything's awful. Everything's ruined—"

"Whoa," she said. "Me. Emergency. My emergency."

Insane as it sounds, I almost felt better for a second that someone else had an emergency. Misery loves company, right? And I was miserable enough that I could use a whole shitload of company.

"Okay, Anya. What's your emergency?"

"Bathroom."

Girl of few words.

I followed Anya into the bathroom, where she did the usual ritual, checking under all the stalls to make sure nobody was there. Jennifer Hess was in stall number three. We could tell by the tattoo on her ankle—a band of flowers going all the way around.

Neither of us said anything.

"This isn't awkward or anything," Jennifer said from behind the door.

"Are you almost done?" Anya asked.

"I didn't know there was a time limit," she replied.

We'd obviously interrupted the poor girl so I felt kinda bad.

"Sorry," I said. "Take your time."

"Or don't," Anya said, giving me a what-the-fuck? look.

Finally the flush came and Jennifer walked out of the stall, adjusting her jeans, glaring at us both.

"We said we were sorry," I snapped at her.

She glared for another second, but she seemed to reconsider and the corners of her mouth curled into a slight smile. "Whatever," she said. "Enjoy your conversation. I don't need to see my head glued to a shih tzu."

She washed her hands and left as I turned to Anya.

"So what's going on?" I asked.

"You first," she said.

"But you said you had a nine-one-one."

"It can wait, you look upset."

"I fucked up," I said. "Really bad."

I lost it then. I didn't even mean to. The tears started streaming down my face before I'd even started to cry. I don't even know if that makes sense, but they were just involuntary. I started to bawl, right there in the bathroom next to where it said "Nicole Herzog does anal" in blue Sharpie. The janitors hadn't cleaned it up yet and for some reason I couldn't stop staring at it on the wall. Even Anya noticed.

She turned around and read the message on the wall, and then looked at me crying, and got this weird, concerned look on her face. "Ooh. So—"

"What?" I sniffed.

"I mean . . ." She pointed at the wall. "Is it . . . um . . . what are you . . ."

Jeez, Anya.

"No! God, no!"

"Okay!" she said. "Hey, I had to ask! You kept looking at it. . . ."

"Ugh," I replied, putting a hand over my face.

"And it occurred to me that I haven't seen you sit down today, and . . ."

"Anya!"

"You *were* walking a little weird just now, and . . ."

"Oh my God!"

"I'm sorry," she said. We both laughed a little, a welcome mood shift . . . but it didn't hold. I didn't even know what Anya's issue was—and as bad as this sounds, I wasn't dying to find out—because mine was cataclysmic.

"Chris hates me," I said.

"What? Why?"

"When he told me about the dog show prank, it was an example of why he couldn't date Skyler anymore. He was telling me exactly what he *didn't* want in a girlfriend. So what do I take from that? *Hey, let's steal her idea and do it to* them. Fucking brilliant, huh?"

"Wow," Anya said. "I didn't know it went down that way. So that's why you didn't tell him about it before."

"Yeah. He feels like I abused his trust and, I don't know, like what we did is just as disgusting as what Skyler planned to do."

Anya was quiet for a bit.

"Say something!"

"Hailes, I want to make you feel better, but . . ." She looked at me empathetically. "I can see why he'd be upset."

"I know," I said. "Like I said. I fucked up."

"You didn't think something like this could happen?"

"I don't know," I said. "This year has just been so crazy. We were doing good things, right? The Invisibles, all the stuff we got from Noel's journal—I was really *proud* of all that, you know? Like we weren't putting up with bullshit anymore, we weren't going out like that."

"Yeah, dude," Anya said. "We kicked ass."

"And this just seemed like the same thing, right? It was proactive. Creative."

"Dahlia did *amazing* fucking work."

"Amazing, right?" I said. "Ten times better than whatever Skyler would have done."

"A hundred times. A million. But she didn't do it."

Ugh. "Yeah," I said. "And Chris said she wasn't even *going* to do it."

Anya looked confused. "What? Like he made the whole thing up?"

"No, no," I said. "I mean . . . she came up with this plan last year,

285

the whole Westminster Dog Show, all the details. She told Chris, he broke up with her, new school year, you and I hang out, Invisibles, all that shit. I guess at some point she just decided not to do it."

"Doesn't matter," Anya said. "She's done enough shit. I don't feel bad for her. That's not the problem. The problem is—"

"That Chris told me in confidence, and I took it and turned it into our prank, totally behind his back."

"Winner, winner, chicken dinner."

We stood there for a second. A freshman we knew from chorus popped in to pee, and she was a nice kid, so we didn't tell her to go down the hall.

I was still feeling sorry for myself, but it occurred to me I was kind of being an asshole—Anya said she was having an emergency, and here I was, making it all *The Hailey Show with Hailey, featuring Hailey.*

"Hey," I said. "I'm sorry, what was your thing?"

"It can wait."

"No, it can't. You listened patiently and pleasantly to my unending tale of sadness and woe. What's the deal?"

She sighed and rolled her eyes, almost like she was embarrassed to talk about it.

"It's Andy," she said, crossing her arms in front of her.

"Okay, so . . . the Andy and Emily thing?"

I don't know whether you could call Andy and Emily the sophomore class's "hot couple"—I would have hoped people would have been calling me and Chris that, at least before today's nightmare—but they'd obviously been going strong. Emily had stars in her eyes whenever she talked about him, and Andy, as best I could tell, appeared to reciprocate.

Anya seemed to be considering her words carefully. "No, not Andy and Emily. Well . . . yes, but no . . ."

"So what?"

"We made up, Andy and me," she said.

"I know. I was there."

A long pause. "Okay. I . . . we . . . it's not *that* kind of made up."

It just hung there for a while. The bathroom door swung open, two girls we didn't know, and Anya made them leave. I forget the specifics, but there was something in there about their asses and a cheese grater if they didn't get out of there right now. Something along those lines. (Cut me some slack. Pretty much everything from that day is a blur.)

Alone again, we just looked at each other.

"So . . . ," I started.

"Yeah," Anya said.

"Wow," I said. "How did this happen? *When* did this happen? *Where* did this happen? *Why—*"

"Last night. He came over, we were talking. We were just talking."

"Yeah?"

"Yeah," Anya said. "And then there was naked."

"Oh my God!"

"Yeah. It just happened."

"That doesn't just happen!"

"Oh, it does," she said with a smirk. "Look, I told you *how* things ended with us and you know *why* things ended with us, but what I didn't tell you is that before the . . . *situation*, we were really happy. Then it got all screwed up, and it really didn't seem like we'd ever find our way back." Then she twisted her mouth and shrugged. "But somehow we did."

"Back up the truck," I said. "What started this?"

Anya exhaled and chewed on her cheek, the way she does when she's contemplating a response. Which she does a lot, that whole contemplating-a-response thing. I'm pretty much surprised she still has a cheek.

"Okay," she started. "This is complicated—"

No shit.

"What are you, a Facebook status? Just tell me what happened!"

"I'm trying to," Anya said, and the whole thing reminded me of trying to extract the truth out of my mom: *If only waterboarding were legal, I could save so much time.*

Anya took another deep breath and went for broke: "Okay, fine. It started because I just really needed someone to talk to...."

"Huh? Why couldn't you talk to me?"

Anya sighed. "Because it was *about* you."

I didn't think anything today was still capable of leaving me stunned.

"Anya," I said in my most measured tone. "What the *fuck* are you talking about?"

She sighed yet again, almost like she was getting paid per sigh.

"Hailey," she said, "I don't know—sometimes I feel, like, over the last month or two—it just doesn't seem like what we talked about, the Invisibles, standing up for ourselves, all that—it just doesn't seem like what we've been all about."

"What do you mean?" I asked. "We were getting our asses kicked by Skyler and her crew. She humiliated you and tossed you aside. I only had to spend a few days with her to realize they don't give a shit about anybody but themselves. We banded together. We used Noel's journal and got shit *done*. We—"

"—started acting just like Skyler," Anya said.

What?

The bathroom door opened—a girl presumably trying to get in a quick pee right before final bell, which Anya and I were obviously going to ignore because we had shit to settle. We both gave the girl a death glare.

"I'll just go down the hall," the girl said.

"Good idea," Anya said.

I was still working through Anya's words in my mind. Acting just like Skyler? Bullshit! We were just standing up for ourselves! We didn't start this fight, but we were damn well going to end it! We . . .

But if I was so proud of what I did, why didn't I ever tell Mom or Dad what was going on? Why didn't I tell Chris what I was planning for Skyler and the minions? Why was I just as obsessed with covering our digital tracks, so Principal Dash couldn't tie us to BitchBook in any way, shape or form, as I was at conceiving the plan in the first place? If you're doing the right thing, should you really be spending so much time setting up alibis and plausible deniability?

Still, the sneaking suspicion that I might have gone a touch too far wasn't enough for me to acknowledge it to Anya. Following Noel's lead had done a lot for me, and I didn't see any way in hell she'd show any weakness here.

"Well, Anya, I'm sorry you feel that way," I said. "But I don't see it like that."

"Well, I do," she said. "And I didn't know how to talk about it with you without pissing you off, so I went to Andy. Look, it's hard to tell your best friend how annoyed you are with so-and-so when that so-and-so happens to be your best friend."

"Wow," I said. "So much for trying to help people."

"Like I said . . . it's complicated."

"Apparently."

I felt a million things: hurt, confused, angry—okay, mostly just those three things, but on the feelings scale it felt like a million emotions, because I didn't know which feeling to latch on to.

But that was determined for me when Anya opened her mouth: "Hailey, you've kind of been a bitch lately."

I was steaming. The rocks in my stomach had turned to hot coals. I knew what I wanted to say, but I held it in check for now.

"Well, don't hold back, Anya. By all means."

"Ugh," she said. "Look, this sucks. And the timing couldn't be worse with you being upset about Chris, but this all kind of stems from the same thing. I went to Andy to talk about my concerns with what we were doing, and then . . . that happened, and now I need to confide in you."

"But, Anya, you can—"

"No," she said. "I can't do it without being honest and being honest is just making us fight when I really just needed my friend right now, which is what started it because I feel like my friend is turning into a completely different person. A total *bitch*."

I didn't know what to say. Everything was falling apart. One minute I felt like I was on top of the world, and the next minute I couldn't do anything right. I didn't know how I could possibly fix this.

And I felt cold. And hurt. And *pissed*.

And I looked right at Anya, and I stepped up close to her, as close as Skyler had been when she whispered in my ear, and this is what I said:

"Well, honey, I'm sorry. I'm sorry that my behavior made you so upset and confused that you had no choice but to fuck your baby daddy, even though he's dating one of your very good friends, so I'm just thrilled I could be your convenient excuse for that shit.

And maybe you're right. Maybe Skyler and I have more in common than I thought. Because I guess when Skyler was telling the whole school you were a slut . . . it's because she was right. It's because apparently *you are a slut.*"

And I walked out of the bathroom.

What made us think that we were wise?

—THE VERVE PIPE

"The Freshmen"

CHAPTER

18

After everything I'd just dealt with, I approached the front door of my house with one thing in mind: Go to bed. Go straight to my bedroom, don't let anything or anyone get in my way. Do not pass Go, and . . . well fine, if someone wants to give me two hundred dollars I suppose I would be happy to collect it on my way to bed. I needed to relax, and rest, and make some sort of freaking sense out of the completely insane day I was trapped in.

And a half second after I was inside the door, that was all shot to shit.

"Well, well," her voice rang out.

I recognized her voice instantly. I mean, of course I did. But it was still weird as hell in this context, given that I wasn't expecting at all to hear the voice of . . .

"Noel!"

She was sitting right there on the couch, and I couldn't help but run over and give her a hug, albeit a somewhat awkward hug. Normally I'd be fine hugging my sister, I mean—we weren't close, but she was still my sister. But I was a bit self-conscious, given all the time I'd recently spent in her shoes. I mean her *actual* shoes, a still decent-looking pair of Calypso flats on my feet at that very second.

I had no idea whether she knew I was still annoyed by her ridiculously curt response when I reached out to her by email. If she did, she showed no indication of it. Instead, she did a typical Noel move—she immediately looked down and checked out the Calypso flats. Of *course* she did.

Throughout our youth, she could pick out anything strange or out of place about my appearance from a thousand yards. When I was twelve, I once trimmed my bangs with household scissors. I only took off maybe an eighth of an inch. I didn't think anyone could tell. Eagle-Eye Noel was on it in seconds: "Your bangs are, like, at a forty-five-degree angle. If your bangs were a table, everything would slide off of it." A year later, when I tried putting on fake eyelashes for the first time, I swear she knew it before she even saw my face. I was coming down the stairs from my room, and she was at the kitchen table looking the other way. Before she even looked up, she said, "Hailey, lose the eyelashes. They're way too big. If you blink once you're going to cause a Category-Four hurricane."

I swear the girl was psychic. Maybe a witch? That might explain some things. But apparently little had changed.

"Thought I gave those to Goodwill," Noel said with a slight glance at the shoes. I wished I could click them three times and be whisked off to Kansas. (Although normally I've never had any interest in going to Kansas. I mean, no offense if you live in Kansas, but seriously: *Kansas*?)

"You did," I managed to utter, feeling the trash-picking shame well in my stomach. "But . . . I appropriated them when I realized that my whole wardrobe—much like my entire life—needed a do-over. And your castoffs were a big step up from anything I had."

"Well, I guess it's lucky we're the same size now," Noel said. "You've really changed in the last year. Your hair, your posture . . . and wow, how about your body?"

I braced myself for criticism—I thought my body looked pretty good these days, thank you very much, but I never remembered Noel thinking much of it.

"Hailey, you look great," Noel said. "Seriously. You've lost weight. Your skin's cleared up too, which isn't easy at your age. I was fighting World War Zit all through sophomore year. I even named some of them."

Wow. This was all so unexpected. Not just a visit from Noel, but apparently a very different Noel from the one I'd last spent any time with. After the email disaster, I wondered whether she'd bother giving me the time of day. Now she was being decent, even almost friendly. Which made me suspicious, because seriously, who acts like that? I planted that in my mental file: What's going on with Noel?

Then again, whatever. I wasn't complaining. It was great to see a smiling face after the never-ending nightmare of this day. Things were finally starting to look up.

I smiled at my sister. "Thanks, No," I said, and Noel smiled at the old nickname. "I cut out sugar, well, like, mostly. No more sodas, no more Pop-Tarts for breakfast."

"No more twelve squirts of ketchup on your hash browns?"

"Hell, no more *hash browns*."

I saw her eyebrow raise a little when I said "hell" instead of "heck"—for the longest time, Noel used to punch me in the arm (not powerfully, but not exactly softly either) if I ever said swear words. But this one she let slide. I guess she recognized we were different people now. And "hell" was the least offensive gem in my swear-word arsenal.

"Well, good for you, Hay," she said, using her nickname for me. "Believe me, it's tough when you get to college. There's a reason they call it the Freshman Fifteen."

It was fun hearing the nicknames we'd used as kids. I'd be "Hay" and she'd be "No," which led to conversations like:

"Hey, Hay, have you seen the remote?"

"No, No."

"Hey, Hay, so you don't know?"

"No, No, I don't know . . ."

And so on. All of which seemed pretty funny when we were kids, but seems unbelievably dumb now. I guess that's just how kids' stuff works.

Anyway, getting back to the present: Noel didn't seem to be in a hurry to address the elephant in the room, so I jumped to it:

"Noel, what the heck are you doing here?"

She gave me a strange look. "What? I'm here for the weekend. Mom didn't tell you I was coming?"

"No," I said, thinking, *That's weird. God, can't anything be simple these days?* "Why didn't you send me an email or IM or something?"

Noel shook her head. "I figured Mom would have told you. And you know how busy I've been. Speaking of which: I don't know if you even noticed—"

I did, sis, I sure did.

"—but when you emailed me about all that stuff before, I had a *lot* going on. I meant to send you back something a little, um, *better*, but I know how it goes in high school. All that stuff seems super-important, but it's not. It all works out. Plus, you're tough."

I felt myself get a little annoyed that Noel was dismissing high school as not being important—that's my whole world, and it sure seemed important enough to Noel to write a whole *journal* about it. Then again, Noel thinks I'm tough? Really? When did that happen?

"Hailey," my mom said. She came bounding into the room, wearing dark jeans and a burgundy cashmere sweater, her hair swept up with a few pieces hanging to frame her face in front. (*My mom really is pretty,* I thought.) "I see you found your sister."

"And I wasn't even looking for her," I said. "Why didn't you tell me Noel was coming?"

"Sit down, girls," she said. She tucked one leg behind her and sat on it, the other leg folded in a normal seated position.

Noel and I exchanged a look, and for once it was like we were on the same side: wondering what was going on.

I sat down next to my mom and Noel sat on a chair. Mom placed a striped throw pillow on her lap and inspected it for a moment, then looked up.

"Hailey, I didn't tell you Noel was coming because I didn't want you to worry. And I didn't discuss what was happening with Noel because I just thought it would be better to talk to both of you in person."

"Are you sick?" I blurted. The thought washed over me in a sudden flood of panic. I felt sick and my hands started to sweat and my heart began to race. Dizziness overcame me, and I tried to calm myself because if she was sick then I'd be totally selfish having a freak-out when she was the sick one.

Breathe, I told myself. *Just breathe.*

"No," she said. "I'm not sick."

"Is Dad sick?" I asked.

"Jesus, Hailey," Noel said. "Why don't you just let Mom talk?"

"It's okay," Mom said, as I glared at Noel. Mom continued, "Things have been strange around here, Noel, and Hailey's probably had a lot of questions. And . . . I haven't tried to answer those questions because I didn't know what I was going to do."

Oh, so it's that, I thought. I felt oddly vindicated—something weird had been going on, I was right about that—and yet terrified at the same time.

"Jeez!" Noel said. "So what's the deal?"

(Look who's the interrupter *now*.)

My mom swallowed hard, and then looked at me and then at Noel. "Your father has . . . he hasn't been faithful." She looked at me and then Noel and then back at me, trying to gauge our reactions.

I was genuinely shocked, even though the reality of the situation was unquestionable. It all made sense. It all tied together. You don't want to think your dog ate the neighbor's chicken, but it's hard to be skeptical when he comes home with a mouthful of feathers.

(Yes, that's the kind of insane crap that goes through your mind when you find out your dad's been cheating on your mom.)

I turned to Noel, expecting a similar reaction. I didn't get it.

Noel's face was white. I can honestly say I've never seen her so taken aback. Her hands were over her mouth like she was praying. Praying to be anywhere at that moment but here.

No one was saying anything. It was the most uncomfortable silence of my life. I felt like the wind had been knocked out of me. My dad had always been my buddy. How could he do this? Why?

Noel took a deep breath. When she spoke, she didn't sound like my sister. She sounded like a prosecutor.

"Did you catch him in the act?" Noel asked, biting off each syllable viciously. "Did you hire a private investigator?"

"No and no," Mom said. "In that regard your father was honorable. He admitted to it."

Finally I found a few words. "He admitted to it because he was sorry? And he said he'd never do it again?"

Mom stood up and brushed herself off. "Girls, I didn't even ask if you wanted anything. Hailey? You just got home; are you hungry? Tea?"

"*Tea?!*" Noel and I exclaimed.

"Just tell us the rest," I said.

"I'm not avoiding," Mom said. "I really just thought you might be hungry."

"Hungry?" Noel leapt from her seat. She started pacing around the room. Her hands were shaking, her face still pale. "Jesus, Mom. Jesus."

"Noel, that's not—" Mom began.

My sister hit her with a death glare that ended the sentence. It wasn't fair. Our mom wasn't at fault here, but I was too upset—and too afraid of Noel the Terminator—to say anything.

My mom sat back down. Noel didn't. She leaned against the doorway, arms crossed over her chest. She wasn't even looking at Mom. Her eyes were darting around like a million things were going on behind them.

Mom stared at the floor. "I just thought . . . you might be hungry . . ."

We'd been through this before, pretty much whenever Mom needed to talk about anything serious—when one of our cats got sick and would need to be put down, when a planned dream vacation fell through because my dad's company didn't give out vacation bonuses that year, stuff like that. I think Mom thinks she's softening the blow by stretching these things out, but in reality it's the most torturous type of torture in the torture textbook.

Noel stood. "*Mom: What's. The. Deal?*"

"Yeah, Mom," I echoed. "What's going on? Dad cheated. Got it. What else?"

Mom sat up a little straighter. "Yes. Well . . . your father met someone, and he seems to be . . . quite fond of her."

This I couldn't quite wrap my head around. "I'm sorry, *what?*"

"He loves her," Mom clarified, the words catching on their way out. She cleared her throat.

"Who *is* she?" Noel asked.

"I don't understand," I said. "When did this happen? Things were okay between you and Dad before we moved, right?"

"I thought so," my mom said. "I mean, look—your father and I have been married for nineteen years. Relationships ebb and flow. But we had a pretty solid run."

"Until he effing screwed another woman," I said. "Oh, dear me, I'm sorry. I mean *ebbed.*"

I expected Mom to jump on me over that—forget about *fucked,* even *effed* isn't the sort of thing she liked hearing in her home, much less from her daughter—but she didn't even react. Even Noel, who was more freaked out than I'd ever seen her, looked at me with her mouth hanging open, as if I were suddenly dressed like Nicki Minaj.

"It's bad," Mom said, her eyes reddening. She dabbed at them with a Kleenex. "But it's not the end of the world."

"Are you divorcing him?" Noel asked.

"We're talking about it," Mom answered.

There my stomach went again. A veritable Cirque du Soleil taking place in my stomach.

"Are you moving back to Westchester?" Noel asked.

"We're discussing that too."

"So that's what I walked in on," I said.

Noel spun to face me so fast I could actually feel the breeze. "You *knew* about this?"

I rocked on my heels. "No," I said. "Just—they were arguing, it was weird. I asked Mom but she didn't—"

"You should have called or emailed," Noel said. "If you thought something—"

"Noel, but I emailed you about a bunch of stuff—"

"Not about *this*!" she exclaimed.

"But a bunch of stuff, important stuff, and you blew it off like it was nothing! 'Oh, don't worry about it, Hailey! High school's no big deal, Hailey! You're tough, Hailey!' *Whatever!* We've barely talked since you left. You dropped off the face of the earth. Maybe if I could get in touch with my one and only sister more than every other leap year, this would have *come up*!"

"Hailey, you have no idea how busy I am!" Noel shouted. She was shaking with indignation. "College is *nothing* like high school. I don't have time for stories about who sat next to who at lunch or why your friend 'liked' a photo on Facebook of a girl you both supposedly hate."

"*Girls!*" my mom yelled. That's something she almost never does, and it startled us both. (Being startled was becoming a regular occurrence today, unfortunately.)

Mom continued, "I know you're upset, but stop taking it out on each other. Noel, Hailey didn't know anything about this. And, Hailey, freshman year at college can be very challenging."

Noel and I glared at each other. This wasn't finished. What was especially annoying was that Noel was being such a bitch to me and she didn't even know about my reading (and employing the lessons in) her journal. Then again, as soon as I thought of that, I felt guilty. I needed to tell her about that before the guilt consumed me. And with this revelation about my parents, I couldn't handle any more stress.

Meanwhile, Mom was still going on about how Noel and I needed to be strong and be there for each other through this tough time, and *blah blah blah*. I'm sure she meant well by going into peacemaker mode, but it also seemed like she relished the opportunity to talk about anything other than our horny, steaming asshole of a father.

"I can't believe he'd cheat on you," I said. I had just been thinking how pretty she is. Not *was*, but *is*. How could he do this?

"Men are dogs," Noel said.

"Not *all* men," my mom corrected.

"Any guy I've ever known who was in a relationship—given the right circumstance and a guarantee that his girlfriend wouldn't find out—would cheat."

"I'll take Depressing Life Lessons for a hundred, Alex," I muttered.

"Girls, I wanted you both here because I want you to be there for each other."

I looked at my mom. "Are you *sure* you're not sick? That sounds like something a sick person says: 'I want you to be there for your sister.' A person says that because she knows she's dying."

My mom laughed. *God, I love her laugh.* "I'm not dying!" she said. "Stop being so morbid."

"Swear?" I said.

"Yes, Hailey, I swear."

I looked at her like I was trying to see if she was lying. I moved my head around, being almost silly, eyeballing her from all angles. Finally I decided I was satisfied. Though heartbroken.

Noel growled, "If anyone should be dying, it should be Dad. Maybe we can make that happen."

"*Noel!*" Mom said.

"Aren't *you* pissed off?" Noel asked. "How long has this been going on? Has this happened before? Is she the first?"

"Yes, Noel, I'm pissed off," Mom said. "But I have other things to worry about than that, like you two. I'm not going to get into all those details. That's between me and him. I know you're upset, but he's your father and no matter what happens between us, he's your father and you're going to respect him."

"You can't demand respect," I said, echoing something I'd heard somewhere. "It has to be earned."

"Where did he meet her?" Noel asked. "Did he know her before you moved? Did you move *because* of her?"

"Ugh," I said. "I feel sick."

Mom just sighed and forged ahead: "Your father is going to want to take you both to dinner tomorrow night. He'll tell you everything he wants to tell you. I just wanted you to be prepared, and I wanted to talk to you first."

"You mean he's not coming home?" I asked.

"Why should he?" Noel scoffed.

"No," my mom clarified. "He's not coming home right now."

"Where's he staying?" I asked. "With his whore?"

"Hailey," my mother said, looking right in my eyes. "You have every right to be angry. But you will speak with a civil tongue in this home, is that understood? And you will not use *that* term with me or your father. Not now, not ever. Got it?"

"But—"

"*Got it?*"

Chastened, I tried another approach: "Do you know her? Have you seen her?"

"I've seen her from a distance," Mom said. "Once. Because I was curious. She's very pretty."

"Is she young?" Noel asked.

"She may be a little younger than me, but she's not, you know . . . *inappropriately* young," Mom said.

"Yes, far be it from him to do something inappropriate," Noel said.

Mom gave her a sideways glance. "Girls, this is tough on everyone. I know it's a lot to process. I know it's incredibly upsetting. But this is the situation. I hope you know this in no way reflects on either of you. We both love you more than anything in the world. This is in no way your fault and we're going to try to work this out as amicably as possible."

"Great," I said, not even trying to hide the sarcasm. It was like she was dictating from *Divorce for Dummies: How to Talk to Your Kids.* "This is not your fault." "We both love you." "You did nothing wrong." Gag me.

"What a dick," Noel said.

"Noel, that's the last one," Mom said. "I'm *not* kidding."

Noel rolled her eyes but stayed silent.

"I'm sorry he did this, Mom," I said.

"I'm sorry, too, baby," Mom replied. "But we'll get through it."

She stood, dabbed her eyes again, and forced a smile. "Now who wants to pig out? Because I, for one, could use some empty calories."

"No," Noel said. "I just want to lie down."

"Noel, sweetie," my mom said, "you need to eat. Come—"

"NO!" Noel shouted, and my mom and I both jumped back. Noel was shaking. Even she sounded shocked by her own voice. Her face had gone from pale to beet red. I understood that she was upset—we all were—but I never expected her to handle something like this so badly.

"Noel?" I said. "What is it? Look, I know this sucks, but—"

"Yeah, Hailey, it sucks. It sucks. It sucks when you come here, here to this house I don't even know. I don't have a home anymore. I thought at least I had a family here, but so much for that. I'm going upstairs in a house I don't know in a city I don't know to try to rest on a bed I don't know, and I'd love to talk to my dad about it, but he's off boning all the Real Trophy Wives of Beverly Hills or whatever!"

This most certainly wasn't the calm, collected character of *How to Be a Hater*. I started to wonder whether that person even existed.

"I know this is weird and hard and all," I began, "but it's going to be okay."

"It won't, Hailey. Think of all the shit you're going through times ten. I told you I was sorry you were having a tough time and I meant it, but you don't know. It's not okay . . . nothing is okay . . . nothing . . ."

And then she was crying and shaking. I stood back, stunned. Mom stepped forward and took Noel in her arms, and Noel collapsed into her embrace.

I walked outside to leave them alone for a bit. I worried about Noel—I guess college wasn't everything, or maybe anything, like I thought it was—but I was having enough trouble trying to process how my dad had screwed over the family. The more I thought about it, the angrier I got.

When I came back in, they were talking, an economy-size box of Kleenex getting one hell of a workout, tissues being extracted every couple of seconds.

It looked like Noel had calmed down somewhat, thank goodness. Both of their faces were red from crying, but they were just talking, even smiling a little.

I wasn't sure how to break the silence. "Um . . . so about those empty calories?"

Noel turned and grinned. It was a beautiful sight.

"Jeez, Hailey," Noel said. "So much for that diet, huh? All it takes is your parents to break up and your face is right back in the trough!"

We all laughed heartily over that, and it felt great.

"So you're in?" I asked.

Noel sighed. "Yeah. I'm due for a 'cheat day' anyway. But I'm not going whole-hog. We can't have *all* the Harper girls getting fat. One of us needs to stay foxy."

I rolled my eyes. Mom pulled out menus for takeout while I opened up cabinets to find the most gluttonous snacks possible.

We were going to try to have fun and, if only for a brief high-calorie carb-carnival, forget the devastating truth—that our family as we'd known it would never be the same again.

Dinner the next night was worse than I'd imagined—and I'd imagined *a lot* of grim possibilities. But nothing could have possibly prepared me for what would come out of our dad's mouth somewhere midway through the meal I was already having a hard time getting down.

We were at a sushi restaurant called Sushi Roku because there are so few things Noel will eat—not that I was complaining, I love sushi—and this place seemed extra nice. It's definitely not Cheesecake Factory. (Which, for the record, I also love. The menu is practically a novel. Or a short story at the very least. A short story about delicious, fairly priced, oversize food. Yum.)

Neither Noel nor I were being particularly warm as my father tried to tell us that people "grow apart." (*But my parents hadn't,* I thought.) Worse, he hit us with "Sometimes it just happens." (Sure, if you add a *sh* to *it.* Because this was the *height* of shittiness.)

I wanted to show solidarity for my mom by not even eating, but the food was just too good. There had been so much emotional trauma over the past forty-eight hours: the prank that blew up in my face; the fight with Chris (we still hadn't talked since); the fight with Anya (see *Chris*); and the tiny little revelation that my dad not only had been screwing another woman, but it looked like this was going to end my parents' marriage. And, let's be honest, I've always had a hearty appetite. Basically, every minute of my life is a countdown to when I'll eat next. The way I feel when a waiter brings my food is probably similar to the excitement of a dude on *Maury* who just got told he's not the father. And it turns out that emotional trauma starts off making you not want to eat at all, and then suddenly, you're famished and devouring plate after plate of sushi and praying you don't get mercury poisoning from eating more raw fish than a hammerhead shark does in a month.

So I found myself with a mouthful of tuna roll, which was much easier to swallow than the ugly truth our dad was somehow trying to make us accept.

Noel and I were mostly handling it by eating our words, because we both knew if we spoke freely it would get ugly fast. Maybe we were too easy on him, because he had the gall to say a bunch of nice things about this nasty skank he'd hooked up with to destroy our world.

"Look, I know this is hard, but I think when you get to know Crystal, you'll see that she's really a wonderful woman," Dad told us. "And, Hailey, she has a daughter your age."

What? I'm supposed to be happy? Welcome this new "sister" into the family? I don't think so.

"Congratulations to her," I said, reaching my breaking point. "So, Dad, let me get this right: In addition to being a home-wrecker, she also scared away her first husband? Or were they even married? Or was he married to someone else at the time? That sounds like par for the course."

"*Hailey!*" my dad said in a shushing voice, looking around. We were in a corner booth that provided some privacy, but it wasn't like we had the place to ourselves.

Dad leaned in. "There is *no call* for that kind of talk," he said. "I know you're upset, but we all just need to be adult about this."

"Well, she's not an adult, Dad," Noel said, "so maybe you should understand that this is a tough time to go through something like this. And maybe you should have thought about that before you planned to hook up with this 'Crystal' woman."

"I didn't 'plan on' anything, Noel," he said. "This just . . . happened. I know it's tough on everyone and I'm sorry about that, but I'm with Crystal now, and I think if you gave her a chance—"

"A chance?" Noel exclaimed. "Why? What do you want us to say? We're so happy that you've been cheating on Mom and found someone you like enough to ruin our family for?"

Exactly! You go, sister!

"I'm telling you because this is how it is," he said. "This is how it's going to be. I'm sorry that it upsets you, and maybe you can't understand now, but maybe later you will. The heart works in mysterious ways."

"Gag me," I said, this time out loud, wanting to stab him with a chopstick. *I wish they made sharper chopsticks.*

Dad exhaled deeply. "Hailey, I only brought up her daughter because she's your age."

And because you're an idiot. A cheating, lying, cheating, cheating cheater.

"Yeah?" I said, wanting to push him, wanting him to feel the rage I felt. "Don't care. She can be sixteen or sixty. She's still the daughter of the slut you cheated on Mom with."

"*Hailey!*" my dad said, grunting, trying to calm himself. "*That's* enough of that. You can be as angry at me as you want, but you will not use words like that about Crystal, are we clear?"

I clenched my jaw, looked down, and stabbed a lone piece of yellowtail with my chopstick.

Noel pointed a finger at our father. I knew she was even more upset than I was, but she wasn't going off the same way. Maybe that's the maturity you get in college. Instead of blowing up the building, you send in a surgical drone strike.

"Dad, how did you expect Hailey to react?" Noel said. "Did you think she wouldn't be disgusted? Even I'm shocked and disgusted, and I'm old enough to understand how guys act once they know the thread count of your sheets."

Whoa.

Talk about a statement designed to provoke. Dad glared at her, and she glared back. But he didn't take the bait. I tried to keep a poker face, but I loved that she went right at him. Coming to my defense was becoming a pattern with her, which was a nice change. Seemed like years since that was the case.

To break the silence after that shot, Noel continued, "So *what* if this girl and Hailey are the same age? What does that have to do with anything? Hailey and I have all the sisters we need. We weren't recruiting for another one. Why on *earth* would we be happy about this? How could that idiotic notion even *occur* to you?"

"I just—" Dad started, and I could see a little pain in his eyes. That was super-rare. Not that I was feeling particularly sympathetic under the circumstances, but you could tell dealing with this was wearing on him too. Of course, that was *his* problem. He started this shit.

He settled himself. "Look, I just want you to know about Crystal and her family. You don't have to like this right now, maybe not for a while. I do understand that. But like it or not, you're going to meet them at some point. Also, it's my understanding that Hailey might actually *know* Skyler, and—"

Wait!

Wait!

Wait, what the—oh my God, this is not happening. This cannot be happening, please tell me this isn't happening, someone pinch me or punch me and wake me up from this awful nightmare.

"WHAT?"

Of course, that was right when the server had come by to refill our beverages and I realized that I'd yelled "What?" so loudly that everyone in the restaurant had heard me, and Noel looked shocked and Dad looked shocked and the server looked triple-shocked for a second and then just turned and skittered off to wherever servers go.

"Um, Hailey—" Dad sputtered.

I grasped at my last straw. "Skyler," I said. "Skyler. Her name is Skyler."

"Well, yes—"

"And it's your 'understanding' that she knows me. You're sure? Do Crystal and Skyler have the same last name?"

"Well, yes. It's—"

don't say it don't say it don't say it don't say it don't

"—Brandt."

Why don't meteors ever land on your head when you really want them to?

This couldn't be real, I thought. I must be having a nightmare or being Punk'd or something. Was this Skyler's final prank? If so, boy, she got me! Come on out, Ashton! Bring Justin Bieber with you! Let's all have a good laugh!

"Dad, please. Please tell me you're kidding," I pleaded.

"Why?" Noel interjected. "What's the deal with this girl?"

"Now, as for Skyler, I understand you two aren't exactly friends," Dad said.

So he knew? He knew he was bedding the evil monster who'd spawned the devil-child who'd become my mortal enemy?

"This can't be happening," I said. I felt dizzy and sick and the circus in my stomach had moved to a more focused desire to now empty all its contents.

"Hailey, seriously, what's the deal?" Noel asked me. "What does he mean?"

Sorry, Noel. I know you're stressed out and confused too, but I can't come to the rescue right now.

I wasn't quite sure what to say. Dad obviously didn't know how ugly things were between me and Skyler. My head was reeling, but I tried to calm myself and see if I could gather some information.

"Dad," I said. "Yeah, I know who Skyler Brandt is. Everyone does. She's like the most popular girl in our class, but why would you say we're 'not exactly friends'? Has Skyler talked about me?"

"Well, no," he said. "Not really, not to me. Skyler doesn't really give me the time of day, honestly. I think she's still a little unsure about my seeing her mother, though I hope she comes around in time."

You're one stupidly optimistic idiot, I thought.

Dad continued, "But you know, I ask Crystal how Skyler's doing, and if your name ever came up, and, well, Crystal has a really hard time getting Skyler to talk to her too. I mean, it's crazy. Like a few months ago, apparently some awful student humiliated Skyler by making a tape that went over the PA system claiming she had, I don't know, some very embarrassing medical condition. You heard about that?"

My heart felt like it would explode. "Uh . . . yeah. Yes. Really couldn't miss it."

"Well, it was just awful. Dreadful. Anyway, Skyler didn't even tell Crystal about it. I mean, this big horrible thing, right? Crystal was out of town that week, so she only heard the voice mail about it when she got back—your Principal Dash was apologizing, said the girl who broadcast it was being disciplined, but they didn't know who made the tape."

"Jeez, Dad, what's the point?" Noel asked.

"I want to hear this," I told Noel. "Dad, go on."

"Well, Skyler hadn't said a word about it to her mother. And when Crystal asked her about it, she just said it was no big deal, that it was 'all taken care of.' Whatever that means. But Skyler's had a tough time."

Oh good Lord, I thought. *Save me the pity party for Miss Popular.* "Okay, Dad, but . . . what does that have to do with me?"

"Oh, well . . . I just meant that she doesn't really confide in Crystal, and certainly not in me. She's a bit of a weird bird. But I understand that early in the school year, Skyler had mentioned your name as someone hanging out with her and her friends. Then when Crystal asked about you later, Skyler said you'd had a falling-out. I thought that was unfortunate—it would have been great if you two were friends, under the circumstances—but I know high school can be weird like that. Things can change pretty quickly."

Tell me about it, I thought. While still disgusted at the idea that my dad was hooking up with Skyler's mom, I was relieved to realize that Skyler hadn't shared much of anything with them—or at least not with my dad. I had enough trouble dealing with school shit without my family getting involved, although I guess the way things were going, we were involved regardless.

Noel turned to me. "Hailey, wait: You used to *hang out* with this girl? Our new . . . 'stepsister'?" She said the last word while making the most bitter-looking air quotes you could imagine.

I looked at Noel, sighing. "Remember in the email when I said the leader of the popular clique took me under her wing? And it turned out to be really stinky and awful and evil under that wing? So I broke the wing and flushed it down the toilet? Yeah. That was her."

"Um . . . yeah," Noel said, sputtering. "Well, kind of . . ."

"Jeez, Noel, did you even *read* it?"

"Yeah, really quick . . . Anyway, so this girl's really, really popular? That's a little weird. I mean, good for you and all, but that's never really been your deal, right? Did you seriously dump them? They didn't dump you?"

I glared at Noel. She locked eyes with me and held that gaze for a few seconds, but then she realized I wasn't backing down. She glanced down at her plate.

"Um, what do you mean it was evil under the wing?" Dad asked.

I gave Dad the same death stare I'd just used on Noel. He seemed to figure out we weren't going to explore that topic.

"Well, I'm sorry you and Skyler had a falling-out," he said. "But, hey, you're both young, smart girls, I'm sure you can get past it."

Gawd, he's more clueless than ever.

"Dad, does Skyler know?" I asked.

"Know what?"

"That you and Crystal are serious. That you're leaving Mom. That I'm your daughter?"

I was praying she didn't. Because if she knew that her mom had stolen my dad away from our family . . . I couldn't bear to think about the smug satisfaction she'd probably feel. That would be the ultimate fuck-you. Game over. She won.

"I don't believe she does," he said. "Crystal and I agreed that it would be right to let you and Noel know first."

Oh really? Crystal and you agreed? How fucking thoughtful of you.

A rock settled in the pit of my stomach. How would that conversation go? Would Skyler tell her mom and my dad all the crazy shit that happened over the past year? That I was behind the announcement? Not to mention BitchBook?

The only upside to any of that: Maybe Dad and this fucking "Crystal" would part ways once they realized their daughters basically want to kill each other. (And seriously, what woman actually uses the name *Crystal*? Is she a stripper? A psychic? Both?)

Dad was talking again, and I tuned him back in: "We hope that you two will become friends," he said. "Who knows? Someday you could be family."

I pushed myself away from the table. Him saying that in all seriousness was more than I could bear. "Can you please take me home now?" I didn't wait for his answer. "I'll be waiting outside."

Noel got up and followed me out.

Nobody spoke on the drive home.

You don't understand . . .

—ALICE IN CHAINS

"Down in a Hole"

CHAPTER 19

Noel and I had pretty much gone straight to my room, where we chilled on the bed and talked. Though Mom had asked us how things had gone, I had no idea how to answer her, and no emotional energy left to even entertain the conversation. My whole life had changed in so many ways in forty-eight hours. I missed Chris and wished he'd return my messages, but no response so far.

In my room, Noel and I hashed out our issues over the email and why we'd barely spoken this year. Talking to Noel was never something that came easy to me. Partially because she was older and cooler and I worried she would judge me and think I was stupid, and partially because we just never had that relationship. But siblings are important (especially as you get older and your parents get older, from what I've heard), so I decided it was time to try to build a closeness that we'd never had. Especially considering everything we'd just experienced in the last twenty-four hours. And what better way to create a new and lasting loyalty with your sister than to admit to having stolen and read her diary?

Yeah, *not so smooth.*

But then, it did feel like our relationship had changed, even in just the couple of days she'd been home. She'd changed since going to college. I'd changed since—well, since using her diary to make some big changes in my life, but life itself had changed the shit out of me all on its own too. Our relationship was different because we were different people.

I didn't dive right into the diary thing. We were both feeling hurt and angry, and it had been a long time since we really caught up, so we talked about college and high school and just some general things. I told her bits and pieces of how sophomore year had gone so far without bringing up the diary per se. But I knew I had to get to it eventually.

Noel apologized again about not being more receptive to the email. Turns out college is a lot tougher and more stressful than I realized. She was stressed out all the time, and even after figuring out high school as well as she had (as I knew all too well), college was a whole different world.

She talked about all the limitations in high school—go here, go there, you need a pass for this, a pass for that, don't leave campus, don't be in the wrong building. They're annoying, sure, but there's security, as she explained it, in those limitations. Once you get to college, no one's forcing you to do this or do that. Show up for class, study and do your homework—or don't. It's all up to you. And that creates a lot of pressure, especially when you're trying to have some sort of life outside the classroom.

I'd never thought of it that way. It made sense. She also admitted she knew high school could be tougher than she'd suggested earlier, and I appreciated that. It was like the first really "adult" conversation we'd had in—okay, I think it's the first "adult" conversation we'd ever had. And, yeah, we talked about sex. That was a little weird at first, but it was fun. She cracked up when I told her about the Altoids incident, but it just made me miss Chris all the more.

After all that, it was going to be a tricky balance between admitting I'd screwed up while also heaping praise upon her: I mean, she'd written the plan of attack for a legion of girls at West Hollywood who basically idolized her. That *was* true. I did have that ego-stroke to work with.

Still, I was petrified. After everything that happened, I needed her counsel. Her journal had all that wisdom, but now I needed more. I knew she was the only person in the world who could possibly help me get out of the ginormous mess I'd gotten into and maybe help rally the troops again—to get us past our petty differences and working together—but I didn't know how she'd react.

Noel had already had an epically bad day at this point, just like I had. Not exactly the best time to hit her with my massive invasion of her privacy. She'd be furious that I'd read her private thoughts and—much, much worse—also read them to ten or so other people. I just prayed that some sort of sisterly love might surface when she saw how bad I felt and how huge I'd screwed up.

So I told her. That's when something shocking happened.

Noel didn't get mad at me.

In fact, she didn't say much at all. I told her everything: how scared I was to move, how I found the diary and it was like a secret angel handshake from the sister I always wanted but never had, how I used her words, her attitude, her clothes to make friends . . . and how once I made those friends, I realized I couldn't stand them. So I forged ahead and used my newfound confidence and attitude to make friendships with people I could relate to—even if they weren't "popular."

I talked and talked and she just listened. Never interrupting, not saying anything, though she did have the most curious look on her face at times. I told her everything from beginning to end, and by the time I was done it was three in the morning and we were both exhausted. At the end, I apologized profusely and told her I'd understand if she never wanted to speak with me again, but she simply told me she wasn't mad, but she was glad I'd admitted what happened. Pushing my luck, I asked if she'd come to an emergency Invisibles meeting I had planned.

Noel smiled slightly and said:

"Hailey, I wouldn't miss it for the world."

I have to admit that part of me worried that she was secretly pissed off and was planning to humiliate me in front of everyone. There were times in Noel's past where that sort of nastiness emerged, though I guess that was true of every teenager at some point—including, quite recently, me. But I decided to hope for the best.

We had the emergency meeting at Sweet Lady Jane, a coffee shop/bakery in West Hollywood that had ridic desserts for us to chow down on. Their cakes were these almost old-fashioned, beautiful floral creations made to perfection with delectable pastel colors *and bonus: you could eat them!* (Which we planned to do.)

Noel wanted it to be a tea party of sorts; it was her idea to go there. My nerves were cranked up to a seventeen on a scale of one to ten, but when we arrived at Sweet Lady Jane, Noel was kind, calm and seemed to take on the elevated goddess-like status that had been unknowingly thrust upon her with a seamless grace. (Of course.)

Needless to say, everyone was freaking out. Here she was: Noel Harper in the flesh. The Invisibles were freaking out. It was like Elvis showing up to speak at an Elvis impersonators' convention.

Anya and Emily were seated as far as possible from each other, because in my infinite wisdom and effort to screw up *every* part of my life, I'd implied to Emily that she should probably not get *too* serious about Andy. Yeah, that was insanely stupid. She figured out the rest in a hostile Q-and-A session with Andy. Needless to say, Anya was even more pissed off at me, and now I'd added Andy to the list of people who hated me. (On the last point, my current attitude was "tough shit": Whatever his history with Anya, he had no right to cheat on Emily. Though I suppose the same argument could be made for Anya, since she was supposedly Emily's friend.)

Kura, meanwhile . . . well, she looked like a mess. Her hair looked like it hadn't been brushed all day, she wasn't wearing any makeup that I could see. (I mean, even I thought she looked unpresentable, and I'm pretty chill. Skyler would lose her mind.) Kura was wearing sunglasses despite being indoors, which is never a good thing unless you're Tom Cruise or an NFL wide receiver or . . . come to think of it, it's *never* a good thing. (Get over yourself, people—you're *inside.)* It briefly occurred to me that I'd been so wrapped up in all my stuff I'd barely paid any attention to her situation lately, but the ugly reality was this: I still had my own crap to handle right now. We all did.

How to Be a Hater had turned into *How to Be Hated* in what seemed like the blink of an eye. And I guess I should have stayed out of Emily's business, but I felt like I owed it to her as a friend to at least give her a little bit of a heads up. Plus, if I'm being honest, I was really pissed at Anya and I'm sure that played into it a little.

So even though everyone was excited, a bunch of us weren't even talking to each other. And while several were giving others the stink eye, Noel stood up in front of the group and said,

"I appreciate you all showing up. I understand there's some tension between some of you so it's a testament to your friendship that you all came. Hailey's told me all about the Invisibles and some of the, um, 'projects' you've been working on, inspired by my journal. Now, I don't exactly recall promoting criminal misdemeanors and even felonies in my journal, but I must give you points for creativity."

Dead silence. That's not exactly what anyone was expecting.

"I mean, it sounds like it's only the good graces of your enemies that kept a few of you from getting expelled over that STD announcement. Car theft? That's a great way to end up in juvenile detention and maybe even end up with a felony or two if they try you as an adult. And the BitchBook thing—very creative. But how none of you ended up having to repeat your sophomore year after that one I'll *never* figure out."

We all looked at each other, guilty as charged, but Noel kept talking.

"Hey, at least none of those girls you pictured swallowing dog shit decided to swallow a bottle of Xanax after being publicly humiliated in front of the whole school, huh? Dodged another bullet there."

"But," Xandra said, "we didn't start it—"

"Well, kid, that's all the reason you need right there," Noel said. "'We didn't start it,' so if someone drops out of school or goes to jail or kills herself, it's not your fault. 'Because you didn't start it.'"

"Noel," I said, "come on, ease up. I get what you're saying, and, yeah, we took things a little too far and we got a little lucky—"

"Hailey, the minute you turn eighteen, you should play the lottery every chance you get," Noel said. "Because you got way beyond lucky. You don't have *any clue* how lucky you got."

She sighed, picked up her diary. The diary we had combed through, memorized passages from, treated like it was our bible.

"Did anyone notice anything *weird* about this diary?" Noel asked.

Nobody said anything.

"Like, that it just . . . stops?" she went on. "Nobody noticed how it just ends abruptly?"

"We were wondering," Dahlia said. "But, you know, people abandon journals all the time. Sometimes they just get tired of them, or maybe they move on to another one."

"Fair enough," Noel said. "Well, that's not what happened here. I abandoned it for a reason. Apparently the only mistake I made was not burning the thing."

You could have heard a pin drop. We'd been living our lives by this journal, and its creator was before us—blaspheming it.

"Noel, what the hell?" I said. "Did you come here just to ridicule me?"

"No, Hailey," she said. "Not at all. I love you, sweetie. And I totally understand how you could get caught up in all this crap I wrote. Hey, I got caught up in it; that's why I wrote it. But here's the thing: Everything you read, that's only half of the story. And the half you read? Well, a lot of that turned out to be bullshit."

Leave it to Anya to appreciate the no-shit approach: "Okay. So what's the deal? What are we missing?"

"Well," she said, "Hailey's told me all about this Skyler—enough to leave me pretty concerned, since I'm going to have to get to know this bitch too. But that's another story."

A few raised eyebrows—I hadn't shared that with the group yet.

"Anyway, I was probably what you'd call a 'Skyler' when I was in school. Maybe not quite as bad, but close. All of that stuff in the diary, I didn't just use it to be self-confident. I used it to knock people down. I used it to get my way and get ahead. And now, whenever I think about it, I feel sick to my stomach."

I looked around at the other girls. They were hanging on every word. So was I.

"There was a girl in our grade named Lisa Gregory, and quite simply, she smelled *bad*. Like really, really bad, like she didn't bathe at all, and she almost always wore the same clothes. Her hair was a mess, like filthy, greasy, oily—disgusting. So, you can imagine we all tried to steer clear, make sure she didn't touch us or get too close or, heaven forbid, talk to us."

The girls all nodded in agreement, leaning forward waiting for whatever was coming next.

"And of course we made fun of her. Because that's what you do when you're in high school. You're mean." She stopped and looked around at all of us. "In high school, we say and do the most hurtful things we can think of, because that somehow makes us feel better about ourselves. But does it really? Do you *really* feel good about yourself when you've hurt another person?"

More girls were looking down now, noticing seemingly fascinating things about their shoes, their shirts, anything to avoid Noel's gaze.

"So like I said, I was the Skyler. I was the 'leader of the band.' So I went up to Lisa one day when she was standing by her locker, and I pretended to be nice to her. It didn't even take any effort. I was nice to this girl just long enough to watch her open her locker and get her lock combination. The next day, before school started, my friends and I filled her locker with everything we decided she must not have access to: shampoo, soap, deodorant, hairbrush, toothbrush, toothpaste, douche and—as a lovely coup de grâce—a note that read: 'Take a hint, or better yet, take a *shower*!'"

Everyone was silent. This obviously wasn't going to be a happy story.

"The next day, everyone knew what we'd done, so there were

lots of kids gathered to watch as she opened her locker. She took a few items out and examined them as half of the school laughed at her humiliation. We thought it was *so funny*. Well, until the next day."

"What happened?" Dahlia asked.

"Lisa was in critical condition in the hospital. She'd tried to kill herself and damn near succeeded."

"How?" I asked. I'd somehow never heard about this before.

"She drank a bunch of her stepfather's bourbon and took some pills she found in his nightstand, got in a warm tub and slit her wrists with a razor blade. Well, not her wrists, really. Everyone says 'wrists,' but really, when you do it right, it's pretty much right up your entire forearms."

"Oh my God," I said, a sentiment echoed by the other girls.

"Yeah," she said. "She survived, but she had these horrible scars that ran up both arms, which you could only see at PE, because she wore long-sleeved shirts all the rest of the time, even on the hottest days. She'd be sweating in the middle of summer, wearing her long-sleeved shirt."

"God," Anya said. "At least she lived."

"Yes," Noel said. "That was lucky. But things almost got worse for her. You think people pointed and stared and talked behind her back before? Now she wasn't just the girl who smelled bad; she was the girl who tried to kill herself. It was a whole new level of hell for her after that."

Complete silence. Nobody touched their dessert.

"So yeah. I was devastated. Obviously she had issues, she had problems, but—what we did, *what I did*, that was what pushed her over the edge. And that's when I stopped writing in my diary. I realized you don't have to tear down others to build yourself up. Once you understand that your success doesn't depend upon the failure of others, well, that's when you really grow up. And you become a whole lot less of an asshole."

There wasn't much more discussion after that. Noel had said all she needed to say. No one even wanted to look at each other. I didn't know what the future held for the Invisibles—if there even was any future—but the pranks, the retaliation, all of that, obviously was over for good.

Noel and I had just left Sweet Lady Jane when I stopped, realizing there was a situation happening right in front of me that I could maybe help, or try to help, and I knew I had to do something. I told Noel I'd meet her back at the house and doubled back to find Kura. We had barely just dispersed but Kura was nowhere to be found. I walked back into the café and asked the lady behind the counter.

"Did my friend, the pretty Asian one . . . did you happen to see her leave?"

"I think she's in the bathroom," she said, and my heart started to speed up, much like I assumed hers probably was.

I knocked on the bathroom door.

Sniff. "Just a second," she said. Sniff.

"Kura, it's me," I said. "Open up."

There was no movement and the door didn't open. So I banged on it. Hard. I finally heard the latch unlock, and the door cracked open. She looked so fragile, I didn't say a word. I just took her arm as we left the restaurant. I guided Kura to a shaded bus bench where we could talk. This probably sounds weird and terrible, because I absolutely wanted Kura to feel better, but there was something strangely soothing about worrying about something other than my own disintegrating life for a change.

Kura took off her sunglasses. Her eyes were sunken.

"Kura," I said, but her name caught in my throat. "You look *really* bad."

"I'm stopping," she said. At least she knew immediately what had me so concerned, for whatever that's worth. "I'm really stopping, I swear."

I'd heard that too many times to believe it. "I'm worried about you."

"Don't," she said. Her eyes darted around—she was looking anywhere but at me. She stood up, jittery. "I really have to go. If I'm late getting home, my parents will flip. You have no idea what Asian parents are like. It's like Godzilla was actually a metaphor for angry Asian parents whose kids were fuck-ups."

I laughed, admiring her ability to be entertaining even in this situation, but I felt frustrated by how helpless I was. She just didn't realize the seriousness of her situation.

"Kura, please, just know that I'm here and that I want to help you, okay?"

"Okaaay," she replied in a mocking tone, rolling her eyes for effect. It was an unnecessary gesture, but it only took a moment for me to realize that was the drug talking, not her.

In a flash, she was up off the bench, striding away. "I gotta run," she said, not even turning back to me.

Part of me wanted to follow her, but what more could I do? I'd given it a shot. And it's not like I didn't have enough problems of my own right now.

I could only hope Kura would get help before things got worse.

That night, I went for a walk while Noel talked with Mom. While Noel was being more open with me about how traumatic everything was for her, the two of them seemed to be forming a bond that I couldn't really recall them having before. That's probably because Noel always seemed so headstrong and independent, which isn't exactly Mom's style. But Noel turned out to have just as much insecurity as anyone—she'd just gotten used to hiding it well. And Mom turned out to be a lot stronger than I ever expected. Noel said her talks with Mom were really helping her get it together. She was even feeling at home here in this strange house.

When I got back from the walk, Noel and I had some ice cream. We talked a lot that night. Even though I felt I'd let her down terribly, she was understanding. She told me I shouldn't have read the diary in the first place, but she hoped I'd learn from her mistakes and the reason she stopped writing it.

"The whole hater thing was going really well for me too," she said. "Well, in a lot of ways. I was already aware that it was causing problems, but I chose to ignore them. And then after the Lisa thing, I was devastated. And I was dating this incredibly wonderful guy, and he dropped me on the spot."

"Wow," I said. "Was he that really tall guy with the two-toned hair who always wore the V-necks? He picked you up on that red motorcycle?"

Noel laughed, but it was the saddest laugh you've ever heard, totally heartbreaking. "Yeah, Tristan. You remember him, huh? He was really sweet. Just an amazing guy. He'd been telling me I was changing, and I wouldn't listen. I thought I knew it all. And then the Lisa thing—he was disgusted, of course. And I was a wreck after that."

"Wow," I said. "I never knew."

Noel shook her head. "Hailey, you remember when I started taking piano lessons after school a couple of days a week?"

I hadn't thought about that in years. "Um, yeah, now I do. I asked Mom why I couldn't come with and she said you needed to focus or something."

"Right. And have you ever in your life seen me play a piano?"

Holy shit. "No."

"Ever seen me show any interest in a piano? Or any kind of musical instrument ever?"

"No. So, where were you?"

"I was seeing a therapist," Noel said. "I was shattered over what happened with Lisa. I felt such horrible guilt, I was having a hard time dealing with it. And I was heartbroken over Tristan too, but more than anything else, I just had no idea who I was anymore. I'd thought I had everything figured out, and all that hard work I'd put into being a 'hater' made me hate *myself* most of all."

I let that all sink in. It was like she was telling my story, all the mistakes, what happened with Chris, everything. Everything except an attempted suicide, thank goodness.

"Did the therapy help?" I asked.

"Yeah, it did," she said. "I had a lot bottled up I had to let out. Heck, I haven't even scratched the surface telling you all the awful things I did, or the whole story of Lisa."

"Like what?"

Noel sighed, seeming to weigh whether she wanted to get into it.

"Well, you can imagine how I felt when I found out about the near-suicide. It actually got worse. A lot more information came out after Lisa was interviewed at the hospital. Detectives ended up arresting Lisa's stepdad because he was abusing her. *Sexually.* From what we heard, the reason Lisa didn't change her clothes or bathe was because that was her way of coping—or not coping or trying to keep him away or who knows what—just expressing a general state of misery, I guess. But whatever it was—there was a damn good reason why she wasn't taking care of herself. And we used that reason to humiliate her and make her even more suicidal than she probably was in the first place."

"If there's any possible silver lining . . . I guess it's that people found out she was being abused though, right?"

"We weren't trying to help her. We were trying to hurt her. It's great that she got help but what we did was inexcusable. We pushed her over the edge. I pushed her over the edge. I was cruel. And I will *never* get over the terrible feeling of knowing how badly I added to her pain . . . humiliated her."

"I don't know what to say," I said, and for a brief moment wondered why we feel the need to say "I don't know what to say" when we don't know what to say. Why don't we just stay quiet?

"There's nothing you can say," she said. "Just . . . don't do that shit, Hailey. Be better than that. That girl will never be the same because of what we did. She will remember that forever. And I'll have to *live* with that forever."

"I'm so sorry," I said to Noel, who had tears streaming down her face now. I wanted to cry too. "I won't. I won't do any of that."

She pushed up her sleeve and showed me the tattoo on her wrist with the "Shine brighter" lyric. "That's also when I got this, remember? Well, it was really a message to myself. To be *better.*"

She dabbed away tears. "It's good to be confident—it's great to be confident—but don't ever be a hater. I lost so much that I'll never get back. But you, you might still have a chance to change things."

"How?" I asked.

"Just be you," she said.

This is my chance to fly.

—VAN HALEN

"Unchained"

CHAPTER
20

It's funny the things you think about when your whole world has come crashing down on top of you. When everything you thought you knew—who your parents were, who your sister was, who you actually are deep down inside—turns out to be a lie. To some degree, a lie you've been busy telling yourself. So, yeah, your mind goes to some pretty weird places.

My mind went to . . . security cameras.

More specifically, an editorial in the school newspaper about security cameras. West Hollywood had them running 24/7 in most of the major hallways and student areas as a deterrent against crime, mischief and . . . well, pretty much all the shit the Invisibles had been up to the last few months and Skyler & Co. had been up to ever since getting to the school.

However, the cameras hadn't been much of a deterrent, seeing as how all that shit went down. And here's why: They weren't actually hooked up to any kind of recording media. No hard drive, no recordable DVD, not even old freaking VHS tapes. Nothing. That was all a victim of budget cuts, thanks to California going basically bankrupt in recent years. There were monitors in the main office that the administrators could glance at throughout the day, but they basically never did, because they had jobs to do too, and thanks to a freeze on faculty raises, they weren't exactly dying to go above and beyond the call.

The fact that the cameras didn't actually *record* was one of the ways the Invisibles had, as Noel noted in no uncertain terms, gotten incredibly lucky. Principal Dash could have torn Anya's alibi over the STD announcement to shreds with video from the hallways . . . but no such evidence existed. Of course, the same thing could have nailed Skyler et al. for fish-bombing my locker, and all the other stuff, so it sort of went both ways. But the point was this: When no one's at the school to look at the monitors, you can pretty much get away with anything at West Hollywood High.

That wasn't the only thing that had been running through my mind of late, of course. This had been the most intense week of the most intense month of the most intense semester of the most intense year of my freaking *lifetime*—which is to say, it was pretty intense. It had been a roller coaster of achievements and disappointments, and lately the disappointments had come fast and furious.

And despite that, I felt a little kernel of hope, thanks to Noel. Sure, in one fell swoop, she'd shattered virtually everything the Invisibles and I had been doing all this time, but the more I thought about it, the more I realized that all she shattered was the illusion that being a hater somehow made us stronger. It didn't. Our friendships made us stronger. Our care for each other made us stronger. Our determination to stand up to powerful people and to challenge our own perceptions of ourselves made us stronger. And we *did* do all that.

It's just all the other shit we'd fucked up. And if I was going to be honest, I'd have to confess I was the instigator for most of it.

So a lot was churning around in my brain as I tried to figure out what the best next step was for me. I'd reached a point where just about all my enemies hated me at West Hollywood, which is acceptable, but all my *friends* did too, which wasn't. And it still killed me that my actions had so completely repulsed Chris. I didn't know if I could fix everything, I didn't know if I could fix *anything* . . . but I had to do *something*.

And I'd love to tell you that everything just got better on its own or that I found the perfect solution to fix everything. If my life were a Hollywood movie, Skyler would have turned out to be the sister I never had, one closer in age, one with everything in common with me, a best friend I'd cherish for the rest of my life. Chris would have overlooked the whole breaking-his-trust thing, because "love conquers all," and everyone has some flaws, right? Anya and Andy wouldn't be mad at me anymore because they knew they were in the wrong for hooking up behind Emily's back; and Emily would get "scared straight" after being busted for shoplifting, but she'd get off with a warning because her parents' lawyer was really good and he also had an incredibly handsome son who happened to be our age and he and Emily would start dating.

Also, Chris would be played by Robert Pattinson and I would be played by Angelina Jolie. Don't worry about the age discrepancy—it's my movie, and also, *come on*—half the stuff Hollywood churns out isn't believable. (Including the reality shows. *Especially* the reality shows.)

But this was real life. And the only thing resembling "Hollywood" was the fact that it was the name of the town I lived in.

I couldn't make Anya like me again. I couldn't make Chris love me—if he did love me, and I'd like to think he did at one point, at least—again. And I couldn't make my dad want to be with my mom again, or at least make him not want to be with Skyler's skank-ass mom.

I can't control other people. But I can control myself, and I can do what I can to show them how I feel, especially if it's on an incredibly grand scale—and even if it requires taking a massive risk, one even bigger than all the risks I took this year.

The planning took longer than the execution, and the execution was going to take me all weekend. First I had to write it, to say exactly what I needed it to say. Then I drew it up, every detail, on my laptop, taking all the proper dimensions into consideration. I uploaded it all to my iPad and also put together extensively detailed printouts.

It was Saturday morning, and I was all packed up and ready to leave the house. I had told Mom I'd be staying with Grace overnight. When she asked why I was packing sandwiches to visit Grace, I told her Grace's family was on this crazy Paleo diet and I wanted to be sure I had the food I liked. She seemed to buy it, or maybe she just didn't want to argue because she knew the whole separation with Dad was hard on me. Whatever the case, I made it out with my backpack full of sandwiches—enough to sustain me for thirty-six hours—many cans of spray paint, some basic toiletries, and all my designs.

It was time to break into West Hollywood High.

Remember all those budget cuts? Like I said, security was not exactly a priority, which is kind of strange considering all the money they put into this school and all the state-of-the-art stuff in it. I hear they even used to have security guards on the weekends, but when you need to keep fire trucks and police cars on the roads, security at a high school—even a really nice high school—goes by the wayside.

As I packed my Mischief Bag—yes, that's what I called it, because that sounds so much better than About-to-Commit-a-Felony Bag—I thought back to my last conversation with Noel. Mom and I had taken her to the airport. As screwed up as things were with our family overall—thanks again, Dad—Noel and I had reached a point where we felt much more comfortable sharing aspects of our lives. Mom and I were closer, and Mom and Noel seemed to have forged a better relationship as well. I guess we all needed each other's support more than ever.

Of course, the irony was that I was about to do something I *had* to keep secret from both of them. And even though Noel might not approve of the specifics, I knew she'd be behind me in spirit. Before Noel left for her gate at LAX, we talked one last time about *How to Be a Hater*.

"You know," I said, "for all the—um—*misguided* advice, there's a lot of positive stuff in there too."

"Of course," she said. "The author's a frickin' genius."

I smiled. "Maybe you should write a *real* advice book one day. Not for haters. Just for, you know, kids who lack self-confidence."

"Maybe, sis," she said. "But I'm thinking something more like teen vampire fiction."

"No!"

She smiled, gave me a hug. "*No*. You stay in touch, Hay."

"I will, No. You stay in touch *too*."

"I will. I swear."

I smiled at the memory. Noel would understand what I was going to do this weekend. Down the line, she might even say nice things about me in the courtroom.

It wasn't exactly easy to break into West Hollywood, but thanks to a couple of our more truant Invisibles, I was aware of a security gap that could easily be exploited on a weekend. So of course I took advantage of this to do some vandalism. Well, that's not what *I'd* call it, but I knew that's what others would. I accepted that going in.

It undoubtedly would cost me my CalArts internship.

It could cost me a suspension.

It might very well end up getting me arrested and sent to juvie.

And before I went through the science lab window and added criminal trespassing to my ever-growing long list of crimes, I asked myself, *Do you really want to do this?*

Hell, yes.

I slid through and went right to work.

I'm sure some artists want to make money. Some want to effect social change. Some want to make people laugh or cry. But I think all artists just want their work to be *seen*.

And the work I did at West Hollywood over the weekend, well, it sure as shit was seen. It was seen by the whole administration when they arrived Monday morning. And even before the administrators tried to round up enough tablecloths to cover it up—before giving up because the sucker was just too *big*—everyone arriving for first period saw it. And they took pictures. And they took video. And they tweeted it and they Facebooked it and they Instagrammed it and they blogged it and they Tumblred it and it was seen. Man oh man, was it ever seen. Only two hours after school had opened—by Dahlia's estimation, and hers is as expert an estimation as anyone's—more than 25,000 people had viewed it, or at least portions of it:

My Enormous Super Kick-Ass Comic Strip Mural.

Which happened to be spray-painted all over the halls of West Hollywood High School.

Not all the halls, mind you, but quite a few of them. It really was epic. I'd poured my heart and soul into it, every detail, painting my ass off all day Saturday and most of Sunday, pausing only to grab some fresh air every hour or so before the paint fumes made me insanely dizzy. (How kids can huff that crap to get high I'll never know, but there's a lot I still have to figure out.)

The gigantic comic strip mural began at the main entrance, and then branched off through the various hallways, culminating in the cafeteria. It was a *massive* piece of art, more like a graphic novel with multiple subplots. The administration tried to find a way to cover it up at first, but Principal Dash and the rest gave up quickly. There was absolutely nothing the administration could do about it short of closing the school for the day.

I'd poured my heart out via Krylon spray paint, weaving an amazing true tale of how a girl wanted to become popular, became a hater and hurt all the people she cared about. It had separate vignettes showing how sorry she was and how much she appreciates Chris, Anya and all of "her" friends.

My goal was to make it funny and touching—hoping to earn the forgiveness of the friends I'd let down. Certain aspects of the strip related to specific people, and I'd designed it so the panel where I apologized appeared right in front of those people's lockers.

Like any good comic strip, it had a narrative that built as you went along. Each panel of apology built up to the final panel in the cafeteria. The huge final panel expressed all my remorse for becoming a hater: my sorrow for all the jerky stuff I'd done over the year (specific facts omitted, mind you—I'm not stupid) and my declaration that being a hater is idiotic. Tearing down others to make yourself feel better is like burning down your neighbors' houses to make sure you have the nicest house on the street. You end up all alone and the view sucks.

If I do say so myself, it was mind-blowingly intricate and pretty damn genius.

What's funny is that I actually skipped the first two periods that day. I knew I would be in a world of trouble anyway, and missing the first two periods wasn't going to make things that much worse. But thanks to the miracles of social media, I didn't miss a thing. I saw the Facebook posts and pictures on Instagram and Twitter as soon as my fellow students hit campus. Pictures, video, you name it—they were all over it. I sat at Starbucks with my iPad and drank my coffee—the barista eyeing me and wondering why this kid hadn't gone to class yet, but not busting me either—enjoying the proceedings, yet also praying I hadn't just written a death sentence for my future high school graduation.

The calls came in pretty quickly from all the people who mattered most. Chris was the first. We didn't hash everything out, not by a long shot, but he told me he loved the panel where I apologized to him and said he was really proud of me for using my artistic skills in such a positive and awesome manner. Well, he probably didn't say it exactly like that, but I can't quite remember, because I was just so happy to hear from him and I was crying and the barista kept giving me the stink eye but I didn't care.

Soon after, Anya called too—leave it to my friends, they all know how to talk their way out of class and make a call when they need to. She was touched by the mural, and as such a creative person herself, she told me she'd have to kick my ass because she was so jealous I'd done such an awesome thing . . . but that would have to wait until I got out of juvie. "Run for it!" she joked just before she had to hang up. "Head for Tijuana!"

I got texts and calls from Andy and Emily and a bunch of the Invisibles, all going on about their amazement, most saying it was the most incredible thing they'd ever seen at a high school, and some saying they didn't know if a student could spend her entire junior and senior year in detention, but I should probably brace myself for that.

Quite honestly, I knew it could be worse: I could very well get expelled. And deep down, I was more than a little scared that would be enough incentive for my mom to make me move back with her if she left California. Sure, that would get me away from the horror of having Skyler as a stepsister—the very idea still made my blood boil—but I did not want to leave. It was a calculated risk, and I took it.

Now it was time to face the music.

Well, pretty soon. I stalled just a little—long enough to miss about half of third period—before steeling myself for what awaited me at West Hollywood.

That turned out to be the smartest thing I'd done in a long time.

Here's what I'd learn later from Mr. Muñez:

Had I been there for first period, I would have been hauled off in handcuffs by the school resource officer and detained at the district's remedial facility while my parents were called. Principal Dash was going to immediately recommend to the school board that I be expelled, an action he felt he had no choice but to make, given the degree of damage, and one the school superintendent would have demanded as well.

In ninety-nine out of a hundred similar situations, that's where the story would have ended. It isn't even a close call: When you break into your school and spray-paint a shitload of it, you definitely get expelled. You almost certainly get charged (as a juvenile, which is only slightly better) with breaking-and-entering and destruction of county property. You take a nosedive into one deep-ass pit that you'll spend years climbing out of. It's a mother.

(No, I don't spend my free time reading legal texts. I looked all this up on Google before I decided to go for it. I had to have some idea of what I was getting into, right?)

So that almost certainly was my fate, and I was ready for it. Not thrilled about it, but ready for it. And as I later learned, that's exactly what was being discussed as first period went on. Apparently anybody who was anybody in the school system was being consulted on this one. And I guess it went on through second period. And then some other people got consulted. And then there was third period, and I showed up at class—and about three seconds later, no shock here, I was *escorted* by my teacher to Principal Dash's office. Not told to go, mind you: escorted.

My parents were already there. This was the first time I'd seen them together since the news of my family falling apart courtesy of dear old dad had come to light, so I wasn't exactly going to take anything he said about a "moral compass" and "knowing right from wrong" seriously. That said, they were both angry. Words like "disrespectful" and "vandalism" and "criminal" were bandied about.

I was asked to explain myself, and I did, but at the end of it all, I told the principal: "Just read the mural. That's my story. That's the best explanation I can give you."

Principal Dash shook his head. "Hailey, for whatever . . . *aesthetic merit* your enormous art piece had, you broke into a school. You permanently defaced school property. Those are serious crimes. The sheriff's office says it's up to the school district to determine whether to prosecute. I'm honestly surprised we haven't been given the go-ahead yet."

"You think I'm going to be arrested?" I asked. Even though I'd prepared for this, the thought genuinely terrified me. I'd seen some of the kids who went to juvie. They were pretty scary.

The principal sighed. "I just don't know. It's not up to me. I'm sorry, but you and your parents should prepare for some very serious consequences. For now, while I'm waiting to hear back from the superintendent, you can go home. You're on indefinite suspension until we get this hashed out. If you need anything before heading straight home, that's fine. Mrs. Turley will escort you to your locker—"

"Is that really necessary?" my mom chimed in.

"Let's just play it safe," Principal Dash shot back, "unless you want me to have your daughter searched for stray crayons and Sharpies."

I saw Chris when we were leaving the principal's office. I gave a hopeful "phone" gesture (holding an imaginary phone to my ear) as subtly as I could and he nodded yes, which was encouraging. I tried to read his face, his eyes, to see if there was a chance that things could go back to how they were. I hoped they could. I wanted that more than anything. But I couldn't really gauge much of anything from that brief moment.

I knew I should be worried about more serious things, like a life of pressing license plates behind bars—I'm kidding, I think—but I couldn't help but think about Chris. I'd have to be satisfied that he agreed to call me later. Assuming I had phone privileges, that is.

Things were *not* pretty when I got home. Mom and Dad must have asked me a million times what the hell I was thinking. I had my printed designs of the mural, and I showed them to my parents. It didn't exactly satisfy them. Mom worried I'd be tossed in jail. Dad worried that the school would sue us for damages. Both worried that a year from now, I'd be working at Burger King and still trying to pass the GED.

More than anything, we waited. And waited. We expected the knock on the door anytime that day, but it never came. No city police, no sheriff's deputies, nothing.

My dad called Principal Dash in the morning. The principal said to sit tight, things were still being discussed. I tried to glean what information I could. Anyone who knows anything about kids knows that electronics are currency, and when someone gets in trouble, those are the *first* to go. (Which is not to say my allowance wasn't also docked—hell, it was *revoked*.)

But though my phone and iPad were taken away, I did have access to my laptop (so I could eventually do my homework), and on Tuesday morning I enjoyed a Facebook page Dahlia had put up called "Free Hailey!" It had photos and videos and comments from tons of people who "Liked" the page—many of them not even West Hollywood students—going on about artistic freedom and the power of art, you name it. And more than a few claimed they would sign a petition for Principal Dash's firing if I was expelled. I didn't think that was exactly necessary—the guy was just doing his job, after all—but I appreciated it.

More good news trickled in over the next few days: Principal Dash advised my mom that after a "spirited and passionate debate among faculty and administrators," the district had chosen not to press criminal charges. (*Thank God.*) However, it would be billing my family for the costs of cleaning up the mural. I remained on indefinite suspension, though I was allowed to contact my teachers for homework.

The school didn't wait for me to get back from suspension and do the repainting myself. They hired contractors to come in and paint over my masterwork right away. Mom told me that would be coming out of my allowance until it was paid off or I got a part-time job or whatever, but bottom line: I would be paying for it.

Friday afternoon, I got another bit of great news from the school: I wouldn't be expelled. I'd serve another full week of suspension in addition to the one I'd already served, but I'd be responsible for all the class work I'd missed in the meantime.

That was just the start of my punishment. I'd be spending long days at school until sophomore graduation: three hours of clean-up detention every day after school. Because my mural was covered up by the time I got back, I would get to clean sinks and toilets, pick up trash on the quad, all that fun stuff.

All things considered, I got off incredibly easy. It was a one-in-a-hundred break. I figured there must have been some angels on my side. As I'd learn just a little later, there were angels on my side, and they had the ear of the school superintendent.

Unfortunately, the same day brought frightening news about Kura.

Xan called to tell me Kura was in the hospital. She'd overdosed on Adderall the night before; her mom found her sweating and complaining of heart palpitations and called 911. When the paramedics got there, Kura was having difficulty breathing. They feared she was having a heart attack, and once they found out how much Adderall she'd ingested, they started treatment to counteract the overdose.

I started freaking out, but Xan had talked at length with Kura's parents and broke it all down for me: Kura was expected to recover just fine from the overdose. Her mom and dad had suspected something for a while, but they weren't sure whether to act or how far to push Kura to get the truth. (I could empathize with that.) They told Xan they'd get Kura into drug treatment right away.

I told Xan I'd plan to visit Kura whenever that was allowed. When I got off the phone, my head was spinning. I had to sit. Kura had gotten so bad she'd overdosed. My thoughts raced: *I should have clubbed her over the head and made her stop that day. I should have gone straight to her house and told her parents. Something. Anything.*

No matter what I'd been going through, I had a responsibility to help my friend. Thankfully Kura survived and would be getting help. She got lucky. But I promised myself I'd never let something like that happen again. I realized something that day: Sometimes the best thing you can do for a friend is the last thing they want you to do.

Meanwhile, Chris and I had spoken only twice, but he came over on the Friday of my suspension week. Grounded means you can't leave, but thankfully they weren't being so heartless that I couldn't see my boyfriend—if he even *was* my boyfriend anymore.

I changed my outfit four times before he arrived—no idea why, at that point he'd seen me in all forms of clothing—but I just wanted to look my best in case he was on the fence about me. I hoped maybe if I looked cute, that could be my saving grace. Silly, I know.

I settled on denim Current/Elliott cutoff shorts and short motorcycle boots—both courtesy of Noel. She was wearing them the Friday before and I complimented her on how cute she looked, so she left the whole outfit behind for me. On purpose! Things really *had* changed. On top I wore a hippie-style blouse, gauzy white with blue embroidered flowers, and I wore my hair down but did two braids out of a couple pieces in the front and then secured them in back to fully achieve my bohemian look.

Chris showed up with Starbucks lattes for each of us. There were napkins and straws and sweeteners in the bag—he'd pretty much covered all the bases. I was surprised he didn't throw in the glass bottles of chocolate and cinnamon while he was at it, but I was the criminal in the relationship—not him.

"It's so good to see you," I said.

"You too," he replied with a genuine smile. "You look pretty. I like your hair."

He noticed. "Thank you." I was certain my smile was way too gummy at that moment but I was too happy to rein it in.

"How's jail been?" he asked, referring to my house arrest.

"Eh," I shrugged. "I finally feel like one of those tabloid stars—all I'm missing is the ankle bracelet. And the fame. And the talent."

"Oh, you have the talent," he said. "That mural was incredible."

"Thank you," I said, then pressed a little: "Incredible enough to earn some forgiveness?"

As we'd been sitting there, I'd taken my Starbucks napkin and torn it into a few pieces. I fashioned a heart out of it and slid it in his direction.

"I'm so sorry, Chris. I got so carried away and I totally abused your trust."

"Yep," he said. Not giving me much to go on.

"I hate that I did it. I promise you I hate me way more than you could ever hate me."

"I don't hate you," he said. *Thank everything that is holy.* "That's very cute, by the way," he said, motioning to my creation.

"Everything got out of hand . . . and it was all from me being stupid and insecure and trying to be someone I wasn't—acting like the people I thought were 'cool.' But the good news is that's not the real me. I think you know that. I hope you know that."

"I do," he said. "I wouldn't have cared so much if I didn't."

"I know," I said. "I just got carried away. Like, way carried away."

"Yeah, you did," he agreed. "That was not the girl I fell in love with."

He loves me? He said he loves me! He loves me!

"I'm so sorry. I hate that I screwed us up so bad."

"I do too," he said.

Ugh. That didn't sound hopeful. Didn't he just say he *loved* me? Did he mean that in past tense?

"Can we both hate how I acted but not hate me? Or let me hate me and you try to like me again?"

I think I confused myself with that one.

"I already told you I don't hate you," he said.

But you didn't say we could be back together!

"I promise you it won't happen again. Nothing like it. I will never betray your trust again. You could tell me what you had for dinner last night and I could be trapped in an enemy prison camp and they could waterboard me and beat me and tell me they'll only let me go if I told them what you ate and I would never tell them."

"That's a little extreme."

"Listen, a lot of people want to know what you had for dinner," I said, hoping to lighten the mood. "And I won't budge."

He looked at me with those gorgeous eyes. I wanted to dive into his eyes and swim around—which would be gross and probably all squishy with eye matter and veins and would probably be the consistency of a hard-boiled egg if I were to take a guess. Enough about that, though.

"Hailey," he said, "everyone makes mistakes. Yours were, you know, kinda *huge*."

"I know," I said, bowing my head.

He sighed. "When you say *never ever*, it's gotta be—"

"Never! Ever! Never ever ever!" I must have sounded like a mental patient. "Chris, I *swear*."

He sighed. Then he cocked his head to the side and smirked at me. "You make it hard to stay mad at you."

"Go with that," I said, and he laughed, which seemed like a good sign.

"Can we just start over? You don't have to trust me completely and I'll just work really hard to prove that I'm not a complete and utter jerk?"

"Yes," he said, hitting me with one more flash of those killer eyes. "We can do that."

Anya was another story. I couldn't wear cute clothes or bat my eyelashes or kiss our relationship back together. She had already suggested an ass-kicking, so when I saw her on Instant Messenger that Saturday, I offered myself up.

> **ME:** hey. anytime you wanna kick my ass, i'm just across the street you know. i'd bring it over for you to take the opportunity but I'm still on lockdown
>
> **ANYA:** uh huh
>
> **ME:** can we make up please?
>
> **ANYA:** not mad anymore
>
> **ME:** lie. total lie
>
> **ANYA:** swear. i'm not. we all have our asshole moments. mine was most of freshman year when i was one of skyler's skanks
>
> **ME:** and then i tried to turn us all into hailey's hater tots
>
> **ANYA:** like i said, we all have our moments we're not proud of. i was a total bitch and I got knocked up freshman year. u didn't top *that*
>
> **ME:** what's up with you and andy these days?
>
> **ANYA:** why, so u can tell emily?
>
> **ME:** okay that's deserved. but no. because ur my friend. and i care. & i miss you. i really really miss you

The silence was deafening. I watched my blinking cursor and I watched to see the words "Anya is typing a message to you" in tiny lettering.

ME: are you still my friend? can we please be friends again?

Aaaaaaand nothing.

My heart sank but I knew we had built enough of a friendship that eventually it could be salvaged. At least, I hoped so.

I tried again the next day via text:

Anya, I'm SORRY. I said some terrible things and I don't have an excuse. I was awful. Please can we just talk? Please? I'm begging. I wouldn't beg for just anybody.

No response. I stared at my phone for about twenty minutes, literally trying to *will* her to write back. Nothing.

Then the doorbell rang. I walked over to answer and saw Anya through the window, flipping me off. I laughed and opened the door.

"Hey, asshole," she said.

"Hi," I said sheepishly, stepping aside. "Come on in."

"Don't mind if I do," she said.

Screw the small talk, I thought. Let's get right at it.

"Can we please move on?" I asked. "I'm *sorry.* I've said so every way I can think of with the exception of skywriting and that's expensive and my allowance is basically docked until the end of time so—"

"What are you sorry for?" she asked.

I thought about it. I was sorry for the things I said in the bathroom obviously, the names I called her, the way I'd behaved. "For everything," I said.

"Be specific," she said.

I knew she cared and there was a chance that we were going

to be friends or she wouldn't even be here—at least I hoped—but she was being hard-core. Not letting me off the hook.

I took a breath and started over, thinking back to everything I could apologize for. I wanted to get it right.

"Every shitty thing I said to you. Calling you . . . what I called you in the bathroom. I didn't mean it. And you and Andy had such a major history that it was completely unfair for me to judge you or say anything about you guys reconnecting. It was stupid. I don't and can't even pretend to know what it's really like between you guys, but it wasn't my place to say anything at all. I was just in my own little world—"

"Ding ding ding!" she interrupted. "*Therrrrre* you go."

"Yeah?" I perked up.

"Well . . . getting warmer."

I got it. It was what I tried to apologize for in my mural, but that may have been a little too, you know, "macro."

I swallowed as the words found their way out. "I was a bitch."

"Yup."

"I became everything we hated."

"Pretty much," she said. "I believe dictionary-dot-com refers to your behavior as becoming a grade-A Skyler-esque bitch."

"Is that the technical term now?" I couldn't help but smile. She was tough but she was real and that was what drew me to her in the first place. She made me be better.

"It is," she said. "I don't *think* they've updated it but I haven't checked lately. Hopefully it hasn't become 'Hailey-esque bitch' yet. That would suck."

"Well, if they used a flattering photo of me next to the definition, I suppose it *could* be considered a certain brand of achievement."

"I'd see to it they didn't," she said. "You'd look like Zach Galifi-anakis."

"Beard and everything?" I asked.

"Yup."

"I guess I deserve that."

Anya nodded.

I sighed. "Well, I think technically one has to remain bitchy for a more prolonged period of time to make it into the dictionary. If, say, one were bitten by the bitch bug and suffered symptoms for just a brief period of time but then realized the error of her ways, perhaps her friends—*and* the dictionary—could give her another chance before condemning her to official bitch infamy. Not to mention looking like Zach Galifianakis."

"Jeez, Hailes," Anya said. "Haven't you ever heard that when the buyer says yes, stop making the pitch?"

"I honestly have no idea what that means," I said. (I really didn't.)

"It means I've bought your line of bullshit," she said, smiling as she said the last word. "I'm sick of fighting. But . . . you're on probation."

"Really?" I sighed, relieved. "Oh, thank God. I know it's hard for you to trust people and I promise I won't screw up again."

"Good. Because I don't give third chances."

"I won't need one."

"You better not."

"Should we hug?" I asked.

"Why?" she replied. "Chris won't take you back? I've told you before, you're not my type. But if you really need to cop a feel, do it fast and don't latch on like one of those needy baby monkeys because *they're* cute. You? Meh."

I grabbed her and hugged her anyway, probably for longer than she wanted, but I didn't care.

* * *

When I returned to school the following Monday, I was feeling pretty chipper. My mural was the talk of the Internet—well, Internet users around West Hollywood, at least—and somehow I'd gotten through it without a criminal record, expulsion or an uncontrollable addiction to huffing spray paint. My friends were talking to me again. Chris was talking to me again. More than talking to me. He *loved* me! Well, he *did* say it once.

But first, I had to report to Mr. Muñez's office, where I knew nothing but bad news was waiting. It was time to get the bad news—the official bad news, at least—about the CalArts internship.

There are other internships, I told myself as I meekly knocked on his door. *You did the right thing. Everything comes at a price. This just had a big price tag.*

"Hi, Hailey," he said. "Please sit down."

I did.

"So," he said, "paint anything lately?"

I let out a little groan. "I don't think I'm even allowed to paint my nails right now."

He smiled. "Yeah, probably not. So I have a question for you."

"Okay?"

"Where were you when school opened Monday morning?"

Shit. "Um, is this, like, 'on the record'? Because it didn't come up with Principal Dash and I—"

"Hailey, don't worry. You're not in trouble. Well, not in any *more* trouble, anyway."

"Okay," I said. "I was at Starbucks, following all the hullabaloo on my iPad."

"Wow," he said. "Saw it all, huh?"

"Yeah, most of it. Why?"

"How did you feel to see all those kids admiring your work?"

"It felt . . . *great*," I said. "But it was more important that my friends saw. I wanted to show them how I felt, that I was sorry for the dumb stuff I did."

"Which you apologized for by breaking into and defacing the school," he said.

I hung my head a little. "Yeah. But . . . sometimes you have to make a big impression, you know?"

"I do," he said. "And here's the thing . . . I'd be remiss if I didn't tell you how impressed I was with what you did."

What?!

"Really?" I sputtered.

"Anyone who couldn't recognize the unique genius of your hallway strip would have to be blind," he said.

"Wow," I said. "Thank you."

"You're very welcome. And I wasn't the only one who was impressed."

"What do you mean, the Facebook page?"

"That and other things. Just in the first couple of hours after school opened, I'd already heard from a number of influential art instructors in Southern California. You were the talk of cyberspace. And I have to tell you, it was one of the most amazing things I've ever seen. I know why you did it, and I think it might have taught some people an important lesson."

"So what are you saying?"

"A lot of people wanted you kicked out of this school after that," he said. "I thought that would be the worst idea ever. I'm not saying you can ever do something like that again—believe me, there is no second chance, you will end up in Juvenile Hall—but I was able to speak up for you when we debated what to do last Monday morning. And later last week, I was able to present emails I'd received supporting you from the various art instructors who had expressed interest. You made quite a splash. Even a local news producer reached out."

"Wow!" I said. "Does Principal Dash know you're telling me this?"

"Well, it's all in your student file now, Hailey. You were going to know eventually. And you should also know that the superintendent's formal decision makes it crystal clear that, let's see, 'if you ever commit another criminal act on school property again, you will be prosecuted to the full extent of the law.'"

He held the paper up so I could see it. Yep, that's what it said, all right.

"Got it," I said, my mind pretty well blown. "Thanks so much for sticking up for me, Mr. Muñez. You're really cool. I'm just sorry I let you down about the CalArts thing."

"Yes, the internship," he said. "So you don't want it anymore?"

"What?" I exclaimed. "What do you mean? I just figured—"

"Hailey," he said, "you're going to be a model student from now on. I don't have any question about that. Because you're smart, and you're smart enough to know that you can't screw around with the school superintendent, right?"

"Right."

"So I know you're going to bust your butt at detention, you're never going to have so much as a single unexcused absence and you're going to work hard at school. And because you're going to promise me right now that you'll do all that, I will personally call the director at CalArts and recommend you fully."

"Oh my God, seriously?" I squealed. "You'll really do that?"

"I can't guarantee anything, Hailey, but I like your odds," he said. "I know a few people there. I was an art major, you know."

Holy crap, no, that was *not* something I knew. No wonder he was so cool. You learn something new every day.

353

I left his office flying sky high. As risky as painting that mural was, it was one of those risks you just have to take sometimes. I followed my heart, and you know what? I couldn't be happier I did.

It was funny how all along I thought that the popularity of the Invisibles was because of the diary. The magical mystical diary . . . filled with all of my sister's secrets. But none of that was true. Everyone was drawn to me for who *I* was. I never should have worried about the popular kids, because I would have been popular on my own terms anyway. (If only it had said anything about *that* in the diary. Guess it serves me right for reading someone else's diary, though. Especially an unfinished one.)

As far as my parents were concerned . . . things were still pretty messy. That wasn't gonna get wrapped up like an ABC Family movie where we all lived happily ever after. My dad had gone from cheating on my mom to having a full-on relationship with this other woman. My mom was considering moving back to Westchester, and although it looked like I could stay here, it would be incredibly weird not to live with my mom anymore . . . much less to have to live with my *dad* . . . much less live with this evil nympho Crystal . . . much less live with her *demon seed* child, effing *Skyler*.

And oh, yes, Skyler. There was a panel in my mural for Skyler, but it wasn't what you might expect. There was no hate in it. It was just a panel of a girl who looked gorgeous, dressed to the nines. Another girl complimented her on her ensemble, and the proxy Skyler's response was "Thank you so much! I really appreciate it!"

Had I ever heard those words come out of Skyler's mouth? Hell no. Had I considered that "thank you" were two words that had never even been uttered from her mouth? Absolutely. But I decided to give my faux Skyler the benefit of the doubt. And as I tried to take a more mature perspective on things, I tried to keep some things in mind: For all of her money and material goods, it did sound like Skyler had a kinda fucked-up childhood, and I wasn't exactly confident the presence of my dog of a dad would make that any better. Also, as shitty as Skyler was to me and my friends, she'd had a couple of chances to really drop the hammer on us, and for whatever reason, she didn't. It might all still be part of her evil plan . . . who knows?

Who knows, I thought. *Well, maybe I should try to find out.*

Now this was a definite Hailey 2.0 move. It was time to talk to Skyler. There was no way in hell we were going to become best friends—other than her fashion sense, I pretty much hated every-thing about her—but one day in the hallway, I asked her to meet me at the Coffee Bean for some Iced Blendeds and a peace talk. To my amazement, she agreed.

I got there first. It was on the corner of Sunset and Fairfax, and there were a ton of cooler-than-you people hanging out on the deck outside, writing their screenplays, hoping to be discovered, looking around to see if there was anyone they might want to ask out on a date. And then there was me. Waiting on my mortal enemy. Hoping a sugary beverage would be a step in the right direction toward not making life miserable for each other next year too.

Skyler walked up wearing dark-blue J Brand skinny jeans, a gray cashmere hoodie and black sparkly Tom's shoes. She turned a few heads, of course, and she reveled in the attention. I was just wearing an old hippie-ish dress, a denim jacket and Noel's boots. Still, my outfit was cute. I had my own style. Name brands aren't always cooler. Sometimes vintage wins.

"Does it ever make you uncomfortable the way people always look at you?" I asked as she sat down.

"I'm used to it," she said. "It will make me uncomfortable when they stop."

I took her point, but that kind of existence was still so foreign to me.

"So," she said. "What's up . . . *sis*?"

It was a shot, sort of, but she didn't seem mean about it. It was just an acknowledgment of how fucking weird this was, our own little "Luke, I am your father" moment.

"You don't beat around the bush," I said.

"Have I ever?"

"No, I guess not," I said. "So, look . . . I'm not expecting miracles here. But as much as I think we'd both be happy to just go our separate ways and move on with our lives—at least I would—our parents are dating. And as much as that grosses me out and as much as I feel like your mom stole my dad from my mom—"

"Stole, huh?" Skyler interrupted. "Hailey, you're not thinking of my mom. She doesn't steal anything. You're thinking of your girlfriend, whatever her name is. The one who can remove a security tag in five seconds blindfolded."

Wow, she's good, I thought.

"Anyway, they were having a relationship before you even moved out here," Skyler said. "I think that's part of why you moved in the first place."

I felt my insides churn. Another deceit from Dad. "I didn't know that."

"Sorry to break it to you," she said.

"Skyler, when did you know? I mean, I just found out. All this time, all the shit between me and you—and it turns out *my* dad was seeing *your* mom? All this time?"

Skyler smiled. Apparently she still couldn't help but enjoy having the upper hand.

"Well, Hailey," she said, "I don't really pay that much attention to who my mom sees. It's honestly rather hard to keep count. Your dad's not the first and—you actually might appreciate this part—I'd be shocked if he were the last. So let's just say I found out at one point and leave it at that."

"My dad seems to think they're in love."

Skyler laughed bitterly. "Yeah. Well, I bet *he* is. She loves some things, but nothing with a heartbeat."

I didn't even know what to say to that, so I moved on: "Fine. I just think we should try to come to some sort of understanding. A real one, not like before. A real truce. So we don't spend every waking hour trying to destroy each other."

"Hmm," she said. "But how do I know I can trust you? How do I know my face isn't going to end up on some farm animal next fall?"

"You don't," I said. "And I don't know that I can trust you. That's where the leap-of-faith part comes in."

She sighed. "I don't like your friends."

That was sort of a tell. As if she were acquiescing to my truce but making it clear that she wouldn't be friends with any of the Invisibles—heaven forbid she lower herself *that* far.

"You don't have to like my friends," I said. "They're *my* friends. They sure as hell don't like *you*. And you don't have to like *me*. I'm just saying maybe we don't do a repeat of the past few months again."

"I *did* like you, once," Skyler said.

"As well you should have," I said. "You don't get to be that popular without having good taste."

She smiled. "Don't get too cocky, Hailey."

"Learned from the master," I replied.

She held up her Iced Blended for a cheers—talk about a moment I'm sure neither of us saw coming—and I held mine up to join hers. We had a truce, albeit an incredibly fragile one, one where neither side really trusts the other, but that's probably true of most truces, right?

They say nothing brings two people together like a common enemy, but they never quite tell you what brings two common enemies together.

I guessed only time would tell.

CAPRICE CRANE is the author of several novels for adults, including *Stupid and Contagious, Forget About It, Family Affair,* and *With a Little Luck.* She was born in Hollywood, but don't hold that against her. She doesn't go wandering around with a tiny dog in her purse. Her mother, renowned film, television, and stage actress Tina Louise, is best known as Ginger Grant from the beloved sitcom *Gilligan's Island.* Her father is former talk-show host and Grammy winner Les Crane. Caprice has worked for MTV Networks as a writer and producer, and has been a music supervisor for film and TV. Her screenwriting credits include *90210* (the new version) and the movie *Love, Wedding, Marriage,* starring Mandy Moore and Kellan Lutz. She lives in Los Angeles and New York City.

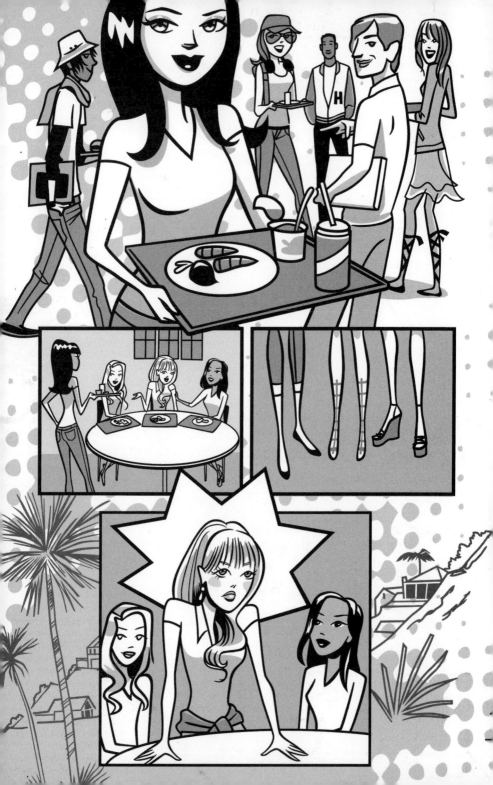